ADVANCE PRAISE FOR
A CONNECTICUT FASHIONISTA
IN KING ARTHUR'S COURT!

"This is not your mother's Camelot! Spicy romance, hilarious thrills, and a heroine who kicks butt in her stilettos—this book is a definite keeper."
—Alesia Holliday, author of *American Idle*

"Marianne Mancusi's debut is super-snappy, pure fun, fast-paced, and even educational—in more ways than one!"
—Melissa Senate, author of *See Jane Date*

"Marianne Mancusi rocks the Round Table with an equal mix of girl power, diva fashion sense, and some wicked, laugh-out-loud humor. Kat Jones is a heroine I'd have drinks with any day!"
—Cathy Yardley, author of *LA Woman*

"Fun, fashion, foul play, and fearless knights. Marianne Mancusi's fresh take on the Arthurian legend is a winner!"
—Michelle Cunnah, award-winning author of *32AA*

"DO NOT TAKE THY RESPONSIBILITY LIGHTLY"

"Something is still wrong."

Oh great. I had a feeling the high priestess'd say that. "Like what?"

"I do not know. However, I pray when thou arrives back in Camelot, thou keeps Lancelot on a short string. Do not let his eyes stray from thee for even a moment."

I frown. "I'm not really the possessive type."

"Katherine, I am not interested in thy traditional habits with men," Nimue rebukes. "The fate of Camelot, and thus thy future, is in thy hands. Do not take the responsibility lightly."

"Okay, okay," I mutter. Talk about putting on the pressure. Normally if a guy doesn't go for me, it's like death to a pint of Ben & Jerry's, not the whole freaking world. I close my eyes, wanting to sleep, wanting to forget everything she just told me.

Everything I can only hope isn't true.

A Connecticut Fashionista In King Arthur's Court

MARIANNE MANCUSI

LOVE SPELL NEW YORK CITY

*To my husband, Aaron, who never
once doubted I could do this. And to my
parents—who always encouraged me in
every endeavor—even the crazy ones.*

LOVE SPELL®

May 2005

Published by

Dorchester Publishing Co., Inc.
200 Madison Avenue
New York, NY 10016

ISBN 0-505-52633-6

The name "Love Spell" and its logo are trademarks of Dorchester
Publishing Co., Inc.

Printed in the United States of America.

Visit us on the web at www.dorchesterpub.com.

ACKNOWLEDGMENTS

First, I'd like to thank my fabulous editor, Kate Seaver, and my equally fab agent, Paige Wheeler, for taking a chance on an unknown writer who decided she'd create a whole new sub-genre her first time out.

I owe much to my critique partner, Marley; The Literary Chicks: Alesia, Lani, and Michelle, (you guys are my heroes!) and the rest of the Chick Lit Writers group. Also my old critique group, Scribes, and the New England RWA chapter. You ladies rock.

Special thanks to everyone at the day job—Channel 7 in Boston—especially my "book club." Hank (a real life fashionista), Mary (yes, I left those scenes in—just for you!), and Chris (my token male reader—thanks for the *Back to the Future* fact-checking!). And, of course, my boss, Nancy, who only winced a little when I announced I was ditching the Democratic National Convention to attend a writer's conference.

Craig for his elite photocopying skills (YNWA!), Ali for all the King Arthur discussions over the years (I Disney Dare yah!), my online gaming buds from Ryuujin EX (for the much-needed stress relief) and my high school English teacher, Chuck Seifert, who told me long ago that I should skip the whole TV news thing and just become a writer. (You were sooo right!)

A Connecticut Fashionista In King Arthur's Court

Chapter One

If Mr. Blahnik could see me now, he'd be royally pissed off. Not that I'd blame the guy. After all, dragging his kitten heels through upstate New York mud is not exactly the reverent treatment four-hundred-dollar shoes deserve.

To be fair, it really isn't my fault. It's not like I volunteered for the assignment. If anyone deserves Manolo's full wrath, it's my editor. She's the one who decided that spending my Saturday with a bunch of no-life weirdoes would be a positive career move.

I originally planned a full day of shopping in the Village, lunch with Lucy, more shopping, then a relaxing train ride back home to my Connecticut condo, where I would lounge by the pool for the remainder of the afternoon.

Instead I am on assignment at King Arthur's Faire. My mission? To write five hundred words on the emerging trend of medieval garb in today's fashions.

I'm Katherine Jones, by the way. But pretty much everyone calls me Kat. Why Kat and not Kathy or Kay or one of the million other nicknames for Katherine, I don't know—maybe it's my eyes. I've got big, green, catlike eyes that turn

1

up at the corners. When I was a kid growing up in Brooklyn, they were my ticket to fame. The guys couldn't stay away—even the ones I wished would.

I've moved up in the world since then. Now, as the twenty-nine-year-old associate fashion editor at *La Style,* my job is to claw through the hype and sniff out the trends. I'm good at it, too. Remember that Louis Vuitton cherry-blossom-purse craze? I broke that story before *Vogue* laid their Chanel-shaded eyes on it.

But does my editor recognize my talent? Uh, that would be a no. In fact, half the time I don't think she even recognizes *me,* though I've been working for the fashion rag for nearly four years.

And so instead of jetting off to Milan to write cover stories on the beautiful people, I usually get stuck doing back-end blurbs that lie lost between tampon ads.

This time it's medieval gear, which, I'm sorry, but I think is ridiculous. I can hardly see J-Lo sporting a pointy veiled headdress, and am quite positive Brad Pitt would not be caught dead in tunic and tights.

My photographer, Chrissie Haywood, seems to have none of these doubts. She's currently traipsing through the mud in a Chrissie Haywood original—a royal-blue velour gown with lace-up corset and cap sleeves. She told me earlier that she made it from a pattern she'd bought off eBay, confirming my suspicions that the Internet really is an evil empire where freaks come together to rejoice in their freakiness. In B.I. (Before Internet) days, if you had an odd quirk, you kept it to yourself. Now you form e-mail loops with thousands of others, bonding together through your common idiosyncrasies.

When I was growing up, my family couldn't afford a computer. But I didn't care. All I needed were magazines: glossy, glamorous, advice-filled pages just waiting to transport me to a world of beauty, majesty, and anorexia—for the bargain price of $3.99. Why waste a grand or more on a plastic box good only for downloading porn?

"Hear ye, hear ye," a barker announces as we walk by his stand. "Whoso shall lift this sword from the stone, the same is rightly born king of England." Or, in this case, will rightly win a plastic Excalibur of his very own. The toy sword emits a piercing scream when slammed against trees, rocks, people—whatever the little brats decide to use as their unwitting target. I know this not because I'd tried my luck at the sword-in-stone thing (I have no burning desire to become British royalty) but because every kid here seems to have already won one and has made it his or her mission to see that I achieve the headache of a lifetime.

I know the story of King Arthur and the Knights of the Round Table as well as anyone, I suppose. Dude pulls sword from stone, becomes king. Marries a total tart named Guenevere who goes off and shags his best friend, Lancelot. What I don't get is why people think it's so goddamned romantic. Having been a victim of an ex-boyfriend's infidelity, I can tell you for a fact there's nothing beautiful about being cheated on and lied to.

We walk past Ye Local Eatery, where for $5.95 you can get a cup of mead (aka Bud Light) with your King's Royale Chicken Bites (courtesy of King Ronald McDonald, if I'm not mistaken). They also feature what I'm sure was a medieval delicacy—pepperoni pizza of the Round Table.

"Here, wear this." To my horror, Chrissie plops a tall dunce-cap thing—complete with lavender polyester veil—over my head. She must have bought it while I wasn't looking. "Now you fit in," she proclaims, as if that had been my goal—rather than my nightmare—all along.

"Gee, thanks," I reply, pulling the hat from my head and examining it with a critical eye. Could Gucci really be planning this kind of kitsch for the fall runway? Chrissie looks hurt as I pick at the hat's seams, investigating the quality or, in this case, lack of it. I could have sewn better during first-year home ec at the Brooklyn community college I went to—and that was the year I accidentally blew up the kitchen! Okay, so I'm a better seamstress than cook.

"You know," Chrissie whines, "you could at least try to have a good time." She twirls around, velour gown flapping in the breeze, as she takes it all in. "It's not exactly torture, you know, hanging out in a medieval village. Could be much worse."

It could, and suddenly is, as the skies open up and rain starts gushing down. Super. We duck into the nearest tent for cover.

"May I read thy palm, milady?"

Oh, great. The tent we pick just happens to be inhabited by King Arthur's very own Miss Cleo. A tiny, wrinkled gypsy type addresses us from behind her crystal bowling ball. She wears a bright, mauve-colored robe bordered with intricate gold embroidery. Gotta give her some props—her costume, at least, looks authentic enough, even though I'm pretty sure I've seen that same crystal ball at Spencer Gifts for $19.99.

I motion for Chrissie to take a photo. "Ooh, yes. Kat, get your fortune read," she replies, misunderstanding my pointing hand.

"No, thanks. I don't believe any of that psychic mumbo jumbo." Sure, I check my horoscope once in a while—what magazine diva doesn't? But anything that forces me to fork over good money for worthless prophecies that could apply to anyone, I steer clear of.

The old crone glares at me with beady eyes, possibly not appreciating the fact that I used the words *mumbo jumbo* and *psychic* in the same sentence. But come on! She must be used to nonbelievers at this point in her career; she looks about eighty. Still, her rather rude stare gives me the creeps, and I contemplate leaving the tent, rain be damned. After a second analysis, I decide the cost of dry-cleaning six-hundred-dollar Armani trousers that I borrowed from the freebie closet at work outweighs being stuck with an annoying old woman who thinks she knows my future.

"Come on, Kat. I'll pay for it and everything." Did I mention Chrissie is persistent as well as enthusiastic? I give in. What else are we going to do while waiting for the rain to end?

Plopping down on the chair, I stick out my arm. A strange chill trips down my spine as the ancient crone takes my palm in her gnarled hands. She traces my lifeline with a long, bony finger as I wonder if I should ask her if she's ever heard of hand lotion. I mean, her hands are pretty far gone, but it's never too late for moisturizing.

"Let me guess," I say with a sigh. "Long life. Success in love. Great career." These fortune-tellers always tell you what you want to hear. After all, spreading doom and gloom isn't going to get them many customers.

"Thou dost not believe." The woman scowls, dropping my hand immediately. "Why would I bother?"

"Look, Chrissie's going to fork over your five bucks," I reply, a little pissed. Who is this woman to cop an attitude with me? She's a lame medieval-fair fortune-teller. Probably doesn't even have her own 900 number. "Just tell me about my illustrious future or whatever it is you do."

The woman sighs—she's really one for drama, let me tell you—and takes my hand again. A sudden fear washes over her crinkly face. "Thou shouldst not be here," she says in an urgent whisper.

"No shit. I should be at Bloomingdale's. Doesn't take a psychic to figure out *that* one."

Chrissie swats me from behind, and I giggle.

"No." The woman looks suddenly fierce. "That is not what I am meaning. I mean thou art out of time."

"Already? I just sat down. You haven't even told me my future yet."

"Not out of time with me. Out of time with life. Thy destiny—it is lying in another era."

You'd think with everyone paying twenty bucks' admission, the fair organizers could have found a better psychic than this. "All I want to know," I say, glancing back at Chrissie with a wink, "is whether I'm going to be rich, successful, and score a really cute boyfriend. Tell me that and I'll be on my merry way."

"Pay attention!" the woman shrieks, and I nearly jump out of my skin.

I try to pull my hand away, but she clutches it tight, digging her long fingernails into my palm. Her beady eyes are wide-open now, but clouded over, her nose scrunched and her lips curling into a snarl. Okay, this is getting a tad bit freaky for me!

"The lines of tragedy are clearly written on thy hand. If thou dost not take heed, *thou wilt surely die today!*"

That's it! I manage to rip my hand from her claws and stand up. "Yeah, sure, whatever, psychic psycho," I spit out. I'd much rather be caught in the rain than listen to this bull. Who does this crackpot think she is, trying to scare me like this? "Chrissie, I'm so out of here."

Chrissie looks from me to the psychic and back again. "Maybe you shouldn't piss her off, Kat," she says in a low voice. "What if she puts a spell on you?"

I can't help but laugh at that one. "Oh, please, Chris," I whisper back. "She couldn't put a spell on a paper bag."

"That is where thou art wrong, my friend," the gypsy interjects, eavesdropping on our private conversation.

"Oh, really?" I ask in my best skeptical voice. "Then go for it. If you've got so much power, give it your best shot."

"*Abu solstice Excalibur!*" The woman suddenly recites her best Harry Potterism at the top of her lungs, following the "magic words" with a rather disturbing cackle. Thunder cracks as she waves her hands with a dramatic whoosh.

Holy shit, what a freak!

The moment passes. I don't turn into a toad. I'm not suddenly sporting donkey ears. In fact, I'm exactly the same Katherine "just call me Kat" Jones I was before she shouted her crazy curse. Except now perhaps a little less mad and a little more amused.

"Good try, sweetie." I pat the gypsy on her embroidered sleeve. "Maybe a few more years at Hogwarts will do the trick." I turn to Chrissie, who still looks petrified. "What now?"

"I . . . I think the rain has let up," she mumbles. "I want to get photos of the jousters."

Jousters, huh? As in sexy men dressed in armor and riding horses? That doesn't sound half-bad. A lot better than crazy fortune-tellers uttering curses, anyway. Determined to change my attitude and show Chrissie a good time, I amicably set the pointy hat on my head and take my photographer by the arm.

"Bring on the jousting!"

The jousting arena is at the far end of the fairground. The organizers set up bleachers on either side, kind of like a high school football field. We're a few minutes early and are able to snag front-row seats.

I steal a glance over at the end of the field, where the men are suiting up. Maybe it's due to my recent guy drought, but boy, do they look good. One in particular sports flowing black hair and a body to die for. He wears a crimson crest on his breastplate in the shape of a dragon. Yum,

7

yum, double yum. I squint to get a better look and wish I had brought my glasses.

"The guy in the dragon armor is playing Lancelot," Chrissie informs me after glancing at her program.

"I'd be his Guenevere any day," I remark, taking in his broad shoulders and arrogant swagger. "I'm definitely digging his whole alpha-male vibe." He looks over, and I flash him a smile, then nudge Chrissie. "Get his picture."

She complies, snapping a few shots using her telephoto lens. "Wow, he looks even better up close," she murmurs. "Maybe you should go talk to him."

I laugh. "No way am I going to lower myself to knight-in-shining-armor-groupie level. Besides, I bet he's dumb as a rock. All brawn, no brains."

"You're such a snob. He could be a rocket scientist on his day off for all you know."

"Okay fine." I rip the camera from her grasp and look into the lens. Unfortunately Lancey-boy simultaneously picks that moment to place his helmet over his head, so I don't get much of a view. "Oh, well," I say, passing the camera back to Chrissie. "Guess it wasn't meant to be." I sigh dramatically. "Though I'll tell you what: *something's* gotta be 'meant to be' pretty soon. I'm like literally a born-again virgin at this point."

Chrissie giggles at my declaration. Easy for her to laugh. She's married to some Jersey-born beatnik and living a happy, hippie vegetarian existence in the Village. She met her poet in high school and has absolutely no idea what the rest of us go through trying to find a decent man in the tri-state area.

It's not that guys don't hit on me from time to time. It's only that lately there hasn't been anything worth hitting back. One would think in Manhattan there'd be cute guys up the yin-yang but no, only on *Sex and the City* reruns. In real life the scene is a lot more depressing.

Trumpets sound, presumably to mark the start of the tournament. Men and women dressed in silly costumes like Chrissie's scramble to find last-minute seats.

"Hear ye, hear ye!" A young man wearing a very fake gray beard, wizard cap, and star-covered gown walks into the center of the field. "Welcome, one and all, to King Arthur's Faire. I am Merlin, wizard of Camelot."

Oh, he's supposed to be Merlin, is he? I snicker, wondering who on earth did the casting for this place. First there was the scary old bag who takes herself way too seriously, and now this teenager posing as an ancient magician.

"Today you will witness feats of wonder that will amaze and entertain. Valiant knights, brave and bold, fiercely fighting to win the favor of their lady, Queen Guenevere."

"Yeah, yeah, we get it. In the name of chivalry and all that shit," I mumble to Chrissie. "Enough intro. Bring on the jousters."

As Merlin keeps talking, I find myself drifting off, unable to concentrate on his long-winded ramblings, his voice lulling me into a strange trancelike state. My eyes blur, and I start to get dizzy. I waver a bit, almost feeling as if I'm going to faint. Odd.

I shake my head to try to wake up, get oriented.

"Are you okay?" Chrissie studies me with concerned eyes. "You look pale."

"I'm fine." The dizziness fades as quickly as it began. "Maybe I'm dehydrated or something. Too many buy-one-get-one-free margaritas last night."

"Let me get you some water." Chrissie rises from her seat and walks toward the refreshment stand. After a moment's contemplation of her extreme niceness, I turn back to the ring.

Merlin's endless speech has somehow miraculously ended, and knights on the sidelines mount their trusty steeds. As they gallop into the ring, the front row seems like it might have been a bad idea. I'm not a big fan of horses and find myself far too close to crashing hooves for comfort.

Two knights line up on either side of the field, grasping long wooden lances capped with steel tips. Each knight is covered in heavy plates of armor from head to toe, offering protection, though not much maneuverability. Even the horses wear armor over their heads, making them look like metal monsters.

A bell rings, and the horses charge, their thundering hooves echoing through my already pounding head. The knights lower their lances, each preparing to bash his weapon into the other, in an attempt to knock him off his horse.

Slam! The lances whack against the shields, splinters flying everywhere. The green-crested knight falls from his horse. He runs to the sidelines and grabs a stick with a chained and spiked metal ball on the end. He swings it, guarding his space, while the blue knight, still on horseback but now wielding a sword, circles him. Gotta admit, the whole thing is rather exciting.

The green knight manages to hook his chain around the blue knight's sword and wrenches the weapon from his grasp, sending it flying. The blue knight jumps off the horse and somersaults to his blade, grabbing it midroll, and stands ready to face his opponent. I lean forward in my seat. I know it's all fake, but it really is a pretty good show.

Where's Chrissie? I look around. Must be a long line at the concession stand. Too bad, 'cause she's missing everything.

After much clashing and bashing of weapons, sparks flying as metal slams against metal, the blue knight succeeds in cornering the green knight, sword to his throat. The first joust is over, the blue knight victorious. High on a far platform, the woman playing Guenevere, wearing a green velour gown and heavy gold metal crown, claps and tosses daisies to honor her champion.

"Blue knight, thou art brave," Merlin declares, this time riding into the ring on a white horse. "But art thou willing to challenge the realm's most gifted sportsman? A knight above all others? I give you Lancelot!"

The crowd cheers and whistles and whoops as the red-dragon knight gallops into the ring, waving a flag with a matching crest. From the starry-eyed gazes of the other women in the audience, it's obvious I'm not the only one who finds him hot.

The blue knight accepts the challenge, mounting his horse and acquiring a new lance from his squire. Another helper hands Lancelot his lance and they line up, ready to charge.

At that moment pain stabs behind my eyes and my vision blurs again, right as the two men are set to run. I want to watch, but instead I'm forced to squeeze my eyes shut, desperate to get rid of the dizziness. The roar of the crowd only makes it worse. I press my fingers against my temples and try to stand. The pain is nearly unbearable. I've got to find Chrissie.

Once I'm on my feet, nausea overtakes me, and I stumble forward, not sure whether I'll throw up or faint. I close my eyes, willing myself to stay conscious. What is wrong with me? All I can think of is the gypsy curse. Her words: *Thou wilt surely die this day!*

That's so stupid. This is just a major coincidence. I've got a migraine. I'm not dying. I take a few more steps to clear my head.

"Get back!" a man yells, and I open my eyes, only to realize he's talking to me. In my delirious walk I've somehow wandered halfway onto the field, right as the jousters have come together for their first run. Suddenly a huge chunk of wood—splintered from one of the lances—flies through the air like a javelin, directly toward my head. I put up my arms to cover my face, but I'm too late. The lance hits me square in the forehead and I see stars, then blackness.

"Milady?"

A sexy, deep voice prompts me to open my eyes. I'm lying on my back on the ground, staring up at the most gorgeous blue eyes I have ever seen. I mean, lots of people have blue eyes, but this particular pair is quite literally the color of sapphires, sparkling in the sunshine. Mmmm.

"How do you fare?" the man asks. His calloused fingertips brush against my forehead as he lifts a wisp of hair from my face. The sensation sends a shiver down to my toes. I drop my gaze and notice the Adonis is wearing a suit of armor with a red dragon crest emblazoned on it. Ah, the guy playing Lancelot. His medieval garb looks a lot more real close up. My very own knight in shining armor. Maybe this whole getting-hit-on-the-head thing could work out in my favor after all. If only it didn't hurt so much.

I force my focus away from those eyes to better assess my current situation. I try to sit, but a stabbing pain at the back of my head causes me to rethink that notion. I lay my head back down and moan. That flying wood must have hit me harder than I thought. Just great. I'm a real damsel in distress now.

"Ow," I cry, closing my eyes in agony. "My head kills. I think I might need a doctor."

"Page, send for Lord Merlin immediately," a concerned

female voice commands in a bad British accent. I open my eyes. Behind the blue-eyed man stands a petite blond woman wearing an authentic-looking purple silk gown and a sparkly tiara. Probably the one playing Guenevere, though I could have sworn she was wearing a different outfit before.

But never mind her. I turn back to my hero, Lancelot. Chrissie was right; he does look a lot cuter up close. His long black hair, blowing in the slight breeze, makes my stomach do flip-flops, despite my headache.

Where is Chrissie, anyway? I try to turn my head to get a better look at my surroundings, but the pain proves too great.

"Rest, lady. The Lord Merlin will attend to your wounds shortly," insists the woman.

I frown. What's this about Merlin? Don't they have a first-aid tent or something? I'm certainly not getting medical treatment from the fifteen-year-old who introduced the jousting.

"Hey," I protest. "I don't want to be treated by some kid." Then again, maybe they have two guys playing Merlin today. One who in his spare time serves as a NYC EMT, hopefully?

"I am not sure what you speak of, lady," the Guenevere wannabe says, furrowing her brow. "Lord Merlin is certainly no baby goat. He is the most powerful druid in all of Camelot, and well versed in the ways of magic."

"Goat? What are you talking about? Oh, I get it. Kid. Goat. You're still doing the role-playing thing." These people really take this stuff way too seriously. You'd think it'd be all fun and games until someone loses an eye—or gets hit in the head with a flying lance. I hope they have good insurance, because if I've sustained any serious injuries, I am so suing this place.

"Could we cut the medieval crap for one second?" I ask, starting to get annoyed. "I'm hurt. I need a doctor. A real one, not a magic one. Maybe even an ambulance." I scan the crowd. No reaction, only blank stares. The Lancelot guy has risen, and I see him whispering with Guenevere.

I fumble for my purse and manage to pull out my cell phone. Screw them; I'm calling 911 myself.

No reception. I forgot we're out in the boonies. They must not even have cell phone towers here. My day is getting better and better. I close my eyes, succumbing to my fate, at least until Chrissie returns. Voices whisper furiously around me, perhaps assuming I'm unconscious and unable to hear.

"Where did she come from?"

"Out of thin air, I should think."

"She is dressed more like man than woman."

"What would Bishop Mallory say?"

"Could she be one of the fey folk, caught between the worlds?"

"Don't be daft; she is as human as you or I."

"Then with what strange talk does she go on about?"

"Perhaps she's mad?"

Sick of the conversation, I open one eye, then the other. A crowd of medievally garbed folk has gathered around me. I check for any nonfreaks, but don't see a single normal-looking soul. Just great.

"Can we go back to the twenty-first century for, like, one minute so I can get help?" I suggest, the pain in my head throbbing. "Then you can go on with your little fantasy world?"

They stare at me as if I'm the village idiot. "Aye, it definitely appears she may be addled," whispers Guenevere to Lance. "Poor child."

I open my mouth to protest, but suddenly the sea of people parts, and an ancient man with a long gray beard and a gnarled cane approaches me. Is this the Merlin guy they were talking about? Well, at least he's not fifteen. Maybe they have different Merlins, like Disney has different Mickeys. I hope this one isn't as crazy as everyone else seems to be.

He studies me with an odd look in his piercing green eyes. "Where did this woman come from?" Okay, not a good sign.

"She appeared from nowhere," Lancelot informs him, evidently not ready to take the blame for his lance's wayward actions.

"Actually," I interrupt, "I was hanging quite nicely on the sidelines when his big lance thing splintered and came flying at my head." No need to admit to my walking out onto the field, in case of future lawsuit. Had I signed any kind of waiver? I hope not.

Lancelot's eyes narrow. He reaches beside him and picks up his lance. Not a splinter on it. Running his hand up and down the smooth shaft, he says, "I know not what the lady is going on about, sire. But she was hit by no lance. As I said before, she appeared out of nowhere, already bleeding when she collapsed onto the field."

My face heats in anger. "That's such a lie. You're only saying that so you won't get sued." I meet Merlin's eyes. Will he believe me? "He probably did a lance switcheroo while I was out cold." What a jerk that Lancelot guy is. Forget the whole knight-in-shining-armor thing, the beautiful blue eyes. Underneath it all, he's exactly like the rest of the sorry male race—from Mars!

"Hmm." Merlin's eyes fall on my abandoned cell phone. He reaches down and picks it up, turning it over and around in his fingers, a look of wonder and surprise clearly written on his face. He presses a button. The responding beep makes him jump a little, dropping the mobile on the hard ground.

"Do you mind? That's a four-hundred-dollar phone," I protest, to no avail. The old man's clawlike hands grab the handset off the ground and stuff it into his robe's pocket. "Hey! That's mine. You can't—"

"What is the trouble here?" a rich baritone voice demands. The crowd parts again, this time also bowing their heads in reverence. A blond, bearded man, probably in his mid-thirties, dressed in red robes and wearing a large golden crown, approaches. He looks down at me and then to Merlin with questioning eyes.

Merlin shoots me a suspicious glare, then turns back to the crowned man with a sly smile. "We've caught an intruder, Your Majesty. A spy from another land."

"Oh, give me a break," I moan, unable to take much more. I'm in pain—physically *and* mentally at this point. All I want to do is go back to Connecticut. Where the hell is Chrissie?

"She certainly does not have the voice of one born in Camelot," the king guy agrees, though his tone is cautious. "And her clothing is very strange indeed."

"She is not a spy, Arthur," Guenevere pipes in. "She is just a girl. I will admit she may be a bit odd. Perhaps simple—or mad, even. But I think not—"

"Spies can come in all shapes and forms, Your Majesty," Merlin interrupts. "You cannot be too careful these days. Many outside the civilized lands of Camelot wish to do you harm. What better plan than to send in an innocent-looking girl to win your heart and gain your trust, all the while feeding back your intimate secrets to her barbarian Saxon lover?"

Oh, yeah, whatever, loser. I can tell Guen doesn't like the

guy either, from the dirty look she shoots him behind his back. Not that Arthur notices. It's obvious he respects Merlin's opinion more than that of his wife. Men. If he's acting anything like the real Arthur did, well, it's no wonder Guenny ends up finding solace in the arms of Lancelot.

"Indeed, we should practice caution," Arthur admits. "Lord Merlin, what do you suggest we do with her?"

"Take me to a hospital. Please!" I beg, starting to get a little worried at this point. Blood's been trickling from the gash in my forehead for at least ten minutes now, and I'm feeling more than a little faint. The throbbing pain at the back of my head hasn't let up either. I might have a concussion. And they're all standing around, acting! It's like a nightmare, but I can't wake up. "Chrissie!" I call, a lump forming in my throat. *Don't cry, Kat. Don't let these losers see you cry.* "Chrissie, please help!"

But Chrissie is nowhere to be found. The only answer I get to my calls is from Merlin, who folds his arms across his chest, a smug expression on his wrinkled face. "I think we should lock the infidel in the tower."

Chapter Two

Wow, this sucks.

As a child I used to pretend that I was a fair maiden locked in a tower, waiting for a handsome knight (played by my rather unwilling snot-nosed neighbor, Billy) to come to my rescue. It was romantic and exciting and all the rest.

In real life I now realize that towers are damn boring. At least this one is. There's not even a TV, radio, or any magazines to while away the time—just a cot in the corner with a small wooden table beside it. The cot's mattress is a glorified bale of hay, and you can only imagine how comfy *that* is. I can only hope that it doesn't have any fleas.

They even took away my clothes. While I lay passed out, someone exchanged my black Dolce & Gabbana netted corset tank and my Armani silk pants for a shapeless, colorless shift dress made out of scratchy wool. Worst of all, they took my shoes! My precious Manolo Blahniks! Seriously, if I ever get out of this tower, I am going to have to kick some major ass.

To tell you the truth, I'm not totally convinced this actually is a tower. Shortly after Merlin's declaration on the jousting field, he sprinkled some kind of strange, sparkly dust over my head, and I blacked out almost immediately. When I woke I was here—a round room with no windows and one solid oak door with a huge lock.

At first I kept thinking that *Candid Camera* or Jamie Kennedy would pop out at any second, tell me I'm all part of a new reality television show and would I just sign this waiver and go on my way. But as hours go by, the chances of that seem more and more remote. The reality—that I've been kidnapped by a group of Dungeons & Dragons lovers who have lost their marbles—starts to sink in.

It's at this point that I begin to get scared. What do they want with me? Why have they imprisoned me? Is this a temporary thing—until the fair's over? Or will they see fit to keep me on a more permanent basis? And if so, why? Oh, God, maybe that's how they recruit the actors—kidnap them and brainwash them into joining their secret cult?

A bit panicked at the thought, I try the yelling-and-screaming-and-pounding-my-fists-against-the-door tactic for a while, but no one comes. How remote is this "tower" anyway? Has Chrissie reported my disappearance to the police? Are there search parties out right now, looking high and low for some trace of my whereabouts?

At least my head's stopped bleeding and the pain has subsided somewhat. Guess I didn't get a concussion after all. Thank God for small favors. That said, I think I may have a scar for life, thanks to someone's amateur stitching job. While there's no mirror here, I can feel the rough thread knitted into my scalp. Luckily my hair will cover it. As long as the Sinead O'Connor look never comes back into style, I'm all set.

However, I am a bit worried about infection. Who knows

if the guy playing Dr. Merlin sterilized his equipment? The thought makes me feel rather ill. Or perhaps that's just my gnawing hunger. I lie down on the bed, feeling a bit faint.

I hear the click of the lock and sit up. "Who's there?"

The caller is a big, burly redheaded guy wearing a tunic and tights and carrying a wooden tray. Thank God. They're not going to make me die of starvation or thirst after all.

My relief dissipates when he gets closer, and I see exactly what he expects me to eat and drink—a huge chunk of white bread and frothy beer, served in a pewter mug. Both are big no-nos on my low-carb diet.

"Dude," I say as the guy sets the food down on a wooden table by my cot. "I can't eat this stuff. I'm on Atkins. Get me some meat or something. Bacon, steak, eggs, anything. Just take the high-glycemic food out of my sight."

The man looks at me strangely, but does not respond. Instead he turns and heads out the door, locking me in with the deadly carbs. Damn him.

I stare at the bread, my stomach making undignified growling noises. Being locked in a tower is one thing. Being forced to devour fattening carbohydrates that will make my insulin level skyrocket and shoot gallons of fat directly into my already way too wide hips? Now that's torture.

"I hear you are displeased with your dinner."

Startled, I look up and see that that guy playing Lancelot has entered the room. His armor is gone and in its place he wears—surprise, surprise—a red wool tunic with embroidered trim, a gold sashlike belt, and tights. I'll tell you, it's a look not many men could pull off and still look sexy. But Lance does it with style.

Damn, why does he have to be so attractive? I should be shaking with fear, not drooling over a freak who has me locked up in a tower. Though it wasn't his idea, I suppose. But still, he went along with it. And he's definitely as crazy as the rest of them. Just cuter. A lot, lot cuter. With really good bone structure, too. And beautiful eyes . . . Mmmm.

"Lady Giorgio? Are you unwell?" He walks over to the bed and sits, studying me with concerned eyes. Such beautiful eyes. No man should be allowed to possess a set that blue. I scrunch my knees up, not wanting to get too close. After all, what if "Old Blue Eyes" is thinking of raping me? Tying me down, ripping the sheath from my writhing body, and taking me like the— Wait! Did he call me Giorgio?

"Who's Giorgio?"

"Is that not your name?" He furrows his brows.

"No, my name's Kat."

"Cat? Like . . . pussy?"

"Not really; I like men," I quip. It's my standard joke for guys who lewdly try to make that connection, but he doesn't seem to get it. I rise from the cot and walk to the other side of the room, focusing my attention on the featureless stone wall—mostly to avoid looking at Lance and contemplating having his babies. *Psycho*, I remind myself. *Cute man is actually psycho.* "My name's Katherine. But people call me Kat for short."

"I suppose Armani is not your surname either."

I whirl around, realizing now where the Giorgio came from. "Oh, please, Lancey." I shake my head. "That's so *Back to the Future* of you. You couldn't think of a more original time-travel joke than that?" I return to the bed, facing him, my hands on my hips. "What were you doing in my pants, anyway?"

He looks confused. "Pants?"

"You know, the expensive, well-designed article of clothing that you so brazenly removed from my body?"

"I assure you, madam, that my intentions were nothing but honorable. I merely wanted to make you more comfortable."

I roll my eyes. "I take it you've never worn Armani

21

trousers, then. Trust me, they're much comfier than this woolen rag." I reach under the shoulder strap to attack an itch. "This thing totally scratches my skin."

He nods, at least seeming to take my complaint seriously. "I shall see if the queen has any suggestions for more suitable attire."

"Yeah, well, while you're at it, see if she's got any suggestions for more suitable food, too," I say a bit crossly, my hunger making me forget my fear. "I'm freaking starving here." Feeling a little dizzy—probably from low blood sugar—I sit back down on the bed, once again careful to avoid touching him.

Lancelot glances at the tray for the first time and frowns. "I beg your forgiveness, lady. I do not know what the cook was thinking, sending you up a peasant's meal. You are our guest. I shall see to it that you are brought the finest slab of venison the castle has to offer."

"Venison?" I wrinkle my nose. "No, thank you. I'm so not eating Bambi."

"Would you prefer fowl to beast, then?" Lancelot asks. "The cook serves up a delicious roast pigeon on occasion."

I stare at him, not sure if he's joking. "I suppose you're going to tell me it tastes like chicken, right? No, thanks."

He shrugs. "There's always the mutton stew. A bit plain, but certainly filling."

"That's lamb, right?" I let out a sigh. "Fine. Sure. Lamb." Normally I have sympathy for "bah, bah, black sheep," but I think I'm going to starve to death at this point, and the lamb stew sounds like the least horrible dish on the menu.

"Very well." Lance stands and walks over to the door, knocking once. The guy who brought the bread and beer peeks his orange mop inside. "John, bring Lady Katherine a bowl of the mutton stew immediately." He pauses for a moment, then adds, "And some spiced wine to wash it down."

Wine? Now we're talking. Though maybe I shouldn't have any. After all, if I ever get out of here, I've got to drive all the way back to Connecticut. And as they say: if you booze and you cruise, you lose.

I lie on my side, propping my head on one elbow, and wonder how long it will be before the man returns. The bread stares back at me. I roll onto my back and study the carb-free ceiling to avoid looking at it. Protein will be here shortly, I tell my stomach.

I feel eyes on me, and I sit up. Lancelot is still in the room, watching me with frank interest.

"What?" I demand, uncomfortable at being stared at.

"I was observing how beautiful you are," he says matter-of-factly.

"I bet you say that to all the damsels," I quip, trying to act cool, all the while my traitorous heart is banging against my rib cage. I gotta get him out of here, and fast. "Don't you have something else you could be doing rather than hanging here with me?" What was it that medieval people did in their spare time? "Any dragons that need slaying, perhaps?"

Lancelot laughs and flops down on the bed, too close for comfort. "Silly girl. You must know that dragons exist only in tales to scare children and entertain kings," he says as if speaking to a dim-witted five-year-old. "They are creatures of songs and romances, but certainly not real as you or I."

"Dude," I say, not quite getting his logic, "if we're talking reality here, how about the fact that Camelot was only a legend, too? I mean, I don't want to burst your delusional medieval bubble, but most historians think Camelot was no more than a rustic hill fort. King Arthur—if he existed at all—was probably this tribal chieftain in A.D. 500—way earlier than chivalry, knights in shining armor, glamorous castles, and all that shit."

To my chagrin, Lancelot chuckles. "You are an odd one, for certain."

I narrow my eyes. "Look who's talking."

"I ask you, then," the knight continues. "If Camelot is a fantasy, then what castle do we inhabit at this very moment?"

"How do I really know this is a castle?" I demand, getting angry. "For all I know we're in the basement of the Poughkeepsie Rotary Club."

"I do not know of what you speak, lady, but I can assure you this is indeed a castle—the very best castle in all the land, home of the mighty King Arthur, son of Uther Pendragon, high king of Britain."

"Fine. If this is really a castle, I dare you to get me out of here and show—"

The stupid servant picks this inopportune moment to return with my food. After taking the tray from him, Lancelot brings it over to the bed and sets it on the side table. I take a look. Lest I harbor the vain hope of being free of carbs altogether, the stew sits swaddled in a bread bowl. But I'm pretty sure I can eat around it. I grab the wooden spoon and dig in, trying to dodge the globules of fat that float on the surface. The meat is disgustingly salty, tough, and way too garlicky, but I'm too hungry at this point to care. The wine's not half-bad, though. I suck down the cupful, my insides warming.

"You know," I say, my mouth regrettably full (a bad habit I've never been able to break), "you seem like an all-right guy, Lance. Cute, too. So why the medieval obsession? I mean, don't you ever get the urge to go live a normal life? Go out drinking with friends, meet a girl, play the stock market?"

Shaking his head, he pretends not to comprehend my words. Then, leaning over, he traces the corner of my mouth with his finger, his touch sending an unwilling shiver tripping down my spine. He pulls his hand away, and I can see he's removed brown stew sauce from my lips. And here I thought he was being romantic. How embarrassing.

"Don't you guys believe in napkins? Or are those yet to be invented?"

"You're not a Saxon spy, are you?" he asks softly, his husky voice effectively changing the subject.

"Funny, no, I'm not. I'm just an innocent girl who got hit in the head with a lance and then kidnapped by psychopaths whose grip on reality is in serious need of some superglue."

He looks at me with pity written on his face. "I am sorry for the way they treat you," he says. "You are far too beautiful to be locked away."

Hope surges through me. "So let me free," I beg. "They'll never know it was you. Leave the door unlocked when you leave, and I'll be on my merry way." I put on my best pleading expression, the one I used back in college with bouncers who questioned my very fake ID. I bat my lashes for effect, hoping it's not overkill. "Pretty please with a cherry on top?"

Before he can answer, the door opens and the woman playing Guenevere enters. Great. There goes my one chance at freedom.

"How is she?" Guenevere asks, her voice wrought with concern. I give her a once-over. She's changed into a crimson velvet gown with fur trim, a long golden sash tied around her waist. Her blond hair is restrained behind some kind of black-netted cap. Up close I realize she can't be older than twenty. They must get college kids to do the acting for these things.

"Better, I think." Lancelot rises from the bed and walks over to the queen, giving her a slight bow before continuing in a low, but audible voice. "She's still a bit incoherent. Babbles on about the strangest things. But if this is madness she suffers from, I have seen nothing like it before."

"Poor child," Guenevere coos, approaching the bed—like I need her pity. And who's she calling a child anyway? At twenty-nine, I'm probably almost ten years older than she is. "Lancelot, leave us. I would like to talk to the lady alone."

No, Lance, don't leave! But, of course, he does. Gotta follow the queen's orders and all, I suppose. As he exits, he looks back, his generous mouth quirked up in a shy smile.

"Till we meet again, my lady Kat."

"Meow," I reply smugly. A shameless flirtation, I know, and one I've overused throughout my teens and early twenties. But I've yet to meet a guy who doesn't go all crazy over it. Hey, if you've got a name like mine, you might as well use it for all it's worth.

I turn to Guenevere and realize she has some kind of clothing in her hand. Not my designer duds, unfortunately.

"Lady, I apologize for the treatment you have undergone at the hands of the barbaric men who run this castle. They know nothing of a woman's needs."

She hands the garments to me. To my surprise and delight I find my cute little Kate Spade purse hidden underneath the clothing. I look up at Guen in astonishment. She smiles, putting a finger to her lips to indicate I should keep the bag return on the down-low. "I have picked out a gown for you from my own wardrobe. I do hope you find it comfortable."

I pick through the articles of clothing. There's a shift dress, like the one I'm wearing, but this one is made of much softer linenlike material. There's also a royal-blue, ankle-length tunic with amazingly detailed embroidery and tiny jewels seeded into the fabric.

"Where'd you get this?" I ask, examining it closely, suddenly the fashion editor again. I trace my finger over the perfect little flowers, songbirds, and butterflies with ruby antenna, all stitched into the sleeves and neckline. What craftsmanship!

"The dress itself was sewn by one of my ladies-in-waiting," she explains. "The embroidery is mine."

"You know, I'm a fashion editor at *La Style*." I look up. "And we're doing a spread on medieval clothing. I'd love to feature this dress."

Gotta give the woman credit; she's a good actress. Not one flicker of recognition crosses her face when I mention *La Style*. As if there's any woman on the planet who doesn't read or at least know about the world's premier fashion rag.

But hey, fine. She wants to pretend? I can play her game. In fact, maybe playing along will convince her to let me the hell out of here. I'll show them that I'm a good actor, too.

"So," I begin, trying on a fake English accent for kicks. "I think thou shouldst know Sir Lancelot was in mine chambers earlier, flirting with me. Thou might wantest to keepest better tabs on thy lover."

If Guenevere looked surprised before, now she's staring at me as if I have a huge-ass zit on my face. "You are mistaken, lady. Lancelot is not my lover; nor has he ever been."

I smirk. "Right. Sure, he isn't. Don't worry; I won't tell anyone." Oops. Forgot the accent this time. Acting is harder than it looks! Oh, well. I'll just play the visiting American.

"Lady, you must be careful what you go on about." Guenevere looks stressed. "I am the queen, wife of High King Arthur, son of Uther Pendrag—"

"Yeah, yeah. I know the lineage. Lance told me. Don't change the subject. Everyone knows you're screwing him."

"Screwing?"

"Screwing, bonking, doing the dirty deed, the wild thing, making love? Whatever you want to call it." I'm almost enjoying the game at this point—especially her horrified face. She really is a good actress. Reminds me of Gwyneth Paltrow, actually, with a little Claire Danes thrown in.

"Making love? I assure you, lady, that is not the case." Guenevere rises from the bed. "Lancelot is my champion, my chosen knight, to be sure. But he is far from my lover. He is like a brother to me."

"Whatever you say, Guenny."

"Besides," the queen says, turning to face me, "I am very much in love with my husband."

"Yeah, well, from what I can see, your husband's a useless puppet at the hands of that idiot Merlin."

Guenevere's eyes widen and she grabs my hand, sinking to her knees. Her voice lowers to a hoarse whisper. "Do not utter such words about Lord Merlin too loudly." She looks around, panic written on her face. "He has his spies everywhere."

"Why's everyone so afraid of an old man?"

"He is no ordinary man, Merlin," she informs me, still using her whisper—perhaps for dramatic effect. "The Christians call him the son of the devil. A cursed druid living backward in time—growing younger as the years pass, instead of older."

"So, like, if he's evil, then why's Arthur all into him?"

Guenevere sighs. "Merlin fostered the king from a young age, taught him everything he knows. Used his magic to ensure that Arthur became high king. The old druid can do no wrong in my husband's eyes." She lowers her gaze, staring at the floor. "But I see a different creature bubbling beneath the surface of the kind, devoted mentor he pretends to be. Merlin knows more than he tells, and isn't afraid to twist the strands of fate to achieve his desires."

"Yeah, I got that impression."

"But, lady, you must not believe that Arthur has any ill intentions. He is kind and good and loyal. He rules with a strong but gentle hand, and the people love him for that. It is only when it comes to Merlin that my husband lacks good judgment."

I'm so carried away with her tale that I almost forget she's making it all up. "Wow, you've really researched this stuff," I tell her, impressed. "Are you like an English-lit major or something?"

She looks at me strangely and shakes her head. "Lady, I must depart. I will come back and visit you later."

"Listen, Guen," I say, grabbing her arm. "Could you please get me out of here? Or at least tell me what they plan to do with me? Is this some kind of weird reality show? If so, how do I get voted off the island? I've got a huge deadline, and my dog hasn't been fed, and, well, I'd really like to go home." Tears of frustration well up in my eyes. "I promise I won't tell on any of you or go to the police. What do you say?"

She gently pulls her arm away. "It is not my right to free you, lady, for I was not the one who wanted to put you in captivity in the first place. But I will promise to speak to Arthur on your behalf. There are times," she says with a sly wink, "when a woman claims power over her husband that no other man, be he mortal or magician, can overpower."

"You go, girl," I say amicably, trying to restrain my sarcasm. She leans over and embraces me in a warm hug. I think about pulling away—I'm not big on hugs—but decide that might piss her off.

"Enjoy the gown," she whispers in my ear. "I will return shortly."

She exits the room, and I hear the lock click behind her. With nothing else to do I shed my tunic and slip on the undergarment and dress, tying it with a silk sash.

Unfortunately there's no mirror in my prison, so I have no idea what the outfit looks like on me. It feels kind of cool, though heavy, with its floor-length skirt swishing as I walk. If I wore a dress like this every day I'd never again have to use the Thighmaster.

I lie back on the bed, resigned to my fate, and pick at the bread bowl, carbs be damned. Too bad the wine has run out. I could use another gallon or two after all that's taken place today. I really hope Guenevere was serious when she said she'd go talk to the guy playing Arthur. I cannot see myself trapped in this room for another day.

I hear the now-familiar click of the lock, and I sit up in bed. Who's here this time? Hopefully not that creepy Merlin. I wait for a minute, holding my breath, but no one enters. I strain to hear noise from outside. Nothing. Walking over to the door, I place my ear to the wood. Silence. Cautiously I press against the door. It creaks open.

After peeking around each corner to ensure the coast is clear, I slip out the door and onto a torch-lit spiral staircase.

Someone has set me free.

Chapter Three

She's buying a stairway to heaven.

For some odd reason the old Led Zeppelin song gets stuck in my head as I cautiously step down the dark, dank, circular stone stairs. Not that the song really applies here; it's more like I'm descending the stairway to *hell*—as in, I'm going down, and if someone meets me halfway I'm sure to have the devil to pay. Besides, I'm not even a Zeppelin fan. I'm sadly still addicted to eighties pop—Duran Duran, Madonna, Depeche Mode. Actually "Depressed" Mode would probably provide a pretty good sound track for this scenario—filling the corridor with the appropriate synthesized doom and gloom.

Round and round and round she goes. Where she stops, nobody knows.

They weren't kidding when they called this a tower. It's totally skyscraper height. Of course, I'm not moving all that fast, since I'm unaware of what's around the bend. I'm *so* not going to risk getting caught again.

The steps end at a heavy, splintered wooden door, which opens into a narrow stone corridor. Only torches, bracketed to the walls on each side, light the room. A slight breeze from cracks in the stone inspires the flames to cast disturbing, flickering shadows on the ceiling.

The whole thing is very Goth, and I'm sure appeals to those who favor black lipstick and vampire fangs. To red-lipped, fang-free me, however, it seems depressing and not at all feng shui. I mean would it be such a crime to throw a few windows here and there to give the place some natural light? Between the hall and that tower room, this place is a total candidate for *Trading Spaces*. Though I wouldn't let whoever decorated it *near* my already very classy one-bedroom.

I tiptoe down the hallway and come to another door. I pull it open a crack and peek through.

On the other side of the door is a great hall. And when I say great, I mean huge, not particularly nice. In fact, it's kind of gross, really. There's a fire pit in the middle of the room, for one thing, making it unbearably smoky. They don't even have a proper chimney for ventilation—just a tiny hole in a very tall ceiling. That has *got* to be against the building's fire code.

A variety of ragamuffins, dressed in what I'm assuming must be peasant medieval gear, huddle around the fire, holding their hands close to the flames. Evidently these people drew the short straws when it came to doling out acting positions. Or maybe you work your way up; year one you're a peasant, year two a servant, and so forth, until you've got enough seniority to apply for the queen or king position. Who knows? All I can tell is that, peasant or princess, the only apparent requirement for acting at King Arthur's Faire is that you have to be certifiably nuts.

They've even got a bunch of mangy mutts running around, begging for food. As one lifts his leg, relieving himself on a wooden stool, I am reminded that my poor black

Lab, Gucci, is at this very moment stuck inside my apartment either desperately crossing her legs or letting loose on my new Pottery Barn sofa. I'm praying for the first, but know her too well not to expect the latter. Good thing for her I'm a sucker for big brown eyes and possess an economy-size bottle of Febreze.

Of course, here a puddle of pee fits right into the whole atmosphere, in good company with the bones and feathers already littering the ground. It's not a bit sanitary, and the sickening smell of smoke, burned meat, and mildew makes me want to barf.

Things look a little nicer at the far right end of the rectangular hall. About a dozen men and women in fancy dress sit behind a long wooden table (surprisingly, not a round table), drinking from silver cups. On the wall, behind the "royalty," hang elaborate cloth banners, all adorned with the sign of the dragon, like the one Lancelot wears on his chest. You know, for a creature they insist is make-believe, they certainly use it a lot in their decorating.

A servant type presents a tray heaped with colorful fruits and cheeses to the head table. A musician sits in one corner, playing some kind of harplike instrument, while another stands at his side, juggling. You can barely hear the music over the raucous voices and laughter that echo through the hall. Everyone seems to be having a blast, even the people stuck over by the dog pee. The only thing I can compare it to is a kind of medieval-themed rave, minus the dancing and drugs.

I have to admit, I'm actually rather impressed by the elaborate setup. I'm no expert, of course, but everything seems so authentic! Not like the fair itself, where half the stuff was totally cheesy. Evidently once the tourists go home, the real party begins.

At the head of the table, on intricately carved mahogany thrones, sit Guenevere and Arthur. On Arthur's right is the old guy playing Merlin, looking unhappy and constipated. On Guenevere's left I see an empty chair. Perhaps belonging to Lancelot? I scan the room but see no sign of the hunk. Oh, well.

Okay, enough voyeurism. How to get out? I shut the door and try to think. I can't just waltz right through the main hall, of course, though this is the only door I've come across.

Or maybe I can! There's got to be a hundred people in the room. With all the noise and smell and smoke, no one's going to notice one little girl waltzing through.

The key will be to do it with an air of confidence, as if I'm one of them, like when I used to sneak into the VIP sections of trendy Manhattan nightclubs. If you walked past the bouncer, head held high like you owned the place, he would assume you were one of the crowd. If you appeared nervous, he'd smell your fear and say you weren't on the list. (Which is *so* embarrassing!) Of course, it also helps to have the appropriate attire. There, that means the latest Versace. Here, they seem to favor long, shapeless gowns. Thanks to Guenevere I've got just the thing. They'll think I'm one of the actors.

I squeak open the door again and scan the room for exits. Aha! To the very left of the hall, far away from the royal table, are two large, wooden double doors. That must be the way out.

I straighten my shoulders and step into the room with a confident swagger. Though I'm sure my outward demeanor is perfect, my heart is beating so loud and fast I'm positive someone's going to hear it. Like in that Edgar Allan Poe story, "The Tell-Tale Heart." Though, of course, in this case it's my own heart, and I didn't murder anyone, and . . . Well, okay, not such a good analogy.

The hall seems endless as I walk slowly toward the doors of freedom. I keep my head low, trying not to meet anyone's eyes.

"I have not seen you around the castle before."

Caught. I whirl around to address the voice, praying it's not someone who will recognize me from the jousting field. The man behind me is short and stout, with beady little black eyes sunken into a fleshy face. He also reeks of beer and is standing way too close. Evidently he's never heard of the two-foot personal-bubble rule.

"Yes, well I . . . art new to these yonder . . . things," I say, giving my best English-accent impression. Must try to blend in.

"You look like a fine lady, you do." As he talks, little droplets of spit fly at my face, and I step back, wiping them away with the sleeve of my gown. Gross. "Where are you from?"

"Er, um, London?" Was London even a town back then? Luckily he nods. Evidently an acceptable answer. Phew. Hopefully he doesn't have any follow-ups. The only street I know in London is Bond Street, and I have a feeling that's more retail than residential.

"Aye," he says, swaying back into my personal space. "My travels have taken me through London. 'Tis a town not fit for dogs."

Now, I'm not really from London, obviously, but if I truly were, telling me that my hometown sucks is not the way to make friends.

"Well, I like it fine. Now if you'll excuse me, I've got to go . . ." Shit, what was it that ladies had to go do in medieval times? Oh, duh. ". . . to, uh, relieve myself."

But he's evidently not buying it. Instead of letting me on my merry way, he grabs my shoulder with a hairy hand, roughly pulling me to him. He smells even worse close-up. "Won't you come to my chambers, lady?" he asks, slurring each word.

"Not in a fucking million years, asshole," I retort, slipping back into New Yorker mode. I think my playing along has merely encouraged him. I struggle to break free, but his hold is too tight.

"At least tell me your name," he begs, pawing at me with ragged, filthy fingernails.

"I don't have a name," I say, looking around to make sure no one's watching. "And you"—I rear back my foot—"don't have a chance!" On the word *chance,* my knee collides with his groin—the world-famous Kat Jones special-delivery-for-disgusting-men-who-don't-get-the-word-*no* move. Works every time.

He howls, releasing me and crouching down in pain. He's so loud I'm sure someone will hear. But while one or two people turn their heads, evidently seeing this guy holding his privates and moaning isn't enough to cause alarm, and they turn back to their dinners.

I make quick strides to the door. Close up, I realize it's flanked with two guards. Here we go. I flash them a breezy smile like I have no cares in the world. They totally buy it, even opening the door for me, like gentlemen.

I step past the doors and into a huge, open, grassy courtyard filled with crumbling statues and surrounded by high stone walls about twenty feet tall.

I suck in a breath of cool, crisp air, thankful to be out of that smoky chamber, and look around. In one corner is a wooden building that looks like it could be a stable. In another is a small chapel. At the far end of the courtyard, under an open iron grate, I see a lowered drawbridge sitting over an actual moat.

So this really is a castle, I marvel, a little perplexed. Where the hell did they take me? I am quite positive there was no castle near the fair. I'm pretty sure I would have noticed. What if I can't find my way home?

Even more worrying, from the look of the sun in the sky it appears to be high noon. Since it was about four in the afternoon when I got hit with the lance, I realize I must have been out an entire day rather than the mere hours I'd first thought. Poor Gucci.

Poor sofa.

The birds chirp merrily from an unseen location as I cautiously approach the drawbridge, not knowing what—or who—I'll encounter there. Two men dressed in leather tunics with chain-mail sleeves and leggings stand at attention on the other side of the drawbridge. Each holds a spear. Obviously some sort of outer guards. This place is like Fort Knox.

"Milady, has the feast ended so soon?" the one on the left asks as I approach, furrowing his thick eyebrows. Up close, I realize he's quite mammoth, with bushy black hair and a full beard. Kind of got the Andre the Giant thing going on. "I had thought it would have lasted hours longer."

"Indeed, I can hardly imagine they would even be through the first course," says the other, a redhead who looks a tad suspicious at my oh-so-innocent presence.

Are they going to try to stop me from leaving? Time to turn on the charm—my specialty. After all, I didn't get voted senior class president because of my vast knowledge of school politics or even my innovative campaign for an annual "bring your dog to school" day.

"Indeed they are not," I say, donning ye olde English accent once again. "However, I was feeling . . . indisposed."

"I am sorry to hear that, milady," says the nice giant on the left. "But surely the queen will arrange a bed for you in the castle where you may retire until you are feeling well again."

Oh, yeah, right. A real comfy bed made out of flea-ridden straw, I'm sure. "Oh, yes, she has offered, kind soul," I say with a dramatic sigh. "But I am more inclined to head home."

"Where might that be, milady?" asks the suspicious one.

I think fast. "Yonder village. Not a stone's throw from here."

"And where is your escort? It is unwise for a good lady to travel these roads alone. They are filled with villains inclined to violate a lady's honor." This from the nice one—a little too concerned about me for his own good. I grew up in Brooklyn, damn it. I think I can face the wilds of upstate New York without a man by my side. But I need to stay in character. Back then women did not kick as much ass. After all, it was way before Tae Bo was invented.

"I dost not want him to miss thou feast, of course. I can take care of mine self, thank thee."

"You talk with a strange tongue, madam," says Mr. Suspicious. Darn. I thought I was doing so well with the accent thing, too. "Are you sure you are from the village?"

Realizing the whole trying-to-act-my-way-out-of-here thing isn't working, I switch tactics, grabbing my purse (which I had tied to the sash around my waist) and pulling out a hundred-dollar bill. This kills me to do, especially since I have no idea now how I'm going to pay my cable bill without it, but I'm desperate.

"Look, dudes, how much are they paying you to stand here? It can't be more than, like, minimum wage, right?" I wave the bill in their faces for emphasis. "Let me pass and Benjamin here goes home with you. No questions asked."

They stare at me and then at the bill. The nice one takes

it and studies it with a close eye. He turns it over in his hands and even brings it to his nose for a sniff.

"A marvelous portrait," he says to the other guard, handing the hundred to him. "On such a tiny canvas." He looks up at me. "I am afraid I haven't the gold to afford such a treasure, milady." He holds it out for me to take back. "But I thank you for showing it to us."

Urgh. This is really getting annoying. "I don't want gold for it. You can keep it. For free. For letting me go."

"Go where?"

"Away from here."

"Where is your horse?"

"I don't have one."

"You cannot walk. The path is long and steep. You would not reach the village by sunset in those shoes."

"Ha! I'm an expert at walking long distances in impractical shoes. You should have been there the day me and my Jimmy Choos took on the steps of . . ." I trail off when I realize they're not listening to my exciting girl-and-her-shoe tales and are instead conversing with each other.

". . . in the name of chivalry it is only right," says the nice one.

"You only want to keep the miniature portrait."

"Not true. My intentions are honorable."

"Fine. Do it if you must."

"Hello?" I wave my hands to regain their attention. "So can I go now?"

"I will escort you to the village, milady," says the nice one. "Just give me a moment to get my horse." He turns to walk into the courtyard.

"Oh, no, you really don't have to . . ." I start to yell after him.

" 'Tis the only way we can rightfully allow you to leave. The queen would not be pleased if we were to let harm come to one of her guests," the other informs me. "In fact, perhaps we should inform the queen that you—"

"Oh! Ha! No need to do that." I laugh nervously. "Your friend can take me to the village. No problem. No sense disturbing the queen." Wow. That could have royally sucked.

The other nods, wearing a smug smile, like he knows full well I don't want to involve Guenevere in the matter. Jerk. He looks like he's going to say something else, but at that moment the other guy reappears, now astride a horse.

He motions for me to mount. Ugh. Did I mention I hate horses? I've also never ridden one—unless you count the merry-go-round at Coney Island—and never had the urge to do so. Growing up, my friends all dreamed of getting horses of their very own. Not me. If someday my prince were to come, he'd be riding a racing-green Jaguar convertible, not a pony. Hey, a girl can dream, right?

Today, however, this equestrian beast seems my only opportunity to escape the clutches of the nerds in shining armor at the castle. So I muster up my courage, bite my lip, and place my hand in the guard's. He boosts me up so I'm sitting sidesaddle in front of him. It's not at all comfortable, and he stinks as bad as the other guy. I hope the village isn't far.

He shakes the reins and the horse breaks into a trot. The up-and-down bumping makes my butt hurt worse than after two hours of spinning class at the gym. Hasn't anyone invented gel saddles like they have for bikes? Though as medieval purists, these guys would probably rather suffer sore behinds than succumb to a modern, comfortable innovation. I don't get it.

I look back at the castle, my breath catching in my throat. Now that we've headed down the hill a bit I can see the building in its entirety. It's huge, seeming to be carved from the very rocky cliff on which it sits. Its whitewashed stone walls rise to what looks to be a hundred feet high. Tall towers pierce the blue sky, their golden spires catching the sun, nearly blinding me with their brilliance. Red banners, proclaiming the symbol of the dragon, flap brazenly in the wind. The scene is breathtaking. It also makes me wonder . . .

Where the hell am I?

Fear shoots daggers through my heart, delivering an unpleasant adrenaline rush that makes me severely nauseated. Something is very, very wrong. There should not be a magnificent castle like this anywhere in upstate New York. In fact, I doubt anything like this exists *anywhere* in America. And the screwed-up thing is that it looks completely new. Shining even. Not crumbling ruins like the castles in Europe. Even the ones they keep up for tourists look a bit rundown. But this . . . well, I've never seen anything like it.

Where am I?

As we descend a steep, rocky path, the horse taking slow careful steps, I really start to panic. My heart is beating a mile a minute, and I contemplate jumping off the horse and making a run for it. But a run where?

Just wait till we get to the village. I take deep, soothing breaths—the kind they teach you in yoga class—and try to focus. At least in the village I'll be able to get help. Call a cab. Get a ride to the airport if they've taken me far away. Oh, man, why has this happened to me? What if I've been taken to, like, Nepal or some other faraway country? Do I even have enough money on my Visa to book my ticket back? Oh, why did I succumb to that last Macy's one-day sale?

After about a half hour of riding, we come to a turn in the road and I look down the path. The sight causes my heart to flutter out of control all over again, breathing exercises forgotten.

The village sits in a grassy valley below, about a hundred yards down. My first thought is that it's very beautiful and tranquil-looking. My second, more horrifying thought is that it looks, even from here, completely medieval. Hundreds of thatched-roof houses dot the landscape, and cows graze in the fields. On the east side of the village sit farms, tended by people walking behind oxen.

Not a train, plane, or automobile in sight.

Unable to sit calmly on the horse a moment longer, I squirm to get down. The guard tightens his grip.

"Let me off," I cry.

"Ah, milady, I am not letting you go until I deliver you to your people in person." He shrugs his broad shoulders. "'Tis too dangerous for a woman to walk this path alone."

"Dude, cut the chivalry shit and let me go." I try to maneuver out of his grasp, but he's too strong.

"No, milady. That would not be wise. The queen would have my head if I allowed anything to happen to you."

"Screw the queen. I want to get off. Now!"

Sudden inspiration strikes, and I reach into my purse and pull out my almost forgotten can of Mace. I lift the safety and spray the noxious fumes directly into the giant guard's face. He cries out, letting go of me to rub his eyes. I slide off the horse and onto the ground, almost spraining my ankle in the process. Then I take off running, ignoring his screaming curses. I should have enough time to disappear into the village before he regains his eyesight.

I run down the path as fast as I can. The flimsy leather slippers Guenevere gave me have no shock absorption whatsoever, and my feet are feeling every step. I'm also very out of breath, suffering major gym-slacker remorse. If I ever get out of here, I vow, I will take seven step-and-sculpt classes a week and even stay for the sculpt part.

I enter the outskirts of the village and slow my pace. The

good news is that there are so many people wandering around, I'll easily be able to lose the guard. The bad news? Everywhere I look, all I see are people dressed in medieval garb. Hundreds upon hundreds of villagers going about their day as if everything is completely normal.

This can't be. I rub my eyes, hoping to wake up from the nightmare. A few castle-dwelling freaks I can believe. But an entire town of people all dressed the same way? These can't be actors. There're too many. Way too many.

What the hell has happened to me?

Panicked, I break into a run again down the narrow streets, desperate to come across even one out-of-place item that will prove to me this is a joke. Or a re-creation. Or *something*. A bicycle. A phone. A hidden stash of Pokémon cards. Anything!

I run by a blacksmith's shop, past a man hammering a sword over a steaming anvil. I pass a bakery, where a woman is hand-grinding flour with a wooden stick. Then a smelly tavern where men overflow onto the streets, singing drunken songs I've never heard. Finally a churchyard. In the center sits a large stone. My pounding head knows the inscription before I even read it.

> *Whoso shall lift this sword from the stone, the same is rightly born king of England.*

This can't be happening. There's got to be some logical explanation. It's a nightmare, but I can't seem to wake up. I've never had a dream so vivid before—or that went on for so long. Maybe I'm in a coma. That's it. When I got hit in the head with the lance I slipped into a coma, and I'm really at Mount Sinai, hooked up to life support.

Or maybe I'm dead. What if this is hell? Some say hell is the culmination of your personal idea of ultimate torture, and . . . well, the idea of living the rest of eternity without flush toilets pretty much sums up mine.

But I can't be dead. My heart's still beating. I feel pain. There's got to be some other kind of logical explanation for this. Anything but the impossible, crazy notion that keeps spiraling uncontrollably through my head.

Thou art out of time.

What if the crazy gypsy at the fair really did curse me? What if she really did have some kind of magical powers?

Thy destiny—it is lying in another era.

I was thinking she meant, like, the seventies. After all, I've always kind of dug disco. I never dreamed she could be talking about the twelfth century.

If thou dost not take heed, thou wilt surely die today!

Okay, I know this sounds completely off-the-wall, lock-me-up, men-in-white-jackets-take-me-away crazy but I have to ask . . .

What if she sent me back in time?

No. That's insane. I refuse to believe it. I'm in a coma. I think I can even hear my mother's voice calling me, telling me to come back to her.

I've run straight through the village and am now approaching some woods. Maybe if I run a little farther I can find another town. A real one with real modern-day people. This could just be a tourist attraction. If I keep going I'll find the parking lot.

As I enter the forest I slow my pace and suck in air, no longer able to run. With heaving breaths I take in my surroundings, praying for something familiar.

A canopy of low-hanging trees blankets the path and blocks out most of the sunshine. Spooky-looking moss drips from the branches, and a disconcerting mist hangs in the air. It's like a scene out of *Friday the 13th*. I try to remember the rules of surviving a horror movie. Number one, you must be a virgin.

Uh-oh.

I come to a small clearing and sink to the ground, unable to rein in my fierce sobs. On my knees I lean against a fallen log, cradling my face in my hands and allowing my tears to fall. I can't remember the last time I cried. I'm a tough chick from Brooklyn, after all. I don't cry like a little girl. But suddenly I can't help it. It's all too scary, too overwhelming, and none of it makes any sense.

What am I supposed to do? Where am I supposed to go? Back to the castle? No, there I was a prisoner. But where else? It'll be dark in a few hours, and I don't have a place to sleep. The guards said it's dangerous for a woman out here alone. What if some bad guy comes and—

"Well, well, well. What have we here?"

Speak of the devil. I look up—way up—at the hugest black horse I have ever seen. Astride the horse is a virtual giant in coal-black armor. He lifts his helmet off his head, revealing an ugly, battle-scarred face, more hideous than the Elephant Man's. His eyes are cold, calculating, with a cruel mouth twisted in an evil smile. Oh, shit. This is not good.

I glance around, desperately trying to assess my situation and develop an escape plan, but find myself surrounded. At least twenty men on horseback circle the glade, all watching me with lecherous eyes. Somehow I get the impression that these are not any of Arthur's loyal Knights of the Round Table, but renegades out for blood. My blood.

I try to stand up, to run, but trip over a sunken root and fall flat on my face. As I begin to rise I feel a sharp metal point press against the back of neck. I reach back to grab the offending object and instant heat burns my palm. I bring my arm forward to examine my hand. Blood seeps through a huge slice of skin—a battle wound garnered from grabbing onto what I suddenly realize is aimed at my neck.

A sword.

"Now, now, my pretty," the black knight coos with an evil chuckle. "I would be loath for you to run away and miss the party." He presses the point of the blade into my neck, and I stifle a cry as the steel pierces my skin. I can feel a trickle of hot blood drip down my back. Tears threaten my eyes again, but I refuse to give the bastard the satisfaction of seeing me cry.

Instead I grit my teeth. "Party? I love parties," I manage to spit out. "Bring it on."

Chapter Four

Okay, if I'd known the so-called "party" was more than a day's trip on horseback, I never would have RSVP'd. You have no idea how uncomfortable it is to be hog-tied to a hairy beast and ride all day down a dusty trail. I'm filthy, I smell like horseshit, and have long ago lost all feeling in my butt.

The never-ending trip's also given me never-ending time to think. And four hours later I'm not any closer to figuring out what the hell has happened to me.

For one thing, the whole time we've ridden I've seen not one sign of twenty-first-century civilization. No planes have flown overhead. We've passed over no paved roads. Here and there we come across these little thatch-roofed huts in the forest, and every single one of them looks medieval. So I'm thinking my original theory of this all being one big reality show is out. It's too grand a scale to be fake. Too elaborate.

Okay, on to options two and three. Either I'm dreaming-slash-in-a-coma or the gypsy's spell really sent me back in time.

Since the whole time-travel idea is so out there, I temporarily decide to give the nightmare-slash-coma theory a turn. I imagine myself lying motionless in a hospital bed, my mother sitting patiently at my side, tears in her eyes, begging me to wake up. After all, I did get hit on the head with a sharp piece of wood. I do remember that.

However, if this *is* true, and I'm really in a coma, I've got a major bone to pick with my subconscious. I mean, would it have been so wrong to go with a coma dream involving sandy white beaches and gorgeous, tanned waiters bringing an endless supply of margaritas to my lounge chair by the water? But no! *My* brain decides a mind trip to dirty, smelly medieval England would be a cool way to while away the unconscious hours.

Sigh. Well, since I'm here, I might as well play along, right? I mean what else do I have to do? Though my dream kidnappers aren't being very cooperative. They refuse to tell me where we're going, and also what will become of me when we get there. I do learn, from overhearing scraps of their conversations, that the black knight isn't only a knight, but also a king named Lot. He and his cronies are from the Orkneys, which is apparently someplace far north. From their accents, I guess my imagination wants me to think they're Scottish, though it lacks the creativity to conjure up kilts, so I can't ask them if they're wearing anything under them to make conversation.

I do try to tell them about my great-grandmother on my father's side who was (or I guess "will be" in this case?) Scots-Canadian—making us practically kin—but they don't seem to care, and at this point they stop to gag me with a stained rag that is not at all hygienic. So help me, if it gives me a cold sore . . .

Oops, sorry. Brain fart. Can't catch cold sores from dream rags! Duh. But at certain moments the whole thing seems pretty darn real—tastes pretty darn real, too, and I almost forget it's all in my head.

Of course, if for some strange reason this *isn't* a dream, then I'm royally screwed. I mean, imagine if it were a real scenario! Kidnapped by a bunch of scary-looking guys who force me to ride all day toward some unknown location in the middle of nowhere. Pretty scary. But I will my heart to stop pounding and my hands to stop shaking. After all, it's only a dream. It's gotta be!

The sun dips beneath the trees, and when we come to a clearing, King Lot decides it's a good spot to set up camp for the night. Oh, great. Camping. *Why, brain, why? You know I hate camping!*

I once dated a guy who was the real outdoors type. He insisted I would love camping if I gave it a try. Since he was way cute, I reluctantly agreed to a weekend trip to the Poconos. Well, after a romantic dinner of freeze-dried "just add water" beef stew, a mosquito-bitten makeout session by a smoky fire that stung my eyes, and a night of sensual in-tent lovemaking, complete with rocks and roots gouging my back at every thrust, I had enough camping for a lifetime and demanded I be taken back to civilization immediately. Needless to say, my poison ivy lasted longer than our relationship.

"Isn't there a hotel or something nearby?" I ask hopefully, as one of the rogues removes my gag. They had hotels back then, right? I think hard, trying to conjure a dream hotel with my imagination. Who knows, maybe I have magic powers in my coma dream. Unfortunately no hotels materialize out of thin air. (Did I mention that this dream really sucks?)

"An inn?" I suggest. "A tavern with rooms for rent, maybe? That way you could even get beer! Come on," I try to cajole. "You know you want a bed and a brew. It'll be so much better than sleeping on the ground. Maybe you'll even meet a nice serving wench and—"

"Och, the fine lady doesna want to lie on the forest floor," Lot says to his men, in a totally unwarranted poor-little-rich-girl tone.

"She can lie on me instead," one of the men suggests with a leer. I shoot him a dirty look. As if!

"Nay, the wee lass will be sleeping in my tent tonight," Lot corrects, sliding off his horse. "Though I canna guarantee she will get much rest."

Catcalls and cheers from the gang. Wonderful. I swallow hard, getting a good mental picture of what he plans to do with me; it's not pretty. Great. First sex in, like, six months and it's going to be with a grisly, gap-toothed, evil knight who smells like a sewer. Well, if he thinks I'll take it like a lady, he's sadly mistaken and had better protect his family jewels with his life. If I get half a chance, dream or not, I will *so* go Lorena Bobbitt on him.

Two men drag me off the horse. As my legs hit the ground they buckle, having lost circulation from the long trip on horseback. I fall with a thud, and pain shoots up my back. I bite my lip; this is no time to cry like a baby—especially since this is only a dream.

They pull me to my feet and drag me over to a tree, then sit me down, my back against the trunk, and wrap heavy corded ropes around my middle.

Big pavilionlike tents get set up, and a couple of men spark a roaring fire. I still haven't woken up. I try all my standard wake-up-from-bad-dreams tricks. I pinch myself, squeeze my eyes open and shut repeatedly, count to three, then four, then pinch myself harder, and go so far as to bang my head against the tree trunk. The masochistic wake-up tactics get more and more violent, but still I remain tied to a tree in jolly old England.

I'm starting to get more than a little uneasy at this point. What if it isn't a dream? The gypsy's words haunt me once again. What if . . . ? No. That's crazy. It couldn't happen. Could it? And if it did, what do I do now?

I wish I had paid more attention in school, read the ends of the Jules Verne and Mark Twain novels, instead of skimming the Cliff's Notes and ending my reports with "if you want to know the exciting conclusion, read the book!" Then I'd at least have a clue as to how you get back to the twenty-first century if you have the unfortunate experience of being sent back in time. Now I realize the only back-in-time thing I ever saw the end of was *Back to the Future*, and Michael J. Fox's trip from the fifties back to the big-haired, acid-washed eighties required a DeLorean going eighty-eight miles an hour. Since cars won't be invented for about another millennium, I don't think I'll live long enough to try that tactic.

Wake up, Kat! Please, please wake up!

It's no use. I can't wake up. And as time passes I'm getting more convinced that the reason why I can't wake up is because I'm not asleep. However it happened, whatever it is, it's too real to dismiss as a nightmare. I can smell. I can taste. I can feel, see, and hear. I'm really here.

Of course, accepting that fact means accepting the fact that I'm in pretty serious trouble. If I'm really here then I'm really tied to a tree. I'm really going to get raped. And I'm really in serious danger of getting killed. Oh, my God. This is horrible. How did I get here? And more important, how do I get back?

Don't even go there, Kat. Just chill out.

Two of the men return to the camp carrying several dead rabbits by the ears. Perhaps it's the thought of my impending doom, but I'm feeling oddly sentimental all of a sudden. I can't help but think back fondly on my bunny,

Thumper, that I had growing up. He was litter-box trained and everything. Used to hop around my room and beg for carrots. . . .

I shake my head. What am I thinking? I've got to focus on my situation, not childhood pets. What do I do? How do I escape? Maybe I can slip out while they're sleeping. Problem is, that's a time period that will occur *after* the disgusting king has had his way with me—a scenario I'd like to avoid if at all possible.

They gut, skin, and skewer the rabbits with long sticks and hold them over the roaring fire. Disgusting. But suddenly the smell of cooked meat permeates the air, and I breathe in. I'm starving. Forget Thumper; if they offer me roasted bunny, I'm eating. In fact, at this point I'd gladly eat a whole loaf of white bread or a big baked potato, Atkins be damned. After all, what difference does gaining ten pounds make if cameras haven't been invented to add ten more? Unfortunately it appears they're planning on being less than generous with the rations. Jerks.

"Hey!" I cry. "How about some food over here?"

"Ah, the lass wants to put something in her mouth," one of the men says with a laugh.

"I'll gladly give her something to suck on," says another, hands on hips and thrusting his groin in the air. "Ye think the wee lass would like a large piece of Orkney meat, perchance?" The rogues roar with laughter. I shake my head in disgust. Men. From the same planet Mars now as they are in the twenty-first century.

"Well, we all know your mother does," I retort, a rather halfhearted attempt at a "your mother" joke.

The man's face darkens. He strides over to the tree and actually hits me! I flinch as pain shoots through my already sore body, but refuse to give him the satisfaction of letting him know. "You shall leave me mither out of this," he growls. "A finer woman never walked the earth."

Gotta love it. "Your mother" insults are apparently time-less. Still, so's a punch in the face. I bite my lip, trying not to cry as pain throbs behind my cheek. Bastard.

As they get drunker and drunker, the men's laughter, tales, and songs get louder and louder. Turns out they don't need to go to a bar because they evidently carry their very own porto-tavern on one of the pack mules. Well, the poor beast will have a lighter load tomorrow, that's for sure.

For a little while I hold on to the vain hope that King Lot may actually drink himself to oblivion before getting me alone in the tent. But soon he stretches his arms above his head and announces his retirement for the evening. The men cheer and whistle and make disgusting remarks not suitable to repeat as he walks over, unties me, and drags me into the tent. I try kicking and screaming but he's too strong.

"D'ya see this dagger?" he asks as he shoves me to the ground inside the tent. The glint of metal reflects the light of a lone candle. I nod, trying not to quiver with fear. I don't want him to know I'm petrified. "Try to escape and ye'll feel it as well."

"What do you want with me?" I ask, pulling my knees to my chest and huddling against the wall of the tent. He takes a seat on the floor and begins whittling a piece of wood with the knife. I swallow hard and try to control my breath-ing. I'll certainly never be able to fight my way out of this one. My only chance is to stall for time. I remember a friend telling me about when her ex-boyfriend used to show up at her house drunk, demanding sex. If she blabbed on long enough, he'd usually pass out before making his move. Lot doesn't look too far from the passing out stage, so maybe . . .

"So," I say, forcing my voice to stay calm and confident. Like I'm trapped in tents with medieval knights all the time and he doesn't frighten me a bit. "Are you going to take me back to your black castle and make me your captive queen or something?" Okay, not very stimulating conversation, but it's a start.

He laughs, totally taking the bait. Even sets the knife down, to my relief. "I already have a queen. Queen Morgause. Arthur's half sister."

"Maybe you shouldn't cheat on her with me then," I suggest, not very hopeful that fidelity means anything to a man like this.

"Aye, but my queen is no longer good for rutting," he explains with a chuckle. "She has borne four sons. Five, if you count—" He stops abruptly, then changes the subject away from the fifth kid. Hmm. Wonder what *that's* about. "Now a man could get lost in her ample flanks."

"Huh?" I scrunch my eyes. "You mean she's gotten fat?"

"I have seen smaller cows grazing in the fields." Lot sighs. "But you," he says, turning to me with a lusty eye. "Ye're ripe for the plucking, you are. Fair and sweet."

"Sweet? Dude, have you had your nose checked lately? I smell like shit right now. I haven't bathed in, like, two days."

Lot shrugs, putting down the knife and wood and crawling closer until his face is inches from mine. My breath hitches in fear. He rakes a grimy hand over my hair, and I shudder, suddenly realizing why he doesn't think *I* smell: he positively reeks.

"Ye're a pretty one, ye are," he says in what I believe he must think is a sexy tone. As if at this point, after taking me hostage and making me ride all day tied to a horse, he actually thinks he can turn me on with a little foreplay. Puhleeze! I ponder kicking him where it counts, but the dagger lying next to him prompts me to behave. This guy is psycho, and I really don't want to piss him off until I'm sure I can get away.

Come on, Kat. Think.

"So let me get this straight." I say, trying again to talk my way out of this inept scene of seduction. Maybe I can make him feel guilty or something. "Your wife is stuck at home with four boys, and you're out in the woods screwing other chicks 'cause she gained a little weight? That's a little shallow, don't you think?"

He scowls but, to my nose's relief, sits back. "They are not four boys, but knights full-grown. Gawain, Agravine, Garheis, and my youngest, Gareth. Strapping, strong lads, all of 'em." He flexes his own huge muscled arms for emphasis. I have to grudgingly admit he does have a good body. Maybe—if he took a yearlong bath, shaved his beard, got a haircut, and made friends with a dentist—just maybe he could be a halfway decent-looking guy. Kind of looks like a hairy Vin Diesel. Of course, it goes without saying that he'd also have to work on his personality and his way with women.

Okay, face it, Kat: he's a lost cause.

"But they didna stay home with me wife. Nay, they joined up with that bastard Arthur and vowed their allegiance to him. Denounced their own liege lord." He pauses, then adds in a hurt tone, "And their da."

I almost feel bad for the guy, but I can also see why the kids wouldn't want to stick around. I don't know what Lot's kingdom looks like—it could be quite charming—but if his own band of knights are any indication, I wouldn't live there for all the purses in Prada. With a dad like Lot, the poor kids probably flew the coop the moment they turned eighteen, if not sooner.

Still, maybe sympathizing with him will get his mind off the task at hand. "I'm so sorry to hear that. Kids can be so cruel," I coo.

"No matter," Lot says, picking his fingernails with the knife. "Now that I have you, that is."

"Huh?"

"By the look of yer clothes ye be a fine lady. Arthur will pay dearly for yer return."

"Actually—"

"Ye, my lady, are the pawn. 'Tis simple. Arthur sends back me boys, which are rightfully mine by blood, and I will give him back his fine lady."

Is that his big plan? Oh, man, he's going to be pissed when he finds out who I am. I clear my throat. "I really hate to burst your bubble, Lotty, but I'm not even from Camelot."

Lot's face darkens. "You what?"

"They had *me* prisoner. Thought I was a Saxon, whatever that is. Which I'm not, by the way. But as far as coughing up four knights for my return? I doubt you'll even get one." I sigh. "You know, you should have asked me while we were closer to the castle. Would have saved you a lot of time and effort in the long run. Then you could have found some other lady running around the woods. Now you've wasted, like, a whole day dragging me out here when I'm not even the one you want."

Lot glares at me, his face beet red with anger. "You tricked me."

Tricked him? Yeah, right. What, was I wearing a sign on my back saying, KIDNAP ME, HOLD ME FOR RANSOM, AND YOU'LL GET YOUR KIDS BACK? Funny, I don't think so.

"I didn't trick you. You assumed. And you know what assuming does, don't you? It makes an *ass* out of *you* and *me*."

Lot's body stiffens with rage. "Are ye calling me an arse, woman?"

I know I should shut up—any normal sane person would shut up now—but I'm on a roll. "If the Manolo fits . . ."

Smack! His hand makes contact with my face, and I realize my big mouth has now gotten me into a lot of trouble. Now not only have I completely antagonized him, I've also announced, in not so many words, that I'm as disposable as a Bic razor. OMG, what have I done? Fear-induced adrenaline pumps through my body. I've pushed him too far. Now he'll probably kill me after the raping. *Stupid, Kat. Very, very stupid!*

Lot grabs the knife and presses it against the hollow of my throat. "Undress. Now."

I can't breathe. And soon it won't matter if I can 'cause I'll be dead and I won't need to. How did I get myself into this mess? Tears leak from the corners of my eyes as I wonder what Gucci will do when her mama doesn't come home. Will they take her to a no-kill shelter where she'll be adopted or send her to the gas chambers? Will I see her in Heaven or do dogs go to a separate place?

I squeeze my eyes shut, begging any and all higher powers that are listening for an immediate miracle. Like, preferably one that sends me back to the future. At this point, I'd also settle for:

a) Lot having an instant heart attack and collapsing at my feet.
b) Lot having a change of heart and letting me go on my merry way, maybe even giving me an escort back to Camelot.
c) Some knight in shining armor showing up at the nick of time and rescuing me from the clutches of

the evil knight. (I know that's not very women's lib of me, but to tell you the truth, I'm only a feminist when I'm *not* moments from being raped and killed.)

d) A and C, or heck, all of the above.

"I said undress!" Lot repeats, this time more threateningly.

"No," I say, wishing my voice wouldn't croak with fear. If he's going to kill me anyway, I guess I'd prefer to die with my clothes on, pre- rather than postrape.

Which brings me to the question: What the hell happens if you die before you're supposed to be born? The metaphysics of the whole thing make my head spin. Will the time come again for me to be born? Or has it already happened? Am I destined to repeat the same circle of fate forever? Or can I skip the fair and thus skip time traveling the next time around? How many times have I already done this? What if I've somehow changed the strands of the time-space continuum and I'll never even be born? But then, if I was never born, why am I here now?

Man, this is making my brain hurt. Who knows, who cares? Bottom line? If I can avoid getting killed, I won't have to worry about what happens if I am. The odds of avoiding death aren't looking so good right now.

"You dare defy me?" Lot demands as his blade scratches at my flesh. I bite down on my lip—hard. Oh, how did I get myself into this mess? Will my face be on a milk carton for eternity? They should have a program where missing adults can be on bottles of beer. Hey, that's a good idea. If I ever get out of here, I'm going to suggest that to the missing-persons guys.

I force my thoughts back to the matter at hand. After all, Lot's asked me if I dared defy him, and I have never been one to turn down a dare.

"Go to hell," I retort, sounding braver than I feel.

Lot laughs. "Wherever ye come from, ye're a feisty one; I'll give ye that." He grabs my wrists and shoves them over my head. With his free hand he runs the knife up the bodice of my dress, succeeding in slicing though the beautiful embroidery.

As he grabs at my breast with a grimy hand, I want to vomit. I settle instead on spitting at him, my loogie landing directly between his eyes. Not very ladylike, but desperate times lead to desperate measures.

He wipes the spit away and laughs again. "I am very much going to enjoy this, I will."

Left without other options, I squeeze my eyes shut and resign myself to my apparent fate. I try to think of a few of my favorite things, the way Julie Andrews does in *The Sound of Music*. Unfortunately, since, in my opinion anyway, being raped by a medieval Scottish king is a little more awful than when the dog bites and the bees sting, thoughts of whiskers on kittens and raindrops on roses don't seem to cut it. And while the old standby daydream of a shoe sale at Nordstrom normally does the trick, this time it is accompanied by the horrific realization that Nordstrom won't be invented for another millennium and therefore I will have a long wait if I want to get any cute mules on markdown.

"To arms!"

My eyes pop open. Drunken shouts cut into the night air. The firelight casts shadows of desperate, scrambling men onto the pavilion's walls. With a worried look, Lot scrambles to the tent opening. After peeking out, he turns back to me. "Stay here, lass. I shall be back to finish what we have started." He leaves in a rush. I roll my eyes. Yeah, right. I'll sit here and wait for you. Sure.

I scramble to the tent's entrance and peek outside, where utter chaos rules. Drunken men trip over equipment as they try to find their swords. Others lay motionless on the ground, having already succumbed to whomever's attacking. Cries of agony replace the jovial songs and tales of the early evening. From the look of the place, the guy or guys doing the raiding are real professionals.

Not willing to go from one captor to another, I pull my ripped gown around me, crawl out of the tent, and attempt to make a run for it.

Out of the corner of my eye I see one of Lot's men coming at me, and I dive out of his way. He trips and falls flat on his drunken face. I think I'm clear until he grabs my ankle with a hairy hand. I kick at him with my other foot until he cries in pain and lets go.

Kat one; ugly Scottish guy zero. Watch out Cameron, Lucy, and Drew—here comes Miss Jones, honorary Charlie's Angel.

Another rogue comes at me, this one waving a sword. He swings. I duck. Then I stick out my foot and karate-kick him in the chest. (Thank you cardio-kickboxing classes!) His armor, and probably the amount he's had to drink, makes him totally unstable, and he topples backward, dropping the sword and flailing like a turtle turned shellside down.

Whoo-hoo! Score two for the twenty-first-century girl! Move over, Buffy; there's a new slayer in town. Actually I guess I wouldn't begrudge the Buffster her vampires. After all, they seem a tad tougher than your average drunken medieval Scotsman.

I grab his sword. It's heavier than I imagined, and I realize I'm going to have more than a bit of trouble if I actually want to use it. Oh, why haven't I supplemented my cardio routine with weight lifting at the gym, like my personal trainer keeps telling me? Then I'd have strong, sword-lifting arms that, as an added bonus, look toned and sexy like Madonna's.

I run around the corner, dragging the sword behind me, then stop dead in my tracks.

King Lot stands blocking the path. He brandishes a huge sword of his own, and it doesn't look like it takes him a lick of effort to do so.

"Ah, pretty, so ye thought to escape, did ye?" He raises the sword. "And here I thought we would have a bit of fun before I killed ye. I guess it wasna written in the stars. A pity," he says, not really sounding all that broken up about it. "Still, I will enjoy seeing you die."

"Oh, yeah? Well, say hello to my little friend," I say, doing my best Al Pacino *Scarface* impersonation. It takes all my effort, but I manage to pull my newfound sword from behind my back and raise it like a baseball bat, ready to swing. I can feel my arm muscles start to buckle almost immediately, and hope I don't have to pose like this for too long.

As cool and tough as I probably look, even I have to admit I'm a bit surprised when his eyes widen and he lowers his weapon, taking a definitive step back. In fact, if I'm not mistaken, his entire body starts to tremble. Aha! So I *do* look scary with a sword. Cool. Now *that's* what the Spice Girls would have called "girl power!" (Well, before they broke up, married rich men, and posed for *Playboy,* anyway.)

I smile smugly and give the weapon another little wave for effect, just to scare him a bit more. Maybe he's never seen a female wield such a mighty blade. The power I hold over him is exhilarating, to say the least.

"Scared of a wee lass, are we, now, Lotty?" I taunt. Maybe I can get him to run away before I have to prove my nonexistent prowess.

I suddenly hear a horse's snort and whirl around. I realize that standing behind me, not two feet away, is a six-foot helmeted knight astride a great white stallion, and holding a mighty silver sword.

Oh.

Okay, so maybe Lot wasn't *so* impressed with my feat of arms after all. Darn. Well, hey, whatever works, right? I drop the sword and step aside. It may not be very feminist of me, but right now my weary arms are happy to play damsel in distress.

" 'Tis a dishonor to attack an unhorsed man," Lot calls to the knight. Like he's one to talk about honor. The guy kidnaps and rapes women for a living. "Stand down and fight like a man."

"Dude, you don't have to," I inform my rescuer. "This guy is already about as dishonorable as they come."

But the knight dismounts anyway, and, with Lot distracted, I decide it's about time to make my move. I scurry out of the line of fire and dive behind a bush to let them go at it. I consider making a run for it, until I notice that the horse's saddle bears the mark of the dragon. I look back over at the knight. Is he who I think he is? He looks about the right build, but it's hard to tell with his helmet on. If it is him, how ever did he find me?

Swords clash and sparks fly as the knights come together in battle. Their movements are slower and more labored than those you see in the movies. Lot has the no-armor, quicker-movement advantage. The other guy has the whole nothing-gets-through-the-steel-plates-and-chain-covering-my-body thing going on. So I'd say all in all, they're pretty well matched.

The dragon knight charges forward, beating Lot back against a tree. The knight swings. Their swords slam together, each man pressing for advantage with all his strength. Then the weapons slide apart and Lot ducks, causing the other knight's blade to crash into the trunk. Lot tries to maneuver behind the knight and stab him in the back, but the knight whirls around, easily parrying his pathetic attempt at a thrust.

They keep fighting, on and on . . . and on. How they get the strength to wind up and swing those heavy blades of steel, I have no idea. And my rescuer must be sweating to death in that armor. Still, they go at it. As quickly as one gets a few steps' advantage, the other forces him backward again. At first it was kind of exciting, but after a while I'm getting a little bored. Hurry up and kick Lot's evil ass, dude.

The swords come together again. And again. I look down at the men's feet, leaping back and forth, and marvel at how they deftly match their footpaths to where their swords must go. It's like a dance almost—one step forward, one step back.

A dance? Suddenly inspiration hits me with all the force of a ten-ton truck. A vision of my junior high Spring Fling dance pops into my head. That night a popular boy in my class had been making fun of me and my thrift-store dress. (Don't ask. I really don't want to get into my sordid, unfashionable past.) Anyway, he got crowned Spring Fling king (yes, the cheesy rhyme was intentional), and everyone was supposed to watch as he danced with the queen. (Who so shockingly turned out to be head cheerleader Candi-with-an-i.) But when the junior high royalty took the stage, *somehow,* strangely enough, a lone tennis ball from who knows where just happened to roll out from backstage right at the moment they were dancing by the edge. The Spring Fling king, named Ming (just kidding—he was really called Rick), stepped on the tennis ball, tripped, and came crashing off the three-foot stage, taking Candi with him. His poor kingship suffered a sprained ankle, a load of humiliation, and a big-time breakup with his broken-nosed

Queen Candi-with-an-i (whose real name I found out years later was Janice). Yeah, baby! It was a total John Hughes movie moment.

Anyway, to make a long story short, let's just say that the incident gives me some inspiration. I obviously don't have a tennis ball this time, since the sport has yet to be invented, but this is a forest and filled with rocks, some definitely the rolling type.

So the next time Lot charges, I casually toss out a nearby stone. Sure enough, like Rick, Lot trips and falls forward. Unlike Rick, however, he suffers more than a sprained ankle and a bad breakup with the head cheerleader. Instead, King Lot falls stomach-first into Lancelot's sword.

Whoo-hoo! As Lot exhales a last stinky breath, I do a little happy dance. It has to be said: we girls from the future definitely kick major medieval ass!

The valiant knight whips off his helmet, and I'm psyched to realize it is indeed Lancelot who has come to my rescue. Man, I'd forgotten how good-looking and sexy he is in his whole shining-armor getup.

"Lance!" I cry, overjoyed. "Dude, where have you been all my life?"

But the look on his face makes me prematurely stop my the-king-is-dead, long-live-the-king celebration. His eyes are stormy as he strides to me and grabs me roughly by the arm.

"By the gods, woman, what have you done?"

Chapter Five

"What have I done? I've saved your life, that's what I've done," I retort, ripping my arm from his grasp. What the hell is this guy's problem? Ungrateful bastard. Thanks to me, the evil king has met his demise. Lance should be throwing me a party, not pacing the ground with a scowl written on his otherwise handsome face.

"You interfered. It was a battle won without honor."

Oh, puh-leeze! "Honor, shmonor. You don't want to admit I saved your life." Honor indeed. Such a *man* thing to say. "You won. Don't you think perhaps the end justifies the means?"

"By the code of my knighthood, 'tis better had I died with honor than be spared by trickery."

"Well, I'm *so* sorry to have dishonored you," I say, making sure my voice drips with sarcasm. "You know, I'm *sure* you could have won by yourself and all, but I was getting real bored waiting around, and . . . well, I couldn't take the chance that Lot would get a lucky break and you'd die. Then I'd be stuck with him again."

I start to kick the king's corpse with my toe, but then

think better of it. As happy as I am to be rescued instead of raped, the sight of an actual dead, bloody body makes me more than a bit queasy. Especially since I played a starring role in the guy's death. If we were in the twenty-first century, the police would probably arrest me for aiding and abetting. But then again, I could argue it was self-defense. After all, he did threaten to rape and kill me.

"What news?" a male voice interrupts. Okay, who's that? Another bad guy? Or a friend of Lance's? Oh, please let it be a friend. I can't take another boring fight scene. Especially if, for some ridiculous knight reason, I'm not allowed to help.

Luckily Lance doesn't look too worried at the question and actually answers the guy. So I'm guessing it must be his pal. "Bad tidings, Lamorak," he says as another knight wearing the sign of the dragon approaches. The new guy, Lamorak, lifts his visor and stares at the body with an expression of sheer horror.

"God help us, Lancelot. What have you done?" he cries.

"Hey," I interject. "Why's everyone so upset about the dead guy? Don't you knights fight and kill people all the time?"

Lancelot turns to me, his eyes flashing fire. "People, aye. The king's brother-in-law, nay. The father of Arthur's dearest knights? Never."

Oh. I can kind of see now how that might be considered a faux pas. I had conveniently forgotten the man's relationship to the gang at Camelot when I made the decision to aid in his death. I was thinking "bad guy" when I should have been thinking "bad guy who is a member of powerful family that is already suspicious of me to begin with." I've seen this kind of thing on TV and in the movies, and it never ends well. I hope Arthur isn't anything like Tony Soprano.

"But he was evil," I say, trying to justify it all. "He wanted to rape me."

"Indeed, Lot was not an honorable man," Lancelot agrees. "However, the king has asked that he come to no harm."

"Now, wait one gosh-darned second. *You* harmed him first," I protest. "You made him bleed."

"The wounds he suffered at my hand were shallow, and I doubt would have even left scars. I had planned to fight him to his exhaustion and then demand that he depart to his kingdom in Orkney and not return to Camelot."

Guess I should have found out his strategy before trying to help. My bad. "Can't you tell Arthur it was an accident?" I query, hoping like hell he's not planning on selling me out to the king. I'm sure I'm in enough hot water for escaping the tower without being arrested for murder, too, thank you very much.

"I could, and perhaps he will believe me and, in time, forgive." Lancelot lets out a long sigh. "But his four sons will demand blood in exchange for the death of their kin. Gawain, the oldest, will be forced to challenge me to fight to the death. He is Arthur's knight and a dear friend to the king; I do not want to have to kill him."

"Wait," I interject, thinking fast. "I've got a plan. What if you go back to Camelot and tell the king that you came upon Lot and his knights and they were fighting this major battle with the, uh, Saxons—yeah, that's it. They're bad guys, right? And, like, you tried real hard to help him, but it was way too late, and Lot was slaughtered by the evil, um, Saxonians, and so, like, you gave him a royal burial, and all 'cause he died with honor and stuff." I smile, pretty proud of my spur-of-the-moment plan.

Lancelot and Lamorak exchange glances. " 'Tis a good idea," Lamorak says at last. "It could work."

"Aye, but to lie to the king?" Lancelot moans. Oh, man, this guy is a regular Boy Scout. If he brings up the word *honor* again, so help me!

"Ooh, ooh!" I pipe in, remembering the most important part. "You can also tell him that I was the Saxon's prisoner, and, like, that way they won't think I'm a Saxon anymore, 'cause you had to save me from them."

"And what if the king commands an army to root out King Lot's nonexistent Saxon killers?"

"Um, well, they'll wander around for a while looking for them, and then return to Camelot and say the Saxons must have taken off back to wherever it is Saxons come from. It'd be easy—especially if you led the rooting army."

"Sir, you forget the real problem here," Lamorak butts in. "Whether or not the king will forgive is inconsequential when you take into account the witch."

"Witch? Which witch?" I demand. "There's a freakin' witch involved now?" You know, for an evil king, Lot had a lot of friends, most of them in high places.

"His queen has been known to practice the dark arts."

"You mean that chick Morgause that he told me about? She's a witch?"

"Aye, Morgause is her given name. But in the under-world she is better known as Morgan Le Fay."

Oh, shit. Even *I've* heard of Morgan Le Fay. She's, like, the major she-villain in all the King Arthur stories. And now I've killed her dear old hubby. Wonderful. Damn it, Kat, why couldn't you have stayed out of it? Let the boys have their little fight and moved on?

"Sir," Lamorak says, "I will ride to Orkney and present Lot's scabbard and shield to the queen and inform her of his most honorable demise. You and the woman should re-turn to Camelot."

"Are you sure this is a quest you wish to undertake,

Lamorak?" asks Lancelot, looking a little worried for his friend. "After all, the queen is no woman to trifle with. If she were to hear your thoughts, see through your lies . . ."

"I am quite aware of the danger. However, I am prepared to face it. Witch or no, 'tis better that Queen Morgause hear the sad tidings from friend than foe."

Lancelot nods. "Your bravery will not go unrewarded, Lamorak."

"I thank you for those words. Godspeed." And with that the knight disappears into the night, leaving me alone with Lancelot.

"We cannot stay here," he says, sheathing his sword into the jeweled scabbard that hangs from his belt. " 'Tis not safe. We must make the journey back to Camelot."

Do I want to go back to the castle? That's a tough one. I think I need more info before making my decision. "As your prisoner?"

"Nay, as a lady under my protection."

"And you won't mention to the king about my sort-of in- volvement in Lotty's death?"

"As far as the king is to know, Lot was murdered by Saxon raiders, as you suggested."

Well, okay, then. Since I'm pretty certain that Arthur won't be sending out a team of forensics investigators to take DNA samples—à la *CSI*—as long as Lance keeps his mouth shut, I'm as innocent as O.J.

So should I go back to the castle? I consider my options.

a) Refuse to go back and risk getting kidnapped again. After all, I'm sure Lot ain't the only evil king in the forest.
b) Refuse to go back and risk getting lost in the woods and dying of starvation, since I have no idea how to snare a bunny rabbit, or which mushrooms

are edible and which make you hallucinate like
hippies do at Phish shows.
c) Refuse to go back and risk getting—

Oh, what the hell, I might as well go back with him.
What else do I have to do? It's not like I've got a hot date in
the forest or anything. And maybe if I go back to where
whatever happened, happened, I'll be able to figure out a
way to make it, uh, unhappen.

"Sure, why not?" I agree. "As long as you can find me
more comfortable accommodations than that ghetto
tower." I might as well draw up some terms of agreement
now. "I'm thinking a nice windowed room with a feather
bed. You got those in the castle?"

Lancelot grins his enticing grin. "I think that could be
arranged, lady."

"Do you always have to call me 'lady'? It's getting kind
of annoying, to tell you the truth. I have a name. Kat. Remember? As in, 'meow, meow, pussy cat'?"

"I meant only the greatest respect, Lady Kat."

I grit my teeth. "Not Lady Kat. Kat. Just Kat. Plain and
simple."

"Plain and simple does not suit you," Lancelot says in a
suddenly serious tone.

My cheeks heat, and I look down at the ground, scuffing
my toe against the dirt. I mean, what do you say to something like that? And what prompted him to say it in the
first place? I thought he was all mad at me for killing Lot.
Now he's giving me compliments. At least, I think they're
compliments.

I decide to bring the conversation back to the subject at
hand. "Do we have to go back to Camelot *tonight*?" I don't
mean to whine, but I'm so tired at this point, all I want to

do is curl up and go to sleep. And the castle is at least four hours away.

"Nay, 'tis too dark to travel far," Lancelot says, pacing. "Mayhap we can find a small cave. . . ."

"Oh, no. No way." I place my hands on my hips. "I've had enough camping for one millennium. I'm not sleeping in a cave."

Lancelot studies me for a moment, his piercing blue gaze boiling my blood. I don't know what it is about him that's got me so worked up, but I'm thinking maybe it wouldn't be *so* bad to share a cave with *him*.

"I am sorry, lady—I mean Kat. I forget myself. You are right. A lady is entitled to a bed." He scratches his head. "There is a village not far off. Perhaps we can find a tavern with rooms to let. Are you fit to ride for a short spell?"

"If it means sleeping in a bed, then hell yeah. I'll ride all night if I have to."

If I have to. As I mount Lance's horse, I seriously pray that I won't have to. Day one in medieval times and I've already had my fill of the equestrian lifestyle, thank you very much. Makes me real appreciative of Betsy, my battered old two-door Honda back home. Betsy may have trouble going over sixty-five miles an hour and a penchant for hitting guardrails, but she doesn't smell like manure and is much easier to steer. This horse—like all horses, I suppose—literally has a mind of its own.

Of course, there are some benefits to riding on Lancelot's horse as opposed to those horses that do not regularly carry sexy knights on their backs. Like the feeling of his muscular arms wrapped around me to hold the horse's reins, for one. Of course, the stupid metal armor he wears kind of limits actual physical contact, but it's enough to feel his warm breath on the back of my neck.

I squirm a little. This guy has a hold on my senses that borders on tyrannical, and my body is desperate to submit. I know it's been a long time since I've had a hot guy pressed up against me, but really, do I need to be this turned-on? After all, I'm probably going to get nothing out of the deal. We all know Lancelot had no other love than Queen Guenevere, whether she wants to admit it or not. Man, she is so lucky! What I wouldn't do to snare a nice, handsome, honorable guy like Lance. I don't think they exist nowadays. Maybe like the dinosaurs, in the twenty-first century, chivalrous men are extinct.

As we ride, I try to make conversation by asking where we are. He tells me the Forest Sherwood. Like in Robin Hood? I ask. But evidently the old "steal from the rich, give to the poor" guy hasn't been born yet, because Lance has no idea who I am talking about. Or maybe Robin Hood is fictional. I can't remember. Of course, in my world Camelot is fictional, too, or at least if it did exist it was nothing like the legends—like the Camelot I've seen with my own eyes. Who knows, maybe the history books got it wrong.

A horrible thought strikes me, as horrible thoughts tend to do when the brain has some downtime to wander. If I really have gone back in time—not that I'm totally convinced, mind you, but let's say it somehow happened—what if my killing King Lot has changed the future? Like when Marty's mom fell in love with him instead of his dad in *Back to the Future?* I mean, how big a change could one medieval guy's death make?

The implications are mind-boggling. For example, what if Lot was supposed to have another kid before he died and that kid's great-great-great-great-great-great-great-great-great-grandson founded Louis Vuitton? What will twenty-first-century rich people pack their Armani in when they holiday in the south of France? And how will those street vendors who make a living selling the fake ones survive? Will they have to turn to welfare to make ends meet? And what if the welfare system can't handle the influx of fake purse sellers and completely collapses, causing millions of children to go without food and shelter?

And that's just a scenario involving Louis Vuitton. What if Lot's future kin was supposed to be a Kennedy? Or Saddam Hussein? I know Lot's Scottish and all, but the English knights went over to the Islamic countries during the Crusades, right? What if Lot was supposed to meet a nice, sweet Muslim girl and have a kid with her?

Man, I can't get my head around this time-travel stuff. I need to find someone who knows the deal. Maybe I'll ask Merlin when we get back to the castle. In that cartoon *Sword in the Stone*, Merlin would hop back and forth from the past to the future on a regular basis. Of course, this Merlin seems a lot less cuddly than the animated one, and yes, I am aware knowledge attained by watching a Disney cartoon is a bit suspect, but hey, I've got limited options here.

Okay, time to make conversation with Lance or I'm going to go crazy with questions.

"How did you find me?"

"I followed you."

"You saw me leave the castle?"

" 'Twas I who unlocked the door."

"You freed me?" I'm a bit surprised by this admission. I had assumed Guenevere did it. "Why?"

"A Kat should not be kept in a cage."

Cute. Real cute. I grin. "What was your real reason?"

"I wanted to learn if you were really a Saxon spy."

73

"And?"

He sighs before answering. "You are odd, 'tis for certain. But a spy? Nay, I think not."

Good. At least someone's on my team now. Maybe he can convince Arthur of that, too. Of course, now he's going to ask me where I *do* come from, since it's obviously not from Saxonia or wherever it is the Saxons live, and I'm so not ready to open up that whole can of worms! If I tell him I'm from the twenty-first century and have actually traveled back in time, he's going to think I'm a madwoman. And if I tell him he's just part of my really long, realistic coma dream, he's going to get offended at my thinking he's not real. Definitely time to change the subject.

"What took you so long to rescue me?"

He laughs. "I am strong, lady. Perhaps the strongest knight in all the land. But even I am no match for twenty able-bodied men on horseback. Lamorak and I waited until they had soused themselves on drink."

"Yeah, well, you made your move just in the nick of time. I was this close to getting raped and murdered."

"I can assure you, lady, I would not have let him compromise your honor."

He's really big on the whole honor thing, huh? I guess that's the chivalry kicking in. But hey, if it saves me from rape by an ugly guy, I'm all for it.

The woods part, revealing a walled city of sorts. "Cameliard," Lancelot pronounces as we ride up to its gates, perhaps assuming I'm interested in a geography lesson, which I'm not. The place could be called Cleveland for all I care, as long as it features hotels with comfy beds. Oh, and food would be nice, too. I'm starving. I hope they won't be serving roast pigeon. I can't stomach the idea of consuming those pesky rats with wings.

At the gates, Lancelot asks the porter about an inn, and

the man suggests a place called the Rusty Nail. Now, I'm all for not judging a book by its cover, but I'm hazarding a guess that a place named after a tarnished metal spike ain't gonna be the Ritz.

After dropping off the horse at his own personal horse hotel (aka stable), we walk down a narrow cobblestone road. The houses' second stories hang over the streets, creating a kind of tunnel-like effect. Rather claustrophobic, if you ask me. I remember hearing stories about how people used to dump their chamber pots out the windows and into the streets, and I start walking with my head up, ready to jump out of the way at the first sign of raining piss.

We come to a dilapidated building with splintered walls and rotting beams. A long metal nail hangs from a post. It's definitely rusty, so I guess this must be the place.

We walk inside. You know how I said I had a sneaking suspicion it wouldn't be a five-star resort? Well, that was what you call optimism. I'm not sure if the traditional hotel rating system allows for minus stars, but if they don't, they might want to make an exception in this case. In fact, I'd give ye olde Rusty Nail a negative three. And that's being kind.

But, it seems, not all medieval men share my distaste for a dirty bar with a sticky floor that reeks of stale beer and puke. In fact, the place is packed with boisterous guys shouting and cheering and singing as they down their pewter mugs of ale. Evidently this is *the* place to be if you're a man living in the lovely town of Cameliard. Well, there's no accounting for taste.

A big, burly guy with a huge beer gut and wild black hair approaches us. A wide smile reveals his dire need for modern dentistry. "Greetings, sir knight and lady," he proclaims, slapping Lancelot on the back. Lance looks extremely uncomfortable. Evidently a bar like this is not a knight in shining armor's scene. "What brings you fine folk to me humble establishment?"

"We have traveled far," Lancelot explains a bit stiffly. "We would like to rent two rooms for the night."

The man's smile falters a bit. "Aye, I would love to accommodate you, I would. But I only 'ave one room available this eve. 'Tis late, you see, and I had no warning a fine knight like yourself would be gracing me with—"

"Is there another inn in town?"

"No, milord. The Rusty Nail is it." The man picks at a tooth with what looks like a chicken bone, making me cringe. I consider reaching into my purse to offer him a toothpick but figure it might raise too many questions. "Though I am surprised you would not seek accommodations with Leodegrance, king of Cameliard. Not that you are not welcome here," he adds quickly, probably worried he's going to lose our business. "After all, the Rusty Nail is a fine establishment in its own right."

Sure it is, buddy. If this place is considered fine, I'd hate to see, uh, unfine. Still, at this point I really don't give a damn about its fineness factor. It's here. It's available. It's got beds and food and alcohol. "Lance," I say, "it's late. Let's just share a room."

Lance looks at me like I've asked him to kill his mother and eat her for breakfast. Geez. It's not like I said, "Hey, Lance, let's go have sex." I mean, what's the big deal about sharing a room? It's just a place to crash. "One of us can sleep on the floor," I add to ease his moralistic mind. Of course, by "one of us" I mean him. I'm so not interested in volunteering for ground sleeping, and after all, he's the chivalrous knight, right? Doesn't that give me, damsel in distress, first dibs on the mattress?

"There is a pull-out truckle bed," the tavern owner informs us. "Perfect for those not interested in getting under the covers with a fine lady." He gives me such an unsubtle wink that I laugh out loud. Lancelot, of course, looks mortified. Man, this guy really needs to loosen up.

"What about food?" I ask. "I'm so hungry I could eat a horse."

"I'm, er, sorry, milady," the owner says, looking seriously taken aback. "The cook is not, uh, serving horse this eve."

Oh, darn, 'cause I was being so literal, too. Guess that expression has yet to be coined. "Well, what *do* you have on the menu then?" I ask. Another blank look. Oh. Menu. Guess they don't know that one either. It's amazing how many twenty-first-century words pop into my vocabulary without my thinking. "What do you have to eat?" I clarify.

"The cook makes a fine roast pigeon," the owner suggests. Doh! I knew it. Suddenly I'm not feeling so hungry.

"Maybe I'll just get a drink. Don't suppose rum's been invented yet?" I ask hopefully, but I'm met with the same vacant stares that I'm getting very used to. Guess that's a no. Darn, I would kill for a mojito right now. "Well, you definitely have wine, right?"

The owner's face brightens. "Ah, aye, milady. Imported from France. The very best in the land. I will open a bottle for you." He runs toward the back room.

I turn to Lance. "Well, all right! Alcohol is on its way. I'm feeling better already. I'll tell you what: I can use a drink after all that's happened to me today. Actually, I can use about twenty."

The owner returns with two cups and a bottle of red wine. I actually prefer white, but at this point I'm not complaining.

I take a huge gulp and my insides warm. The tension of the day fades away with my next sip. My third makes me almost forget what century I think I'm in. (By the way, I'm taking big sips and refilling my glass; I'm no lightweight. Kat Jones can hold her liquor.)

I'm suddenly not a bit tired and feel strangely ready to party. I push nagging concerns to the back of my head. The ones that say I should be worried and scared. What good will it do to stress about the situation? It's not going to get me back to the twenty-first century. If I'm here, I might as well make the best of things and have some fun. If I wake up from my coma, or miraculously go forward in time, at least I can say I made the most of my stay in jolly old England.

"Perhaps we should bring the bottle to the room," Lancelot suggests, touching me on the arm. I'm getting the impression he doesn't dig the bar scene.

"No way," I cry. "We should stay and hang with these fine gentlemen of Cameliard. Besides," I add, tripping over a stool on my way to a vacant table, "it's empty." I hold the bottle upside down to prove my point. A barmaid appears at my side and deftly replaces the empty bottle with a full one.

Great service. What a nice bar. With nice, fun people. I take a swig from the new bottle. Glasses are so overrated.

"I do not think it is appropriate for—"

"Dude! Will you lighten up? I mean, really! I'm the one who should be freaking out here. But I'm having a good time. Do you even know how to have a good time, Lancey?" I see the barmaid out of the corner of my eye. "Hey," I cry. "A cup of mead for my friend here. He needs to get drunk. Like, really badly."

She nods and returns a few minutes later with a mug of frothy brew. "Drink!" I command. Lancelot, after a doubtful sniff, complies.

A musician with some kind of hornlike instrument steps

up on a corner stage and starts tooting a lively tune. The men cheer, as if delighted to see him. I give my own salutation, raising my bottle high in the air. "Whoo-hoo!" This place is pretty cool. I don't know what I was thinking before. I mean, sure, it's technically a dive bar, but hey, there are a ton of Jersey clubs that are a hell of a lot worse. I've got a real good buzz going on now, too. Maybe it's drinking on an empty stomach.

The music is pumping. It's not exactly techno, but it has a good beat. I could dance to it. Hey, maybe I should! You know, like, let's get this party started? Show the medieval dudes how it's done? I take another swig of my wine and climb over the table.

I'm a good dancer—lots of experience in high school and college. In fact, I once figured out where to go dancing six out of seven nights a week—a feat that was great for my social connections and body (dancing burns a ton of calories!), but lousy for my wallet. Of course, at the moment my feet don't seem to be moving quite the way I want them to, and I keep finding myself tripping up. Oh, well, it's not like I'm on *Dance Fever*. Who cares if it's not fancy footwork? No one here knows the difference.

Actually, that's kind of a liberating feeling. For once in my life there's no one to impress. No one I need to worry about thinking I'm uncool. I don't give a damn what anyone here thinks of me, and that includes cute-but-boring Lancelot. If I want to act like a fool, I can. And no one from Manhattan ever has to know. What a beautiful thing.

Several of the men, who were staring with shocked faces, have now come out to join me. Their movements are clumsy at first, but they gradually, under my instructions, start feeling the beat. I feel like Rose in that *Titanic* movie, when she goes below deck to dance with the regular folks.

"Come on, Lancey, *dancey!*" I cry, waving my arms in the air. But Lancelot only shakes his head, determined to be a party pooper. I grab one of the greasy men's hands and twirl around.

The men evidently dig the twirling thing, and soon I find myself being spun by multiple partners, each eager to have his turn. I start to get kind of dizzy. Maybe I need more wine. I grab the bottle off the table and take another swig.

"Come on, Lance!" I beg, grabbing his hand. "Dance with me." He pulls his hand away. Spoilsport.

The men around me are dancing like medieval men probably never danced before. I wonder how much effect my teaching them to dance will have on the history of the world. I mean, would teaching them the Electric Slide lead to world peace, World War III, or just a bad dance-craze footnote in history? Since I'm not sure, I decide against it. After all, in my opinion the whole line-dancing thing is stupid no matter which millennium it's danced in, and besides, it's not like the band's playing disco.

You know, I'm having too much fun to worry about these kinds of future consequences anyway. If I'm stuck in the past, I'm making the most of things, damn it—unlike those heroines in my mother's romance books who go back in time just to fall in love. You never read of them getting drunk and getting down. But I'm a liberated woman of the twenty-first century. And tonight I'm going to party like it's 1999.

Oh, and if this is just one long-ass dream, it doesn't matter anyway. After all, I'm probably paying a thousand dollars a night for my hospital bed in Mount Sinai. Might as well enjoy my coma.

"Whoo-hoo!" I cry, after a particularly long stretch of twirling. "The twenty-first-century girl of the future rules the dance floor!"

I stop, realizing everyone is staring at me. Realizing the

music has faded away *before* I yelled out the intriguing fact that I am from the twenty-first century. Suddenly Lancelot is at my side.

"What did you say, woman?" he demands, grabbing me by my arms. . . .

Chapter Six

Ohhhhhh, my head. Like jackhammers drilling into my brain. Ohhhh. Eyes still closed, I press my hand against my forehead, willing the pounding to stop. But neither instructions to brain nor forehead touching seems to do the trick. Pain continues uninterrupted. Ohhhh.

What did I do last night? I remember flickering images of the weirdest dream ever. Like I was sent back in time. To the days of King Arthur! Dancing at some bar? Ha! I wonder if someone spiked my Cosmo with roofies or something. What day is it, anyway? Am I supposed to be at work? I'm so not going to work.

Ohhhhh.

Okay, Kat. Come on. You're the hangover queen. Get it together. Face the day. Step one, open your eyes.

I do manage to force one eye open for a brief moment, but the brightness of the morning makes me reconsider the benefits attributed to sight, and I quickly shut it again.

My skin is all clammy, and I'm simultaneously cold and hot at the same time. And my stomach is doing major flip-flops, starving and nauseated simultaneously. This has got to be the worst hangover I've ever had.

Delaying the idea of opening my eyes and getting up, I try to remember more of my dream. Parts of it seem so real. Other parts are real foggy. Like the bar scene—I don't really remember much of it. Oh, but there was a really cute guy. Lancelot. Yes, yes, the same one from the Round Table. Ha! Where does my brain come up with these things? What would Freud say? Repressed sexual childhood fantasies about an honorable alpha male who is nothing like my I'm-running-out-for-cigarettes-and-never-coming-back father?

My stomach churns and I realize I'd better make my way to the bathroom in case I throw up. On the count of three I will open my eyes and sit up in bed.

One, two . . .

Okay, maybe the sitting-up-in-bed part was too ambitious. I have managed to open my eyes, though, and they're slowly getting adjusted to the light. I stare at the ceiling, made of heavy wooden beams crisscrossing one another.

Not my ceiling.

Suddenly it's a lot easier to sit up in bed. Where am I? Some guy's house? Did I meet a guy last night? What if he was the one who gave me roofies? Did I get date-raped? Oh, Kat, what have you gotten yourself into *this* time?

I look around, desperately taking in my surroundings. A sparse room. A rickety wooden table in one corner. A suit of shining armor lying on the wooden floor. A tall candle-holder in—

Wait a second! I whirl my head back around. A suit of shining armor lying on the wooden floor? Oh, no. No, no, no, no, no, no, "No!"

"Kat, what is wrong?"

Guess I said that last *no* out loud. A man, presumably the armor's owner, bursts into the room, sword drawn. My jaw drops. Lancelot. A real, live, definitely-not-a-figment-of-my-imagination Lancelot. He glances around the room, looking ready to challenge any danger. It'd be funny if it weren't so horrifying.

"Oh, my God, oh, my God, oh, my God!" I curl back into the bed, scrunching up my feet into a fetal position and pulling the blanket over my head. "Oh, my God. It isn't a dream. It isn't a dream! I'm still here. I'm in medieval times. Oh, my God!"

This can't be real. This can't be real. It can't be real. I can't really be here. This has got to be a joke. Somehow. My friends are playing a joke. Like that movie with Michael Douglas, *The Game*. It's just a game. It's not real. It can't be. I can't have gone back in time. It's impossible. Those things don't happen. Oh, my God, I'm going to throw up for real this time.

I lean over the bedside and start coughing, a prelude to my hurl. I feel Lance's hands pulling my hair from my face and see him thrust a chamber pot under my head as my stomach heaves and I vomit the foulest-smelling liquid I have ever smelled. Ohhhhh.

I lift my head. Lancelot lets go of my hair. I lie back on the bed, defeated, staring at the ceiling. He sits down on the edge of the bed and gently brushes a few strands of wayward hair from my face.

"You drank too much wine last night," he says in a quiet voice. Wow, he must think I'm a real class act. I'm surprised he's even still here. Probably feels sorry for me and my totally pathetic self. Well, join the club.

"No duh." What does he care? What do I care? I should have drunk myself to death. At least then I wouldn't be here. Though I wonder what happens when you die in the past. Do you die in the future, too? Or are you never born? I try to think of something else. Anything. These questions are too philosophical to contemplate while I have a killer hangover.

His cool hand feels good against my sweaty forehead. Am I running a fever? "Where am I?" I ask, a little fearful of the answer.

"A tavern called the Rusty Nail. In the town of Cameliard." His fingers run through my hair, the nails lightly scraping my scalp. Feels nice. Why is he being so nice to me? Most guys would totally ditch a girl after she acts like such an alcoholic fool.

Man, you never read this kind of scenario of those *romance* back-in-time books. Those heroines are always beautiful and virtuous and long-suffering. They would never, ever even consider getting hammered and dancing on tables in front of an entire bar of men, including the not-at-all-drunk hero. (Oh, no! Did I really dance on tables last night? Idiot! Idiot!) No, those heroines stay clean and sober, and when it comes time for the love scene, they're passionate and gorgeous and smell like honeysuckle and rose petals. I, on the other hand, am so nasty and dirty and gross right now, I'm sure Lancelot would rather vomit himself than consider getting me into bed.

Not that I want to sleep with him. I don't. Not really, anyway. Well, I mean, I wouldn't mind if we were in another place and time—"your place or mine" takes on a whole new meaning, doesn't it? Yes, I suppose if Lancelot were a Wall Street exec that I met on the elevator, I'd be very interested in making his acquaintance. He's a little strait-laced for me, but maybe that's what I need. Some stability. Someone to gently remind me that I will regret the great idea of table dancing in the sober light of morning. There's just something about the guy that I find so appealing. . . .

Earth to Kat! Come in, Kat! Houston, we have a problem. And we should not be thinking about what-ifs, but be concentrating on what the hell we are going to do.

I look up at Lancelot, nearly losing my cool when my eyes lock on his. God, he is *so* gorgeous. *Stop it, Kat; focus.* How much can I trust him? Can I tell him the truth? He seems like a nice guy and all, but will he really understand?

"What I guess I'm really asking is . . . um . . ." Should I really do this? Explain what I think has happened to me? He's going to think I'm crazy. Really freakin' crazy. Like lock-me-up crazy.

But hey, maybe I *am* crazy. I remember this *Buffy the Vampire Slayer* episode when she wakes up in a mental hospital and learns she's really not a slayer of vampires and everything in the last few years of her life has been a psychotic delusion. Maybe I'm in a psycho ward right now, wearing a straitjacket and mumbling curses under my breath.

That's it. I'm probably crazy. 'Cause everyone, except Einstein, I guess, knows you can't go back in time. How did this happen to me? And if I really am back in time, how do I get back to the twenty-first century? I want to go back. Really, really badly.

My eyes well up with tears. I hate crying, but I can't help it, and at this point I don't feel like I should have to justify it. I mean, have you ever woken up early in the morning after a night out and remembered you've crashed at a friend's place? All you want to do is go home, but the effort of getting out of bed and driving there in your current state is too much to bear. You know you should go back to bed, sleep it off, wake up, and go order the Grand Slam breakfast with your friend at Denny's once the sun rises. But at the same time all you can think about is crawling into your own warm, soft, private bed and hugging your teddy bear tight until you drift off into dreamland, where your head doesn't hurt a bit. (Yes, I sleep with a teddy bear. Deal with it.)

Well, imagine that feeling multiplied by one thousand and then add in the fact that you're not a twenty-minute car ride from home but a millennium away—without a clue as to how to get back. I mean, let's face it: hungover or not, you'd cry too if you woke up and found yourself stuck in a time where toilet paper has yet to be invented.

"What do you want to ask, Kat?" Lancelot prompts me with a tender voice. He takes an embroidered handkerchief from a small bag tied to his belt and blots my tears. For a medieval knight, he really is a nice guy. Honorable. Stable. Loyal. The kind of man I should look for in my real life, instead of the I'm-in-a-rock-band-and-have-no-job losers I always end up with.

But should I tell him I think I've traveled back in time? He's going to think I'm majorly screwed up in the head. But, then again, what do I have to gain from his thinking I'm normal? And truly, I'm sick of keeping all these crazy thoughts to myself. I need desperately to share.

"This is going to sound insane," I say, offering the disclaimer up front. "But what I was asking is *when* am I? 'Cause to me it seems a lot like I'm back in the days of King Arthur. And that's a time zone I don't belong in."

Lancelot looks surprisingly unpuzzled, and he continues to stroke my hair. His touch is comforting, supportive, and gives me the courage to go on.

"What would you say if I told you I was really from the twenty-first century—like, a thousand years into the future? And that somehow I have traveled back in time?"

Instead of freaking out, Lancelot offers a fond smile. "I would say you already told me that last night. About thirty-five times, in fact."

I stare at him in shock and awe. Did I really already spill the time-travel beans while drunk off my ass the night before? I know I have a tendency to babble and, worse, repeat my babble when drunk, but would I really have told him that I was a girl from the future not once, but thirty-five times? Oh, man, I am never, ever drinking again. Never. That's it. Kat Jones, teetotaler, that's me from now on.

"And . . . what do you think about my, er, evidently often-repeated revelation?" I ask, desperate to know at what level on the Richter crazy scale he places me. Does he think me a harmless freak? Or a dangerous psychotic?

"I was trained in Avalon by the Lady of the Lake, Nimue, high priestess of the mother goddess who gave birth to the world," Lancelot says in a reverent tone. "She taught me that time is but a wheel, ever rotating. We rise and fall through birth and death, only to be reborn once again."

His words are pretty, but also pretty meaningless. "So," I say, trying to discern the gist of what he's saying, "are you trying to tell me that you *believe* me?"

He shrugs. "I gave the matter much thought while you slept. Closely examined the strange objects you showed me from your reticule. While it would be quite easy to categorize you as mad, those items are certainly not from this time or place. So whether you have come from another world or another time, I know in my heart you truly do not belong in the here and now."

"Well, what do you know? Guess I got the whole time-travel confession out of the way already, and I don't even remember the awkward task of doing so." And now he believes me. Gotta say, that was so much easier than I thought it was going to be. Go figure.

"The only other thing I can think of is that you're totally a product of my imagination," I can't resist adding. I have to introduce *something* new into the conversation that we've evidently already had many times over.

"Ah, lady. Do you think it so?" He leans down and presses his lips against my forehead. The touch sparks an electrical shock through my entire body. Oh, my God. He lifts his head. "Did you conjure that from your imagination as well?"

Nope. Don't think so. Felt real anyway. Really real. Like, way more real than even a real kiss should really feel like. I look up into his amazing blue eyes. So beautiful and so kind. So gentle and yet at the same time strong. The type of man who could fight all day for my honor and still make sweet love through the night.

"Thanks for believing me," I say, bowing my head from his gaze. I'm too caught up in him. I need to focus. The pounding in my head's making it difficult. I wish I had packed some Excedrin in my purse. Wonder what the standard medieval headache remedy is?

"Of course," he replies. "However, you must keep in mind that not all in Britain follow the path of the goddess. The Christians are slowly gaining in numbers; even our dear King Arthur has named Camelot a Christian kingdom. They will not believe you are who you say you are. More likely than not they will call you a witch and wish to burn you at the stake. Better that you act as if you belong in this world."

Good point. I need to keep a definite low profile. "Where should I say I'm from?" Since my medieval geography is worse than fuzzy, I'm in need of suggestions.

"My kingdom is across the sea in Little Britain," he says. "Mayhap I can call you my young sister. This way I can serve as your knight protector, without question as to your background and honor."

"Yeah, but everyone who was on the jousting field knows you didn't recognize me when I first showed up," I say, pointing out the logical flaw in his otherwise pretty good plan.

"Aye, but I was sent to Avalon as a young boy and have not returned to Little Britain in more than fifteen summers. It would be easy to see why I did not know you, nor you me."

"Oh. Yeah. That would work then." I nod, then instantly regret the head movement as pain shoots down my neck. "But I've got to ask: Why are you helping me? Why not just leave? You don't owe me. If anything, I've been a royal pain in your butt."

Lancelot looks at me thoughtfully. "I am a knight, lady. 'Tis my job to help maidens who are in need of my services."

Oh. Well, okay. I guess it's just a chivalry thing. For a moment everything seems good. We've got a plan. I've got a new sexy brother—eat your heart out, Jerry Springer. Then I realize it doesn't really matter if anyone buys the idea of my belonging in medieval times, because I don't want to belong here in the first place.

Depression sets back in. I've got a great life back home that I want to return to. A prestigious, if not high-paying, job, supportive friends, a fuzzy dog who I'm sure most desperately wants to go out to pee.

"The thing is, though, Lance"—I sigh—"all I really want to do is get back to where I come from. Got any insights on that one?"

Lancelot thinks for a moment. "On the way back to Camelot we could make the journey to Avalon. If anyone is to know how to get you back to your world, the Lady of the Lake will. We shall consult with her."

"Okay," I say a little skeptically. Like, really, how the hell's she going to know? Are time travelers an everyday occurrence for the pagans of medieval England? Doubt it. And as far as I'm concerned, it's going to take more than medieval hocus-pocus goddess worship to get me back to the future. Where, oh, where is a time machine when you need one?

I sigh and resign myself to giving the priestess a try. After all, it's not like I've got a plan B. "When do we leave?"

"You do not appear well enough to travel," Lancelot says, looking concerned.

"I'm fi—" I try to sit up and simultaneously feel pain in my head and nausea in my stomach. I lie back down. "You're right. There's no way I can get on a horse today."

"We are very near the castle of King Leodegrance, Queen Guenevere's father. It was too late to announce our presence last night. However, this morn we will be welcomed." He looks around the room with a rueful grin. "I promise the accommodations will be more suitable for a lady than this hovel."

"Hey, I was just happy to not have to go camping." I pick at a broken fingernail. I'm in desperate need of a manicure. Well, that and a shower. I seem to remember reading somewhere that they didn't bathe in medieval times. I hope that was a myth. I can't go on much longer without washing up. "Do you guys bathe?" I blurt out, crossing my fingers for an affirmative answer. Oh, please, please, say yes, and don't say yes, then tell me it's done in a freezing-cold river.

Lancelot's eyes dance in merriment. "Aye, of course. Only the lowest of all peasants are content to live like the swine. I am sure that the ladies-in-waiting at the castle will be able to prepare you a lovely hot bath."

Phew! Hot baths. Thank God for small favors. "Then what are we waiting for?" I ask with a grin. "Let's go hit the castle."

"Hit?" Lancelot furrows his brow. "I hardly think we would want to damage the very place where we desire welcome."

"Er, never mind." I laugh, the thought of the bath making me feel a tiny bit better. "It's a twenty-first-century expression. I have lots of them. Bear with me."

Ah. Now this is the life. I'm lying in a huge Jacuzzi-size wooden tub, the water heated by a nearby fire. Fragrant rose petals float on the surface, making it a positive aromatherapy experience. As I soak, my troubled mind drifts away with the dirt.

Sure, I'm still stuck, a stranger in a strange land, but things could be a lot worse. I could still be Lot's captive. I could be dead. I could be still throwing up. Instead an herbal remedy has eased my bad head and settled my stomach. I've been assigned two palace maidens to attend to my every need, which included serving me a heaping plate of sweet grapes and yummy goat cheeses before my soothing bath. Not a bad setup. I am determined to see my cup as half-full.

When we first arrived at the palace, we were welcomed like royalty. Evidently Lance is a big deal in the knight world, and well-known throughout the land. You should have seen all the ladies-in-waiting giggling like schoolgirls when he approached King Leo's throne. You'd think the guy was Brad Pitt. Of course, I got a few dirty looks; maybe they were worried about potential competition. Like they even have a chance. I've got many, many years of "How to win a guy without even trying" magazine research at my disposal; they've never even taken a *Cosmo* quiz.

Interestingly enough, it turns out that Guenevere is also in town, visiting her dad. Evidently Arthur was pretty pissed when he heard I'd escaped, and Merlin tried to pin it on Mrs. King, so she figured it'd be better to lie low and make herself scarce for a few days.

Once I've had my fill of soaking in the tub—the last of the ground-in grime expunged from my body—I climb out. It's cold in the chamber, but before I can even get goose bumps, two maids surround me with warm, thick towels. It's a full-service establishment, this place, I'll tell you what.

They lead me to what I assume is a luxurious room for medieval times and pronounce it my chamber for the extent of my stay at Camelaird. Now we're talking!

I circle around slowly, taking in the space and all its antiquities. Real glass windows line one wall, letting in warm sunshine. Rich, unbearably soft furs blanket the wood floors. The walls are decorated with brightly colored embroidered tapestries, depicting knights and ladies, fight scenes, and courtly love. But the ultimate coolest part? An actual canopied bed, draped by heavy red velvet curtains.

I always wanted a canopy bed, ever since my Barbie doll got one for Christmas in 1982. That Barbie, she had it all— her own town house with hot-pink furnishings, a Corvette, even a golden palomino horse named Dallas. (Where she kept the horse while living in a town house, I have no idea. . . .)

Of course, material possessions aren't everything. Thinking back, I realize the poor little rich doll was stuck living a chaste existence with a plastic-haired, non–anatomically correct Ken, who was so obviously gay—never even noticing his girlfriend's stunning figure and breast implants. However, I am convinced Barb must have been getting some action on the side. Maybe with my brother's much manlier G.I. Joe? Otherwise where did her so-called "little sister"—like anyone believed *that* one—Kelly come from?

One of the servants lays out several gorgeous embroidered gowns and asks me to choose. They're really pretty, but also really colorful, and truth be told, I'm more of a black kind of girl. I mean, come on. Is there anyone in the world now who doesn't see black as the ultimate color for clothing? It goes with everything. It's slimming. It's always in style and always appropriate, except for weddings, though now some of the more urban "I dos" have even decreed this an outdated *former* faux pas. Oh, and did I mention it's slimming?

However, since it doesn't appear I have much of a choice, I decide to go for a red silk number with long bell sleeves. It laces up in the front with green ribbon—very Christmasy—and is thus more fitted than a couple of the other options. I hope it will make me look a little thinner, but since there are no mirrors anywhere, guess I'll never know for sure if it's working. Oh, well, what do I care what people think I weigh, anyway? I keep having to remind myself that here, I have no one to impress. Not even Lancelot. Really.

Ignoring my protests that I have dressed myself for more than twenty years and probably can manage to do so at least one more time, the two servant girls strip me of my towel and dignity, then pull a silky sheath dress over my head. From what I've now gathered, the sheath is like medieval underwear, as in you always wear it under your clothes. I, myself, prefer the type of underwear that actually provides some sort of support. I'm not Dolly Parton, by any means, but wearing a bra sure does help cut out the jiggle. Especially when one is riding on horseback, as I found out the hard way. Maybe if I end up stuck here for a while I could invent the equivalent of the Wonderbra. Why, I'd be a hero for medieval woman everywhere. The men probably wouldn't raise too much of a fuss, either!

The girls instruct me to lift my arms so I can put my hands through the sleeves of the dress. It goes on like a bathrobe and ties in the front. While one girl bends down to straighten the hem, the other starts lacing up the bodice, pulling the strings a bit too tight for my liking. Reduced lung capacity for the sake of fashion. Yuck. Oh, well, I'll deal. It's not like I'm going out to run a marathon or anything.

"Good morn to you, Lady Kat."

I look up. Guenevere has entered, dressed in a gorgeous creamy white gown with golden trim that matches her long, flowing blond hair. An exquisite brooch secures the ends of a long violet cape that drapes behind her, dragging on the floor as she walks. On her fingers she wears a great many heavy silver rings, and a tiara, glittering with gems, sits on her head. She's so beautiful that my breath catches in my throat. Not that I'm a lesbian, mind you, but as a magazine editor I can definitely recognize beauty when I see it. The girl could be a model. Well, a petite one, anyway. Stunning. No wonder she's queen. Arthur probably snatched her up the moment he laid eyes on her.

"Hey, Your Majesty, how's it going?" I ask casually. From our previous conversation in the tower, I've decided the girl's probably pretty cool, so far as medieval ladies can be considered.

"Leave us," she commands the servants in a regal voice. "I will help Lady Kat get dressed myself." The two girls bob in curtsy before making a hasty exit. Gotta hand it to the queen: when she talks, people listen. I'd love to have that kind of power!

Once the doors shut behind them, Guenevere gives me a big smile. "How do you fare?" she asks, grabbing the laces of my dress and tying them together in a bow. "I trust you found your bath comforting?"

"It was heaven."

" 'Tis my desire that you feel most welcome in my father's house," the queen goes on. She pulls a matching red velvet cape from the pile of dresses and drapes it around my body, fastening it with a silver dragon pin. "Especially after all you have had to go through."

"Yeah, I've had a rough couple of days; I'll give you that."

After pronouncing me beautiful, the queen plops down on the bed and pats the side, inviting me to join her. I sit, a little reluctantly. How much should I trust this woman?

"I must tell you, Lady Kat, that it is my heart's dearest desire to hear the many stories you can tell about where you've come from and what it is like in your world."

"You've been talking to Lance?" I ask suspiciously, making a mental note to berate my knight in shining armor the next time I see him. I thought we were keeping this time-travel thing on the down-low! So why are we spilling the beans to Mrs. Arthur?

"Never fear," Guenevere assures me in her light, musical voice. "Like Sir Lancelot du Lac, I have also been trained by the priestesses of Avalon. I am a worshiper of the great mother and believe that it *is* possible to travel between worlds and through the strands of time."

"Oh. Well, you're one step above me on that one." Man, these guys have totally bought into the time-travel thing without a bit of skepticism. Makes me want to mention the Brooklyn Bridge I've got for sale. "I still can't quite believe it myself."

"Tell me, lady, what is the future like?" Guenevere begs, eagerness dancing in her blue eyes. For all her queenliness, she's still a girl, I suddenly realize. An idealistic, sweet, young girl. Suddenly I feel old and jaded. "I must know! Is it too wonderful for words?"

Hm. What part of the future does she want to know about? I mean, should I inform her that she and Lancelot are destined to get caught in a compromising position? That their betrayal leads to the downfall of Camelot? Or should I gush on about the modern wonders of indoor plumbing, stretch fabric, and vodka-and-Red Bulls?

No, I'd better keep on track—warn her about Lancelot. Seems more important than, say, an in-depth discussion of the miraculous invention of deep-dish pizza, no matter how good it tastes—compared to, let's say, horse.

"You want to know the future? I gotta tell you, Guen, it's not looking so good for you and Lance. In fact, you might want to stay away from the guy. From the movies I've seen, King Arthur's knights, who are, like, totally jealous 'cause Lance is such a good knight, persuade Arthur to pretend to go hunting so you think you're alone in the palace. You go to get some action—I mean, you go make love to Lance— then they charge in on you and catch you together in his bedroom. They"—I clear my throat, not wanting to bear the bad news—"sentence you to burn at the stake."

Guenevere laughs—not a chuckle either, but a full-on, bellyaching laugh. She falls back onto the bed to continue her unabashed snickering, not taking me a bit seriously, obviously, and I feel a bit offended. Maybe I should have introduced her to the concept of microfiber purses and air-conditioning instead.

"I'm trying to warn you," I say a bit crossly.

She attempts to control her giggle. "I am sorry, Lady Kat. I do not mean to find amusement in your prophecy. 'Tis only that I cannot imagine myself making love to a knight like Lancelot."

"Why not? He's attractive enough." This is too weird. Why doesn't she like him? All the books say she's supposed to be totally obsessed with the guy. So what's with her indifference? I don't get it.

"Aye, he is a handsome knight, indeed," she says, staring up at the canopied bedpost. I watch her closely, looking hard for some kind of hint that she's hiding her true feelings. But her face is an open book, and I'm not reading any lusty bedtime stories whatsoever. "Many a girl in my court is much affected by his charms. But he does not make my heart flutter. As I said yesterday in the tower room, if anything, the man is a brother to me." She pulls herself back to a seated position. "Besides, I love my husband, Arthur," she adds, her eyes shining as her thoughts evidently fall to the king. "He is noble and wise. Great. Handsome. Loving. The best man a wife could ever hope to have."

"Well, that's good," I say with a shrug. Evidently the legends were wrong. Go figure.

"Besides, if anyone were in danger of losing her heart to Sir Lancelot, I should think 'twould be you." She says the last part with a sly grin on her face.

"Me?" I try to put on a shocked face. "No way. He's an old stick-in-the-mud. I have no interest in him whatsoever." As I speak the words, my traitorous brain meanders back to Lancelot's dramatic rescue scene. His hot breath on my neck as we rode on horseback to Cameliard. The sizzling kiss he planted on my forehead to prove he was not a figment of my imagination.

Nope, not interested at all.

"Lady, you may deny your feelings as long as you wish," Guenevere says, now positively smirking like a Cheshire cat. "But I saw with mine own eyes the way you two looked at each other when you first approached the court. I know what I see when it comes to matters of the heart."

"Okay," I confess. "Maybe I'm attracted to him. But really, I am so not getting into a relationship with a guy who's, like, literally a thousand years older than me." I shake my head. "Seriously, Guen? All I want is to go home—with no complications."

"Very well." Guenevere rises from her seat. "Then shall we ready ourselves to join the king, my father, and the knight Lancelot—the one you do not care for at all—in the dining hall?"

I stare at her. "Are you kidding?" I cry, horrified at her suggestion. "You think I'm going to let him see me before I fix my hair and put on makeup?" The queen grins widely, and I realize what I've implied by my preoccupation with beauty in the context of coming face-to-face with our favorite knight. Doh!

Okay, so maybe I'm a teensy bit into Lancelot after all.

Chapter Seven

After extensive medieval preparation time, during which Guenevere somehow manages to pull my shoulder-length shag into two small braided buns that she assures me is the latest fashion, even though to me it screams Princess Leia, which is never good, we walk down to the dining hall.

The room is smaller than the great hall of Camelot—cozier, too. There's a roaring fire at one end, but the ventilation seems a bit better than at Arthur and Guen's place. On the wall hang tapestries depicting fair maidens feeding white unicorns. At the center of the room sits a large circular table.

The hall is empty except for Lancelot and King Leodegrance, who are conversing quietly by the fire.

"Ladies," greets the rather heavyset king as he sees us approach. He takes my hand in his and kisses it gallantly, his white beard tickling my skin. Then he approaches his daughter, planting a kiss on her cheek. "You are right on time for dinner."

I turn to Lancelot and watch his jaw drop as he stares at me. Guess I have to resign myself to the fact that the

Princess Leia look may indeed work on guys in medieval times. Though perhaps it's the Christmas-colored dress. Or maybe he's just easily impressed.

If only he could see me in my little black Stella McCartney number with my deliciously strappy Jimmy Choos. I wore the ensemble to the Fashion Awards last year, and even Joan and Melissa Rivers gave me a thumbs-up. A proud moment in the life of a fashionista.

"Kat!" Lancelot cries, making swift strides to reach me. He takes my hand in his and brings it to his lips. I try to smile demurely, like a proper medieval chick would, but inside I do a happy dance for the effect I'm obviously having on him.

"Hey, Lance. Check me out." Now that Guen's told me she's not interested, I can't resist a little harmless flirting. I twirl around, my gown floating in the resulting whirlwind. "I clean up nice, huh?"

"You look as radiant as the morning star," he replies quite seriously, giving me a once-over with reverential eyes. Now, that's a line I'll admit might sound pretty darn cheesy when spoken by a twenty-first-century guy at a beer bar. But here, with the Gothic castle atmosphere and Lance's painfully earnest face, it's sweet. Really nice, actually. A girl from the future doesn't usually get this kind of unabashed worship. I blame women's lib.

"Thanks. You're looking pretty tasty yourself," I compliment him, looking over his red wool, belted-tunic ensemble. He's tied his shoulder-length black hair back into a ponytail, revealing killer chiseled cheekbones, and now smells of patchouli. Normally I don't dig the hippie fragrance, but on him it kind of turns me on. Hell, on him that cheap-ass Stetson cologne they always advertise nonstop at Christmastime would probably turn me on. He just has that effect on me. I so wish I could take him back to the twenty-first century. He'd look amazing in Armani and smell heavenly with the tiniest spritz of Jil Sander.

"The lady is too kind." He bows his head. Then he glances over at Guenevere, who is standing beside me with an amused expression, taking it all in. Color drops from his face. "Oh, er, lady, uh, Queen," he stammers, evidently realizing he should probably be giving some props to her royal majesty, too. "I did not mean to fall remiss in relating tales of your beauty, as well."

Guenevere laughs her musical laugh. "'Tis clear to all, sir, why your eyes would be so blinded. I take no offense, delighting in the fact that you admire my handiwork in preparing Lady Kat for dinner." In other words, she's taking full credit for my makeover. "Shall we dine?"

"Oh, yes, please," I pipe in. "I'm famished."

We walk over to the rich mahogany circular table, set for dinner with decorative goblets and wooden bowls. The table's huge. The four of us take up only the smallest section. As ruler of one of the smaller kingdoms, Leodegrance explains, he rarely has to set all the places.

"It's a beautiful table," I remark, running my hand over the smooth wood. A servant places a pewter tray in front of me, along with a spoon. I notice Lancelot reaching into his boot and pulling out a knife. Evidently this is a BYOB (bring your own blade) kind of establishment. I'd ask to borrow, but after looking at the grime ground into his utensil, I'm thinking knifeless is the way to go.

"Aye." King Leodegrance smiles proudly. "The table is made of rare wood from a far Eastern land, and was imported to Britain by the Romans when they occupied our lands. 'Tis one of the many objects of interest left behind, and a rare piece indeed; you will not see many other round tables in the entire country."

Round tables? My hand stops abruptly, and I look down

at the table with new eyes. Could it be? Then why is it here and not at King Arthur's pad?

"Doesn't Camelot have one?" I'm met with blank stares. "You know, like King Arthur and the Knights of the *Round* Table?"

"Knights of what?" Lancelot asks in a puzzled voice.

"Never mind." Did the legends get that one wrong, too? First Guenevere has no interest in Lancelot, and second, the knights don't even sit at a round table. Interesting. Very, very interesting.

As the servant reappears, this time carrying a tray piled high with sliced meats, I contemplate the situation. While I'm not eager to hook Lance and Guen up anytime soon, I don't think it would hurt to try to get some round-table reality going on. And no, I'm not being selfish by wanting to keep the knight and queen apart. Those two getting together leads to the destruction of Camelot, which would be a bad thing. It has nothing to do with my slight crush on Lance. Really.

"You know, Guen, this table would look great at Camelot," I suggest oh, so casually. As if her agreeing or disagreeing won't shape the future as we know it. "Arthur could use it when he hosts meetings with all the knights."

"But why?" Cocking her head in question, she asks, "Why wouldst our knights wish to reside at a table round, as opposed to one of the rectangular shape?"

"Why?" I repeat, thinking fast. Hmmm. Why *was* it that the round table was so important? I mean, it must have been important or the stories would never have bothered mentioning it, right? But what were its benefits? Why would no other table do? Damn it, Kat, why didn't you pay more attention in school?

As I try to think, I can't help but watch Guenevere grab a piece of meat off the platter with her fingers and shove it into her mouth. Horrifying. She's a queen, and she has worse manners than my uncle Donny.

Thanksgivings at Uncle Donny's Hoboken house are always a treat. (And yes, I'm being very sarcastic!) I stare at my plate and try not to watch as he slurps his beer and chews with his mouth open, spittle flying as he speaks before swallowing. The sight is literally nauseating. You can't help but notice, either, since he always sits at the head of the table. He insists, saying it is his house and therefore he is the head of the—

That's it! I'm a genius!

"The table must be round so no knight gets to sit at the head," I explain proudly. "Makes them all of equal status."

Understanding nods all around. "'Tis a good idea," Guenevere says, addressing Lancelot with a smile. "This way you and Sir Agravaine can no longer argue over the coveted position." She turns to her father. "That is, of course, unless you object to giving up an object of such value."

King Leo smiles indulgently. There's no doubt from his expression that Guenevere is daddy's little girl. Why, I bet he's never been able to resist giving up whatever her heart desires. And, of course, she made dad proud—marrying the high king of the land and all. I'm betting that being the queen's father ain't such a bad thing when Leo has to deal with his enemies. Worth a table or two, at the very least.

"The table is yours, my darling," he says. "Do with it as you wish. 'Tis a fine suggestion, and I will be quite willing to dispatch twenty men to ship it to Camelot in the morn. If you will excuse me, I will go about the preparations." He rises from his chair and exits the chamber.

Well, what do you know? I've created a legend. What would have happened if I hadn't gone back in time? I wonder. Would they have eventually decided to ship it over themselves? Or . . . An uncomfortable thought strikes me. What if I'm *supposed* to be here? What if all the legends are based on *me* changing things? But then how would I know of them before they happened? Well, I guess not before. Just before in my time line. What if this is all a big time loop, and I've been making this journey a billion times over, like in that movie *Groundhog Day*? Of course, he remembered his time looping. And he only looped back for one day, not one millennium. Oh, and he had to do it over and over until he got it right. God, what if I'm supposed to get something right? Because of my pitiful lack of medieval history, I have no idea what's even wrong to begin with! If this is the case, I'm royally screwed.

I shake my head to clear my thoughts. Sometimes I think I have adult ADD, the way my brain wanders off on crazy tangents. Like one time I was at this fashion show and I was supposed to be watching the runway, but couldn't help think of how the lighting made the models look even skinnier, which led me to think about how some department stores must pay a lot of money to install skinny dressing room lights, because I know when I bring the item home it never looks the same on me, which got me to thinking, I really shouldn't have eaten that last piece of pizza last night, which reminded me . . .

Oh, sorry. But see what I mean?

"So are we heading to Avalon tomorrow?" I ask, trying hard to scoop up a slice of meat with my spoon. How many years until forks are invented? "Go meet with this lake lady?"

"Aye," Lancelot says. "We shall leave at first light. 'Tis a day's journey at most."

"You are making a pilgrimage to Avalon?" Guenevere

105

asks, her eyes lighting up. "I have not been to the sacred isle for many summers. Would you allow me to accompany you?"

Seeing as she's the queen and all, I doubt that either Lance or I have much choice in the matter. Still, it's nice she presented the idea as a question. Also, I wouldn't mind having another chick to chat with in case we run into some bad guys and have to sit through a long fight scene again.

"Sure. That'd be cool."

Guenevere scrunches her eyebrows in confusion. "D'you think it so? But the weather has been so warm of late."

I burst out laughing. I'll never get used to talking medieval. "Oh, sorry. In my time we say 'cool' to mean something good. So by me saying 'that'd be cool,' I mean that would be a good thing if you came with us."

"So heat is not well liked in the future?"

This is tougher to explain than I thought. "Well, no. It's just an expression. To confuse you even more, if someone's good-looking, we'd say, 'Wow, he's hot.' And that's a good thing."

"Kat, I think thou art very hot." Guenevere tries it out shyly.

"No, no, no." I shake my head, trying not to make her feel bad. "You don't want to say it to another girl. Then people'd think you were a lesbian."

"Les-been?"

"A woman who loves other women."

"I love other women. My recently departed mother, for one. My ladies-in-waiting are also very dear to me."

"Yes, Yes, I know." I sigh. "But do you, uh, lie with them at night? Like you would with your husband?"

Guenevere raises her eyebrows in shock. "Of course not."

"Then you're not a lesbian."

"In the future women make love to other women?"

"Yup. And men to men. In fact, most of the good-looking guys are gay . . . the male version of lesbian."

"Aye, we have that here as well." She nods. "Many a lord has been caught coupling with the young, fancy lads of the palace."

I glance over to Lance, who looks a bit pained by the subject matter. Macho medieval homophobe.

"Really?" I grin. "What about knights?"

"Well, yes. I have heard tales of knights who, on long, lonely crusades . . ." Guenevere babbles until Lancelot clears his throat—extra loudly. "But certainly not Lancelot," the queen adds quickly, perhaps afraid I got the wrong impression. I hadn't, but find it amusing to see Lancelot turn beet red. "He is quite the man with the ladies."

"I'm sure that he is," I say with a smile. I turn back to Guenevere. "Anyway, to get back to your first question, yes, I'd be delighted to have you accompany us to Avalon."

"Then 'tis settled," Lancelot butts in, seeming anxious to keep with the subject change. "We leave at first light."

The next morning I'm woken up by a servant girl, who tells me the caravan to Avalon has been prepared and will be setting off as soon as I'm ready. I had no idea the trip involved a caravan. Truth be told, I'm not even sure what she means by that—the only Caravan I've even seen is the Dodge kind.

Once again the maid insists on helping me dress. This time I choose a bright yellow dress and matching cape with hood. I think I'm actually getting used to walking in heavy, bulky gowns at this point, though if we get a really hot day, I'm going to be sweating to death. No deodorant. Ew.

The maid leads me down the steps and out of the castle. There I see about twenty horsed men, including Lancelot, and a brightly decorated, portable tent. A horse in front and a horse behind support the litter with long wooden poles slotted into each saddle. Seems to me they should have put wheels on the thing, but what do I know?

Guenevere pokes her head out from inside the tent and gestures for me to come inside. After giving Lancelot a little wave of greeting, I peek behind the curtains and am amazed to find a plush little chamber inside, big enough for two to sit comfortably. I climb in and plop down opposite the queen, settling into the soft furs that line the floor.

"Now, this is the way to travel," I remark. "Much better than a stinky, bouncy horse."

About an hour into the journey, I take back my optimistic statement about the litter beating out horseback in the comfort category. It's bumpy as hell and has given me major carsickness . . . er . . . I mean, litter sickness with all its rocking back and forth. It's all I can do to hold down the nausea swimming through my stomach.

Guenevere, on the other hand, is not affected in the least by the jarring ride. Guess she's used to it. Bubbly and happy, she babbles on and on, relating stories of derring-do—this knight smiting this other knight who then smote still another knight in retaliation for the first knight's smoting and smiting. There's the compelling story of "how Sir Palomides jousted with Sir Galihodin, and after with Sir Gawain, and smote them down," for example. Then, there's the thrilling tale of "how Sir Marhaus jousted with Sir Gawain and Sir Uwaine and overthrew them both." Oh, and let's not forget the classic "how Lancelot slew two giants and made a castle free." At first I pay attention to this one, since it involves Lance, but once I find out the so-called "giants" probably wouldn't even make the NBA, I drift off again.

On and on she goes, each story running into the next, sounding exactly alike, until I'm ready to jump out of the litter and into the nearest lake to drown myself before I have to hear another.

It's not really her fault. She's trying to pass the time. And by her animated voice, I can see the stories fascinate her, and she wants to share. It's just that when I'm already feeling nauseated, the last thing I need is an enthusiastic, non-sick traveling companion. It's kind of like being on an airplane next to the old lady who won't shut up about her grandchildren, but even worse, 'cause I don't have an iPod to wear.

"Wow, your knights have done some cool stuff," I say, finally catching her between stories. Maybe we can summarize and move on.

"D'you not have knights in your time?" she questions.

I think for a moment before answering. "Well, technically we do. I mean, they do in England, anyway. The queen can knight whomever she wants. But lately she seems to favor aging rock stars and actors over those in the 'rescue damsels in distress' line of work."

In fact, the idea of Sir Elton John or Sir Paul McCartney participating in this sort of smiting and smoting is kind of funny. Though isn't Sean Connery a knight, too? Him, I could see dressed in the armor. Remember that 1995 movie where he played King Arthur? The former 007 looked so sexy in his role as the once and future king that it seemed ludicrous to believe Guenevere would pick Richard Gere over him. They should have had Johnny Depp play Lancelot. He's a hottie. Or maybe Heath Ledger. He was good in that other knight movie. But then again, he was probably too young in 1995. . . .

"That reminds me of another tale," Guenevere declares, interrupting my *First Knight* recasting. "It is titled, 'how Sir Gareth fought with a knight who held within his castle thirty ladies, and how he slew him.'"

And so it goes. More stories. Sigh. This is going to be a very, very long trip.

* * *

After what seems an eternity of riding and storytelling, we finally come to a stop. After a few moments Lancelot peeks his head into the litter. "We are at the village," he says.

Thank goodness. I couldn't spend another nauseated minute in that box. I tumble out, my legs unsteady from being tucked under my body for so long. Lancelot catches me as I stumble, and for a moment I simply enjoy the feeling of his strong hands grasping my waist. Maybe I should feign a sprained ankle so he'll have to carry me. Nah, that's a little too tacky, even for me.

I look around. We've stopped at the outskirts of a sleepy village sitting on the shore of what appears to be a large lake. The land surrounding the village is green, but real swampy—kind of like Alligator Alley in Florida. The lake itself is blanketed by swirling fog. Thick as pea soup, my mom would say. The sun has nearly set, giving the fog a reddish glow.

"Avalon lies across yonder water," Lancelot explains, pointing into the fog. "Shrouded by mists, the holy land, protected. No man can approach its shores unless he be so trained to navigate through the fog. The villagers who know the route guard the secret with their lives."

Wow. Sounds kind of spooky when you put it that way. I shiver a little. Good thing I'm with Lance and Guen. I'm thinking I'd have a hell of a time trying to convince the locals I deserve to set foot on their holy ground.

"Some say the villagers are not human at all," Guenevere adds, stepping out of the litter. "But descended from the very fey folk."

Oh, so they're fairies, are they? Sure. But hey, everyone has their own beliefs, right? Who am I to say fairies only exist in, er . . . fairy tales? After all, last week I would have said the same thing about time travelers.

"Art thou in need of transport?" A tiny, ancient-looking

man, supported by a gnarled cane, hobbles out of the mist. With dark skin and shimmering white hair, he looks like no one I've ever seen before. Something about his eyes— otherworldly, I guess you'd say, though it's hard to pinpoint why. Maybe the fairy theory does have some merit after all. I check his ears and am disappointed to find they're not pointed.

"Aye. We will pay well for passage to Avalon," Lancelot says, reaching into his cloth change purse and pulling out a golden coin.

"You may pay well, indeed." The man takes the coin and shoves it into his own change purse. "But passage is granted only to those deemed worthy by our Lady of the Lake."

"My worth has been tested by my lady," Lancelot says, pulling up his sleeve to reveal a stunning dragon tattoo on his forearm. The beast looks almost alive as he flexes his muscle. "And found not wanting."

The man studies the body art with a critical eye. "The tattoo of du Lac," he says in a revered whisper. "It has been many years since I have seen one who bears the mark." He turns on his cane and begins hobbling toward the shore. "Follow me, oh blessed of our lady. I shall secure you passage."

Well, all right. Guess it helps to have knights in high places on your side. Lance pulls down his sleeve and gestures us to follow the man into the mist. Guen and I step into line behind him and a couple of the other caravan guards, and trail behind.

"A man must be a great warrior to bear the mark," Guen whispers to me as we approach a long wooden barge. "And trained in all the ways of the high druid sect as well. Lancelot is not only a champion at arms, but could easily serve as a spiritual leader, should he choose."

So he's multitalented then. Interesting. And here I'm

thinking he's got more brawn than brain. Maybe I've misjudged him.

Guenevere stops right before we board the barge. "I have dear friends in the village I wish to see before making the journey to the isle itself. Go with Lancelot, consult with the lady, and I will see you in the morn."

"Okay. Have fun," I say. She squeezes my arm affectionately, and I feel guilty for thinking bad thoughts of her and her stories earlier. She's a nice girl, just from a different millennium, meaning different ideas of what's entertaining. I need to be less closed-minded. After all, I'm invading *their* world, not the other way around.

"Enjoy the company of Sir Lancelot," she whispers into my ear before letting go of my arm and disappearing with her bodyguards into the mist.

I step onto the barge. Lancelot is standing at the far end, his back to me, staring into the shroud of mist. As the old man digs his oar into the lake bottom to push us away from shore, I trace the outline of Lancelot's broad shoulders with my eyes.

The voyeuristic pleasure of watching him unaware soon consumes me. He's quiet. Contemplative. It's obvious, even to dense, self-absorbed little me, that this place holds a special magic for him. Suddenly I long to know his thoughts. Explore his mind. See what makes this tall, dark, silent knight tick.

As we silently glide through the waters, the fog thickens and I can no longer even see my hand in front of my face. I make a decision: if we end up with any downtime on the island, I will make an effort to get to know Lancelot a little better.

If he wants to get to know *me*, that is.

I know I've behaved like a spoiled teenager ever since I

got here: getting wasted, dancing on tables, throwing up. He must think I'm a total loser, the medieval equivalent of white trash. I've sure acted like it. Just 'cause I'm in a strange place doesn't give me free rein to do whatever I choose. When in Rome, do as the Romans do. Or as the medieval English do, in this case. I should be trying to fit in, not bucking the trends. Whether I like it or not, women in medieval times didn't do the shit I've been doing. And I've probably totally embarrassed the one guy who's so nicely volunteered to help me out. It's not like he's getting anything out of the deal.

Why *has* he been so nice to me, anyhow? I mean, fine, he probably thinks I'm good-looking or something, but there are plenty of other hot castle chicks he could choose from. Judging from the reception he got at King Leo's place, he has his pick, too. So why is he set on protecting little twenty-first-century me?

Unable to bear the silence any longer, I call out to him, "Lancelot?"

"Yes?" The fog obscures my vision, and I can only hear his sexy voice—I cannot see him at all. The only other sound is that of the oar dipping into the otherwise still waters. It makes the conversation strangely erotic.

"Tell me about the Lady of the Lake."

"She is beautiful. Wise," he says slowly, his rich, deep voice slicing through the fog. "A mystical being born of the fey folk. Kind. Full of love."

A pang of jealousy shoots through me. Why should I be jealous of some old woman who lives on an island? Maybe it's something in Lancelot's words, a kind of worshipful tone that no one on earth has ever, ever used when talking about me.

"You said she raised you?"

"Indeed. She and her priestesses take in many a young girl to train her in the ways of the goddess. But I am the first and only boy to have grown up on Avalon's holy shores."

"Oh." Silence again. A slight breeze picks up, causing wisps of hair to tickle my face. I want the moment to continue, for our strange, intimate, blind conversation to continue.

"Why are you helping me?" I'm suddenly desperate to know.   .

"You needn't ask that, lady."

"Yes, I *do* need to. I've got to know," I insist. "I've been nothing but an embarrassment and problem since I arrived."

" 'Tis untrue."

" '*Tis* very, very true," I cry, suddenly feeling quite sorry for myself. "In fact, I'm willing to bet you've never, ever had to deal with a drunk, table-dancing damsel in distress in all your years as a knight. I bet everyone you've rescued before is, like, sweet and demure and nice and thankful for your help." I'm practically shouting at him now, I'm so worked up. I can't believe how pathetic I am, how pathetic I must seem to him. "You should be running in the other direction instead of going out of your way to help me out. If I were you—"

Out of nowhere roughened hands cup my chin, and desperate lips crush my own. I gasp in surprise—lost in my self-pity, I didn't even hear him approach. I can't see him, even with my eyes wide-open. The mists have robbed me of my vision, the rest of my senses conquered by him alone. His hands find my waist and yank me closer. His mouth, his lips, demand total submission. Blood pounds in my ears, drowning out the silence of the lake. His scent, patchouli, mixes with musky desire. I'm weak. Powerless. Overwhelmed. Breathless. All at once. Can't explain. Don't want to.

Just want to feel . . .

Like this . . .

Forever . . .

So I kiss him back.

Remember *Titanic*? The sweaty palm pressed against the glass after Rose and Jack make love? A simple symbol, wordlessly capturing ultimate desire. I thought it beautiful then. It's the only thing I can compare this to now.

What happened to the cynical, self-absorbed girl who thinks romance was invented to sell chocolates and sappy cards? The girl who has sex, but doesn't make love? The girl who abhors public displays of affection, and believes marriage is an evil institution thought up by misogynistic men who want to control women? Well, at this moment she's taking a little time off. Some well-deserved R-and-R. The new and improved romanticized version of Katherine Alyssa Jones is presently lost in the ecstasy of it all, and no, I don't think I should have to apologize for it!

The barge hits land and I'm jarred forward into Lancelot's arms. For a moment he holds me, as if physically unable to let go. I am his willing captive. Then his hands drop. His lips pull away from mine. I am alone once again. An emptiness—an extreme loneliness—shoots a torturous ache through my stomach.

"I am sorry, milady," his voice stammers through the fog. "I—I shouldn't have. . . . I forget myself. Please forgive me. That should not have happened."

Yes, it should have! That was, like, the most romantic thing that *ever* happened to me. I mean, I've had my fair share of passionate moments. But none can top an invisible kiss by a valiant knight in the middle of a mist-shrouded lake. Suddenly I see why medieval literature and movies are so popular. There's something about knights—this one in particular—that is so damn appealing, so freaking romantic I can barely stand it.

My legs are still unsteady as we step off the barge and onto the mossy ground. I look up and see a light piercing through the mists. A woman dressed in a simple white, beltless gown and no shoes stands on the shore, holding a lantern. Her long blond hair falls to her lower back, and her eyes, reflected in the lantern's dancing light, shine with an unnatural glow.

"Welcome to Avalon," she says in a voice of tinkling Christmas bells that you could very well imagine belonging to a fairy. "My lady has been expecting you."

Chapter Eight

Expecting us? How can she be expecting us? We certainly haven't called to make an appointment. And considering we decided to make this trek only, like, twenty-four hours ago, I don't think anyone's had time to warn her.

Lancelot doesn't seem surprised at all by the white-robed maiden's words. Like, duh, he thinks she's magical. Of course he'd buy into the idea that she knew we were coming. But really, for all we know, this greeter priestess has been hanging out for days on end, under strict orders from her mistress to pretend to recognize any and all visitors and let them know they were expected, even though they weren't.

The girl (for she is, I realize after taking a closer look, only about fourteen years old) turns and starts walking up a mossy incline, her long blond hair swishing behind her. I glance at Lance, who motions that we should follow.

She doesn't say a word as she leads us into swirling white mist, guided only by her single candle lantern. It's kind of scary, to tell the truth—the darkness, the spooky owls hooting in the trees. My pulse is racing, and I long for the modern wonders of street lamps and neon lights. Even Vegas, in all its tacky glory, would look good to me right about now.

It seems like we walk for hours, but maybe it's because I have no point of reference. My quad muscles tell me I'm climbing up and up a huge hill, like on one of those never-ending StairMaster things. Lancelot informs me they call it the Tor, a magical hill, evidently. Surprise, surprise. Like everything else in this freaking place.

The mists pull back, and we reach a circle of thatched huts sitting in a grassy clearing, surrounded by dense forest. Nothing glamorous like a castle for the lake lady, I guess. Poor thing. I can't imagine living my whole life on a Starbucks-free deserted hill in the middle of nowhere. Especially with no TV. What does she do in her spare time? Magic tricks can entertain someone for only so long.

The maiden stops and points to one of the nondescript huts. "Thou may enter there."

Lancelot nods and thanks the woman. "Blessings of the goddess be upon thee," he says.

"As on thee, master," the girl returns with a small smile. I see her give my knight the once-over. Another total knight groupie. Add druidic girls on magical islands to the list of Lancelot fans. If this guy lived in the twenty-first century, I swear he'd have to be an actor or rock star. I guess knights were the rock stars of their time. Or maybe *sports hero* would be a better comparison, on account of the jousting matches.

Lance pulls open the slatted wooden door and gestures for me to follow him as he steps into the one-room hut. Inside, tiny dragon-shaped candle lamps scattered around the floor give off minimal light, their flames casting dancing shadows on the walls. (Pretty, but a total fire hazard.) Other than that, the room is empty. Not a single piece of furniture. How does the lake lady live with no furniture? I can understand going with a minimalist decor, seeing as she's like a druid chick and they're all one with nature and stuff. But you'd think she'd at least need a bed, a chair. A kitchen table.

"Why dost thou seek audience with our lady?"

The voice startles me. In my lack-of-furniture musings, I hadn't noticed anyone there. But yes, another white-robed girl, nearly identical to the first one, stands at the back of the hut, her arms crossed over her chest.

Okay, here's a thought: If the lady's been expecting us, wouldn't she already know the reason for our visit, too? Still, I'm determined to keep my mouth shut. Let the natives believe whatever it is they want to believe. As long as I get home in the end, that's all that matters.

Home? Am I starting to delude myself into thinking that this lady can help me? More likely this whole thing is a big waste of time. On the other hand, I guess it's pretty cool coming here, seeing this Avalon place with my own eyes and all. And let's face it; I've got nothing better to do.

"We have come to seek the lady's wisdom on the matter of traveling through time," Lancelot explains.

Well, all right. Guess we're not being subtle about our mission. I wait for the girl to hide a laugh or at least look vaguely amused, but she never loses her serious expression. I should be used to it by now, but it still amazes me that these people believe this stuff without even the slightest doubt.

"Wait here. I will inform the lady that thou seekest an audience." With that she disappears, slipping behind a crimson velvet curtain at the far end of the hut. Oh, so there is another room. Maybe her furniture is there. This place is a lot bigger than it looks from the outside.

Lancelot reaches over and squeezes my hand in reassurance, an intimate gesture that implies that we're in this together. "You needn't worry," he says in a low voice. "The lady is as kind as she is wise. She will be able to help you; I am sure of it."

I steal a peek at his handsome face, and realize he's watching me with those eyes of his. He smiles tenderly, sending my pulse racing once again.

Maybe it's because I'm so out of my element, lost and alone, that I feel this close to him so soon. I'm usually more of the "keep my distance" type of girl. I mean, I'll sleep with guys, no prob. In fact, I really like sex. However, I'm so not into the unpack-all-emotional-baggage-the-second-you-meet-the-guy style of dating. My friend Lucy meets a guy, and after the first date she's already poured out her soul and picked out china patterns. Scares a lot of guys off. I, on the other hand, am first out of bed and first out the door the next morning, my lover literally begging me to return his phone calls. Don't know why; it's not, like, premeditated or anything. I just feel the need to leave. Fast. My shrink says it's due to the whole absentee-father thing. Thanks a lot, Dad.

Anyway, to get back on topic, around Lancelot I already feel very vulnerable, very involved, even though all we've done is kiss. I wonder why. The only thing I can blame it on is the circumstances. He's saved my life, and I am stupefied to think what would have become of me without his involvement. If he hadn't rescued me from Lot, I'd have been raped and killed. If he hadn't guided me to Cameliard, I'd be still wandering around lost in the woods. Probably would have ended up as lunch for a grizzly bear.

I owe him everything, and have given him nothing, and still he holds my hand in reassurance that everything is going to be okay. It's like I can—and this is too weird to even mention . . . in fact, I never use the phrase—but I really, really think I do this time, and I'm not afraid to say it for once in my life. . . .

World hear me now. Kat Jones, about to say three words she never, ever says.

I trust him.

I know, I know, for a moment there it sounded like I was going to say I loved him. But I'm not going to get carried away here. This is real life, not some fantasy romance novel. And after all, I barely know the guy.

Returning, the girl pulls aside the curtain and steps into the room. "The lady will see thee now," she says. "Lancelot, I trust thou still knowest the way?"

He nods and expresses his thanks with another goddess-blessing-type remark. Since I don't know any goddess blessings, I simply say, "Thanks and ditto," to which, of course, the girl responds with a confused look. Man, I've got to get Lance to teach me the medieval lingo so I don't appear to be such a tacky American tourist all the time.

Keeping hold of my hand, the knight slips behind the curtain, and I follow into a darkened hallway. A secret passage! Cool. I always loved the idea of secret passages. When I was growing up, my friend Donna lived in this old Victorian house from the 1800s, and at the back of her bedroom closet there was this tiny secret crawl space we used to play in. It led to her mother's room, but we used to pretend it was the doorway to Narnia, like in *The Lion, The Witch, and the Wardrobe*.

Lancelot pulls a flaming torch out of a wall bracket, and we start walking downward. It's like a mine shaft, with earthen walls and floors supported by wooden beams. Yikes. Is this safe? As much as I like secret passages, I've never really dug caves. A bit claustrophobic, I think. Plus, it smells pretty musty in here. Needs a good dousing with Lysol.

Having no choice but to keep going, I buck up, squeeze Lance's hand a little tighter, and start down into the darkness. This is turning out to be quite the adventure.

The path eventually evens out. We're deep underground now, walking in a long corridor, the torch providing the only light. I pray it doesn't blow out—I'd be truly freaked if we had to find our way in pitch-blackness. Why didn't I stick a flashlight in my purse? Oh, yeah: I assumed I'd be surrounded by electricity all day. Go figure. It's funny, really, the modern conveniences one takes for granted in the twenty-first century.

The passage finally ends at a small, nondescript wooden door. Lancelot lets go of my hand and turns to face me. "Behind this entrance lives Nimue, Lady of the Lake. Go through. Tell her everything you have experienced. Then ask if she can help you."

"Wait, you're not coming with me?" Suddenly I'm a little more scared, and I realize my hands are trembling. I shove them behind my back. Be brave, Kat. After all, I'm the girl who once walked through Central Park barefoot at one in the morning wearing a red party dress and carrying broken heels. Of course, I was sixteen then, and wasted with liquid courage.

"No. I would be a distraction to you both. But do not fear: I will not leave you. I will remain outside this door, waiting for you to return, no matter how long you take."

"Okay." I sigh as I try to muster up some bravery. My heart's slamming against my rib cage. What am I afraid of, anyway? Compared to everything else I've faced in the last days—capture, near rape, a hangover from hell—this is totally minor.

Lancelot nods and opens the door for me. As I step

through, I gasp out loud. I can't help it. I've entered a huge—I mean absolutely mammoth—cavern, and it's beautiful. More than beautiful. There are no words to describe its majesty. The ceiling drips with rainbow stalactites. Light refracted from billions of crystals almost seems alive as it dances throughout the cave.

But the thing I notice the most is the treasure: gold coins, diamonds, rubies, sapphires, crowns, necklaces, jewel-hilted swords, all piled high, spilling over their chests. Everywhere I turn there are more priceless items. I've never seen anything like it. Not even in *Pirates of the Caribbean*. Man, this lake-lady character is filthy rich! I wonder if it's too vulgar to ask for a souvenir to put one of these pieces up for auction on eBay . . .

"Welcome, Lady Katherine."

The low, purring voice startles me from my treasure gazing. I look over and see a dark-haired woman sitting beside a deep, sea-green pool of swirling water that matches her emerald eyes. She wears the same type of white, beltless robe as the other girls, but there is something different about her. I don't know how to explain it exactly, but she has, like, this aura around her. She practically glows. And her face, so unlined, so beautiful . . . it's hard to look at. She could be a thousand years old or a girl of eighteen. It's impossible to tell.

"How did you know my name?" I ask, feeling suddenly very, very afraid. I haven't introduced myself. And I'm almost positive Lance hasn't called me by name since we arrived on the island.

"I know many things," she says in her hypnotic voice. She's like one of the Sirens, the supernatural beings who lure men to crash their boats on the rocks in that *Odyssey* book. Good thing I hate sailing. "I am Nimue, Lady of the Lake."

"I'm, er . . . Kat Jones. Lady of the twenty-first century. But I guess you already know that."

I feel like I should be bowing or something. She's so beautiful—she looks like a goddess. Not that I've ever seen one, but if I imagine what one would look like, she'd be it. I'm trying to think of what movie star I can compare her to, but she's so much more striking than any of them it would be an unfair comparison to make. Maybe multiplying Angelina Jolie's looks by about a million would come close. She has the same huge, almond-shaped eyes, full lips, and long hair. But while Angelina can look bratty and pissed-off, Nimue radiates inner peace.

"Yes," she agrees, nodding her dark head. "But what I do not know is how thou found thyself in our time."

I shrug, absently kicking my foot against a gold chest. How can I explain it? I really have no idea myself. "Some gypsy put a curse on me. Don't know if that has anything to do with it." I tell her the whole story, trying hard not to use any slang (since she wouldn't understand) or say *like* between every other word (since she would, like, probably find it, like, annoying).

"I see." Nimue is silent for a moment after I've finished. "Come; sit by me," she says at last, as if she's made a tough decision. She pats a spot beside the pool. I walk over and park myself where she directs. I can feel heat rising from the green pool and breathe in a distinct sulfuric odor. Must be like one of those hot mineral springs they have at Yellowstone Park.

" 'Tis a reflecting pool," she explains, as if hearing my thoughts. "Some call it the Pool of Dreams." She dips her white hand into its waters and stirs. "Gaze into it, and tell me what thou seest."

Leaning forward I'm immediately mesmerized by its whirlpooling currents.

"Uh, green water?"

"Look deeper. Much, much deeper." Nimue's voice seems very far away, her words . . . almost hypnotic. I stare harder and find my eyelids suddenly unbearably heavy. I shouldn't be tired.

Must keep looking at pool.

My vision blurs.

When it clears I'm not in the cavern anymore, but outside in the open air. The open air of Times Square, in fact, which, if you take into account the skyscrapers and people, isn't really that open after all.

Am I home? Was it that quick? I feel a twinge of regret as I realize I never got to say good-bye to Lancelot. Will Nimue at least let him know I've gone so he doesn't stand at the doorway waiting for me?

Stop thinking of Lancelot, Kat. You're home!

I can't believe it. I look around, trying to shake the weird feeling that's come over me. What now? Maybe I should head over to Grand Central Station and catch a bus to Connecticut. I can have my car towed back from the medieval fair, I guess.

It all sounds like a lot of work. And for some reason I feel very tired, drained, almost . . . depressed. Weird. I should be dancing for joy, not moping about. I got what I wanted.

Still, she should have at least given me some warning, maybe rename the Pool of Dreams "the Pool of Traveling Back to the Twenty-first Century Without Telling You First." At least then people will know what to expect when they look into its depths.

But I'm back! Back, back, back. No need to try to look at the cup as half-full, because the cup is more than half-full. In fact, it's overflowing with fullness.

Speaking of cups, I could really do with a cup of coffee. A triple venti nonfat latte from Starbucks will wake me up.

I look around. There's a Starbucks on every corner, they say. Well, maybe every other corner. None on this one. I walk down the street. It feels weird to be back. Weird to see people dressed in normal, everyday twenty-first-century clothes. Weird for me to be wearing ordinary twenty-first-century clothes. What *am* I wearing, anyway? I look down at myself. Yikes. Have I gained weight? And what's with the frumpy turtleneck?

As I walk, I keep half expecting a knight on horseback to charge through, and am actually surprised to see a punk-rock mohawked bike courier whiz by instead.

It's weird; I almost feel sad. Disappointed. Not that I wanted to stay in Camelot, but still, it feels . . . unfinished somehow.

Where is that Starbucks? In fact, not only can I not find a Starbucks, I haven't seen a single coffee-serving establishment for three blocks. I'd even take a cup from a greasy diner's pot at this point. One that's been burning on a hot plate all day. And trust me, that's saying a lot, coming from a coffee snob like myself.

Actually I'd better make it iced coffee. It's real warm out for September. I glance at a newspaper to check the date. Huh? June 21. The first day of summer . . .

Of next year!

I stare at the date, rub my eyes, and stare again. According to this paper, a whole year has passed since I've been away. I've lost a whole year of my life! This is horrifying. Especially when you take into consideration that the year lost was the last year I could give my real age. Oh, my God—I'm thirty! *Thirty!* The big three-oh. Oh, my God. It's the second anniversary of my twenty-ninth birthday.

That Nimue chick has fucked up big-time, sending me back a year too late. What does this mean? What about my job? Have they replaced me? Was it with Barbara? I can deal with being replaced, but not by Barbara. The girl doesn't know Gap from Gucci, or Hermès from H&M.

I actually think being sent forward in time is worse than going back. At least if you go back, you're not missing out on anything. But to lose a whole year of my life . . . The implications are horrendous. Knowing that I'm thirty is horrendous. Does your birthday count if you don't remember celebrating it?

My eyes blur again. Oh, what now?

When my vision clears, I find myself no longer in Manhattan. No longer thirty years old. Instead I'm walking through a decrepit graveyard. The sun hides behind a cloud, and the smell of decay and death is nearly overwhelming.

Oh, no!

"Wait," I cry. "I was home. I was home!" What's happening to me? Did I wish my way back in time again? I take back everything I said about going forward being worse than going back. Losing a year is much, much better than being stuck in a place with no Marc Jacobs. Even with that cheesy turtleneck.

Even with turning thirty.

Please, please, I want to go back.

I glance around. Gravestones mock me with their ancient death dates. I'm back in medieval times, all right. But this is worse than before, due to the fact that now I don't even have Lancelot by my side. How am I going to find him? I'm utterly alone. I now realize exactly how much I've come to depend on the guy. He knows where to go, how to act, whom to talk to. I know nothing. I look around, desperate to find something, anything familiar-looking.

"Nimue!" I howl at the top of my lungs. "Bring me back! Now!" I know yelling probably isn't the best way to seek help from the lake lady, but I can't help it. I'm too mad to mind my manners. "Please?" I beg, lowering my voice to a whimper.

No answer. It's as if I'm the last person on earth.

The wind whips up, ripping through my gown. (Yes, I am again clothed in a gown, which would be devastating if I hadn't recently been wearing that awful turtleneck.) I run blindly through the courtyard, accidentally snagging the dress's silk material on dead branches that litter the ground. Tears streak down my cheeks, but I don't care.

Where am I? When am I?

I keep running until I trip over a rock I didn't see and go flying head over heels, smacking my arm against a gravestone. The contents of my purse spill onto the ground.

"Ow!"

Majorly pissed-off now, I slam my fist into the offending gravestone, realizing only afterward that punishing it actually inflicts even more punishment back on me. (The gravestone being, as its name implies, made of stone.) Jarring pain shoots from my fist all the way to my shoulder. Damn it!

I pat the ground, searching for what has fallen out of my purse. Tampons, a tube of lipstick, a compact, a pen—wait! A compact? Ooh, I have a mirror! I didn't have a mirror back in medieval times, did I? I mean, the original medieval times, not this medieval times. No matter, I have a mirror; that's what's important. Suddenly I feel a tad bit better, knowing I can now see what shape I'm currently in, though I'll admit I'm a bit scared to look.

I open the compact, ready to gaze upon the worst Medusa look in the history of Medusa looks, including the one in *Clash of the Titans*. And she was one ugly woman!

But before I focus on my reflection, sunlight pours out from behind a cloud, hitting the mirror at exactly the right angle. The flash of light blinds me for a moment, and I have to look away. The light reflects off the mirror and onto the gravestone that I hit my arm against, lighting its inscription.

HERE LIETH QUEEN GUENEVERE OF CAMELIARD.

"What the hell?" I drop the compact and stare at the grave. Guenevere's dead? Dead? She's not dead; she's in Avalon. Isn't she?

A heavy gloom washes over me. Not only am I still stuck back in time again, but evidently I've now fast-forwarded into some future past where my only medieval friend is dead. This gets better and better. And what about Lancelot? Is he dead, too?

My eyes blur yet again.

As my vision returns, I force myself to stay calm. I'm beginning to see a pattern forming here. The last thing I remember is staring into the Pool of Dreams. So, rationally speaking, this could be one big, crazy dream. Really, I'm still in Avalon, in the beautiful chamber. The Lady of the Lake still sits by my side. Lancelot still waits patiently behind the door. Guenevere, very much alive, giggles with girlfriends in the village, perhaps relating more of her knight-in-shining-armor tales to a thoroughly bored audience. The idea is almost comforting. It's funny how you get used to a place. I should hate Camelot and all the rest. But instead I'm relieved that I'm still there. At least, I think I am.

Anyway, this brings me to the question, Where have my dreams brought me now? I look around. Aha! I recognize this place from photos.

Stonehenge.

I watch from a slight distance as black-robed men chant and sing, performing some kind of ceremony. A young girl with straight red hair stands in the center of the circle, naked. I step closer to get a better look and notice that her hands and feet are bound. The tallest of the robed men walks forward.

"Sacrifice for the future, sacrifice for the past. Goddess, accept this virgin offering—"

Are they going to kill her? I can't let them kill her.

"Stop!" I cry. The men turn and stare at me. Okay, that was pretty stupid, Kat. Yeah, let's interrupt the knife-wielding, human-sacrificing guys' ceremony. Good idea.

"Interloper," the tall one announces. "Kill the interloper."

Oh, shit.

I try to run but my feet feel like they're cemented to the ground. *Wake up, Kat! Wake up!* Can I die in a dream? Will I die in real life if I do? In *Nightmare on Elm Street* that's how it works. But that's only a movie, right?

The men are gaining on me, raising their sacrificial knives. I want to tell them I'm not a virgin, but my tongue won't work.

Wake up, Kat! Wake up!

My eyes blur, and when my vision clears I realize I'm in the lady's chamber again. I gasp, barely able to breathe. Nimue takes me by the shoulders and pulls me close. My heart's beating a mile a minute as I bury my face in her shoulder, tears falling unchecked.

"Oh, my God," I say, panting. "That seemed so real. I really thought I was going to die."

"I am sorry thou had to experience that," Nimue apologizes. "Usually a priestess undergoes much training before she is ready to look into the Pool of Dreams. But in this case there was no time. Tell me, Lady Katherine, what was it that thou saw?"

I relate the strange, dreamlike scenes in a trembling voice, still pretty freaked out. I mean, this wasn't like I was just seeing visions in an underground pond. I experienced it firsthand. Some sort of magic? I don't believe in magic. Then again, I don't believe in time travel either. This trip has really opened my eyes to a lot of things; that's for sure.

When I'm finished telling Nimue my dreams, she does a hell of a job explaining what each of them means. She's a regular Freud. Basically, she says, when someone like a gypsy puts a curse on someone, they also imprint a way to undo the curse on the unconscious mind. By hypnotizing me, Nimue can draw the imprinted symbols to my conscious thoughts and then interpret them.

"Each dream tells thee something important," she explains. "The first dream tells thee when. Thou said it was the first day of summer, no?"

"Yeah. June twenty-first."

"While I am unfamiliar with thy calendar, I do know summer solstice is one of the most powerful days of the year. Surely powerful enough to break the curse."

"When's the next summer solstice?"

"Nine moons from now."

"What?" I ask, incredulous. "I have to wait that long to go back? Are you sure we can't, like, do it like during winter solstice instead?"

Nimue gives me a pointed look. "Was it snowing in thy dream?"

I sigh. "No." Man, I can't believe I might be stuck here for nine months. This sucks. Though, on the bright side, it does give me time to get to know Lancelot a little better. . . . Hmm.

"The second dream symbolizes the who," Nimue goes on, folding her white hands in her lap. "Since thou art not trained to invoke the power of the solstice sun, a sworn priestess of the goddess must perform the ceremony for thee. Thy light points to Guenevere."

"Guenevere can't do the ritual," I protest, placing my hands on my hips in indignation. "She's, like, a queen. And she's not even that old. Can't you do it? I mean, really, if someone's going to send me forward in time, I'd like to be sure they know what they're doing. This is not something I want to fuck up."

"Did Queen Guenevere not tell thee? She has trained long ago in the ways of the goddess," Nimue informs me with a fond smile. "In fact, I had hoped she would replace me someday as Lady of the Lake. However, the great mother had other plans. Guenevere is fully capable of performing the ritual. Thy dream insists that she do so."

I think fast. "Maybe I made a mistake. Maybe it wasn't really Guenevere's grave. . . . In fact," I say triumphantly, "I think it was yours. Yeah, it definitely read, 'Nimue, Lady of the Lake.' Sorry. You know how it is when you try to read without glasses."

"Katherine, do not trifle with the prophecy," Nimue rebukes me in a serious tone. "This is thy future. Dost thou not realize the wrong interpretation can leave thee stuck here forever?"

"Oh." I gulp. "Well, now that you mention it, I believe it *was* Guenevere's grave after all." What was I thinking? The last thing I need to do is screw up the ritual.

"The third and final dream tells the where. Thou dreamed of a circle of mammoth rocks on a grassy knoll. Thou call it Stonehenge. While the name means nothing to me, the description is very familiar indeed."

"What is it for?" I ask eagerly. Wow, I'm finally going to learn the mystery behind Stonehenge. When and if I get back to the twenty-first century, I can tell the world—write a best seller, go on a ten-cities-in-ten-days lecturing tour. The mysteries of Stonehenge revealed, for the bargain price of $29.99.

"I do not know."

"What?" Damn it, there goes my life as future rich lecturing-slash–book-writing person. "I thought the thing was built by the druids."

"The stone circle has been in existence for thousands of

years," Nimue explains. "No one knows for certain why it was built."

"You got any theories?"

"Legend says that when a small city called Atlantis fell into the sea, a few Atlantean survivors came to Briton and assembled the structure. Some say 'tis a magical doorway to the heavens, and the idea was to bring back their kin who had perished in the floods."

Oh, great. The Lost City of Atlantis. Like *that* theory's going to fly with the book-buying crowd at Barnes & Noble. Puh-leeze.

"Did it work?" I ask skeptically. I mean, I know it didn't—couldn't have. But I'm curious to know what she believes.

"No one knows." Nimue shakes her head. "The Atlanteans disappeared the very day the structure was completed. Some say they met local maidens and had families, settling in as Britons. Others believe they were killed by wandering raiders. But . . ." she says, her eyes shining as she relates the tale. I can tell she's saved the best theory for last. "Some say they learned the secret of the stones and were transported to another world entirely."

"Hey, you never know." I shrug amicably. Once again, I have to come to grips with the fact that these people will believe absolutely anything.

"No matter," Nimue says, back to business. "At the right time, the right place, with the right priestess to guide the way, a portal to thy world may open."

"You sure winter solstice wouldn't work?"

"Katherine . . ." Nimue warns in a don't-mess-with-me voice.

I sigh. "Okay. Fine. Thanks."

"Thou may send Sir Lancelot in now," Nimue requests. Evidently I'm dismissed, my audience over. After reiterating my thanks, I slowly walk over to the door. Then I turn, remembering.

"What about the ugly turtleneck?"

"I am sorry?"

"In my first dream. I was wearing a god-awful shirt. Does that mean anything? Like, am I supposed to wear an ugly outfit on the day of returning?"

Nimue is silent for a moment, then says, "Perhaps clothing that does not belong to thee may interfere in some way with thy journey home."

Oh, okay. Now she's stretching it. Obviously she doesn't want to lose face here by not knowing. I like my theory better, and decide to make sure I'm wearing some unattractive shift dress or something on the day I return.

I exit the chamber, deep in thought, trying to quell the excitement bubbling through my veins. Will it work? Am I a fool to believe I can simply stand in the middle of Stonehenge on the first day of summer and suddenly be transported into the future? I mean, it seems impossible. Stupid, even. But somehow I got here—something else I used to think impossible. I guess I'll have to wait and see. As much as it sucks, I have no other options at this point.

"She wants to see you now," I tell Lance as I come through the door.

"Are you all right?" he asks, his eyes clouded with worry. I realize I'm still pretty shaken up, my hands still trembling.

"Yeah, yeah. I'm fine. Get in there and see what she wants," I say impatiently. No need for him to see me freaking out.

He nods, accepting my lie, and enters the room. I pretend to close the door behind him, but leave it open a crack so I can watch. I know—I'm being nosy. Sue me.

Lancelot walks up to the lady and gets on one knee before her, bowing his head and taking her hand, pressing his lips to it.

"My lady."

Nimue smiles down on him before gently pulling her hand away. "It has been too long since thou came to visit me, my knight. Do castle duties keep thee away?"

"I apologize, my lady," Lancelot says, looking guilty. "Arthur has been determined to make Camelot the best kingdom in all the land. That means constant quests. I've traversed the country a dozen times since I've last come to Avalon. Rescued maidens fair, fought rogue knights and Saxons alike, even spent time in the Far Eastern lands, searching for the Holy Grail the Christians believe to be the cup their Christ offered up at his Last Supper."

Wow, sounds like he's been one busy knight. Nice of him to take time off to help me. Though technically you could file this adventure under the "rescued maidens fair" category. All in a day's work, I guess. Is this merely another job to him? Or something more? What if he kisses all his damsels? For all I know, the romantic scene could be his traditional MO.

"And what of this girl brought to me this eve?"

"Lady Katherine. D'you think you can help her?" Lancelot asks, looking anxious.

She looks at him with kind, almost motherly eyes. "My dearest knight," she says fondly. "Didst thou find true love at long last?"

Lancelot blushes fiercely. "I am merely helping her find her way. Any knight would do the same."

I raise an eyebrow. While I wasn't expecting a complete confession of love and devotion, his too-quick denial makes me think there's something more to the story. I look at

Lance, then at Nimue. Were they lovers? No, the lake lady's got to be much older than him. Well, she doesn't look any older, but she is head lady and all. Besides, didn't Lance say she raised him? Maybe they've got an Oedipal thing going on. Ew.

"Sir Lancelot, thou knowest thou cannot lie to me," Nimue says with a smile. "Why dost thou always try?"

"I am not in love," Lancelot insists, a frown planted on his lips. "With her nor anyone else. I am a knight of Arthur."

"Hmm," Nimue says, dropping her gaze to stare into the Pool of Dreams. Its emerald-green water froths as she drags a finger through the current. "Perhaps the waters reveal something that is to come, instead." She looks up. "If thou hast not fallen for her yet, 'twould be better if thou never did. Bring her back to Camelot, aye. I would not have thee desert her. But then go on one of thy quests. Make thyself scarce until her day of departure."

I frown. If they were once lovers, is this, like, a tricky ploy to try to get him back? Still, I have to admit she's right. Why bother hooking up when a few months down the road I'm going home? It's not fair to him for us to get involved and then for me to take off.

"But why?" Lance asks. I'm glad he doesn't just say, "Yes, okay, no problem."

"I see great danger, great heartbreak in thy future, my dearest knight. Should thou choose the path of love, it will not run smooth. That is why I have begged thee in the past and will beg thee once again: do not give in to the pleasures of the flesh. Keep thy heart caged and thy virtue intact. The very foundation of Camelot depends on it."

"How could that be so, milady?" Lancelot asks. "Is not the path already set by the goddess? How are we to change it?"

"Thou art right, my little one," says Nimue with a sigh,

suddenly looking like an old woman. She rises and pats Lance's shoulder with a white hand. "Though not so little anymore," she adds as Lancelot stands, revealing his six-foot frame. "It does not matter what I say. The great garment of our existence has already been woven long ago. Whatever thread thou wilt choose to follow, the end shall be the same. I merely wish to save thee from misery along the way."

She pulls Lancelot down to her level and kisses him on the cheek, whispering something too soft for me to hear. I lean into the doorway to get a better listen, but to my utter embarrassment lose my balance and end up falling flat on my face into the room.

I look up from my sprawled position to find Lancelot and Nimue staring at me, frowning, obviously realizing I've eavesdropped on the entire conversation. I'm totally busted!

Doh!

Chapter Nine

"I must say, I have found most felines art more graceful than thee, Kat," the Lady of the Lake says, raising a delicately arched eyebrow as I scramble to my feet, my face pulsating with my hot blush. I'm mortified. What will Lance think of me? I knew I shouldn't be listening in. After all, you know what they say about curiosity killing the Kat.

"Sorry," I mutter, brushing off my gown.

"My dearest knight," Nimue continues, turning to Lance, "I can see thy attentions are needed elsewhere. Go now. May the love of the goddess ever light thy way. May thy steps along life's path be ever true."

"As with you, my lady," Lancelot says, bowing before turning to me. He gestures to the door.

I wave a good-bye to Nimue, grateful she isn't too pissed about my intrusion, and head out. As we walk through the mine shaft, my mind wanders back to the prophecy. Will it work? Will I actually be able to get out of here in nine months? Nine months is such a long time. Especially if it doesn't work. And what happens if it gets screwed up? Do I have to wait another year?

Can I deal with living at Camelot for nine months? Will they let me live in the palace? Or will they stick me in the village? Will I have to get a job? I don't think my magazine experience is going to come in very handy here. I guess I could find work as a seamstress. I'm actually fairly handy with a needle and thread, although I don't usually sew by hand, and obviously they're not going to have sewing machines. I couldn't be a cook. I can't even boil water. What else? Hmm. What about those ladies-in-waiting? I think I could handle a job where the only skill necessary is that of sitting around a castle looking pretty.

I'm about to ask Lance whether he knows of any openings amongst the waiting ladies, but we've come to the curtain that separates the secret passage from the regular hut. I step through, and the girl who allowed us entry welcomes us back.

"I trust our lady has helped thee with thy quest?" she asks. Like it's any of her business.

"Aye," Lancelot says, much more diplomatic than I. "I thank thee for arranging the meeting."

"Of course, sir," the girl says, bowing her head. "Will you stay at Avalon tonight, or should I call the ferryman back to take you to the village?"

Lancelot glances over to me. I shrug. Here, there—it's all the same to me. The beds are going to be made of bales of hay, and neither place features free HBO.

"Why don't we rest here for the night?" Lance decides.

"Very well." The girl nods. She opens the front door to the hut and steps outside. We follow. "Yonder lies the House of the Maidens," she says, pointing at one of the huts. "You may find a bed inside. Lancelot, would you prefer to lie in the house of your boyhood?"

"Aye," he agrees. "Nothing would please me more."

Wait a sec. Sleep? It's way too early for sleep. It can't be later than, like, nine o'clock. Though my sense of time is a bit fuzzy without the cool and oh-so-retro Swatch I usually wear. Still, it's definitely prime time, not bedtime.

"I'm way too excited to sleep," I tell Lance. He smiles indulgently.

"As am I. Shall we take a walk instead?"

"Sure." We've already walked miles, but what else are we going to do? Not watch Must See TV, that's for sure. Besides, this way I'll have Lancelot all alone. Maybe get a chance to resume where we left off at the barge.

I catch the maiden frowning a bit, like she's jealous of his attentions toward me. *Hands off, druid girl. He's mine.*

"Very well. I will leave thee to begin my evening prayers. Sir, thou knowest well as any how to find thy sleeping quarters . . . should thee still choose to sleep there."

After accepting Lance's oblivious thanks to her not-so-subtle implication, the maiden retreats into one of the other huts. Good riddance. I slip my hand in Lancelot's and look up into his blue eyes.

"Where should we go?"

He glances down at our clasped hands, furrowing his brow. Then he pulls his hand away in order to scratch at his ear, and doesn't choose to resume the hand-holding once his supposed itch is satisfied. I'm totally dissed. Kind of hurt, too. What's with the change of attitude? Is it 'cause of what Nimue said?

"If I remember right, the moon lights a pathway to the very top of the Tor," he says. "Perhaps we should take that route."

Well, at least he's not changed his mind about walking. Maybe he's waiting for us to be alone—doesn't want to be all PDA in case anyone is watching.

"Sounds good to me. Lead the way."

We pick up the hidden trail behind one of the huts and begin to climb. At first neither of us speaks. But it's not like that uncomfortable silence you get on so many first dates. More like sharing a quiet respect for a place of beauty and allowing the crickets to provide a peaceful ambient sound track. It's like one of those nature tapes my mom used to play me as a kid to get me to go to sleep. (No real crickets where we lived in Brooklyn.)

The full moon casts a dreamy yellow glow on the land, and I gotta say, as I look around, I'm totally overwhelmed. I had no idea a place of such transcendent beauty could even exist.

Everywhere I look I see wild, tangled roses climbing the hill, weeping willow–like trees dusting the ground with their moss-covered branches. Lightning bugs twinkle, making it appear as though the landscape is literally sparkling. The air is crisp, cool, but not too chilly.

The scent of roses becomes stronger as we climb, a sweeter fragrance than even my favorite Clinique Happy perfume. If I could bottle this smell, I'd make millions.

The path ends at a grassy clearing on the very top of the hill. We must be at the highest point of the island now, above the white mists, which still blanket the land below.

I'm getting carried away with description. But this place totally blows my mind. It's so beautiful—another world. And, after years of living in neighborhoods with trash-filled streets, neon billboards, and garish twenty-first-century architecture, it's a refreshing vision of how amazing the world can actually be.

Does this hill still exist in the twenty-first century? Do people still visit here? Do they know what it was? Do they recognize its importance? Its power? Or is this just a place where English soccer hooligans come to down Bass ale and smoke pot? Are the jagged boulders now stained with messages designed to inform all that *Ali loves Bobby* and *MRM was here, '99?*

Sometimes I hate the millennium I live in.

"The mighty Tor," Lancelot announces. He finds a seat on a small boulder, kicking out his legs and stretching his arms lazily above his head. I haven't seen him so relaxed, so unguarded as he is here, now. He must be feeling the same magic as I.

"It's amazing," I say, meaning it. I twirl around, my gown flapping in the slight breeze. Thick forest surrounds the clearing at every angle, hiding even the path we came from.

"As a boy," Lancelot says, "I'd spend many an hour here at this spot, practicing my swordsmanship." He smiles. "As the only lad on an entire island of women, it was hard to find someone to spar with. The poor trees received much abuse from my handmade wooden sword. If you look closely, some may still bear the scars."

I laugh, feeling at ease, peaceful. I wander around the edge of the clearing, searching for battle-scarred tree trunks, surprising a little bunny rabbit grazing at one end. My Thumper would have liked it here.

"Too bad I wasn't around back then," I say, turning to Lancelot. "I used to be quite handy with a wooden sword. Growing up with three older brothers made me a total tomboy." My eyes fall on a long stick lying nearby. I reach down and grab it, wielding it as if it were a mighty blade. "I would have been happy to play swords with you." I lightly poke him in the chest with the stick's tip. "Of course, I would have won."

"D'you think so?" Lance asks with a grin. He jumps to his feet, eyes searching the ground until he finds a branch sword of his own. "D'you think you could beat the best knight in all the land?"

"Is that a challenge?" I ask, delighted. I raise my stick.

"I would not want to injure you."

"I'd like to see you try." I smack my stick against his, remembering my childhood games in the neighborhood. Of course, we used to pretend they were light sabers out of *Star Wars*, not swords. But I'd be crazy to even *try* to explain sci-fi and outer-space stories to Lance. Hell, the guy probably thinks the world is flat.

"Right, then. A challenge has been issued. A fight to the kiss."

"To the kiss?" I giggle. "I've never played this version of swords. Sounds fun."

"Aye," Lancelot says in an overly serious tone. "The one who can successfully kiss the other on the mouth first wins the challenge." He pauses, then adds, eyes sparkling, "Unless you prefer we play to the death?"

"Nay, fair knight," I cry in my best British accent. "I accept thy challenge to fight to the kiss."

He laughs softly, then raises his stick. "I did warn you, lady."

"En garde!" I cry, dancing forward, swinging wildly. He easily parries my thrusts with his own stick. I charge again. Blocked. I try to sneak around the side. He's too quick. I think the fact that I've caught the dreaded giggles has interfered with my normal stick-swordsmanship skills. Or maybe it's 'cause I'm out of practice. I did give up the sport more than twenty years ago.

"Surrender!" I demand, stumbling over the long hem of my dress.

"Never," he says, laughing along with me. He slashes at my stick, bending it back. I'm losing—really losing. The guy knows his stuff. No wonder he's the best knight in the land.

Time for some Kat Jones illegal stick-sword-fighting tactics. I grab his stick with my free hand and break it in two.

"Ha-ha!" I crow, triumphant. "I win." I press my sword into his flat stomach. "Without any sense of honor whatsoever! Whoo-hoo!" I drop my stick and jump on him, throwing my arms around his neck. My sudden movement catches him off guard, and we both come tumbling down to the grass. I'm on top of him now, and we're both laughing so hard we can barely speak. "Now to claim my prize." I lean down to press my lips against his, trying to quell my giggles.

But before lip contact is made, I squeal in surprise as he rolls me over on my back. Now, on top of me, his leg pressed between mine, he looks into my eyes, suddenly quite serious.

"First rule of a knight," he says, his voice low and husky. "Do not celebrate until you are sure you are victorious." He leans down and kisses me hard on the mouth. It takes my breath away. He pulls back, his eyes flashing his delight. "I believe 'tis I who should be celebrated as winner."

"Cheater."

"And breaking my sword in two is seen as fair play?" he queries, rolling onto his back.

"Yeah, yeah." I stare at the galaxy above me, my heart still beating wildly and lust coursing through my veins. *Must slow down, Kat. Look at the pretty stars.* When I was growing up in Brooklyn, the stars were not often visible, and only the brightest could be seen. Here there seem to be billions—tiny crystals embedded into the black sky.

I glance over at Lancelot, who is also lying still, also gazing into the heavens. What's he thinking? Does he want me as much as I want him? *Focus, Kat. Don't want to rush into things, scare him away.* I doubt many medieval women make the first move.

Silver light steaks across the sky. "Ooh," I cry. "A shooting star. Got to make a wish!"

"A wish?" Lancelot asks, turning to face me, propping his head up with his hand, his elbow on the ground.

"Yeah. In my time we wish on shooting stars," I explain. "There's even a poem. 'Star light, star bright, first star I see tonight. I wish I may, I wish I might, have the wish I wish tonight.' "

Lancelot reaches over, tracing my cheek with a calloused finger. It sends chills down my spine—lots of chills. The good kind, mind you. Really good.

"What did you wish for?" he asks.

I turn over on my side, our faces inches apart. "Now, now, Lance," I chide, unable to resist a mischievous grin. "If I told you, it wouldn't come true."

He laughs softly, his breath warm and sweet against my face. How does one achieve such nice breath when toothpaste won't be invented for centuries?

"Well, we would not want you to lose your wish, now, would we?" he asks in a raspy voice. Oh, no. He's right about that one! I shiver as he runs a finger along my shoulder, down my arm.

"Never," I murmur. Why won't he hurry up and kiss me again? Is this some kind of chivalrous thing? Or is he worried about what the lake lady told him? I mean, I know he kissed me to win the duel, but that was a quick one. No tongue even. Not the kiss he'd give his mother, but not a long, lazy lover's kiss either.

I decide that if that's what I want, it's up to me to get this party started. So, wrapping my hand around the back of his neck, I pull him close, shut my eyes, and press my lips against his. I can feel his surprise as our mouths make contact, his initial hesitation, his eventual acceptance. I part my lips a little, allowing him to explore my mouth. His tongue is soft, reverential as it traces my lips and then

145

delves in for deeper discoveries. Almost as if he's amazed I'm allowing him free rein. My own mouth—heck, my whole body—has already completely given in to the delicious torture his tongue invokes. How do the romance heroines say it?

His touch stoked a fire deep in her loins.

I never really got what loins are, but I know exactly where *my* fire's been stoked.

As he kisses me, his hands wander as he runs his fingers through my hair, then drags his nails down my back. He explores my hip, my outer thigh, his fingers leaving a trail of heat in their wake. Then he moves higher, finding what I'm dying for him to find: my breast.

He caressed the tip of her delicate womanly pillow until it budded into a diamond-hard peak of perfection.

As he drags his thumb across my fabric-covered breast, I squirm against him, shivers of exquisite torture ransacking my body. I want him so badly right now, I can't stand it. I'm usually not a nature lover, but making love to a breathtakingly handsome guy on the top of a secret hill on a magical island . . . can it get any more romantic?

He's so gentle with his exploration. There's no rough fumbling, no rush to rip my clothes off. Just worshipful caresses and soft, sweet kisses. God, I can't stand it.

He reached under her skirts, his throbbing member piercing her sweet rosebud.

Okay, that last part didn't really happen. Believe me, I would very much *like* the rosebud-piercing process to begin, but he's taking his time. My body's impatient. I mean, don't get me wrong: I appreciate the foreplay. But at this point I'm ready. More than ready, in fact. The throbbing inside me is unbearable, and I'm dying to move on to the next part. To satisfy the ache that consumes me down to my toes.

I want him inside me. Desperately.

Maybe if I give him a little encouragement . . . I pull up my dress and grab his hand, guiding it to where I want it to go. Third base, baby.

"Make love to me, Lancelot," I murmur, not bothering to hide my need.

Suddenly his hand jerks away. His lips jerk away. In fact, everything that is him jerks away—far away, like standing-up-and-walking-to-the-other-side-of-the-clearing far away. Damn it! I sit up, pushing down the folds of my skirt and smoothing my hair.

"What's wrong?" I demand.

"I cannot do this."

"Why not?" I scramble to my feet and stalk after him. He stands at the edge of the clearing, his back to me. I mean, what the hell? "Is it 'cause of what that Nimue lady said?"

"Perhaps." He sighs deeply.

"Lance," I say, trying to rationalize. It's tough when my heart's still beating a mile a minute. "This thing between us has nothing to do with any prophecy. We're two adults here. No one has the right to say what we can or cannot do." I place a hand on his arm. "Besides, she never has to know."

" 'Tis not just that," he says, his voice not hiding his anguish. "I am a knight. My loyalty to the king is absolute. I need no distractions."

Distraction? Okay, now he's pissed me off—big-time. I withdraw my hand and plant it on my hip. "Is that what you think of me?" I question him, angry. "I'm a *distraction*?"

Lancelot paces the ground, a distraught expression overwhelming his otherwise stunningly handsome face. "Yes . . . No . . . I do not know." He runs a hand through his long black hair, yanking on the ends. "You are more than a distraction, but you completely distract me."

I squint, not quite sure what to make of that statement. It sounds complimentary, right? Romantic even. But still cryptic. I'm a twenty-first-century American, damn it. I need everything spelled out.

"Lancelot, what do you think of me? Really. I mean, am I just another one of your damsels in distress?"

He turns to look at me, his eyes wide and his expression horrified. "No! Is that what you think?"

"I don't know what to think. I don't know you well enough to know your habits. But I'm trying to be realistic here. Let's face it: You're a gorgeous knight. It's, like, so obvious all the girls in the land adore you. You could have anyone."

"I do not want anyone," he insists. He grabs my hands in his and looks me straight in the eye. "Truth be told, I have always wanted no one. Until I met you."

"Why?" Maybe if he gives me a reason, maybe if he explains, the doubt raging through my body will be sated. I want to believe him, but what if this is what he tells all the damsels? I already have plenty of twenty-first-century unrequited crushes; the last thing I need is to develop one on a medieval knight in shining armor.

"Why you?" Lancelot shakes his head in disbelief. "How can you ask that? Do you not see what you do to me?" He lets go of my hand and stares off into the black woods, as if they could hold the answer. "You are different from anyone I have met. Your bravery, your determination. You are like a dancing sprite from another world, more clever and more spirited than even the fey folk. Your laughter lights up the darkest night. You are not afraid to dance in a room full of strangers. You are like a firefly—brilliant, shining, but not to be caught and caged."

I sit listening to his analysis, breathless with desire. No

one has ever uttered stuff like that to me before. Sure, I've gotten a lot of "Hey, babe, you're real hot" and "Kat, you're totally dope." And the world-famous "Are you a model?" (Okay, so no one's actually said that to me.)

But Lancelot has not mentioned one word about what I look like. He's actually telling me what it is about me on the *inside* that he likes. It's not things that I've pretended to be to make him like me, like so often with other guys. He actually—and this blows my mind completely—likes me for me!

"I had no idea you felt like this," I say, lowering my eyes to stare at the ground.

"I know. It's maddening that I couldn't share it before now. I have tried to fight it. I am a knight, sworn to my king. I cannot have a woman displace my loyalties. But oh, how can I bear not having you?"

"Why can't you have both?"

"I beg your pardon?"

"Why do you have to choose?" I ask, cocking my head in question. I really don't get it. Like, Arthur expects his knights to stay celibate? A little unrealistic, I think. "Can't you have a lover and a job?"

Lancelot thinks for a moment. "Knights should be free to go on quests, to save those who need to be saved. To fight for honor and not be distracted."

"I see." I sigh. "Well, I wouldn't want you to go against your king." Great, Kat—now you've gone from your usual I-don't-work-at-all-and-live-off-my-parents type to a complete workaholic whose job requires he not have sex. You sure know how to pick 'em.

Still, something about his refusal doesn't make sense. There's got to be more to it. A horrifying thought strikes me. "You have . . . had sex before, haven't you?" I ask.

He face reddens at my direct question, but he nods. "When I reached manhood, the Lady of the Lake taught me how to please a woman."

Aha. I knew there was something between the two of them. Is this the real reason for his hesitation? I try to keep my irrational jealousy from rising like bile to my throat. "So you two were an item? What happened?"

"Item?"

"Lovers," I clarify my twenty-first-centuryism.

"Nay, we were not lovers, though we committed the act of love on several occasions. She is more a mother to me than anything else."

Okay then. No wonder he's so screwed-up about what he wants. The only person he's slept with was a woman he considered his mother. Now there's a *Jerry Springer* episode waiting to happen. I don't know what's worse: the idea that he could be a virgin or that he's had sex with his mom.

"So you never had a real lover? Have you ever been in love?"

Even under the moon's dim glow, I can see his face redden. "Nay," he says. "As I told you, I am a knight of Arthur, sworn to his side."

"Well, not that I'm all that experienced in the matter"—I don't want to come off sounding like a slut—"but making love to someone you care about, someone you're attracted to, is quite a different thing. Sure you don't want to try it? See how it goes?" I try to sound casual, but inside I'm dying.

"Yes. I mean no," he stammers. "I mean, I am sure that I do not."

Hmm. He's going to need a little convincing. A mischievous idea comes to mind—one that involves showing a little skin. I loosen the drawstrings of my gown and seductively drag the corner of the fabric down, exposing a bare shoulder. I thrust it out, like I've seen the models do.

"Are you sure that you're sure?"

He bites the bottom of his lip, staring at my naked shoulder. "Aye."

Okay, step two. I kick off my shoes and slowly hike up my skirt, exposing bare shins. Don't they have an ankle fetish in this era? Or was that Victorian times? I point my red-painted toes—at least my pedicure hasn't worn away yet—and rub them against the inside of his calf. He squirms uncomfortably and steps back.

"Really sure?" I purr. This is kind of fun.

"A-aye." His voice is unsteady now.

Time for step three in my great Lancelot seduction. I circle his waist with my arms, clasping my hands above his butt, and knead his lower back. Then I lift one leg, wrap it around his thigh, and press my body tight against him. I stand on tiptoe on my other foot to reach his ear and breathe out slowly.

"Really, really sure?"

"Aye, yes." His voice says one thing, but I can feel now that his body is saying something completely different. I'm going to win this one, and I can't wait.

Lowering my leg, I untie his belt and grab the hem of his tunic. He doesn't resist as I pull it over his head. His breathing is quite erratic now, as if he's run a marathon.

I run my fingers down his chest, rejoicing in his muscle tone, his perfect six-pack abs. His skin is hot to the touch. I stop right before I get to the top of his tights.

"Really, really, really sure?"

"Goddess forgive me," he moans, and grabs me. Forcefully, he slams me against a tree, his mouth quite literally devouring mine, his hands engaging in a flurry of activity—

grasping breasts, lifting skirts, pulling down his own tights. No longer gentle, no longer sweet. A raw act of possession, of domination. I am his slave, his conquest.

He's inside me now. Plunging, kissing, thrusting, touching. I wrap my arms around his neck, digging my nails into his upper back. My breasts crush against his chest, the friction of fabric against skin sending an agonizing throb down to my toes. I lift a leg and wrap it around his waist, allowing for a deeper thrust. My back rubs against the rough trunk but I don't care. I'm too caught up in the moment, the sensation, the unquenchable inferno of him inside me.

Rough, wild, crazy medieval sex. Amazing.

My world is spinning out of control, my brain cloudy, my body burning liquid fire. His mouth leaves a trail of fiery kisses down to my neck, greedily, as if I'm his first meal in years, in forever. For a moment there is no time travel, no alternate reality. There is only the here. The now. The fire. The hysteria of delight that consumes me utterly.

It's all too much, and before I can stop myself, before I can wait and make it last longer, I'm at the top of the roller coaster, over the edge, culminating with an intensity I've not felt since I actually rode my first roller coaster.

"Oh, God, Lance!" I cry, knowing I probably sound like Meg Ryan faking it in the restaurant—except I'm not faking. I'm coming. Hard. Fast. Burning. Oohhhh! Have I ever come like this before? I don't remember it feeling like . . . Ohhhhhhhhh!

Lancelot lets out his own cry as he finishes moments later. He collapses against me, holding me close, his breath deafening in my ear. "Oh, Katherine," he murmurs, covering my neck with soft kisses. "Oh, my lady."

After a moment of savoring the post-lovemaking ecstasy, I pull away from the tree, now realizing that our encounter has caused serious damage to the back of my dress. The rough bark practically shredded the fabric. Worse, I've got major trunk burn on my back. Oh, well—it was worth it; that's for sure.

"See, I told you it's more fun with someone you're attracted to," I point out, though I do realize "I told you sos" are probably not the best pillow talk. But hey, I don't see any pillows around.

Lancelot pulls up his tights and grabs his shirt from the ground. "I have never . . ." he says, still breathless. "I mean I . . ." He shakes his head and then looks at me. "You are truly stunning." He kisses me on the forehead. "Thank you."

"No problem." I try to sound casual, but I'm literally still shaking from the encounter. Encounter? Let me rephrase. I'm literally still shaking from the best sex of my entire life.

"Though I would like to stay here all night, we should go back to the circle," Lancelot says, slipping his hand in mine and squeezing it. The sweetness of the gesture nearly overwhelms me. " 'Tis getting late, and we have a long trip back to Camelot tomorrow."

Camelot. The word fills me with dread. Do I really want to go back there? What if Merlin decides I should be locked up again? "Can't we stay here at Avalon?" I ask. "This place is so beautiful, so magical. I never want to leave."

"Nay," Lancelot says, shaking his head. He pulls me gently toward the path. "I must get back to Arthur."

"Vacation's over." I sigh.

" 'Tis odd," the knight muses as we walk down the pathway. "As a boy growing up here, all I dreamed of was someday leaving." He smiles down at me. "Now, being here with you, I wish I could stay forever."

Aw. He really has the nicest way of putting things. I love that about him. One of the many things I love about him.

He's such a great person: nice, sweet, honorable, loyal. Sexy as hell. Why can't there be guys like this in my millennium?

Sadness washes over me as I realize the implication of that thought. I'm going home. Nine months from now, but it's going to happen. I'm going to leave Lancelot behind. I will never, ever see him again. Ever.

He'll forget about me and probably hook up with Guenevere, like his destiny foretells, and I'll be stuck dating some boring twenty-first-century stockbroker who doesn't have even a speck of romanticism in his bones. Sure, he'll buy flowers after the first date, but as time goes on he'll forget our anniversary, cheat on me with his secretary, and finally leave me for a twenty-something blonde who drives a red Ferrari.

Okay, so maybe that's speculating a bit, but the facts remain. I belong in the twenty-first century. I'm leaving. I'm going back. Lancelot belongs here. He's staying. He's not coming back with me. Therefore, I can't get attached to him. I can't come to depend on him. I can't make him important in my life. *I can't ever fall in love with him.*

Oh, God. What if I already have?

Chapter Ten

After only a brief brushing of lips—a not-at-all-sufficient revisit to our recent erotic interlude—Lancelot says good night, and I reluctantly enter the House of the Maidens, where I've been assigned to sleep.

Inside it's like summer camp: Bunk beds three stories high climb each wall. Giggling girls, ranging in ages from six to sixteen, stare at me. One of the older ones, already sporting the long blond hair/white robe uniform the full-grown priestesses do, shows me to an empty lower bunk. Great. I hope neither of my young upper bunkmates still wets the bed.

I'm not sure if I should blame the long, bumpy day of traveling, the Pool of Dreams, or the wild and crazy sex, but I'm exhausted. In fact, I don't even bother to remove my gown as I curl up onto the straw mattress and pull a tattered wool blanket over my head.

It's funny. Back home my mom always called me Princess and the Pea, due to my complete inability to fall asleep without at least three-hundred-threadcount Egyptian-cotton sheets and a fluffy feather pillow. Guess I'm getting used to the lack of luxuries. The pillow here *is* made out of feathers, I think. However, since it still smells like a live chicken, it's not exactly a perk worth mentioning.

At first I'm sure the whispering girls are going to keep me up, but the second my head hits the pillow, my eyes close and I'm out like a light.

I'm lying in a luxurious canopied bed piled high with brightly colored silk pillows. The bed's embroidered curtains are drawn, and I feel like I'm in a cozy cave.

I roll over to find Lancelot by my side, naked in all his manly glory. I draw in my breath. Has there ever been a man so magnificent?

"Hello, lover," I say slyly, unable to resist dragging a finger down his chest. I lustily look into his eyes, but then notice the tears.

"Why are you crying?" I ask, puzzled.

He smiles—a sad smile that breaks my heart. "I was thinking how much I will miss you when you are gone."

I furrow my brows. Huh? "Where am I going?"

"Why, home, of course." Now it's his turn to look confused. "Do not toy with me, Katherine. I cannot bear it today."

Sadness consumes me, and tears slip unbidden down my own cheeks. Lancelot leans into me, kissing away each individual tear with tender lips.

"I love you," he whispers. "No matter where you go, no matter how far away you are, I will love you. Forever."

White flash.

I'm no longer in bed. I'm in a chamber alive with torchlight. Guards. Shouting. Screams. Swords drawn. Chaos everywhere.

I see a porter rushing by. "What's going on?" I demand, grabbing his sleeve.

"Treason," he answers, his eyes wide. "The queen has been caught with her favorite knight. With Lancelot."

"What?" I cry. Lancelot and the queen? No way! He loves me, not her. Me! "There must be some mistake!"

"No mistake, lady. She was discovered in his very bed." The porter shakes free of my grasp and runs down the hall.

What the hell is going on?

White flash.

I'm outside, standing by the jousting field. However, instead of a tournament they're having a bonfire. But it's not the kind where you toast marshmallows and drink beer, celebrating the joyous arrival of summer.

This fire's made for burning a human being.

Sticks and logs are piled up five feet tall. On the top, an eight-foot wooden stake juts into the sky.

Tied to that stake is Guenevere.

She has been stripped of all her queenly glory. Dressed in rags. Bound hand and foot. Her face is pale, beautiful, noble. No tears. No begging for her life. Proud. Determined. Accepting of her fate.

But I can't accept it.

"No!" I cry, running toward the pyre. A guard grabs me by my arms, ripping me backward. I turn to him, struggling to free myself, and notice tears in his eyes.

I turn back to the scene and watch as another guard steps forward, carrying a burning torch. He lowers the torch to the pile of sticks and the flames lick at the wood.

"No!" I cry. "She's innocent. Innocent! Guenevere!"

"Katherine! Katherine! Wake up!"

I open my eyes, wildly looking around. I'm in the House

of the Maidens. Lancelot is kneeling beside me, a worried expression on his face. The other maidens crowd behind him, watching with interest. From the look of things, I've roused the entire island.

"Lance!" I blubber, thankful to have been awakened from my nightmare. "Have I been screaming out loud?"

"Shhh," he hushes. "I am here now." His voice is thick with concern. He strokes my hair, his touch cool against my burning forehead, and suddenly I realize my entire body is drenched with sweat.

"I had the worst dream," I babble weakly, unable even to sit up in bed. "Guenevere. They were going to kill Guenevere."

"I think she could have a touch of the ague, sir," pipes in one of the maidens before Lancelot can comment.

He looks worried and turns to the maiden who spoke. "Are you sure 'tis a fever?" he questions. "Could she not be experiencing the sight?"

What's he talking about? The sight? What's the sight?

The maiden shakes her head. "Sir, I hardly think one such as she could receive the Mother's gift. It takes years of training before one is worthy of such an honor. More likely than not 'tis but a fever-induced dream."

"Lance, I don't feel so well," I interrupt, trying to keep up with the conversation. The faces above me blur in and out, and I feel sick to my stomach. What's wrong with me?

"Hush, Katherine," Lancelot whispers. "Stay still." He turns back to the girls, his face stormy. "Do not simply stand there like fools. Get her a cool compress. If she has a fever we must try to bring it down. Has your training taught you nothing?"

Chastised, several of the girls disappear. I struggle to remain conscious. I don't want to pass out again and resume the dreams where they left off. Where Guenevere gets killed.

My eyelids are unbearably heavy. My body feels weighted down with lead. "What's wrong with me?" I ask, fighting the nausea that seeks to overwhelm me.

I feel worse than when I was fifteen and my friend Sara and I robbed my mother's liquor cabinet, each downing about a fifth of straight vodka. I had to go to the hospital to have my stomach pumped later that night. Oh, God, they don't have hospitals here! What if I'm . . .

"Am I dying?" I ask, grabbing Lancelot by the neck of his tunic. "Tell me the truth."

He shakes his head, but I see tears at the creased corners of his eyes. "Nay," he whispers. "A dream. Nothing more." He turns back to the girls. "Summon the lady. Ready the sickroom," he demands, his voice harsh, cold. "Now!"

Several girls, wearing frightened expressions, hasten to obey. Fear clutches my heart. Something's wrong. Very wrong. The sharpness in his voice, the moisture in his eyes. What's happening to me? I was fine only hours before.

No longer able to hold my eyes open, I close my lids and drift into blackness, into horrible, fitful dreams, always vivid, real. Always the same.

Guenevere to be burned at the stake. For treason. For sleeping with Lancelot.

I wake in another bed, this one made of the softest feathers. Not in the House of the Maidens. Somewhere else. How did I get here? The room is lit by a hundred candles set on little stools and tables and on the wall, surrounding me with dancing fire. I try to focus my eyes, but the landscape insists on staying blurry. I look to my left and see Lancelot still sits by my side, clutching my hand in his. I can see his fingers stroking my wrist, but I can't feel his touch.

What is wrong with me?

I close my eyes again, unable to fight the overwhelming

sleepiness that consumes me. I've never been so sick. Ever. I feel worse than the time I got mono in high school and had to stay out for three weeks.

I drift off, unwillingly inviting the dreams to return, to haunt me without relief until I want to scream—and maybe I do. I'm not sure what's real anymore and what's in my head.

Guenevere, being burned at the stake. Because she has had an affair with Lancelot. My Lancelot.

I'm back to consciousness, at least for a moment. My body's burning with fire, and not the turned-on-romance-heroine kind, but that of a raging fever consuming my body. What do they give sick people here to help them? I hope they don't bleed me, like some historical societies did. In history class we learned that they used to attach leeches to people's bodies and . . . Ugh. I'm not even going to think of that. I'm going to close my eyes and sleep it off.

No. Must stay awake. Don't want to dream again.

Is this relentless dream trying to tell me something? Something I need to know? Have I somehow developed a medieval version of *The Shining*? Should I tell Lance? Nimue? Guenevere herself? I know these people take dreams very seriously. I don't want to worry them unnecessarily.

I drift asleep again. And again I dream.

I wake up with no idea how much time has passed. I open my eyes to see Nimue deep in conversation with Lancelot at the other end of the room. At least, I think it's Nimue. It sounds like her, but her appearance has changed somewhat. No longer majestic and regal, the priestess now looks haggard and old. She runs a hand through graying hair. What happened to her? Where did all her beauty go?

" 'Tis most like the fever, Lancelot," she insists, though her voice sounds troubled.

"I do not believe it," Lancelot answers in a sharp voice. "If 'twere the fever, then why now? Why so soon after looking into the Pool of Dreams?"

"'Tis not connected."

Lancelot shakes his head. "She is not a priestess. She has had no training. Yet you allowed her to look into the pool. What did you expect to be the outcome?"

Nimue lets out a long sigh. "Thou brought her to me."

"I brought her to you in faith that you would take care of her. Had I known you would endanger her life, I would have never allowed it." He's furious now, and I can't help but feel a tingle of pleasure at how protective he is of me. And he's stayed by me the whole time I've been at death's door. Most guys I've dated won't come near me with a ten-foot pole if I tell them I have a tiny cough. "I don't want you to get me sick, too," they say, refusing to come over even to open a can of chicken soup, plop it in a bowl, and nuke it for a minute or two. Lancelot would probably go kill me a fresh chicken—or at least a pigeon—if I asked him for soup, no questions asked.

They sure don't make men like they used to.

I turn back to their conversation. After all, Lancelot said something about endangering my life. Is my life in danger? Chills crawl up my spine. Will I die? I don't want to die!

"Thou art letting thy personal feelings cloud thy judgment, little one," Nimue tells him.

And what's wrong with that?

"*You* are letting your power cloud your humanity," Lancelot retorts, kicking at a stool. Yeah, you tell her, Lance! He rubs his thumb against his unshaven chin. "What is wrong with her? Tell me now."

Nimue paces, her steps eating up the distance between the hut's makeshift walls. "I could be wrong, but . . ."

"What? Tell me!" Lancelot grabs her by the shoulders and whirls her around.

"Behave, knight!" Nimue says, her eyes wild. "I am still thy priestess."

Lancelot drops his hands and bows his head. "I beg your forgiveness, lady," he says, his voice matching his repentance. " 'Tis only that I am worried. She is so pale. The girl, once so full of life, lies near death's door. I must know why."

Nimue's face softens. "I know, little one," she says. "I will consult the pool myself. I will see if I can determine what ails her."

I close my eyes again, my heart pounding its fear against my rib cage. This is terrible. They think it's some kind of sickness from looking into the Pool of Dreams? Did I mention how gullible these medieval people are? Why can't anyone see the obvious answer? I've evidently caught some rare medieval disease. Like the plague, maybe. Didn't medieval people have the plague? Spread by rats or something? I haven't seen any rats. Unless they crawled on me when I slept. Oh, man. How creepy can this get?

Worse, they don't even have any antibiotics here! No medicine. No emergency surgical procedures. I'll probably die here in Avalon.

The thought fills me with dread. I've come so far. I can't die now. Now that I've found a way back home.

Oh, please don't let me die in Avalon.

I drift asleep again, and again I dream—the same torturous, repetitive dream. I'm really getting sick of it, to tell the truth. I wish I could at least have some variety. Maybe throw in a lying-on-the-beach-sipping-frozen-margaritas dream once in a while? Why does my brain insist on replaying the same horrible scene over and over again, like some broken record?

Guenevere, tied to a stake. Set to be burned. For treason. For sleeping with Lancelot.

"Katherine. Wake."

I open my eyes groggily, relieved to be awakened before the part of the dream where the flames begin to rise. Before I hear Guenevere's screams.

I look up to see Nimue sitting at my bedside.

"Nimue," I murmur weakly, reaching out to touch her arm. "Where's Lancelot?"

She frowns, as if I have no business asking. "He rests," she says finally.

"What's wrong with me?" I ask. "Am I dying?"

She shakes her head. "Nay, thou art not dying." A pause, then: "Katherine, listen to me. I need thee to tell me what thou hast dreamed."

"Is it a vision?" I ask. I'm ready to believe anything now. "It seems so real."

"Tell me!" she demands, raising her voice a bit.

What's her problem? Where's the nice, sweet lake lady whom everyone loves and adores? I think about not telling her, but what good would that do? I'm too weak to argue, anyhow.

"The dream's always the same. Guenevere is arrested for treason. She's slept with Lancelot. Betrayed the king. They burn her at the stake."

"Do they actually burn her?" Nimue asks. I pause, thinking, trying to remember. The Lady of the Lake grabs my shoulders, her nails digging into my flesh. "Do they?" she asks, almost hysterical.

"N-no," I stammer, suddenly quite frightened. "I always wake up before she dies." I close my eyes. "But I hear her screams. They're . . . terrible screams."

I feel Nimue shaking me by the shoulders, and I open my

163

eyes to meet her fierce expression. Now she seems more like the Wicked Witch of the West than Angelina Jolie.

"Guenevere is a sworn priestess of the goddess," she informs me in a tight voice. "She has been placed in Camelot, placed with Arthur, to combat the spread of the Christian religion. She knows how important she is to the future of our people. She would never betray her destiny for mere carnal pleasure. What thou hast seen is but a dream. Not a vision. 'Twill never happen." She pauses and then adds, perhaps for emphasis, "Never."

"Well, actually . . ." I begin to say, not sure at all whether I should bring up the point that I'm *from* the future and don't really need some dream or vision or whatever it is to tell me what " 'twill" and " 'twill never" happen. "According to all the legends I've read, she *does* sleep with Lance. And her doing so leads to the destruction of Camelot."

Nimue lets go of my shoulders, her face morphing from anger to deep sadness. She lets out a long sigh. "I know."

"What?" Huh? Didn't she just say it " 'twill never happen"? Now she's saying she knows it will? Okay, now I'm, like, so lost it's not even funny. "What the hell is going on here?" I demand, my confusion overpowering my sickness.

"Katherine, canst thou keep a secret?" Nimue asks.

Secret? Now there are secrets? "Uh, I guess . . ."

"Thou hast met Merlin, correct?"

"Yeah. Old guy. Took away my phone. Do you think he'll give it back? I don't mean to sound shallow here, but it's a four-hundred-dollar-phone with a great James Bond ring tone."

"Merlin and I have long sought a way to save Camelot from its ultimate destruction," Nimue says, artfully ignoring my phone question. "For we too have seen the signs of what is to come, due to Guenevere's foretold betrayal of country and king. For countless years we've consulted oracles, researched the stars, everything. All to determine a path that does not lead to the end of the line of Pendragon and the rise of Christianity in Britain."

"And?"

"What I am saying is that thy presence here is no accident."

"What the hell are you talking about?" My heart pounds in my chest the way hearts do when you realize something really, really important is going to be said in the next few moments.

"That gypsy at the fair?"

"Yeah? What about her?" I grit my teeth. *Get to the point, Nimue.*

" 'Twas I."

"Yeah, right. Give me a break. I mean, I may be sick in bed and hallucinating, but I'm not stupid. For one thing, the gypsy at the fair looked nothing like—"

Nimue suddenly covers my eyes with her hand, obscuring my vision.

"Hey!" Angry, I reach up to swat her hand away. "What the hell are you doing?"

She offers no resistance, and I remove her hand from my eyes. When I do, my gaze falls on a familiar face now peering down at me.

The gypsy!

"Oh, my God! Oh, my God!" This cannot be happening! I'm still dreaming. Maybe? I hope. Oh, my God—*she* brought me here? I start to scream but Nimue claps a hand down on my mouth. Her grip is too strong; I am too weak from my illness.

"Katherine, thou must listen," she pleads, her face fading back to its more familiar Nimue/Angelina Jolie face. The effect is fascinating, though at the same time utterly horrifying. "After scouring the universe, I found the stars all point to thee as the only soul able to win Lancelot's heart. To ensure he will never fall in love with Guenevere and thus spark the destruction of Camelot."

She tentatively lifts her hand from my mouth, ready to cover it again should I scream.

"You fucking bitch!" I spit out, squeezing my hands into fists and struggling to sit up in bed. "You fucking, fucking bitch! You tore me from my fucking twenty-first-century life and dumped me here in the Middle fucking Ages just to fucking further your own fucking religious agenda? Well, fuck you. I refuse to play any more of your fucking reindeer games!"

Wow, I don't think I've ever used the word *fuck* so many times in a row. Still, the circumstances definitely call for harsh language, and if I could think of a harsher word I'd be using that too.

"Send me the *fuck* back," I demand, raising my fist and adding one more *fuck* for good measure. "Now!"

"No," Nimue says quietly.

"Now, bitch!" I clasp my hands around her neck in an attempt to throttle her, but I'm too weak to do any damage, and she easily takes my hands in hers and places them by my side. Exhaustion from that tiny effort overtakes me, and I'm forced to lie back down. She's so lucky I'm not feeling well. Otherwise she'd be a dead woman.

"I cannot take you back now. It must be during the summer solstice. *After* the scheduled date of Guenevere's betrayal."

"There's a betrayal schedule?" I moan. Man, these people are nuts! Though organized, too, I guess. "I'm going to tell Lance and Guen everything," I say stubbornly. After all, *they're* my friends, not Nimue the face shifter and Merlin the phone thief.

Nimue raises an eyebrow. "Will you?" she asks, back to

YES! ☐

Sign me up for the **Historical Romance Book Club** and send my THREE FREE BOOKS! If I choose to stay in the club, I will pay only $13.50* each month, a savings of $6.47!

YES! ☐

Sign me up for the **Love Spell Book Club** and send my TWO FREE BOOKS! If I choose to stay in the club, I will pay only $8.50* each month, a savings of $5.48!

NAME: _____

ADDRESS: _____

_____

TELEPHONE: _____

E-MAIL: _____

☐ **I WANT TO PAY BY CREDIT CARD.**

☐ VISA   ☐ MasterCard   ☐ DISCOVER

ACCOUNT #: _____

EXPIRATION DATE: _____

SIGNATURE: _____

Send this card along with $2.00 shipping & handling for each club you wish to join, to:

**Romance Book Clubs
20 Academy Street
Norwalk, CT 06850-4032**

Or fax (must include credit card information!) to: 610.995.9274.
You can also sign up online at www.dorchesterpub.com.

*Plus $2.00 for shipping. Offer open to residents of the U.S. and Canada only.
Canadian residents please call 1.800.481.9191 for pricing information.
If under 18, a parent or guardian must sign. Terms, prices and conditions subject to change. Subscription subject
to acceptance. Dorchester Publishing reserves the right to reject any order or cancel any subscription.

JOIN NOW!

her demure voice. "And thou thinkest they will believe thee over the wise Lady of the Lake? I raised them since they were small children." She clears her throat. "Besides, if thou tell them, I will not give Guenevere the ceremonial words that will send thee back to thy twenty-first century. Thou wilt be stuck in Camelot forever."

If I thought I felt sick before, now I'm really going to puke. "Why all the deception?" I ask. "Why not just tell Guen and Lance it'd be better if they never hooked up? I'm sure they'd understand."

"Mayhap. But mayhap it would spark the desire of forbidden love, the most powerful love of them all. What if they decided they cared not whether Camelot was destroyed, as long as they had each other? Then 'twould be all for naught. We cannot take such a risk."

"And so you decided to bring me into the picture," I conclude. "I gotta ask you, though—couldn't you have found someone a little closer? I mean, I can't be the only girl in the history of the female race whom Lance would fall in love with over Guenevere."

"We did try," Nimue says. "First we introduced him to a beautiful princess named Elaine. The lass was quite smitten with our knight the moment she laid eyes on him. But he had absolutely no interest in her. In the end she took her own life to still her grief."

I grimace. "Ouch."

"Then I myself attempted to distract our knight with love," the Lady of the Lake continues. "I took him to my bed and showed him the ways of the flesh. I thought perhaps satisfying his male lust would be enough to keep him from seeking love in the arms of the queen." She shrugs. "But after only a few nights, he tired of the game."

"And so then how'd you make the jump to me?"

"Time was running short. We consulted the Pool of

Dreams. 'Twas there I first saw thy face—a vision: Lancelot and thee, delighting in each other, the very same night that he is destined to be caught with the queen. I knew then, no matter what I had to do, I must bring thee here. Thou remain the only hope for the salvation of Camelot."

"Wow. That's some heavy shit," I say, totally not knowing what to believe at this point. And I thought the whole time-travel thing in and of itself was fucked-up. I had no idea an *X-Files*–size conspiracy lay behind it. Something occurs to me. "Okay, I've got a question. If you're so hot on getting Lance and me to fall in love, why did you tell him to stay away from me when you two were talking in your caverns?"

The corner of Nimue's mouth kicks up in a smile. "As I said before, there is nothing more sweet than love that is forbidden."

Man, she is a clever one, isn't she? She knows from looking into the future that Lancelot digs the forbidden-love stuff, which is why he's "scheduled," as she puts it, to have an affair with Guen. So instead of telling him to stay away from the queen, she tells him to stay away from me, knowing full well that will drive him right into my arms.

If Nimue lived in the future, she'd be one good shrink. Or someone's mother.

Which brings me to my next question. "By the way," I ask, trying to sound casual, "how does one go about bringing someone back in time?"

Nimue shakes her head; she's clearly not going to tell me. "Some mysteries are better left unrevealed, Katherine. But know 'tis not an easy task, and not one to be done on a whim."

Damn. Guess I won't be starting timetraveltours.com when I get back, then. Another great medieval moneymaking opportunity down the drain.

Focus, Kat. This is your life here, not some multilevel-marketing business scheme.

"So Merlin's been in on this the whole time, too?" I ask. Question three of the three million I am dying to ask her. "Why did he lock me in the tower, then?"

"Because we knew that Lancelot, being a chivalrous knight, would let thee out." Nimue smiles. "Leading to a time when the two of you would be alone. A time to fall in love with each other."

"Wow. You guys thought a lot about this, didn't you?" If I weren't so pissed at being played as their pawn, I'd be impressed by the elaborateness of their plan. I mean, coordinating a twenty-first-century kidnapping—that alone must have taken some doing.

"Katherine, I know 'tis troublesome for thee, but do know that our intentions are nothing but honorable. We wish only to save our land. Save our people." Nimue's eyes take on a distant look. "Help us, Katherine Jones. Thou art our only hope."

"Yeah, yeah, Princess Leia. Me and Obi-Wan. Only hope. I know." I shake my head. This is so freaking bizarre I can't even get my head around it all. "I just wish someone had asked me first. Then I could have at least packed a decent overnight bag with toothpaste and tampons."

Nimue laughs softly as she studies me with those emerald-green eyes. Before she can give a response to my rather witty statement, a knock sounds at the door. She instructs the visitor to enter the hut. One of the white-robed blond priestess clones comes, bearing a mug filled with a steaming liquid.

"Here, drink this," Nimue says, taking the mug from the priestess and putting it to my mouth. The priestess exits.

I purse my lips and make a face. "What is it?"

" 'Twill stop the dreams. And 'twill make you well."

Yeah, right. I wasn't born yesterday. It's probably poison or something, knowing this lady. Well, actually, I guess it wouldn't be, since she needs me to help her. Considering all the trouble she's gone through transporting me a thousand years into the past, I guess I'm safe as can be. She obviously needs me alive.

"This will really make me better?" I ask, giving it a suspicious sniff. As much as I'd like to tell her and her plans to go to hell, the bottom line is that she's the only one who can help me get back to the twenty-first century. So I have to humor her—for now.

"Aye."

"Okay, then. Cheers." I down the liquid. It tastes like shit. "So what about the dreams, anyway?" I ask, suddenly sleepy again. This stuff works quick.

"Not dreams. Visions. Visions of what will happen to the queen if thou dost not succeed in winning Lancelot's heart."

They certainly do put a lot of stock in the supernatural. Then again, Nimue's admitted she knows how to transport people back and forth through time, and can change her facial features at a moment's notice, so I guess it's paid off for her. I wonder if I asked real nicely if she'd give me Kate Moss's bone structure.

In any case, I don't want her overly concerned just 'cause of some weird dream I had. "You know, I wouldn't worry too much," I tell her, stifling a yawn. "I mean, I have fucked-up dreams all the time. They never come true. Even the ones I wish did. Like one night a couple weeks back, I dreamed me and Brad Pitt met in this dark alleyway, and he threw me against the wall and—"

"But"—Nimue interrupts my erotic-dream retelling before I even get to the good part where Brad rips off my clothes—"this time thou had the visions after looking into the Pool of Dreams . . . a bad omen that 'tis more than a dream. Also, the fever that rages inside of you makes me even more suspicious." She narrows her eyes. "Something is still wrong."

Oh, great. I had a feeling she'd say that. "Like what?"

"I do not know. However, I pray that when thou arrive back in Camelot, thou keep Lancelot on a short string. Do not let his eyes stray from thee for even a moment."

I frown. "I'm really not the possessive type."

"Katherine, I am not interested in thy traditional habits with men," Nimue rebukes. "The fate of Camelot, and thus thy future, is in thy hands. Do not take the responsibility lightly."

"Okay, okay," I mutter. Talk about putting on the pressure. Normally if a guy doesn't go for me, it's, like, death to a pint of Ben & Jerry's, not the whole freaking world. I close my eyes, wanting to sleep, wanting to forget everything she just told me.

Everything I can only hope isn't true.

Chapter Eleven

Tweet, tweet. Tweet, tweet.

What, have I awakened in a Hitchcock movie? There must be a million birds chirping good morning outside my window. Their cacophony might sound musical to some, but to this city girl, it's damn annoying.

Fine. I'm awake. Good freaking morning to all.

I open my eyes, feeling strangely cozy in the warm, soft bed. I take stock of my physical well-being: no headache, not nauseated, not tired. In fact, I feel great. I attempt to sit up in bed. I'm still feeling pretty weak, but much, much better. Guess that shitty-smelling potion worked.

"Katherine, are you awake?" I look over to see Lancelot rising from a stool in the corner. He looks terrible, like he hasn't slept in days. Was he really *that* worried about me?

He reaches the bed and kneels beside it, placing a hand on my forehead. "Your fever is down," he says, his eyes shining with his relief. "Thank the goddess."

No, I'm thinking it's more like *fuck* the goddess. As in, Nimue worships the goddess and wants to continue doing so, which is why she needs to make sure Guenevere doesn't cheat on Arthur, leading to the fall of the rule of Pendragon and the rise of Christianity, which is why I've been summoned from my very comfortable twenty-first-century life.

So, yeah. Fuck the goddess.

"I was so worried, my darling." Lancelot lowers his head to rest on my stomach. I brush his tangled black hair with my fingers, rejoicing in the silky feel of the strands.

His darling. He called me his darling. This should make me feel warm and fuzzy inside. But instead, now that I know how he's being manipulated by forces he can't begin to understand, I feel bad and sick about the whole thing.

I want to tell him the truth, tell him we're all pawns in an evil game, but I don't even know how to begin. And besides, like Nimue said, he probably wouldn't believe me. It'd make him hate me, and then he'd find solace in the arms of Guenevere. Nimue would never help me get back to the twenty-first century.

I feel selfish for thinking like this, but I can't help it. I belong in the twenty-first century and really don't want to stay here forever. Even if it means staying with Lancelot, which in this case it wouldn't. I'd be stuck in medieval times and I wouldn't even have the love of my favorite knight in shining armor. Nimue's certainly got me over a barrel; that's for damn sure.

"She is awake?"

We're interrupted by the joyous cry of a familiar female voice. Guenevere bursts into the hut, her face lively and happy. "Oh, Kat, we thought you would d—"

Lance shoots her a warning look. She stops midword, but I get the picture.

"In any case, 'tis so good to have you with us once again," she coos, sitting on the other side of the bed. "Now we can travel to Camelot, and I can show you my kingdom. You didn't get to see much of it on your last visit. You will love it, Kat. I know you will. I understand Lady Nimue has figured out a way that *I* can help you get home. What an honor for me to be a part of it all! I will learn the required ceremony well, Kat. Never fear; I will practice at every free moment. You shall go home, and I will be the one responsible for sending you there. I shall miss you, of course, but . . ."

As she babbles on in her musical voice, an overwhelming sadness settles in the pit of my stomach. So innocent. So sweet. My brain flashes back to my dream, my relentless visionlike dream.

Guenevere, burned at the stake. For treason. For sleeping with Lancelot.

I look from the queen to my knight. Would they? Could they? I now know from Nimue's words that Guenevere's marriage to the king is nothing more than a political arrangement to keep the Christians out of Camelot. So does that mean her heart does not really belong to Arthur? Could she fall in love with Lancelot? Am I really the only one who can stop their budding romance?

I guess I'm doing the right thing. This way Guenevere won't be burned at the stake, like in my dream. She'll remain the naive but happy, girlish queen until her dying day. And I can be with Lancelot, even if it's for only nine months, and then I get to go home. A win-win situation for all.

So why do I still feel like everything's wrong? That changing history could be a very bad thing, no matter what it gains me personally? Like maybe I should possibly mention to Lance and Guen, my only two medieval friends, what has been planned?

Too many questions—they're making my head hurt again. I shake the foreboding thoughts from my mind and smile at Lance and Guen. I ache for their innocence, suddenly feeling old and drained. But for their sake I try to stay upbeat. Why should they suffer for things they haven't even done yet?

"Well, then, what are we waiting for?" I ask, keeping my voice bright. "Cam-e-lot-ah here we come!" I sing, paraphrasing the old California song. "Right back where we started from."

And then I realize, as I watch Lance and Guen exchange bemused looks at my bad singing, that nine months later I'll be right back where *I* started from. The good ol' twenty-first-century USA.

So why am I not all that excited?

While I'm eager to get back to Camelot, Lance and Guen insist we stay at Avalon until I regain my strength. Fine by me. I don't have any pressing plans. And what better place to waste time than on an enchanted island?

From what Guen says, I have been deliriously sick for two whole weeks. While I don't remember the time passing, the shape of my body makes me inclined to believe her. I feel like I've lost at least ten pounds. Happy-dance time! Some good has come out of the ordeal. Though, knowing me, I'll probably gain it all back and then some once I start eating again. It's so tough to stick to Atkins when low-carb energy bars have yet to be invented.

After a few more days of being stuck in bed, I start getting restless. I'm feeling much better, and I can tell my strength is returning.

"Lance," I whine when he comes for his morning visit. "I'm so bored. Can I go outside? I'd like to see Avalon in the daytime."

He smiles indulgently. "The lady has already permitted it. I have arranged for us to go riding, that you may see the island in all its majesty."

"Riding?" I wrinkle my nose. "Can't we walk? Honestly,

Lance, I'm not really one for the whole horseback thing." I know I'm being a baby, but I can't help it. Riding with someone else holding the reins I can handle—though barely. But I'm so not going to be in charge of steering the thing.

I guess it stems from the incident at Billy's birthday party when I was five. His mom hired a guy to give pony rides in the backyard. I was petting the pony's nose while eating ice cream, when a cat ran underneath its legs. The pony reared up in fright, succeeding in knocking me over, scaring the shit out of me, and basically scarring me against horses for the rest of my life.

"Riding horses is a necessary part of life. You must learn to get over your fear," Lancelot says, interrupting my fond childhood reminiscing.

"I didn't say I was afraid." I frown as Lancelot raises a skeptical eyebrow. "Just . . . don't like them."

"Kat, you are a very brave woman. But you must learn that fear is not something to fear."

"Um, FDR would have disagreed with you. In fact, he said, 'The *only* thing we have to fear is fear itself.'"

"I do not know this FDR," says Lancelot. "But I do know that you will feel better once you have conquered your fear of horses. Perhaps you will even enjoy riding."

"Yeah, right. So not going to happen."

"I have saddled a fat Welsh pony for today's lesson," Lancelot continues, ignoring my comment. "The beast cannot run much faster than you or I. She is sure of foot and will not stumble." He rises from his seat beside me. "Get dressed and meet me at the stables," he says in a voice that leaves no room for argument.

Ooh, I love it when he gets all alpha male on me. Makes me think of what he must sound like when he's commanding Arthur's army to battle. I study his broad, sculpted backside as he exits the room. Yum. It's worth getting on a horse in exchange for some alone time with him.

After donning a simple, unadorned riding dress, I join Lancelot at the stables (which smell to high heaven, let me tell you!), and there is, as the knight promised, a gray pony with big brown eyes and a long black mane. She's kind of cute, actually. Much less scary than the huge warhorse that Lancelot rides. I stick out my hand—tentatively at first. The pony nuzzles her nose into it.

"Hi, cutie," I whisper.

"Her name is Eleanor," Lancelot informs me. "She is old and lazy. She will give you no trouble."

"Hey, don't insult poor Ellie here," I protest, pretending to cover the pony's ears. "I'm sure she's got a lot of life left in her."

Lancelot laughs. "There is only one way to be sure, mi-lady."

"All right, all right. Help me up."

Lancelot places his firm hands around my waist, and I rejoice in the sensation as he boosts me onto the pony. It's been way too long since I've felt those strong hands ravaging my body. Maybe if we find a nice quiet place on the ride . . . Hey—am I sidesaddle?

"No, no, no!" I protest. "I'm not riding like some girl."

"You *are* a girl, and you will ride like one," Lancelot tells me firmly. "Besides, this is Avalon. They have no saddles for men here."

I frown. That sucks. It's hard enough to ride a horse straight-on. Now I have to look to my left to steer the thing. It's going to totally strain my neck; I know it.

Lancelot mounts his own steed and motions for me to follow him out of the stable. Luckily Ellie here seems to get the drill and follows without my having to do any steering.

We head down the path into the trees. The air is cool and

crisp, and the sun warms the top of my head. I breathe in and delight in the sweet smell of honeysuckle. It's so nice to be out in the open air after weeks of being cooped up sick in a cabin. Maybe this horse thing wasn't such a bad idea after all. I reach down to pet Ellie on the neck, and she nickers her own delight.

Avalon, I discover, is even more beautiful in the daytime, dressed in emerald green with multicolored flower ornaments decorating the landscape. Crystal-clear pools of water lie around every bend, many sporting waterfalls cascading into their depths.

As we walk, I ask Lancelot to tell me stories about his life, about Camelot. He complies, spinning fantastic tales of the brave young Arthur, who pulled the sword from the stone to become king of all England. How he drove the Saxons to the coast and united the British tribes into one nation of relative peace. His eyes shine as he speaks of the king; obviously Arthur has made a good impression on him.

It's really nice talking to him like this. Listening to his stories. Not worrying about the ever-mounting sexual tension between us, or the issues that passion brings up when it comes to the future. Today we're living in the moment. We're two people without pasts or futures who are simply out for a pleasant ride and enjoying each other's company. It's such a nice feeling.

He doesn't try to dominate the conversation, either, and asks plenty of questions about me and my world. He's especially fascinated by the concept of our democratic government and how even the lowest peasant has the same vote as a nobleman. He also listens attentively to my admittedly bad explanation of our judicial system.

"So the king does not rule on matters of disharmony; rather everyday peasants decide the fate of the accused?"

"Yeah. Well, they call it a jury of your peers. And everyone takes turns serving on it, not just the peasants, as you call them. Unless you can come up with a really good excuse."

"And why is this way better than ours?"

"Well, I guess it's 'cause it's not just one high-up guy who gets to decide what happens to you. Twelve people have to agree that there's enough evidence to convict you. It cuts down on wrongful accusations, I guess. Gives the accused more rights. Like, what if he didn't do it? Or what if the king didn't like him?"

Lancelot nods his head, looking thoughtful. "I should like to share this idea with Arthur when we return, if you do not mind. He is looking to introduce a fairer system of justice to Camelot. I think he will entertain this notion with great interest. I will not, of course, inform him that it came from you, since you are to be presented to him as my sister. 'Twould seem quite odd to him for a woman to talk of politics and justice."

"So I take it we're keeping the time-travel thing on the down-low when it comes to the king?"

"Yes. He is a Christian and might condemn the idea as witchcraft and have you burned at the stake."

I gulp. "Good plan then, brother Lancelot."

He laughs heartily. "Aye, sister. Let it be so."

We ride on, and I realize I'm really enjoying this horseback thing. It's so pleasant to be outside in the fresh air, exploring the island without having to hike and get all out of breath. Ellie plods along at a steady pace and isn't even that bumpy.

I ask Lancelot to tell me another tale of Camelot. He complies, describing how he first came to the kingdom, young and eager to serve the king. Arthur welcomed him as a brother, though he was largely untrained in the ways of knighthood. A wonderful, kind man is the king, he says.

I sigh happily. Lancelot ain't so bad himself. He's brave.

Strong. Loyal to the king. When he spins his tales he doesn't speak badly of others. He's not gossiping about who does what at court. He's a genuinely good person. And it's a refreshing change.

It's funny: all my life I've been attracted to jerks. Anyone who treated me well was automatically not good enough—someone to walk over and abuse. Instead I'd give my heart to total losers who would do the same to me as I did to those nice guys. I'd end up heartbroken, alone, and ready to swear off guys forever.

Now I meet the most interesting, kind, wonderful guy ever, and of course he has to live in a different millennium.

"How are you enjoying your ride?" Lancelot asks, breaking me out of my reverie.

"It's all ri—" I start, then change my mind. "It's wonderful." With Lancelot I can speak the truth. I don't have to hide under my tough-girl front. I can admit that I'm wrong, and he's okay with that. "Though a little slow." I grin in challenge. "How much horsepower you think Ellie here's got in her?"

"Shall we see?" Lancelot asks, his eyes twinkling. "There is a beach not a stone's throw from here. A good place to learn your horse's power."

"Cool. Let's go."

We break out of the trees and onto a long stretch of sandy beach. The blue waters sparkle as they lick the sand. Eleanor whinnies and her steps become light. She must like the beach, too. Probably easier on the feet than all those rocks and roots in the woods.

Lancelot shows me how to flick the reins to get the horse to break into a trot. I flick, remembering only after Eleanor breaks into a full gallop that I forgot to ask him how to get her to slow down.

The wind whips through my hair as Eleanor takes off

down the beach. It reminds me of the time I rode on a boyfriend's motorcycle, only much bumpier. It's hard to keep my balance, riding sidesaddle and all, but I crouch down, burying my chest in Eleanor's neck, and try to be one with the horse.

The beach scenery blurs on either side. I rejoice in the feeling of wind, of speed, of freedom. It's pure ecstasy. Why didn't I ever try to ride a horse before? This is great! When I get back to the twenty-first century, I'm so getting a horse. Can you keep horses in your garage if you convert it to a stable?

Suddenly Eleanor stops short—on a dime, actually. And I, not expecting the instant reduction of speed, follow the laws of motion and am flung forward. Pain shoots through me as I'm thrown onto the sand.

I swear, clutching my ankle. I look up at Eleanor, who is casually munching a tuft of grass. Was that why she stopped? She was hungry? "Thanks a lot," I mumble.

Lancelot is beside me, sliding off his horse and crouching to my aid, his face dark with concern. "Are you hurt, Kat?" he questions.

"My ankle," I say, pointing to the appendage in question. "I think I might have sprained it."

"Lady, I am so sorry," he says as he presses his cool fingers along my anklebone, feeling for a break. "I should not have let you gallop when you had not the experience."

"Are you kidding?" I ask. "That was freaking awesome! The feeling of losing control and letting the horse take you? The wind tickling your every extremity? I loved it! I'd totally do it again!"

"You are not discouraged by your fall, then?" Lancelot questions, looking a bit puzzled. "I should have thought you would never want to set foot on a beast again after—"

"After a tiny fall? Puh-leeze, Lance. Haven't you heard

the expression 'get right back on the horse'?" I laugh, then wince as my ankle throbs in response. "If anything, it makes me more determined. Besides," I say, hobbling to my feet, "don't tell me you never fell off a horse."

"Aye," he agrees. "I've been thrown many a time, while training new stallions to be warhorses. But you are a—"

"A what? A woman?" I scrunch up my face in disgust. "Look, Lance, you've got to realize that in my day and time we women are no longer considered the weaker sex. In my world I'm your equal. I can do anything you can do." I pause, thinking. "Except pee standing up, of course."

Lancelot laughs—a full, hearty, throw-back-his-head kind of laugh. Then he grabs me in a fierce hug and squeezes me tight.

"Hey, watch the bruises," I protest.

"You are too wonderful, Lady Kat," he says, loosening his hold. "Proud, brave, determined. The women in court are so boring, with their gossip and embroidery and songs. They would never have remounted a steed after being thrown. They'd snivel and sob and beg me to call for a rescue party with a litter to carry them home. I have longed to meet a woman with the fortitude of a man, but never thought she existed."

"Well, in my time we're a dime a dozen," I say, feeling my cheeks heat.

"Do not fool yourself, Katherine. You are one of a kind. And, dare I say it, very beautiful as well. My lady, it is an honor to be in your presence."

He bows low. Midbow I grab his head between my hands and kiss him on the forehead. He grins and soon his lips find mine and we're kissing—enthusiastic, happy, exuberant kisses.

"My lady, I'm sorry," he says, breaking away after a moment. "You make me lose my senses. We should not—"

"The only thing we should not do is stop." I grin.

"But the Lady Nimue—"

Oh, yeah—he still doesn't know. He's going by what Nimue said down in the cave. But I know now that it was all a ruse—making it attractive forbidden love. I know that she wants nothing more than for us to have an affair.

My joy dampens somewhat at the thought. But it's not like I'm tricking Lance. Not really. I started to fall for him long before I realized there was a conspiracy-theory plot for me to do so. Still, I feel like a total louse, and something inside gnaws at me, making me desperate to tell him the truth.

At the same time I realize telling him everything would only hurt him in the end. He might begin to doubt my true feelings for him, think I've been in on the whole thing with Merlin and Nimue from the get-go. That I seduced him on purpose. How could I then explain that I really do care about him? That our relationship, if you can call it that, is extremely special to me? That I'm beginning to fall in love with him?

Yes, I'm using the L-word. And I truly mean it, too. Lancelot's so unlike any guy I've ever met. I know I've said that before, but it's so true. Most twenty-first-century guys are crude, or selfish, or boring. Lance is none of these things. He's attentive, loving, sweet—a complete gentleman. At the same time, he's fun and sexy and completely entertaining. He's the kind of guy I'll want someday as a husband. The kind who comes around once in a lifetime.

It's not that I don't want him with Guenevere because it means the end of Camelot. I don't want him with her because I want him with *me*. And so the question burns in my heart: when the time comes for me to go home, how am I ever going to leave him?

"Look, Lance. Do you want me?" I ask, looking into his hungry eyes.

He nods. "More than anything," he says.

"Are you married? Engaged to someone else?"

"No."

"Me neither. So we're both consenting adults. Don't fight it. What will be, will be." I lean forward and kiss him, hoping my words and mouth will be enough to sate him.

They are.

Chapter Twelve

The next day Nimue pronounces me well enough to travel back to Camelot. I'm disappointed. I would have liked a few more days to master this horse thing, but Lancelot promises he will give me lessons back at King Arthur's pad. There, he says, he will find me a proper horse—no more ponies for me. I'm thrilled at the idea of having my own horse, and can't wait to get back in the saddle again.

So we say our good-byes to Nimue, cross the misty waters, and rejoin our caravan on the other side of the lake.

The ride back to Camelot is predictably long and rough. I want to ride on horseback, but Lancelot insists my ankle needs time to heal. Inside the litter I try to rest, hoping to regain my strength. Guenevere seeks to entertain me with more of her knight-in-shining-armor stories, and surprisingly I even find myself somewhat interested.

"Can I ask you something, Guen?" I query between stories, as we bump along inside the litter.

"Of course," she says promptly. "Anything at all."

"Do you really love Arthur?"

She smiles shyly. "Aye. With all my heart."

I'm tempted to believe her. After all, I've never met such an honest, forthcoming girl. She's completely genuine, guileless. But appearances can be deceiving, and I remember the Lady of the Lake's words. I have to know the truth.

"Nimue told me your marriage was a political arrangement. That you were sent to keep the Christians from taking over Britain."

Guenevere's face falls. She stares down at her small white hands. "She told you that?" she asks in a quiet voice, the smile completely vanished from her face.

"Yes. When I was sick."

Guenevere sighs. "Aye. Then I guess 'tis all right to tell you. 'Tis true. I never thought I would know a man. I was trained as a priestess of Avalon. Chosen to become Lady of the Lake when Nimue tired of her duties." She picks at a fingernail. "But then one day Nimue called me to her chambers. She and Merlin were standing by the Pool of Dreams. They told me they had consulted the pool and that it prophesied a different fate."

I try to hide my scowl at their obvious manipulation of the poor girl, who just sought a simple life.

"All I wanted to do was stay at Avalon," Guen continues in a sad voice. "I love it there. It's so beautiful. So peaceful. But they gave me no option."

"They ordered you to marry Arthur."

"Yes. The Pool of Dreams foretold that I would become high queen and lead my people in the ways of the goddess." She looks up at me, her eyes wide with her innocence. "Truth be told, Kat, I was frightened to death. At only fourteen summers, I had yet to know a man. And now I would be sent to marry one I had never even met. And a king at that. It was not what I wanted, to be sure."

Bastards. Anger bubbles in my stomach as I imagine how

scared and confused she probably was. Why, she was just a child! When I was fourteen I hadn't even kissed a boy yet.

"How much older is Arthur?"

"He is ten summers older than I," Guenevere informs me. "When we were wed he was twenty-eight, and ready to take on a wife. I, on the other hand, came shyly to our marriage bed."

That's like statutory rape—Nimue and Merlin pimping out the kid in order to further their religious goals. Horrible.

"But," Guenevere continues, "do not think things are still as they once were. While at first I feared Arthur, I grew to love him in my own way. He is a kind, fair man, and has been very generous to me. He is also a wonderful king and has brought much peace to the tribes of Britain. If my company brings him pleasure, then perhaps in some small way I have contributed to my people's happiness as well."

"Well, that's good." At least he's not some abuser. *That* I wouldn't stand for. Not after what my stepdad did to my mother. Yup, if Guen even *hinted* that Arthur treated her like shit, I'd find a way to kick his royal ass, high king or no.

"But I feel I have failed them all," Guenevere continues, a tear slipping from the corner of her eye. "For I have never been able to grow the seed of Pendragon. Never been able to produce an heir."

Hmm. I was kind of wondering about that. Six years of sex with no birth control . . .

"Oh, sweetie, don't cry," I say, reaching over to give her shoulder a comforting squeeze. "Lots of women can't have kids. Maybe you guys could adopt one."

Guenevere looks up, puzzled. "Adopt?"

"You know, like an unwanted orphan baby. A kid whose mom died in childbirth or something. You could raise him as your own."

"Oh, no." She shakes her head. "The child must be of Arthur's blood to pass down the royal line of the Pendragon. If I were never to bear a child, the line would end. Unless," she adds in an even more despondent voice, "he was to find another woman who could bear him the son he has always desired. I've heard the rumors, Kat. His advisers have suggested he put me away and choose a new wife. One who can produce an heir."

Poor Guen. Maybe Nimue should have considered bringing an infertility specialist back in time instead of me. I bet if she and Arthur had a kid, the girl wouldn't be so interested in straying. She'd be too busy with midnight feedings and diaper changes to carry out a romance on the side.

I wish I could help her, but a degree in fashion doesn't really qualify me as a baby-making expert. Well, except when it comes to the old-fashioned way of doing it. There I could probably give her some pointers, as long as she promised not to practice on Lancelot.

"I'm sorry, Guen," I say, trying to console her. But really, what can I say? That in the twenty-first century, women don't define themselves by their ability to get pregnant? That you can be a successful, childless woman with a full life? I'm not stupid. Right or wrong, she knows as well as anyone that her whole purpose in this medieval life is to have a kid—keep the royal gene pool alive. And who am I to say that's not important?

At the same time, I don't want her beating herself up about it too much. After all, it could be Arthur's fault that they haven't conceived. Is it so outrageous to believe that the Once and Future King could have a low sperm count?

"In truth, 'tis nice to have another woman to share this with," the queen says, smiling through her tears. "I must keep it a secret from the other ladies at court. For all they are to know, Arthur and I are deeply in love and plan to have many children in the near future. Were it to get out that my womb has shriveled, as I fear it must have, then it could lead to much unrest in the kingdom of Camelot. Others may begin to vie for their place as Arthur's successor."

And lead you into the arms of Lancelot, I think. Talking to her gives me a much clearer picture of what must have transpired to instigate her betrayal of Arthur with Lance. The legends never made it clear, and until now it had always seemed stupid to me that'd she go off and cheat on dear, honorable Arthur.

But now I hear a different story. First she gets married off to this dude she's never met at age fourteen. Then he pressures her to start popping out the kids before she even hits her twentieth birthday. And she can't even talk about it to anyone, 'cause if she admits it, the whole country could fall apart.

I'm, like, almost thirty and have yet to even find a guy I *want* to have kids with, and the only pressure I get is from my Italian *nona*, who brings up her lack of great-grand-babies once a year at Christmas.

No wonder Guenevere ends up falling for a dashing knight who smiles in her direction and wants nothing from her but love, sweet love. Who wouldn't? Makes me almost want to hook her and Lance up together.

Almost.

It's probably midnight by the time we arrive at Camelot's mighty wrought-iron gates. Since it is so late, Guenevere tucks me into one of her adjoining chambers, promising me a proper suite of rooms come morning. Who cares? I could sleep outside on a rock at this point.

The next morning a dark-haired woman wearing a plain-cut brown dress wakes me by opening my canopy bed's curtains and letting in the sunshine. After closing them

again—a swift reaction to my sunlight-induced groans—
she introduces herself as Elen and tells me she has been assigned to serve me during my stay at Camelot. Guenevere
has instructed that she help me dress for court, which evidently will be in session any minute now.

How cool. I've never had my own maid! Well, once my
old roommate and I hired Merry Maids to clean our apartment before we moved out so we could get our security de-
posit back. The poor woman had to spend over ten hours
sterilizing the place, and afterward I heard she quit her job
and moved to Haight-Ashbury to live with the hippies, saying she never wanted to clean anything ever again. Hey, cre-
ative people are never neat.

Anyway, now I have my own maid. My personal maid.
Sometimes I feel this medieval world ain't half-bad. If only
someone would invent low-fat frozen yogurt, I'd be all set.

After choosing from an enormous variety of gorgeous
gowns, I select a sky-blue one made of the softest silk. I've
spent weeks wearing the same clothes over and over when I
was sick, and it's refreshing to change into something new
and clean, though I long to put on a comfy pair of Seven
jeans and an old cotton T-shirt.

Elen even brushes my hair and pulls it up into one of
those pointy veiled hats, reminding me of the one Chrissie
bought at the fair.

It's funny, really. That day seems so long ago, almost like
it was part of some other life. This world, with all its vi-
brant colors, magic, and romance, sometimes seems more
bona fide than the actual millennium in which I have spent
the majority of my existence. Weird.

I am escorted down a winding staircase that opens into a
long, rectangular stone hall with high ceilings and no windows. Well-dressed men and women line each side, socializ-
ing below colorful tapestries depicting dragons, unicorns,

and the like. Down the center a red carpet leads from the main double-door entrance to the other end of the hall, where Arthur and Guenevere lounge on two enormous carved wooden thrones. To Arthur's right, a curious Merlin watches my approach from his own thronelike chair. I offer him a little wave and wonder whether he'll give me back my cell phone now—seeing as I'm on his and Nimue's payroll and all. I mean, sure, I can't actually call anyone with it, but my downloaded version of phone Tetris sure would help pass the medieval time.

Arthur looks noble, powerful in his simple red cloak draped over a plain-cut tunic. Even without the circle of gold around his head, I could have pegged him—he has this kind of air about him that screams *king*. At his side hangs a sword, a shining steel weapon encased in a jewel-encrusted scabbard—what I assume to be the legendary Excalibur. How cool is that? To see the actual Excalibur up close and personal! Just as long as he doesn't try to use it on me.

Guenevere looks radiant in queenly purple silk, a heavy diamond-set tiara atop her blond head. She smiles and waves when she sees me. "Lady Kat!" she calls, gesturing for me to approach. I do, wondering if I should bow, and then decide to do so just in case. I sink to my knees in front of the throne, allowing the dirty floor to get the better of my elegant gown. Great. They obviously don't have dry cleaning here, and I don't know how the dress will stand up to being scrubbed in a nearby lake.

"Your Majesties," I murmur, hoping I'm coming close in terms of what Arthur expects in greeting. I should have quizzed Guen the day before as to courtly manners.

"Rise, Lady Kat," Arthur commands in a regal voice. I stand up again, looking at him. He's a pretty handsome guy, actually. Big, blond, blue eyed. Kind of Vikingish.

"My queen tells me that you are the sister of my most valiant knight, Sir Lancelot."

"Yes, my lord," I say demurely. I still don't like lying like this, but Lancelot and Guen both insist that if I can't name my parents and family lineage, the court will think I'm a foreign spy and will either lock me up or cast me out. And since the Jones family of Brooklyn won't fly in this case, I've got few options other than to pretend I'm kin to Lancelot.

I glance over at Merlin who has so far managed to keep his poker face. I doubt he'd be so silent and serene if I hadn't agreed to go along with him and Nimue's big plan. He totally looks like a sell-you-down-the-river-if-I-don't-get-my-way type of guy.

"Any relative of Lancelot's is a friend to Camelot," Arthur says, breaking out in a huge smile. "Welcome, Lady Kat. You may stay with us as long as you desire. I know my queen, for one, has expressed hopes that your visit will be a long one."

Guenevere grins broadly at the proclamation and looks so excited that for a moment I think she might jump out of her chair and hug me.

"We are deeply regretful that we did not recognize you during your first visit to our humble kingdom," Arthur continues, "and hope you will forgive us for locking you in the tower. You must understand, we take the safety of Camelot very seriously here."

"No big deal, don't . . ." I start before remembering my medieval grammar. I clear my throat. "What I mean to say is that I have already forgotten the incident."

"Still," Arthur insists, smiling over at his wife, "let us make it up to you. If it pleases my queen, I suggest a banquet be held tonight in Lady Kat du Lac's honor."

I wonder what the heck he means by "du Lac," until I remember that's Lance's last name. *You're his sister,* I remind myself. And that means no lustful looks from across the hall.

Must keep relationship secret.

You know, I can already see how this setup could cause some serious problems. Sure, we agreed on the sister thing, but that was before Nimue said I needed to become romantically involved with him. I mean, how am I supposed to be his lover and his sister? This is going to be tougher than I originally thought.

Merlin suddenly rises from his seat. "An excellent suggestion, your majesty," he says, clapping his wrinkled hands together. "A banquet would be most fitting for our honored guest. I shall see to the preparations myself." He bows low and before Arthur can open his mouth, the wizard flees the chamber through a back door. Almost as if he's in a hurry to get the hell out of Dodge. But why?

As if in answer to my unasked question, the door at the far end of the hall swings open. I turn around to see a knight in full armor enter the throne room, followed by a heavyset woman dressed all in black. My first thought is, How can I get myself some of those black dresses? I'm sick to death of all the bright colors I'm stuck wearing.

My second, more serious thought is, Why has everyone in the court let out a simultaneous gasp of horror as she approaches the thrones? Who is she? I step aside, allowing her to stand tall in front of the king and queen. Looking over at Arthur, I can see he is no longer smiling, and his face has lost most of its color. His kind eyes have morphed to cold steel. Guenevere sits, looking confused, obviously also unaware why everyone seems so shocked at the visitor's presence.

Hearing a noise, I look back to the doors and see a teenage boy, probably about eighteen years old, walk into the court, wearing matching black tunic and tights. He has a slight build, longish brown hair—sort of an early Beatles cut—chiseled cheekbones, and walks like he has a stick up his ass. My friend Serge back home would be absolutely *dying* (in a good way) if he saw this guy. Trust me, I have very good gaydar.

The young man walks up to the woman and stands by her side. She smiles over at him in a motherly way and then turns to address the king. I notice she does not bother to bow.

"Arthur, my dear little brother. It has been too long."

"Morgause," Arthur notes, tight-lipped. "What brings you to Camelot?"

Morgause? Uh-oh. Like King Lot's wife and Arthur's half sister, Morgause? Aka Morgan Le Fay, the witch whose husband I "accidentally" killed?

Oh, shit.

"Your brave knight Sir Lamorak brought news to the Orkneys that my husband, King Lot, has perished in battle," she says in a gravelly voice.

I let out the breath I didn't realize I was holding. Phew. She has no clue I was the one responsible. So why is she here? I bite my lower lip. What's this woman going to say?

"I am sorry for your loss," Guenevere offers, really looking as if she is. Guess Lance forgot to mention that little part of our adventure to her.

Morgause shoots a blatant dirty look at the queen, then turns back to Arthur. "Since I have a champion no longer, I would hope thou, as my brother, would grant me one favor."

"Anything," Arthur says, squirming on his throne. What's going on? What's he so afraid of? I know she's a witch and all, but what is it that she holds above his head?

"Anything?" she asks, effectively dragging out the suspense.

"Aye. Name it, be it half my kingdom, and I will grant it, dear sister." The way he says *dear sister* makes me believe Morgause is anything but.

"Ah, my request is nothing as grand as that," Morgause says with a smile. She puts her arm around the shoulder of the young man at her side and pushes him forward a bit so he stands at Arthur's feet.

"Greetings, sire," the boy says, a bit shyly.

"Allow me to introduce you to Mordred," Morgause says with a twisted smile. "Your son."

Chapter Thirteen

The court erupts with murmurs as everyone tries to talk at once, buzzing at this bizarre twist of events. After all, it's not every day the high king's sister waltzes in and presents the king with the bastard son no one had any idea he had.

But the loudest cry of all comes from Guenevere's side of the room: a half scream, half moan as the queen stares, openmouthed, at the teenager before her.

"It cannot be," she whispers, her face as white as a ghost, twisted in agony. She looks as if she's going to pass out, and I really can't blame her. Poor girl. She's been trying for years to give Arthur a kid, an heir to Camelot. Then his sister shows up one day and basically says, "Oh, by the way? Arthur has a son already, and he's full-grown." In front of the whole kingdom. How humiliating. Poor Guen.

Courtly manners be damned—I hurry to the queen's side, kneel by her throne, and squeeze her shoulder in what I hope is a comforting gesture. "Shhh," I hush her in her ear. "Don't let them see you upset."

I glance over at Arthur, who still sits there, a dumbstruck expression on his face. Evidently it's a big shock to him, too. So who, I wonder, is the mother? Some damsel in distress he screwed before meeting Guen? Judging from the fact that the kid looks about eighteen, and Arthur's thirty-four, he'd have to have been a teenager himself when he planted his royal seed in this kid's mom. Guenevere herself would have still been in diapers—if they have diapers in this century. I guess she can take some comfort in the fact that it's not like he cheated on her.

Mordred himself looks rather uncomfortable, probably due to the fact that he's in court, surrounded by about fifty gaping strangers. Poor guy. He shoots a stressed look at Aunt Morgause.

"Mother . . ." he whines.

Mother?!

Arthur groans and flops his head in his hands as the court breaks out into furious chatter once again. My mind whirls as I try to figure out what the heck I'm missing here. Mother? How can Morgause be his aunt and his mother? He must mean adopted mother, right? Right? Arthur couldn't have . . .

Could he have? Ew!

Guenevere trembles against me, burying her head in my chest. I can feel her trying to rein in her sobs. "It's going to be okay, sweetie," I whisper in her ear, brushing a hand over her golden locks. Of course, I have no idea how this optimistic statement could possibly be true. It's clearly not going to be okay, and everyone here, especially Guenevere, knows it.

Guen turns on Arthur, her face twisted in rage. Gone is the bubbly girl queen, and I wonder, under the circumstances, if she'll ever regain her sweet innocence again.

"Tell me this woman lies," she demands, her once musical voice icy and cold. "Tell me you did not father a child with *her*. Your very *sister!*"

Oh, man. This is *so Jerry Springer*. I'm waiting for them to start throwing thrones any second now. Though I'm not sure who Guen would like to hit first, the sister or her husband. I glance over at Morgause, who I realize is trying to hide her smile. She's actually enjoying this! Bitch.

"Be still, woman," Arthur commands. "This is not a discussion to be had in front of the entire kingdom."

Whoa! That's a confession if I ever heard one.

"So it's true," Guen hisses, at least keeping her voice down this time.

I watch as Arthur tries to surreptitiously brush a hand to his eye. Is he crying? " 'Twas a mistake," he whispers so only she—and I, since I'm standing beside her—can hear. "I did not know 'twas my sister. She bewitched me long ago, during the feast of Beltane, wearing the face of the goddess herself. Seduced me to her bed. The next morning I was horrified to find 'twas her. I left immediately and have not seen her since that day. Merlin made sure she stayed far away from me by marrying her off to King Lot."

Oh, good one, Kat. I knew aiding and abetting in Lot's death would come back to haunt me. If the evil king had lived to fight another day he probably would have headed home and played father to Mordred. Taught him how to rape and pillage, or some other useful evil-king-in-training skills. After all, he had been griping that all his other sons had abandoned their dear old dad. Now my well-meaning actions have probably ruined Guenevere's life.

Arthur's still talking, still pleading. "I swear to you, my love, I had no knowledge that our encounter produced a child." He lets out a soft moan and makes the sign of the cross. "May God forgive me!"

Guenevere shakes her head. " 'Tis not God's forgiveness you need, Arthur," she says loudly, spitting out his name as if it were poison, "but that of the poor boy who stands before you." She gestures to Mordred, who's shuffling from foot to foot, looking completely freaked out by the whole encounter. Guess it's not every day you find out your father and mother are siblings. I feel bad for the kid. " 'Tis not his duty to pay for his parents' sins," Guenevere continues. "Will you now claim him as your rightful son and heir?"

"Guenevere," Arthur hisses furiously, eyes wide, pleading. "You know that I cannot. If I claim him, if I acknowledge him as heir to the Pendragon line, then our future child will be left with nothing."

The queen stares at him, hatred distorting her face. "Our child?" she asks loud enough for everyone in the court to hear. "*Our* child? We will have no child, Arthur. Is it not obvious that I am barren? If your seed be so fertile as to impregnate your very sister, surely 'tis I who have no gift of life in my womb. You might as well recognize your bastard son, for you will get no child from me."

My heart aches at the pain in her voice. Poor girl. Poor, poor girl. I can see so clearly now why she and Lance get together. I almost want them to, after all she's been through. She needs someone to take her in his arms, comfort her, gently kiss away her humiliation, and promise her love in a life that's done nothing but hand her cruelty.

"Guenevere, my love," Arthur begs, reaching his hand over to clasp hers. She rips it from his grasp and cradles it protectively in her lap, her face stony. Then she slowly and deliberately rises from her throne and storms out of the room. The crowd murmurs excitedly. This is like one big soap opera to them.

Arthur frowns after her retreating figure. *Go after her!* I beg him silently. But no—like a typical man, he gives up too quickly. Instead of chasing after his distraught wife, the king turns back to the court, to Mordred, who stands fiddling with the hem of his well-cut black tunic.

"Well, then," Arthur says, his voice artificially cheery. "What remains to be said? Welcome to Camelot, my son."

Even with the interruption of the king's incestuous kin, it seems the show must go on. Or, in this case, the party that's being thrown in my honor. Though now I'm sharing the bill with Prince Mordred.

After court's over, I find Guenevere's room and bang on her door, begging her to let me in. A servant girl opens the door a crack and tells me the queen wishes not to be disturbed. I try to talk the girl into it, even attempt to bribe her with a cool silver ring I found in my room, but she won't budge. I next decide a little physical force is in order and try to grab the door and push it open. She slams it on my knuckles.

Bruised and defeated, I head back to my little in-castle apartment. I've been moved to a pleasant suite of rooms, complete with roaring fire and canopied bed. My personal maid (I love saying that!), Elen, escorts me to a tub room, where I bathe in a hot bath of rose petals and spices. I try to enjoy it, but I can't stop thinking about poor Guenevere and this whole disturbing scenario.

At the same time, I'm dying to meet up again with Lancelot. He's been away all morning hunting, and so I don't even know if he's heard about Arthur's surprise guest yet. I wonder what he'll say. Will he feel bad for the queen, too? Will he try to comfort her? Is that when they get together? I wish Nimue had given me a better idea of exactly where and when the two hooked up. It'd be a lot easier to plan things out.

As I step out of the tub, an ache settles in my stomach. Will Lancelot fall in love with Guenevere? It seems like he loves me, but how can I be sure? He hasn't said that he does. And besides, even if he is, love can change. You can be in love with someone one day and someone else the next. Or you can be in love with two people at once. What if he's not out hunting after all? What if he's in Guenevere's chambers right now? What if that's why she won't answer the door? The ache starts burning a hole in my stomach, and I rush to dress. Elen begs me not to rip the delicate silk sleeves as I shove my arms through.

I break out into a run down the hall to Guenevere's chambers, breathless with worry and anticipation. Could Lancelot be in there? A flash vision of the two of them writhing in each other's arms pounds through my brain. Would he betray me like that? Hot blood pulses at my temples.

I reach the locked door and pound on it with my fist. "Guenevere!" I cry. "Open this door!"

I hear a click of the lock and ready myself to slam my body's weight against the door the second it creaks open. I see a crack of light and push. The door swings wide and I fall through the open passage, tripping and ripping the skirts of my once beautiful silk dress.

Guenevere stands at the doorway, fully clothed, looking somewhat amused through her sadness. "If you wanted entrance that badly, Kat, you should have said so."

I grimace, my face hot with embarrassment. "I wanted to make sure you were okay." I feel like a rat for being so suspicious. Here the queen has learned that her husband not only screwed around with his own sister, but had a kid with her, who will now become the heir Guenevere could never provide. And I'm worried she's shacking up with my boyfriend.

She nods her head and gestures for me to come in. The room is simple, but elegant, dressed all in purple silk. Of course, Lancelot is nowhere to be seen. My imagination totally got the best of me.

Guenevere sinks into a wooden chair, looking down at her white hands.

"Listen, Guen," I say lamely. What does one say in this kind of situation? I try to remember a good *Jerry Springer* final thought. "I know this sucks and all, but chin up. So Arthur's got a kid. Big deal. Doesn't mean he doesn't love you. Doesn't mean you're still not queen. Sometimes life doesn't deal you the cards you'd like. But you've got to turn those lemons into lemonade." She probably has no idea what I'm talking about. Heck, I'm not sure I do either.

"I know, Kat. I will be fine. Do not worry about me," she says in a brave voice. " 'Twas just a bit of a shock, as you can well imagine." I watch as she tries to surreptitiously wipe away a tear.

"Yeah, no doubt!" I agree. "That one definitely came out of left field."

"But"—the queen looks up with a small smile—"I do not want my personal sorrows to dampen your stay at Camelot. After all, tonight is the banquet. Sure to be a fine feast. And," she adds, her eyes twinkling through her tears, "your so-called brother, Lancelot, will be in attendance. Surely a brother-sister dance is in order, do you not think?"

I grin. "Hell, yeah."

She smiles wistfully, looking into the distance, as if the wall behind me holds the answers to all life's mysteries. "You are very lucky, Kat. The way Lancelot looks at you . . . I have never had a man want me before. Not like that. With such hunger in his eyes. Such adoration. Love." She shakes her head. "I envy you a little."

My heart breaks at her words. I can't stand it. It's not right. It's not fair. Lancelot's supposed to be giving *her* those looks. She's supposed to find happiness in *his* arms. And instead, because of Nimue's and Merlin's selfish personal agendas, she's left to fend for herself all alone in this cruel medieval world. And I have selfishly agreed to hoard all the love that rightfully belongs to her.

On the other hand, if she does get together with Lance, according to Nimue's "betrayal schedule" (man, I still love that one), they've got, like, eight and a half months before getting caught. Before Guen gets sentenced to burn at the stake.

I've heard it's better to have loved and lost, but is it better to have loved and *died*? I look over at her grieving face. What would she want? A year of happiness or a lifetime of pain and suffering?

And why am I the one stuck making this decision?

After much arguing, Guenevere insists that I go to the royal banquet, though she herself will not be attending. I tell her I'd be happy to skip the event and hang with her in her chambers, but she won't take no for an answer.

"After all, Lancelot will be there," she teases.

So Elen and I set out to get me dressed. I can tell the maid's pissed that I ruined my last gown already, but since Guen's provided a whole roomful of dresses, I don't really see what the big deal is. I think she likes to complain. After she's gotten over whining about the torn fabric, the girl selects a cream-colored gown with sheer sleeves and a braided silver rope that crisscrosses my chest and back, then comes around to tie around my waist. Very Miuccia Prada–like. I wish I had a mirror to look in so I could get the whole effect. Elen wants to do something with my hair, but I shoo her away. I'm sick of wearing hats. Tonight my hair swings free, roots and all.

A knock sounds on the door. Elen frowns at the interruption, but goes to answer it. She pulls the door open, and I look behind her to see who's come to visit me.

Lancelot.

My heart thumps as he steps into the room wearing a leather tunic over a billowy red shirt. Fresh from hunting, it appears. His tousled hair and five-o'clock shadow tempt me, and I can barely resist the urge to throw myself in his arms, kiss the life out of him, and then suggest we go test out my new bed. Any thoughts of him comforting Guenevere are completely out the window. He's mine. All mine.

But a glance at the frowning Elen tells me I need to behave myself around my "brother." Damn.

"Lady Katherine is not ready yet," Elen informs him curtly, making me realize that while having a maid sounds cool in theory, it can actually be a big pain in the butt.

Lance shoots a sexy smile my way. "I cannot imagine her beauty improving beyond what I see with mine own eyes."

Standing behind Elen, I make throat-slitting motions with my right hand, trying to mouth the reminder, *Brother and sister*, to him. He furrows his brow in confusion, having no idea what I'm trying to do. I give up. What does Elen care if a brother calls his sister beautiful, anyway? After all, this is the castle whose new heir is the product of a sibling relationship.

"It's okay, Elen," I say, touching the maid on the shoulder. "I'm ready as I'll ever be. You can take off now, and I'll give you a shout if I need anything else."

Elen stiffens. "There will be no need to shout. My own chamber adjoins your bedroom. I shall wait there for your call." She turns and walks into my bedroom and through another small door on the left-hand side.

Damn it, she's going to be right next door? So much for a little prebanquet loving. Having a live-in maid sucks.

Time for plan B. I put a finger to my lips and motion for Lancelot to follow me out into the hallway. We walk down the corridor until I find the medieval equivalent of a broom closet.

Once inside the small storage chamber, I shut the door

and waste no time wrapping my arms around Lancelot's neck, pressing myself against his rock-hard body. He leans down, his lips connecting with mine.

"I've missed you," he murmurs between kisses. His hands wander down my back until he cups my bottom, pulling me closer. I can feel exactly how much he's been missing me, and rejoice in the effect I have on him.

His mouth traces my jawline, then dips lower, finding my neck and devouring it like some hungry vampire.

"I've missed you, too, *brother*," I quip as his right hand finds my breast. I gasp at the tingling feeling his thumb invokes as it rubs against my sensitive flesh. "Mmm, very, very much indeed."

He laughs softly. "I cannot believe I will have to restrain myself in court. How will anyone not be able to see how much I desire you?" He pulls at the gown's neckline, exposing a bare shoulder and covering it with fervent kisses. "My sister."

"I doubt anyone really cares," I say, digging my nails into his back, practically breathless with desire. "These days everyone's doing the brother-sister thing. We're, like, right in style."

Lancelot stops kissing me, pulling away. His eyes cloud with a question. "I do not understand."

Oh, yeah. He's been hunting. Hasn't heard the latest. While I'd rather have my way with him first, I resign myself to filling him in on the details of Morgause's visit. When I come to the part about Mordred, his jaw literally drops.

"A son? Arthur has a son? By his sister?" He rakes a hand through his black hair.

"Yup. As you can imagine, poor Guenny's very upset," I continue. "I've tried to comfort her, but—"

"The queen must be devastated," he says. "I should go see her."

I frown. "She told me she wants to be left alone."

"How can anyone who has heard such news know what they want?" Lancelot asks. "I am her knight. I must attend her."

With that, he darts out of the storage chamber without even so much as a "see you later." Probably right into the arms of Guenevere.

Good going, Kat.

With little else to do, I head back to my chambers and collapse on my bed, curling my body into a large feather pillow. I try to shake the image of Lancelot and Guenevere alone together in her bedroom. He loves me, I try to remind myself. Well, sure, he's never said those words, exactly. But I'm, like, his girlfriend, and he's a loyal, devoted guy. Not the type who goes and cheats on people. Especially not with a married woman.

I can't help thinking about the last time I had a guy cheat on me—back in college, with my best friend, in my own bed. My stomach still feels queasy as I remember catching them in the act. But Brian was a twenty-first-century scumbag, and my friend a total hippie, free-love slut. Not all guys would do such a thing. Lancelot wouldn't. Would he?

Man, I hate having all these trust issues. I'm, like, total damaged goods. I don't even know why Lance likes me in the first place. Probably just a sexual thing. He's using me 'cause I'm available and willing. I bet he never gives me a second thought once I go back to the real world. Or maybe he and his knight buddies will have a good laugh about the pathetic futuristic chick who let him fuck her against a tree.

Before driving myself absolutely nuts with self-pity, I close my eyes and manage to drift off into a troubled sleep. No dreams, though. In fact, I haven't had a dream since drinking Nimue's potion.

Sometime later Elen wakes me to say, in an irritated tone, that I've almost slept through my own banquet. Damn it! I rush to get ready and arrive at the banquet hall fashionably late. Well, I arrive at what *I* would consider fashionably late, which seems to actually be extremely late, since most of the food has already been consumed by the time I get there. When I look at the leftovers, I decide I haven't missed much.

Arthur invites me to take a seat at the head table, unfortunately next to Mordred. He even introduces me to the kid in a way that suggests he thinks it'd be a way-cool idea if the two of us hooked up. As if! Of course, to Arthur this probably seems a perfect scenario. What better bride for the future high king than the sister of his number one knight? Guess he doesn't get the fact that Mordred is way too young for me, and also so obviously more into dicks than chicks.

Speaking of my dear "brother," I scour the room, hoping to catch a glimpse of Lancelot's handsome figure, but he's nowhere to be found. A wave of disappointment washes over me. I assumed he'd be here. The rest of the kingdom is. Well, except for Guenevere, of course.

Guenevere.

Lancelot.

Oh, no. No, no, no!

I take a deep breath and will my rapidly beating heart to behave. No use getting all worked up over something that's probably a figment of my overactive imagination. Just because Lance and Guen aren't at the banquet doesn't mean they're off screwing around in her chambers. Even though that's exactly where Lance was headed the last time I saw him.

"Have you seen Lancelot around?" I ask Arthur, who sits to my left.

The king shakes his head. "Not since this morn."

"I hear your brother is a fine knight," Mordred butts in from my right.

I turn to him, a bit annoyed by his interruption. I have to find Lancelot and Guen. I don't have time to play nice with the boy prince.

"Yeah. He's pretty good." I turn to Arthur again, but Mordred grabs at my sleeve.

"D'you think he would teach me if I asked him?"

"Sure. I guess." I shrug. "Arthur—"

"Because I should very much like to learn to be a knight someday. Lancelot is so fine. So brave. The best knight in all the land."

I roll my eyes. I can see where he's going with this. He doesn't want to play swords. He wants to . . . well, play with Lancelot's sword.

"Dude," I say, patting his arm. "I hate to break it to you, but he's straight."

"I beg pardon?" Mordred cocks his head. "Straight?"

"Yeah. He doesn't swing your way. He plays for the other team. He's a breeder."

"What does that have to do with . . . ?"

"Look, Mordy. I understand why you think Lance is a stud. Everyone does. But trust me, he's not gay." Blank look. How can I put this delicately? "He doesn't, um, lie with other men."

Finally a look of understanding—mixed with horror.

"Does the lady suggest that . . . that I . . . By the gods!" Mordred says, his voice high and angry. He rises from the table, looking like he's about to throw a hissy fit. Oh, man. I should have kept my mouth shut.

"Look," I say, hoping to placate him. After all, he's Arthur's son, and heir to the throne—not someone I want to make an enemy of at Camelot. I gently pull him down to a seated position. "I didn't mean to imply that you were . . . you know. Not that there's anything wrong with it," I add hastily. "I mean, I have some great gay friends back home. Serge, for example. Best friend a girl could have. After all, who else would honestly tell me if my butt was looking fat, or if I was better off wearing strappy sandals or mules with a particular Dolce and Gabbana skirt?"

I realize I'm babbling. He has no idea what I'm talking about. "What I mean to say," I try again, "is that I'm not trying to question your sexuality or anything. If you want Lance to teach you to be a knight I'm sure he'd be happy to."

Mordred stares at me for a moment, and then his face breaks out into a dapper smile. "Aye, very well. And what of you, sister of Lancelot? Would thou be interested in teaching me any *lessons?*" He leers at me, grinning, and actually gives me a cheesy wink. "I have been told I am a very good pupil."

Oh, my God, he's trying to hit on me! Could it be he's really not gay? No, he *has* to be. I have perfect gaydar. I picked my uncle John out of a lineup years before he came out of the closet. Just to be sure, I steal a peek at his shoes. Perfect match to his beige tunic. I'm so not wrong. He must just not realize it yet. Wow.

"No offense, Mordy," I start, mentally trying to summon all the "How to reject a guy in a nice way" articles I've read over the years. Problem is, I usually skipped those articles and went straight to the more pertinent "How to survive *being* rejected in a nice way" ones. "But I'm not interested in starting a relationship right now. It's not you," I add hastily, lest he get offended. "It's me."

He sighs, deeply and dramatically. He's *so* not not-gay. "Have you already given your heart to another, then?"

I have to think for a moment on how to field that one. If I say yes, he's bound to follow up with a "who" question. If I say no, he's going to want to know what's wrong with him. I'm doomed.

"Actually, yes," I lie, making my decision. "A lover back in, um"—where was I supposed to have come from again?—"Little Britain. We are engaged to be wed."

"I see." Mordred looks disappointed, but like he's buying it. He gets up from the table. "Please excuse me." Evidently now that I'm taken, I'm not worth talking to. Typical. He walks over to the other end of the table to where his mother sits stuffing her face.

Arthur leans over to me, having overheard the convo between me and Mordred. "I did not know you were betrothed, Kat. Who is the lucky fellow?"

Oh, great. I know I'm going to regret this. "A fine gentleman," I say, digging my grave a little deeper. "Named Serge." Of course, the real-life Serge would be more interested in Mordred than me, but because of my recent gay-is-okay spiel it was the first name that popped into my head.

"It is lovely to hear about two young people in love," Arthur says with a sigh. "I do not know if Queen Guenevere will ever forgive me for what has transpired today."

I give him a rueful smile. "She will," I assure him. "It just takes time."

"She was but a young girl when we were first wed," Arthur says, staring at his plate and picking at a chicken bone with his dagger. "So sweet. So shy. So very beautiful." He sets the knife down on the table. "I fell in love with her the minute I laid eyes on her."

Well, that's interesting. Arthur loves her. And I can tell he's being totally honest. His wistful eyes give it away.

"You must understand, Lady Kat, the incident with Morgause happened many, many years before I even met my Guenevere. And while many a king might find it pleasing to take on a lover, since I married the queen I have never lain with anyone else. I love her with all my heart and soul. She is the sunshine in my otherwise dark and tormented life.

She gives me the courage and will to rule Camelot. Without her, I am nothing."

I raise an eyebrow at the declaration of love. Does Guenevere have any idea he feels this way? If she does, she hasn't let on to me about it. Then again, men can be so close-mouthed. I'm willing to bet twenty bucks he hasn't told her any of this.

"Does Guenevere know?"

"Pardon?" Arthur cocks his head.

"The stuff you're telling me. Do you ever say that to Guen?"

Arthur absently rubs his beard with his thumb and forefinger, lost in thought. "Unfortunately, I do not believe I have declared my love to her for some time now," he says, his voice sorrowful. "At times, being high king causes me to be somewhat remiss in my husbandly duties."

"Don't beat yourself up about it," I say, playing shrink. "Sometimes when you're married for a long time your career can get in the way. You get busy. You stop hanging out together. You begin to live separate lives." Man, I sound like a self-help book. "But it's never too late. Well, I mean, sometimes it is, but in your case I bet it isn't. Guen just needs some TLC right now. Uh, that's tender loving care." I pat him on the arm. "Why don't you go tell her how you feel?"

"You are right. I must speak with her," Arthur agrees. "Immediately. Where is she?"

Which brings us back to the real twenty-four-thousand-dollar question. "Last I saw, she was in her bedroom."

Arthur nods. "Page," he calls to one of the young boy servants. "Attend to the queen's chambers and ask her if she will join me."

Probably would have been a lot better if he went himself, but hey, at least he's making some sort of effort. I hope

Guen will appreciate it. If she's not busy banging Lance, that is. Jealous worry creeps back into the pit of my empty stomach. I suck down a goblet of wine and try not to think about it.

A few minutes later the page returns—alone. The king rises from his seat. "Why do you return without the queen?" he demands.

The page bites at his lower lip, not looking like he enjoys his role as bearer of bad tidings to the king.

"The queen is not in her solar, milord," he says in a trembling voice.

"Well, then, perhaps she is taking a walk," Arthur reasons. "Go and look for her in her gardens."

"The thing is, milord," the page says, still stammering, "the queen's maid has informed me that the queen has left Camelot altogether." He swallows hard. "Promising never to return."

Chapter Fourteen

Hang on, Kat. No need to panic. Just because Guenevere's gone doesn't mean Lancelot went with her.

"She's taken Lancelot with her," the page adds helpfully.

Okay, panic time. "Bastard!"

Oops. Did I say that out loud? The entire court turns and stares at me, then at Mordred.

"No, not him," I correct, annoyed. "Lancelot."

Man, Nimue was right about keeping the guy on a short leash. I give him time off to go visit the queen for one teensy-weensy afternoon and now they've both run away from home.

I clench my fists at my sides. How can he do this to me? *Such* a scumbag. Such a typical man. One minute he's all, "Oh, my darling, my darling," and the next he takes off with Arthur's wife. I am so going to kill him when I see him again.

"Lady Kat, have you information regarding this disappearance?" Arthur demands. Gone is the sweet Guen lover. He's back in high-king mode. And he looks pissed. To give him credit, it must be pretty darned embarrassing to find out in front of the whole kingdom that your wife ran off with your number one knight.

"You've got to be kidding me," I retort, a little insulted. "You think I'd allow her to run away?" *Or let Lancelot accompany her?* I think, but don't say.

Arthur nods thoughtfully. "Aye, I would think that you would have more sense than to let her go. However, the same might be said about Sir Lancelot. He is loyal to her to a fault and at times forgets that I am his king." He rises from his seat. "Guards, summon the knights. Saddle my steed. I want the entire country scoured if need be. Leave no stone unturned. My wife and Lancelot must be found." The hall erupts into action. When the king speaks, people listen, let me tell you.

But this kind of random looking doesn't really appeal to me. I need more information before I lead my own search party. After all, the kingdom of Camelot's at stake here, not to mention my all-inclusive first-class ticket back to the twenty-first century. I must find the queen and her knight before they do any relationship consummating.

Without bothering to excuse myself, I pull up my skirts and run to Guenevere's chambers as fast as my medieval slippers will carry me. (Which is admittedly faster than my Manolos would have, given the absence of the three-inch spiked heels.)

The door to the queen's apartments, luckily, is already open, saving me the trouble of having to slam my body against it this time. I burst in to find the same maid who had barred my entrance before, sitting quietly in a chair doing needlework.

"Wh-where is she?" I demand, bending over to rest my hands on my thighs—an attempt to catch my breath from the sprint. Being sick has done nothing for my stamina. I should start jogging around the castle or something.

The maid lifts her eyes and studies me seriously. "Where is whom?"

Oh, so she wants to play games, does she? I'll introduce her to one the cops play in the twenty-first century. We call it interrogation.

I reach down and grab her by the neckline of her dress, yanking her to her feet. She drops her needlework and squeals in protest.

"I demand that you let me go!" she says, clawing at my hands.

I smile what I hope looks like a crazy, sadistic grin. "Not until you tell me where the queen is."

"Never." She purses her lips together in defiance.

Okay, now what? I can't really hurt her. Well, technically I can, but look at all the trouble I got in last time, when I inadvertently helped kill King Lot. And he was a bad guy.

Time for plan B. I let go of her and nod my head.

"Very good."

"I beg your pardon?" the young maid questions, squinting at me in confusion.

"Guenevere said you were loyal to her. Guess she was right," I explain in my most businesslike tone. "She sent me to test you. To make sure you would not, even under threat to your life, tell anyone where she's gone."

The idiot maid beams, her brown eyes alight with joy at the compliment.

"What's your name, miss?" I query, straightening her neckline for her.

"Ina, milady. I have been with the queen since she first came to the palace. And I would rather die than let anything happen to her."

"Yes, yes. Of course," I say in an absent voice. I study her thoughtfully for a moment. "Though you gotta wonder: if you two are that tight—that close, I mean—then why didn't she take you with her?"

Ina looks slightly offended. "She would have, lady. But Lancelot—" She stops, probably wondering if she's revealing too much.

"Yeah, I hear you. I know how those knights can be," I say, not missing a beat. Damn it, where did they go and what are they up to? I mean, if Lancelot's supposed to be, like, my boyfriend, why wouldn't he at least give me a heads-up before going away on a "business trip"?

"Oh, no, milady. Nothing against Lancelot," Ina hastens to explain. "He likes me."

"Yeah, yeah. Of course he does."

"He simply said that I was not needed, since Guenevere already *has* servants residing at Camelot Cottage. Therefore I should stay here to tell whoever comes calling that the queen has left."

"I see." *Bingo!* I restrain from hugging her. After all, I'm supposed to already know this information.

"However, they promised they will send for me when they are settled in." She sniffs, tears welling up in her eyes. "I miss her already."

Hmm . . . Now that I know where they are, what should I do? Go after them? How will I find my way? I obviously can't MapQuest it this time.

An idea does one of those lightbulb things above my head. Seriously, sometimes I'm such a genius, I can't stand it.

"Cheer up, Ina. That's why I'm here."

"I beg pardon?"

"Yeah, they told me to come collect you on my way to the cottage. Guess Guenevere couldn't bear to have you gone. So pack your bag and let's be off."

"Oh, milady!" Ina's eyes shine through her tears, making

me feel a little guilty about my deception. But desperate times call for desperate measures. "I shall pack at once."

"Cool. After you pack, can you hook us up with some transpo—I mean, can you acquire some horses for the journey? You do know the way to the cottage, don't you?"

Ina's face falls. "I am sorry, milady. I do not."

Sigh. So much for that plan.

"But my brother, who lives in the village, does," she adds helpfully. "He could be our guide."

Whoo-hoo!

"Great, Ina. You arrange it all and come to my room when you're ready. Third door down to the left. I'll be waiting." I pause. "And Ina, I don't have to remind you to keep this all on the down-low . . . er, to keep quiet, that is." Man, talking medieval is exhausting.

She nods enthusiastically, and I turn to walk out into the hallway and head for my suite. I hope Ina will be quick about it. I've got to get to Camelot Cottage soon, before something bad happens.

I need to get there before Guenevere and Lancelot start falling in love.

Ina's brother, a short, dumpy-looking dude with stringy black hair, does a decent job of leading us to Camelot Cottage. We get lost only once. Despite my pleadings, he refuses to ask for directions. Guess that annoying male trait goes back a ways. But to give him some credit, he does eventually find the trail again, and about an hour later we cut through a clearing and find the cottage.

Cottage is really a misnomer for this place. It's more like a Mini-Me of Camelot the castle: white stone walls, small turrets waving dragon flags. It's even got its own little moat around it. Cute.

217

I have to say this Camelot Cottage looks nothing like the same-named Catskills establishment I once stayed at. Despite its adorable name, the New York one turned out to be nothing more than a no-tell motel, like dozens of others on the street. The lumpy bed even had one of those cheesy vibrating things. Since it rained most of that vacation, my boyfriend and I went through a lot of quarters.

There had better not be any bed vibrating taking place in *this* Camelot Cottage.

I climb off my horse and race to the front door. Will I catch them in the act? My heart squeezes, and I realize my hands are shaking. I pray that I'm wrong, but how can I be? The heartbroken queen took off with her favorite knight—the one, lest I forget, *destined* to fall in love with her. What else are they going to be doing? Playing Yahtzee?

I push open the door and burst inside. As my eyes adjust to the darker room, I scan the scene—a cozy little space with simple wooden furniture and a roaring fire in its stone fireplace. The queen is at the far end, seated by the fireplace, staring into the flames. Lancelot is nowhere to be seen.

"Where's Lancelot?" I demand. Guenevere whirls around, startled. Her face breaks into a huge smile.

"Kat!" She jumps up from her seat and runs over, throwing her arms around me in a big hug. "How ever did you find me? I'm so glad you did. I did not mean to run off and not tell you, of all people, where I was to go. But I fear 'twas a rash decision and there was no time. I meant to send a messenger at first light; really I did."

She's happy to see me? She's been fornicating with my boyfriend, and she gives me this kind of welcome? I bite at my lower lip and repeat my question: "Uh, where's Lance?"

She beams. I try to discern whether it's an innocent beam

or a you-mean-the-man-who-just-made-love-to-me? one. "He's out hunting for dinner and should be back very soon. You will stay for dinner, will you not?" she asks.

"Uh, yeah, sure," I mutter. "Oh, your servant Ina's outside, by the way."

Guenevere's face lights up again. "Really? Oh, Kat, you are too wonderful to bring her here. There is a caretaker who could serve me, but she is old and half-blind—nothing like my wonderful little Ina. I must go out to greet her at once." The queen brushes past me in her haste to go see her maid friend.

Left alone in the cottage, I immediately start my sex investigation. Of course, I can't look for used condoms in the trash or anything like I would have back in my own time, but there's got to be some evidence of the dirty deed around.

I find a bedroom and start my search there. The bed's made—a good sign. Still, the furs could have been smoothed over afterward. I pull down the covers and take a sniff. No hint of Lancelot's patchouli scent—just a musty, old smell. No one's slept here for a while. I look for abandoned clothing on the floor. Nope.

Maybe they haven't had a chance yet. But are they planning to? That, as Hamlet might say, is the question. Still, Guenevere did seem pretty happy to see me. Would she be that overjoyed if she were planning a lovers' tryst with my boyfriend? After all, she knows we're a couple.

Do I have this all wrong? Hope surges through me. Oh, please, please let me be wrong.

"What are you doing here?"

I whirl around and smack into the hard chest of Lancelot. I look up, right into his puzzled blue eyes. He looks so good. I can't believe I've actually missed him in the short time he's been gone. I want to wrap my arms around his neck and kiss him senseless. Throw him on the bed and have my way with him, enjoying each and every one of his two thousand body parts, as they say in the Lever 2000 commercial.

I shake my head clear. There will be no two-thousand-part explorations until he comes up with a damn good explanation as to why he took off with the queen to a remote cabin in the woods. And his answer had better be good.

"The real question would be, what are *you* doing here?" I demand, hands on hips, trying not to care so much. This is why I never get into serious relationships. I hate this powerless, desperate feeling. I take a step back, trying to stop the electricity that crackles between us.

He sighs, scratching his chin. "I am sorry about that. I had no choice."

No choice? There's always a choice. "You could have at least told me you were going."

"I tried," he says, and I can't help notice how tired his eyes look, crinkling at the corners. "Your maid, Elen, told me you were sleeping and were not to be disturbed. She is rather firm, that one. When I tried to protest, she threatened to call a guard. Because of the queen's situation, I could not draw more attention to myself."

I frown. "I am so firing her when I get back."

"My darling," he says, stepping toward me and reaching up to stroke my head with his hand. I pull away, taking another step back. He sighs and withdraws his hand, a defeated look on his face. "I am sorry my leaving troubled you so. I would have been back for you as soon as the queen settled in."

"Yeah, but why'd you have to go in the first place?" I ask sulkily, flopping down on the bed.

He runs a hand through his hair, frustrated. "'Tis my job, woman. I told you before. This is the very reason Arthur asks that his knights stay celibate and loyal to the order." He's pacing now, staring at the floor.

"What, so they can run off with his wife?" I'm being difficult, but I don't care. I'm mad. Mad at him for being loyal to the queen. Mad at myself for being mad that he is.

"Kat, listen to me." He kneels at my feet, taking my hand in his. "I care for you deeply. But my position requires I be loyal to my queen above all."

"And what position might that be?" I ask, ripping my hand away. "Doggy style? Missionary? Oh, wait, you're more of a standing-up-against-a-tree kind of guy. Does Guenny like that one?"

He looks horrified, and rightly so. I'm such a bitch. He's done nothing to suggest that he has any sexual intentions toward the queen. Nothing. But I, knowing the future, can see what lies deep in his heart, even if he's unwilling to admit it. And that puts me in a tough spot.

"I do not understand," he moans. "Why are you saying all of this? Have I done anything to make you doubt me?"

I can't take it anymore and decide to come clean. "Look, Lance. I'm from the future, right? Well, I know exactly what happens in the legend of Camelot." I rise from the bed, my hands fisted in fury. I stare down at him. "You and Guen hook up. You become lovers. So whatever you're feeling for me now, forget about it. You're supposed to love Guenevere, not me."

"Lady, how can you say this?" he cries, scrambling to his feet. "Guenevere is the queen. Arthur's wife. She and I could never become lovers, even if I wanted it. Which I do not," he adds quickly.

"Yes, you can. And you do. Of course, it leads to the destruction of the whole kingdom, and Guenevere gets sentenced to death. But hey, don't let a little death and devastation distract you from your destiny."

"I don't want Guenevere. I want you." He grabs me by the waist and pulls me tight against him. His face is desperate, anguished, lonely even. "Why can you not accept that? Why must you torture me with your words?"

I feel the tears start welling up in my eyes, and I angrily try to squeeze them away. But it's no use, and they start to flow.

"Let me go." I try to squirm out of his hold.

"How can you punish me for something I have not done?" Lancelot asks, refusing to acknowledge my request to be freed. "A thing I swear to you now I'll never do?" He wraps me in his arms and I give in, pressing my face into his warm chest, trying to choke back my sobs. "Please believe me."

"I want to. I do," I say. It's true. I do want to believe him. But how can I when I have this major Cassandra complex? It's not like I suspect a boyfriend's cheating through women's intuition. This case of infidelity is on record in a hundred historical texts.

Texts that have not yet been written.

Have I changed the future? Is Lancelot being honest? Will he love me until his dying day and never once steal a lustful glance at the queen? Or should I go with the destiny theory? Is Lancelot predestined to fall in love with Guenevere? In that case, why do I even bother trying to stop it? I should walk away now and save myself any future pain and suffering.

But I can't. I'm in too deep now. I love him. I need him. I want him with me for as much or as little as he can give. I wrap my arms around him, allowing my fingers to caress the small of his back, rejoicing in his hard, muscular body.

"I'm sorry," I whisper.

He turns a bit, deftly shutting the door without letting

me go. Then he picks me up in his arms, as if I weigh nothing, and carries me over to the bed.

"Let me prove my loyalty to you," he murmurs, laying me down on top of the furs. "If it takes all night, I promise you I will."

"What about dinner?" I ask as he traces my lips with his finger.

He smiles. "There is a cook. The queen will be well fed."

"And you? Won't you be hungry?"

"I have everything I need for sustenance right here beneath me," he says, his mouth leaning down to devour mine.

Ditto.

After hours of yummy lovemaking followed by even yummier hours of lying together, caressing each other tenderly, I'm about convinced that my knight really does have no interest in the queen and was merely doing his job.

"What are we going to do about Guenevere?" I ask, tangling my fingers in his chest hair. "I hate to see her so unhappy. And she certainly can't live here forever."

Lancelot sighs, staring at the ceiling. "I do not know. Mordred's arrival came as a terrible shock to her."

"That's the understatement of the millennium. I thought she'd keel over right then and there." I shake my head. "Poor thing."

Lancelot props himself up on his side, meeting my eyes with his own. "I wish she could be as happy as I am right now."

Aw. I smile and drop my gaze. He's so sweet I can't stand it. Once upon a time I'd be horrified to be this doted on. I always went by the Groucho Marx theory of never wanting to join a club that would welcome me as a member. In the same vein, a guy who was in love with me must be a loser. I was always looking for the one who was out of reach. As if his acceptance of me could make me cool. Of course, if he ever did by some remote chance fall for me, then he automatically slipped into the uncool category. So basically there was no winning.

But this, for some indescribable reason, is different. I still respect, desire, and, yes, love Lancelot, even though he constantly declares his feelings for me. Is this how it's supposed to be when you find "the one"?

It *would* be my luck. Spend my whole life searching for "the one," only to find out the reason I can't find him is because he lived and died over a thousand years before I was born. Figures. I wish someone could have told me that from the get-go. It would have saved me the agony of a lot of awkward blind dates and tears from reading "Dear Kat" breakup letters.

I just feel so comfortable around Lance. So safe. So warm and fuzzy. He's amazing in bed. He's strong. Protective. Loving. Sexy as hell. Sweet. Caring. Did I mention sexy?

He leans into me, kissing the hollow of my throat. My breath hitches. Here we go again. But wait . . .

I gently push him away. "We haven't finished talking about Guenevere."

"I want to talk about this," he says, planting a kiss on my nose. "The most adorable nose I have ever had the pleasure of kissing. Wherever did you acquire it?"

I giggle. "Stop changing the subject."

"Or mayhap we should speak of your ear." He traces the outside with his index finger, sending chills down my spine. "A maddeningly beautiful receptacle for sound."

"Stop it!"

"Or"—he grins wickedly—"let us speak of your mouth." He gently pinches my lower lip with two fingers and pulls it down. Then he leans in, his tongue running along the inside of my lip. "The most luscious instrument of all."

I erupt in giggles, destroying the moment. I roll over onto my back. "Guenevere. We must talk about Guenevere."

"What is there to speak of?" he asks, reluctantly resigning himself to the task at hand.

"How can we make her happy?"

"I do not know."

"Well, are you happy?"

"Aye, very." He smiles. "Happy with you in my bed." He leans in to kiss me again, but I playfully push him away. He groans.

"Focus, Lance," I scold. "Now, we're both happy cause we have each other. Therefore, we need to find Guenevere a lover to be happy with." I roll onto my side to face him. "You know anyone single at the castle? I know Mordred is, but that might be a little awkward, him being her husband's son and all. I'm thinking we should probably be steering the love away from the family. They've got enough insider trading going on as it is."

"But Guenevere cannot take on a lover," Lancelot says in a horrified voice. "She is married to the king."

Of course. He's exactly right. Duh. What on earth was I thinking? I succeed at keeping Guen and Lance from getting together, only to get her burned at the stake because she fell in love with some other random dude that I set her up with? *Think, Kat.*

An idea comes to me. "Maybe we should try to get her back together with Arthur. I was talking to him in the banquet hall today, and he was pretty adamant about how much he loves her. If we could get the two of them together, maybe they could make up for lost time or something. If Guen would forgive him for the whole Mordred thing . . ."

" 'Tis a hard thing to forgive."

"Well, not really. I mean, he did it way before they were

married. It's a little disturbing; don't get me wrong. But he swears he hasn't cheated on her."

"Perhaps, then, it may work."

"Then it's a plan. We get Guen and Arthur back together. It'll be good for everyone. Them and the whole kingdom."

"And us." Lance grins. "For I will no longer have to accompany her when she decides to abandon the castle."

"Yes. And I won't have to come track you down," I admonish him, poking my finger into his chest.

"But I like when you do that," he says saucily. "Very much indeed."

"Oh, really?" I ask, pressing my lips against his. "What about this?" I say, coming up for air after the kiss. "Do you like when I do this?"

He groans. "Very, very much." He leans in for a second taste.

Talking time is now officially over.

A rooster crows, effective as an alarm clock with a broken snooze button, and I groggily crawl out of bed. Lancelot is evidently a deep sleeper—the annoying rooster doesn't rouse him. Careful not to wake him, I tiptoe to the door, pull it open, and slip out into the main room of the cottage.

Guenevere rises from her seat at the table and smiles at my approach. "Kat," she greets me. "Good morn. I trust you slept well. Or," she adds with a wink, "not at all?"

I grin ruefully at her not-so-subtle hint.

"The caretaker's wife has not yet risen," Guen says. "So there is no food prepared. I can wake her if you like."

"No need." I slip onto the bench beside her. "I'm not really hungry."

"I should think you would be famished after the night you had with Sir Lancelot," Guenevere teases.

I grin sheepishly. "Yeah, yeah."

"Kat, I am thankful to have you here, but why did you come?" she questions.

My face heats. I can't tell her the real reason. It's too embarrassing, for one thing. I mean, what am I supposed to say? "I came here to make sure you don't seduce my boyfriend like history says you do"?

"Arthur sent me," I lie.

Guenevere furrows her brows. "He did?"

"Yes." I nod enthusiastically, a plan forming in my head. "He was quite upset when he learned you had taken off."

"Then why did he not come after me himself?" she asks. "Too busy with his sister?" She spits out the last word. Ouch.

"No way, Guen." I shake my head. "He's got no time at all for that witch. In fact, the only reason he hasn't kicked her out of Camelot yet is 'cause he's afraid she'll put an evil spell on you."

Guenevere's eyes widen. Did I mention I'm a damn good liar? I had lots of practice in high school with my strict curfew-setting mom. "What kind of spell?"

I hate follow-up questions that require additional lying. "I don't know, Guen. He didn't say. A bad one, I'm sure. Real bad. Like turning-you-into-a-frog bad."

"That was good of Arthur to protect me, then," Guenevere says thoughtfully. "He has always been a good protector." She stares into the distance.

"He loves you, Guen," I say—truthfully this time. "He told me so. He called you the sunshine of his dark life. Said he couldn't bear to live without you. And he swears he hasn't taken on any lovers the whole time you've been married."

Guenevere turns to look at me, and I realize her eyes are glistening with unshed tears. "Really?" she asks. "He said that to you? Tell me the truth, Kat. I cannot bear to be lied to again."

"I am telling the truth." At least about the last part. "Look, Guen. The whole thing with Mordred happened ages ago. You can't really hold that against Arthur, can you? In my time it's really common for people to bring kids from other marriages into the relationship. Sure, it's tough, but a lot of time the kids and the stepparent become really close."

"I did feel bad for Mordred," Guenevere admits. " 'Tis not his fault, and he looked so lost standing there. So confused. Like a lamb on slaughtering day."

Knowing Mordy a little better, I don't share her fond recollections, but I keep my mouth shut.

"What about Arthur?" I ask, trying to steer the conversation away from the kid and back to the relationship.

Guenevere stares down at her hands. "I was always scared to let myself care for him. After all, our partnership was formed to secure the kingdom, not because of any sense of love. Though I do know he reserves fond thoughts of me. After all, he kept me as his wife even after it became apparent that I could not conceive the heir he wanted. Most men would have put me away in exchange for a more fertile spouse. But love me?" She looks up, tears spilling down her cheeks. "I never dared dream that he would love me."

I smile, placing my hand over hers. "He does love you, Guen. He just doesn't know how to express it. You know how men are. Well, maybe you don't, actually." A thought strikes me. "Never fear. I can explain the mystery of men to you right here, right now."

"You can?" Guenvere's eagerness shines through her tears. She leans forward in anticipation of my words.

"Yes," I say, suddenly feeling quite wise. "All the complexities of mankind can be boiled down to one simple statement."

"They can?" I think the queen's actually holding her breath.

"Yup. Guenevere, my darling, all you need to know is this: Men are from Mars, and women are from Venus. . . ."

Chapter Fifteen

After my quite detailed paraphrasing of the main points of the John Gray classic and several other best-selling self-help books, I manage to convince Guenevere that trying to make her marriage work instead of running away over something that happened eighteen years ago might be a good thing. By the time Lancelot wakes, she's already packed and ready to move back to Camelot.

I smile as she eagerly relates to Lancelot all I've told her. If this magazine-editor thing doesn't work out, at least I have a career in marriage counseling to fall back on. He, on the other hand, looks completely baffled at her newfound vocabulary of codependency, self-esteem, and midlife crisis. But then again, most twenty-first century guys are, too.

We arrive back at Camelot later that afternoon, and Arthur looks so happy to see Guen I think for a moment he's going to faint. When she waltzes up to him and plants a passionate kiss on his mouth, I'm almost sure he will. But somehow he manages to retain consciousness long enough to scoop her effortlessly into his arms and carry her off to his royal chambers, where I'm sure the two of them will sit and talk politics until dawn.

Ah, love.

Summer turns to autumn, and the castle gets cranking with preparations for winter. And that doesn't mean hitting Wal-Mart to stock up on everything under the sun; they've got to do it all from scratch. There's meat to be caught and smoked, blankets to be woven, grain to be ground and made into bread.

I try to make myself useful, but Guen has assigned me kitchen duty, which is not really my forte. More often than not I'm just in the way, and the cook shoos me out. I end up spending a lot of time with Lancelot, riding around the countryside on horseback.

I'm actually becoming a darn good horsewoman, if I do say so myself. Lance assigns me my own horse, which I dub Dior (after my hero, Christian), and even teaches me how to jump. At first it's totally scary—after all, if Dior throws me and I get hurt, I obviously can't go to the emergency room. But at the same time it's so darn thrilling—flying through the air on a horse—that in the end, I decide it's worth the risk.

We have a blast together, Lance and I. With him there's no pretense of having to act cool and aloof. I can totally be myself. I love that. I only hope he feels as free with me as I do with him. There is one thing that worries me a little, as our relationship deepens: he's never told me he loves me. To be fair, I haven't told him either—I so don't want to be the one who says it first! But I hope upon hope that he does. At least a little bit. 'Cause by this point I'm totally head over heels.

Honestly, I'm really starting to get used to this living in-medieval-times thing. Sure, there are things I miss: venti caramel macchiatos from Starbucks, microwaves, Seven jeans, central heating, and David Bowie songs. But many things I don't: alarm clocks, McDonald's burgers, reality TV, and country line dancing.

Sometimes I even wonder if, when the time comes, I'll want to go back. I mean, I can't help but imagine staying here, marrying Lancelot, and having some little Knights of the Round Table of our own. It wouldn't be so bad, honestly. But at the same time I miss my friends and family. I don't know if I could bear never seeing them again. Of course, by that token, how can I leave Lance? It's a total catch-22. I try not to think about it too much, but seriously, at times I lose major sleep over the whole thing.

One day Lancelot and I are out in the stables, grooming our horses, when the king's trumpets sound, summoning us to court. We exchange glances. What could this mean?

After all the nobles and knights are gathered, King Arthur calls out a courier, who has been standing in the back. The man looks like he's been riding for days, dirty and exhausted.

"What news have you, sir?" Arthur asks from his throne. To his right sits a well-dressed Mordred, in his new place of honor beside the king. Guenevere is not present; she's busy still organizing the winter preparations. A little workaholic, that queen, let me tell you.

"The Saxons who reside on the eastern shore are restless," the courier replies, still sounding a bit out of breath. "They've been attacking the good King Pellinore of Listinoise, raiding his people's livestock. The king begs Your Majesty send an army to oust the barbarians from his lands."

A cheer rises from all the knights.

"Why are they so happy?" I whisper to Lancelot. To me, the words *bad guys attacking* would seem a negative thing. But what do I know?

Lancelot frowns, his face troubled. "They are happy at the prospect of taking up arms," he whispers back. "Under King Arthur's peaceful rule, many complain of boredom. Evidently they would rather risk being run through by a sword than be forced to spend their lives at home with their wives and children."

We watch as the king rubs his beard with his thumb and forefinger, deep in thought. "However, Arthur is not of this mind-set," Lancelot adds. "After spending his younger years at war, uniting Britain by the sword Excalibur, he now longs for a land of peace, even amongst the savage, un-civilized Saxons."

"But at the same time, he can't just have them go around killing his subjects' cattle," I conclude.

"Aye." Lancelot nods. "So he is stuck, as you are so fond of saying, between a rock and a hard place."

I think for a moment, then get an idea. "Hey, Arthur," I call out. "Why don't you try to go mediate with them?"

The entire court turns and stares at me. As a woman I'm supposed to keep my mouth shut in court. But obviously no one else is going to speak, and hey, if I have a good idea, why should my being of the fairer sex mean I have to keep it quiet?

"What is it you propose, Lady Kat?" Arthur asks, ac-cepting my break in protocol. After my single-handedly saving his marriage, he owes me a favor or two.

"I think you should go talk to their leader and find out why they're breaking the peace. They've got to have some reas—"

"Lady, go back to your embroidery and leave war talk to

the men," Mordred interrupts. "There is no speaking to the Saxons. They are uncouth barbarians who care for nothing but violence."

"Whatever, dude!" I protest. Did I mention what a pain in the neck Arthur's son turned out to be? He alternates from hitting on me to insulting me on a daily basis. Also, he's so eager to become king someday that he has an opinion on everything. And he riles up all the bored knights with his brazen "when I'm king of Britain" speeches behind King Arthur's back. He's a total thorn in his father's side.

"Nay, my son, Lancelot's sister is right," Arthur says in my defense. I give Mordred a triumphant smile. He sneers at me. "Mayhap the Saxons have a reason to be breaking the peace."

"They could be starving, and have, like, no food for winter," I propose. "After all, they're stealing cattle, not murdering townsfolk."

"True." Arthur nods. "The oracles have predicted a long winter. Perhaps they worry for their children."

"May all their bairns die of starvation. I will make a necklace of their bones," Mordred says gallantly. The knights cheer.

"Silence!" Arthur commands in a loud voice. That shuts them up. Arthur is, of course, still king, even though the knights aren't all into his peaceful ways. "Hear this," he says, addressing the courier. "Tell King Pellinore that I will raise an army of five hundred, along with my closest knight companions. We will camp on the borderlands, and I will request an audience with the Saxon leaders. I will attempt to learn the reason for the attacks. If they are unwilling to talk, then we will fight."

More cheers from the peanut gallery. I know they're betting on the fact that the Saxons are uncivilized barbarians who have no idea how to talk peace. I hope Arthur will be able to prove them wrong by uniting the Britons and Saxons under one rule. I mean, it's got to happen at some point in history; how else would the whole WASP thing come to pass?

After court breaks for intermission, I find Lancelot at the back of the room. He looks distressed.

"Hey, Lance," I greet him. "What's wrong?"

He frowns. "Mordred. That boy is trouble. He should never have been declared Arthur's heir. He is nothing like his father. May Arthur live forever; I cannot imagine Mordred taking the throne."

"Yeah, he's a total jerk, huh?"

"He riles up the younger knights against the king. It is treasonous. But Arthur will not hear it. He loves his son and is blind to his evil ways."

"Well, at least Arthur won this round," I say, trying to sound optimistic.

"True. Though you do know what this means, do you not?" Lancelot asks.

I sigh. "You're going with them."

"Aye. I am Arthur's first knight. I must stand by his side during negotiations."

"Do you have to?" I don't mean to be selfish, but we have such little time together. "How long is this going to take?"

"It could take months."

"Months?" I cry. I'd been thinking days. "How many months? I'm only going to be here for, like, seven more."

"I cannot predict. It depends on whether or not we go to war," Lancelot says, leading me down the hall.

"Can I come?"

"Nay. The king would never allow it."

"This sucks," I pout. Lancelot opens the door to his chambers and ushers me inside. After he closes and locks the door, he takes me in his arms. I press my head against his solid chest. "I am so going to miss you."

"Aye, my darling," he whispers. "No more than I will miss you."

The army and knights take off, leaving us womenfolk stuck at the castle. Merlin's here, too—he's too old to fight in a war and, according to Arthur, too valuable to risk losing. But the old magician spends the majority of time holed up in his tower and we barely see him. At one point I approach him to do magic tricks for the court—in an effort to help pass the time in an entertaining fashion, you understand. But he refuses me outright. You know, for an all-powerful wizard, he really comes across as an old fuddy duddy.

The next month is boring as hell. Because I have no job, I find myself with a lot of downtime. After all, being a lady-in-waiting isn't that demanding a career. It's a lot easier than being a magazine editor, anyway, which involves writing and interviewing and traveling. Ladies-in-waiting . . . well, they pretty much just wait, though for what I've yet to figure out.

I do consider throwing myself a big birthday bash when the date arrives, but then decide against it. After all, it's unlikely anyone can make me a birthday cake with my favorite sugar icing and I figure I'm not *really* turning thirty this year since I've technically not even been born yet.

So yep, winter in Camelot is no fun. First of all, there's no central heating, obviously, and the castle is always damp and freezing. It's also extremely boring. With the wind whipping up the snow, no one goes outside. Instead they stay huddled together by the fireplace, content to embroider everything in sight and spend hours weaving boring tapestries. As if the walls aren't already tackily covered in them.

There's not even anything to read. The ancient scrolls in the library are all written in Latin and unfortunately smarty-pants me took French as a foreign language in high school, saying, Why should I study a dead language like Latin?

"Guen," I say on one particularly brutally boring day. "I can't stand it anymore. I'm going completely stir-crazy."

"Aye," she says sympathetically, looking up from her embroidery. She must have embroidered every dress in the kingdom by this point and never seems to get bored with it. "The winters here are long, I know."

"It's a beautiful day outside. I'm going riding."

She looks shocked. "Kat, you know that you cannot. It is too dangerous."

"I'm not afraid of a little snow. Besides, Dior has four-hoof drive." I laugh at my little joke, wishing that once in a while someone would get my humor.

"I do not mean from the snow. The danger comes from the marauding bandits and enemies of the king. Do you not remember what happened the last time you went out alone? You were kidnapped. This time Lancelot will not be there to save you."

"I don't need a man to save me," I retort, my feminist side quite offended. "Besides, that time I was on foot. Dior is, like, the fastest horse in Camelot. No bandit's going to be able to catch me while I'm riding him."

"At least take an escort," Guenevere begs. "A company of guards to protect you."

I frown. "They'll cramp my style. Listen, Guen, don't be a worrywart. I'll be fine."

She shakes her head, knowing better than to bother arguing. "Do what you will. But please, for my sake, be careful. I do not want to be the one to answer to Lancelot if anything were to happen to you."

"Yes, Mother," I say sarcastically, then bite my tongue. Calling Guen *Mother,* even in jest, is cruel.

After apologizing for my stupid joke, I head for the stables and saddle Dior. He's delighted to go out riding—chomping at the bit, you might say—and soon we're off.

The day is cool and clear. The fur cloak keeps me warm enough, and Dior's clearly psyched to be running free. Evidently he's been suffering from the same cabin fever as I have. We head down into the valley and then circle around the village to the paths in the woods. The scene is breathtaking—a winter wonderland. The pure white snow blankets the landscape, with no black dirt from cars to dirty it up. Icicles drip from tree branches. In delight, I start humming a Christmas carol, until Dior starts snorting in protest over my admittedly bad singing voice.

As Dior carefully makes his way through the icy woods, we come across what in the summertime is a gentle stream. A peasant woman, her face obscured by a hooded black cloak, is on her knees, trying to break the ice with her white fist. She's not having much luck.

"Ma'am," I call down to her. "What are you trying to do?"

She looks up and I see her face. She's got a million wrinkles, and her eyes seem to recede back into her skull. When she sees me, she bows low. "My lady," she murmurs. "I was merely seeking to fill my cup." She lifts a hollowed-out wooden bowl for me to see. "But the ice has swallowed the river."

Poor woman. There really was a huge class difference back in the Middle Ages. Not that there isn't in the twenty-first century, but at least most people have running water. Well, in America, at least—I guess that's not true in some third-world countries. Okay, fine. We're totally as classist in the twenty-first century, if not worse.

"Hey, I know. I'll have Dior—that's my horse," I explain, petting Dior's neck, "stomp on the ice and break it for you."

The old woman's face alights. "Oh, milady, please do not feel you must go through all that trouble to help an old woman."

"It's no trouble," I insist, feeling rather magnanimous. Why, if I were a ruler of medieval Britain, I'd be the one who helped all the peasants. The people would love me. I'd be known throughout the land as Katherine the Generous.

I instruct Dior to step forward, and his hooves easily break through the ice, revealing the running stream below. The woman gets on her knees and fills her cup, bringing the liquid to her dry lips. I feel like a superhero.

"Thank you, milady," she says, gushing with joy. "I did not know what I would do before you came. Please accept my gift of thanks." She reaches into her robe pocket and pulls out a small, shiny apple.

My mouth waters at the sight of it. It's been a long time since I've gotten to eat any fruit, and I'm probably halfway to scurvy by now. One of the things that sucks about medieval times is that there's no supermarket to get fresh, imported produce. If you can't pick it off a tree, you're not eating it.

"But I don't want to take your food," I protest, remembering that she's the poor starving peasant. "I was happy to help."

"Please do not disgrace me by turning down my gift," the woman begs. "It is an honor to share the fruit of my labor with such a fine lady as yourself."

"Well, when you put it like that, how can I refuse?" I laugh, reaching down to take the apple from her outstretched hand. She watches me eagerly as I take a large bite. Yum! The cool, crisp juices from the fruit delight my every taste bud, and I'm already taking another bite before I even swallow. "This is a good apple," I say, my mouth full of fruit. Then I realize I'm talking to no one. The old woman's disappeared. That's weird.

I finish the apple and toss the core onto the snow. It's biodegradable, so it's technically not littering. Then I urge Dior to keep walking.

As we walk the trees grow denser, blocking out most of the sunshine. I feel like we're in a dark cave. Still, we press onward. I begin to feel a strange tingling in my head and my stomach. A sort of nauseous, sleepy feeling. The side-lines of the path begin to soften around the edges. But still Dior presses onward.

I think about turning around, going back to the castle, but I find I lack the energy to voice the commands. My tongue is thick in my mouth, swollen. What's wrong with me? My brain is slow even to form the thought. One part of me thinks I should be panicking, but my heartbeat seems too lazy to race.

The apple. Was there something wrong with the apple? The hobbled old peasant woman I'd helped? Why had she been trying so hard to get water under the stream? Why didn't she simply scoop up a cupful of snow for refresh-ment? Too late I ponder how a peasant woman in the Mid-dle Ages acquired a shiny, red, delicious apple in the middle of winter, when all of the castle's fruits and vegetables are soft and moldy.

Tricked? Poisoned?

You know, I should have paid more attention to my fairy tales as a child. This is exactly what happened to Snow White: she ate a poisoned apple given to her by an old peas-ant woman, then fell asleep until she got kissed by the prince. If I fall asleep, will Lancelot kiss me awake? And would that work, anyway, considering he's not a prince?

Or would Mordred have to be the one who kissed me? Gross.

Dior stops. I look around. We've come to a small clearing. The snow has disappeared. In fact, it's rather warm and humid here. I know I should be urging him back to the castle, but instead I end up sliding off my horse and looking around.

The trees that surround the clearing seem to close in on me, their branches extending into creepy animal claws. The sky darkens, and I hear strange music in the rustling of the wind.

The whole landscape seems to sparkle and fade in and out of focus. The only thing I can compare it all to is the time I took acid at this party back in college. Except that was really cool, and this is terrifying.

I'm so tired. Maybe I'll sit for a moment. Or lie down. I need to take a nap. And it's so warm here. The pine needles blanketing the ground are soft. What happened to the snow?

I close my eyes. My last thought before drifting to sleep is whether I'll ever wake up, and I feel wonder at the fact that I really don't care if I do.

Chapter Sixteen

I do wake up. Unfortunately I don't wake up where I fell asleep or back at the castle or some equally nonbad place. In fact, I have no idea where I am.

I sit up and quickly take note of my surroundings, ignoring the pounding headache beating a painful rhythm at the back of my brain. I'm on a straw cot in a small circular room. It looks a lot like my original room in Camelot—the tower—but it's not. I climb out of bed, realizing someone has changed me out of the doeskin leggings and fur cloak I'd worn out riding. I'd be pissed off at this, except they've replaced the clothing with a black silk gown. Finally, back in black! Oh, dark color, I've missed you so.

But enough about fashion. The big question is, Am I here because someone has rescued me or because I've been kidnapped? I walk over to the door and pull.

Locked. Guess that answers that question.

Oh, who's kidnapped me *now*? This sucks. I can't believe this is the third freaking time I've been held against my will. Being a chick in the Middle Ages sure isn't very safe. And this time there will be no Lancelot to rescue me, since he's off fighting the Saxons. Wonderful.

The door opens and a very large, rather familiar-looking woman walks in, shutting the door behind her. She must weigh about three hundred pounds, and is dressed entirely in black. On her head is a huge, gaudy tiara with tacky colored gemstones. It's like she's worried that someone might mistake her for a person other than a queen and is trying to overcompensate for something.

"Madam," I say, attempting to be polite, "where am I?"

She smiles—not the nice, kind smile that one would hope for, but more of a sickly, evil-looking smile. "The name of this place matters not. Only know this: you are my prisoner, and you will be sacrificed for your sins on the night of winter solstice."

"What?" I cry, horrified. "You've got to be kidding me!" She wants to *sacrifice* me? Like, literally? Did they even do that back then? And what the hell "sins" have I committed?

"Do not play innocent with me, Katherine du Lac. I know exactly what you did. I put a truth spell on Lamorak, and he told me everything."

"Who the hell is Lamorak?" I ask, then remember. Lamorak was the knight Lancelot sent to tell Queen Morgause that her husband was . . .

Uh-oh.

"You're Queen Morgause," I say, putting two and two together. I realize I should have remembered her from when she brought Mordred in to see Arthur. But that day I was more interested in checking out incest boy than his mother.

"Some call me that. Others use my faerie name, Morgan Le Fay." She laughs—make that an evil cackle.

Oh, this is not good. I'm in the captivity of Morgan Le Fay, über-bad witch in all the King Arthur stories. Worse, she seems to believe I killed her husband. Which techni-cally could be argued was a complete accident.

My heart is beating wildly with fear, but I try to play it cool. Maybe I can negotiate—talk her out of it.

"Look, I'm sorry about your husband's death. But it was a total accident. You can't go by what Lamorak says. He didn't even see it. He came by after Lot was already dead." She's not looking any more convinced, so I decide to try an-other tactic. "Besides," I say, "I don't know why you'd be all worked up over the incident. Really, I did you a favor. You should have heard what he was saying about you be-hind your back."

Morgause or Morgan or whatever it is she wants to be called narrows her eyes. "And what might that be?"

Ah, caught her interest. "Oh, he was saying all this stuff about how you were no good in bed anymore since you'd gotten, er . . ." Wait—am I going to insult her more by say-ing this? "Since you've, um . . ."

"Gotten fat as a pregnant pig?" Morgause/Morgan asks.

A bit relieved, I nod. "I don't think he used those words exactly."

"Lot was a tyrant of a king and a horrible husband," the witch admits. "In fact, truth be told, I loved him not. Still, he kept me in fine jewels and allowed me to run his kingdom while he was off raiding and raping. Without him I must re-linquish power to one of my sons—brats, loyal to Arthur, the lot of them. The independent kingdom of Orkney will now become nothing but another one of Arthur's provinces. So in my thinking, your actions are responsible for the de-mise of a kingdom. And therefore I believe you should pay."

"Don't you think Arthur will be a little pissed if he finds out you killed me?" I ask, trying to stay brave. "After all, I'm Lancelot's sister."

244

"He will not know what happened to you. Nor will anyone at Camelot. For all they know, you have been eaten by wolves."

Damn. She's right. *Dear God, Kat. How are you going to get yourself out of this one?*

This sucks the big one. I still can't believe that I'm freaking captured for the third time since I've been in Camelot. I mean, really, that seems a little excessive, don't you think? Of course, this time things are much, much worse, 'cause, like, no one has any idea where I am, and also there's that whole I'm-going-to-sacrifice-you-to-the-goddess thing, which is clearly bad.

Why, oh, why didn't I stay in the castle like a good medieval chick? Why did I once again have to prove that I am a liberated twenty-first-century woman? Why was I such an idiot that I thought eating food that came from a stranger would be a good thing to do? Stupid, Kat. Truly, truly stupid.

I miss Lance. I wonder what he'll think when he comes back from the peacekeeping to find out that I disappeared without a trace? Will he go out and look for me? By then it will be way too late. I'll be dead—sacrificed to some pagangoddess type. Will he mourn me? Find comfort in the arms of Guenevere? How long will it take him to get over me?

I toss and turn in bed night after night, unable to find comfort in sleep. When I do manage to shut my eyes for a few hours, I have fitful, longing dreams for Lance—being in his arms, having him whisper his love, only to be torn from his embrace with violent force. When I wake up I literally ache for him. It's such a weird, un-Kat-like feeling. Maybe it's because I'm pretty vulnerable right now—being this close to death and all.

I wonder if Lance is having the same kinds of thoughts and dreams as I am. When he's guarding Arthur from the Saxons, is he wishing he were back at Camelot, where he believes me to be? How much of his day is spent thinking about me?

I feel totally pathetic for wondering, but I can't help it. There's a lot of downtime being locked in a tower. In fact, I'm totally bored. There's absolutely nothing to do. I'm actually wishing I had some of that awful Camelot embroidery to work on. At this point having a needle and thread would rate right up there with going on a free Neiman Marcus shopping spree. I mean, I can be in fear of my life only so many hours of the day. The other twenty three and a half I'm going out of my mind with inactivity. After all, I'm from the MTV generation.

After one particularly long day, the door creaks open and Morgause/Morgan appears. She's dressed in yet another black outfit, but this one looks pretty formal. She wears a long black veil as well, obscuring her ugly face. Behind her are two beefy-looking guards.

"Tonight is the night of winter solstice," she announces. "When the old ones sacrificed a virgin to ensure a fruitful season." Her mouth is covered by the veil, but I can almost hear her evil grin. "This year you will be that sacrifice."

"Listen, Le Fay," I say, trying to keep the tremble out of my voice. "I gotta tell you, I'm not a virgin. In fact, I've had sex with, um"—I do a quick finger count—"nine different guys." Wow, that sounds like I'm a total slut. But I will gladly claim to be the whore of Babylon if it saves my skin.

"One so young as you has had that many lovers?" She sounds shocked.

"Hey! Look who's calling the kettle black," I say, a bit offended. "At least I don't sleep with family members."

"No matter," she says, quickly changing the subject. "I care not for the rigid rules of the old ones. Nor do I really believe the goddess will bless any crops. It is enough to see you die."

Shit. There goes that argument. I've got to get out of here—fast. I look around for a weapon and find only a cup of water left over from my lunch. I grab it and throw it at the witch in an irrational hope that the rules of Oz apply, and she'll suddenly start melting like the Wicked Witch of the West. Unfortunately for me, she gets wet but not a bit melty, and now looks even more pissed. Damn!

Morgause/Morgan gestures to the guards, who proceed to throw me down on the bed. I try to kick them, but one grabs my legs, effectively pinning me down like a mental patient in four-point restraints.

"Let me go!" I cry. What a waste of breath. Like they're going to say, "Oh, okay, since you asked so nicely, sure, we'll stop obeying our evil queen's commands and set you free." Not a chance.

They pull my hands behind me, and one ties a slipknot around my wrists. Then they do the same to my feet until I'm hog-tied. They lift me up and carry me out of the room.

I'm going to die.

Tears blind my vision as they lead me down the steps and outside the tower into the woods.

I'm going to be sacrificed.

The sound of druid chanting fills the air. We come to a clearing, and the guards lay me down on what appears to be some sort of sacrificial altar. I look around. Men dressed in black cloaks surround me, still chanting an evil-sounding chant.

I'll never see my family again. My Lancelot.

"Please," I cry. "I'll do anything. Just let me go." I have

Marianne Mancusi

no pride at this point and try begging for my life, knowing it's all pointless. I have zero bargaining power. Nothing they'd want.

I'm going to die.

I look up. Morgan stands above me, holding a long silver knife high above my head. The veil has fallen back from her face, and she stares down at me with evil eyes, chanting loudly in some foreign language.

Lancelot. My love.

I close my eyes. Funny, but I'd rather not watch as the knife comes crashing down, splitting my throat in two. I pray to God that death will come quickly, that if there is a heaven, I could go there instead of some druid-sacrifice hell. I can barely breathe, I'm so paralyzed with fear.

Please, God. Someone. Save me. Please. Please, plea—

"We are under attack!"

The chanting suddenly stops, replaced by cries of pain, cutting into the night. I open my eyes, straining my neck to see what's going on from my prostrate position. Men in black cloaks run frantically about, and I see them fall one by one, screaming in agony.

My heart thuds in my chest. Am I being rescued? By whom?

"No! He will not save you," Morgan cries, raising the knife. But before she can bring it down, thus ending my life, she screams and falls forward, landing on top of me. I'm crushed by her three hundred-pound frame.

Bleh!

I squirm around, trying to get her off me. Blood—her blood—splashes onto my gown and face. It's like a scene from *Friday the 13th*. Totally gross. But, of course, much better than if it were, say, my blood.

Suddenly the witch's lifeless body is pushed aside, and I'm swept up in strong arms—arms I'd know anywhere.

"Lancelot!" I cry.

The helmeted knight looks down at me for a moment, nods, then mounts his warhorse, still holding me like a baby in his arms. He urges the horse forward, and together we gallop into the night. Behind us I hear the druids screaming, but the horse easily outgallops their chase on foot.

After about ten minutes of high-speed horse riding, the knight slows his steed with a low-voiced command. The horse comes to a stop, and the knight slides off, pulling me down with him. He places me gently onto the ground and removes his helmet. I cry in joy to see the familiar black hair tumble from his helmet. Lancelot. I knew it was him! He pulls out a knife from his boots and cuts my bindings. As soon as I'm free I fall into his outstretched arms, rejoicing in everything that is him: his hot breath against my cheek, his musky scent, his solid chest.

"Oh, Lancelot," I sob, unable to hold back the tears. "I thought I was going to die. They were going to kill me. She knew I killed her husband, Lot, and she said—"

"Hush, my darling," Lancelot whispers, his words tickling my earlobe. "She is dead. And you are safe."

"How did you find me?" I ask, pulling away to meet his beautiful eyes. I see that he too is crying. I reach up to brush a tear from his stubbled cheek. "I thought you were negotiating with the Saxons."

"Aye," he says softly, running a hand through my hair. His touch gives me the chills. It's been too long since I felt him. And I honestly thought I never would again. " 'Twas a strange course of events that brought me to you." He leans in to kiss me on the cheek. "We were camped out on a hill-top, waiting for negotiations to begin. Things were uneasy, and Arthur had told us to stand guard; the Saxons could reject our treaty of peace and attack at any moment. I drew last watch and they bade me sleep till 'twas time to take my post. I went to my pavilion, thinking of nothing but how I missed you. How I longed to touch you again. To hear your sweet voice in mine ear. To-ride and talk and make love."

I sigh contently. He did miss me. How could I have doubted it?

"I fell asleep soon after, thoughts of you still occupying my mind. That is when the nightmares began to take hold. Ugly visions of you, collapsing on the forest floor. You, locked in a tower. You, sacrificed on that altar." He shudders as he remembers. "Then I opened my eyes and saw Nimue standing before me, as clear as you are here now. I knew not if I still dreamed or had awakened.

"She told me you were in grave danger and that if I loved you, I must go to the Forest Perilous immediately, or I should never see you living again." He swallows hard. "I woke soon after and did not know what to do. 'Twas coming on the time of my watch. And the next day I was to stand by Arthur's side as he conducted the negotiations. I was at a loss, truly. Should I disobey the king, my liege, for a vision? What if 'twas nothing but an ill dream, brought on by foul rations?"

"You chose me," I whisper in wonderment. The workaholic, the one who insists the king comes first, obviously decided to abandon his lord and come rescue me—even though he wasn't even positive that I needed any rescuing. I'm touched. No, that's too small a word for what I feel. I'm honored. Even that does not describe the depth of my feelings.

"I chose you," he agrees, leaning forward to kiss me softly on the lips. "I will always choose you."

If this were a movie, this is where the music would swell. This is the "You had me from hello" in *Jerry McGuire*. The "We'll always have Paris" in *Casablanca*, and a thousand other cheesy movie one-liners that always make me burst into tears over the power of love that, until this moment, I thought existed only in Hollywood's imagination. But now, as I feel like my heart has grown three sizes (like the Grinch after he heard all the Whos down in Whoville singing that annoying Christmas song even though they didn't get any presents), I realize that true love really does exist. And that I feel it for Lancelot.

"I love you, Lancelot," I murmur.

I'm saying it first. I never say it first. It's too much of a risk of getting hurt. I would normally rather die than have a guy stammer and stutter after I open up my heart. But now I can't help it. I think if I didn't say it, my new big heart would have literally burst.

He pulls me close, burying his face in my neck. "Kat, my darling. I am truly honored to hear those words. I have waited so long to say them myself. I was afraid you would think me rash to declare my feelings for someone I knew not long. But I am deeply and utterly in love with you. I cannot even remember how I once lived an empty, lonely life before you came into it, and dare not think of a future without you by my side."

He loves me! He loves me! I want to dance and sing and spout poetry, I'm so excited. Instead I kiss him. Long. Hard. Passionately. Wanting to eat him alive. He loves me. He truly, truly loves me. He risked everything to save me.

The thought sobers me for a moment, and I pull away from our kiss. "Will you be in trouble?" I ask, a little worried. "Is Arthur going to be all pissed at you for abandoning him?"

He frowns. "I should think so. My act was one of treason. But the king is a kind, just man. When he hears that I acted only to protect my sister, I see not how he could fault me for my actions."

251

"You've got a point. And I'll back you up."

"However, I must tell you, my love—even were it that I am stripped of my very knighthood, 'twould have been worth it to save the life of my true love."

"Your true love. I like the sound of that." I grin and kiss him again. Arthur and his knights will have to wait. Lance and I have some catching up to do first.

Chapter Seventeen

After dropping me back off at Camelot with a stern warning never to leave the castle by myself again—as if I hadn't already learned my lesson from kidnapping-and-near-death-experience number two—Lancelot prepares to head back to Listinoise in case the peace talks are not going well. But before he can even change clothes, a courier arrives to the palace with a message for Guenevere.

"The king sends his love, my queen," the courier says, reading from his scroll. "And says he was able to ratify a new treaty of peace without any violent negotiations."

"Praise be to the goddess," Guenevere exclaims. She's been acting all tough, in control, and queenly, but I know in her heart she's extremely relieved to hear that her husband's out of harm's way.

Since the army is on their way back, Lancelot decides to stay in Camelot. He's a bit distracted, but I'm sure it's only due to the fact that he knows he's going to get ripped a new one when the king returns.

To keep his mind off of it, I decide to sew together some leather strips and create a crude-looking soccer ball. After all, I know for a fact that sports cheer guys up from just about anything. (Well, except when their team loses, and they end up walking around like big babies for weeks on end, moaning about the stupid, biased umpire.)

"We'll make this end my goal," I say, pointing to the space between two crumbling Roman statues in the courtyard. "And that can be yours. When you get your ball through those posts, you get a point. Whoever has the most points wins."

Lancelot nods, grabs the ball from off the ground, and runs through the goal. "Point?" he asks.

I sigh. "No, no, no! I forgot to mention you can't use your hands. Just your feet. And we really need a goalie—someone to block the goal." I look around and see Gareth, the youngest of the Orkney knights, and the only one not sent to Listinoise. I explain the concept, and he eagerly takes his place at my goal. Lancelot, in the meantime, recruits his own squire to stand guard in his end.

As we start playing, more and more knights, squires, young women, and children ask to join. Soon we have a whole team, an audience of older men and women, and a pretty good game going. Everyone's really into it, too—cheering and jeering at all the right moments.

Hey, I've just invented team sports! They should name something after me. Maybe the courtyard could be the Kat Courtyard. But then again, I'm sure it would be only a matter of time before it gets sponsored, and they totally sell out and change Kat Courtyard to Bob the Blacksmith Courtyard or something equally inane. Not worth it.

As I'm daydreaming about courtyard naming, Lancelot puts a David Beckham–worthy cross past me and right to his teammate, who proceeds to slam the ball into the back of our net. (Well, what we're pretending is a net, anyway.) The two cheer their victory, and Lancelot sticks his tongue out at me. He's having fun and not torturing himself over abandoning Arthur. That's good.

Already winded from running around (after three months of being stuck in a castle and a tower, I've lost most of my cardio ability), I switch places with an eager teen who wants a turn at what is fast becoming the coolest thing in Camelot since sliced bread. If they were to actually have sliced bread, that is.

I guess I shouldn't be surprised. After all, they *are* from England, future home of the soccer (or as they call it, football) obsessed. Maybe if I started a league, the bored knights will get out all their aggression on the field and not be so war hungry. Then Mordred would have no leverage in gaining the knights' loyalty to him over Arthur.

I have another ulterior motive, too: to aid my British friend Aaron back home, who literally cried the day Brazil knocked England out of the 2002 World Cup. With my help they should do better next time around. After all, I'm giving them nearly a thousand years' head start.

I consider teaching them baseball, but I decide it's not worth bothering. In fact, it'd be a complete waste of time, considering that when America has a World Series it forgets to invite the rest of the world.

Suddenly the trumpets blow, succeeding in ending what might otherwise have been an endless game, since I kind of forgot to introduce time limits.

"The king returns!" announces the trumpeter. "He is within sight."

Cheers erupt from the soccer players. They rush off to their chambers, preparing to dress in their best clothes for court. Lancelot's happy sports face crumples into a mask of sorrow mixed with fear.

"Lance," I say, laying a hand on his arm. "Everything's going to be fine. We're talking Arthur here. He loves you like a brother. He's totally going to understand that you did what you had to do."

"Aye," he says, not looking a bit convinced. "He may understand. But what of Mordred? I must inform the lad that I have slain his mother. He will want blood payment for the crime. He may challenge me."

"He won't." I snort. "He's too much of a coward to fight you man-to-man. He's all into his designer tunics and big talk. I've never seen him pick up a sword in his life. And if he is idiot enough to try it, you'll whip his fancy little ass in no time."

"But he is the king's son," moans Lancelot. "I cannot kill him. Or maim him even."

"Look, Lance, you're beating yourself up over something that hasn't even happened," I say, sliding easily into self-help mode. "That kind of unhealthy, negative thinking can lead to major stress and even physical health problems." Wow, I sound pretty smart. I should write a book when I get back to the twenty-first century.

He looks at me, eyebrows raised. "Ah, well, you should know, always worrying about a relationship developing between the queen and me."

I blush. "Yeah, well, that's different. I'm from the future. I know you and Guen are supposed to have a thing. I mean, I hope you never do, but, well, all the storybooks say—"

He takes my hand in his and pulls it to his lips, pressing down in a fervent kiss. The sudden gesture sends a thrill down my spine and makes me completely lose my train of thought.

"I do want you to know," he says earnestly, meeting my eyes, "that whatever happens, I do not regret my actions. I would save you all over again if I had the need to. I love you, Kat."

"And all you need is love," I say back, plagiarizing the Beatles for lack of other witty, romantic repartee.

I can only hope I'm right.

"His crime is treason against my father, King Arthur, high king of Britain. He deserves to be banished from Camelot."

I'm surprised to hear quite a few court attendees murmur their agreement at Mordred's brash statement. The young prince's popularity in Camelot is increasing, and he's evidently set on using that power to get rid of the knights who remain loyal to his father. Knights like Lancelot. And Lance's leaving Arthur's side to rescue me gives Mordred the perfect excuse to try to oust him.

I bite my lower lip. This is not going well. Lancelot has stood before the court and explained his actions. He has begged pardon of the king. Now Arthur has opened up the floor to hear opinions on how he should rule. It's his attempt at democracy—my idea. Now I wish I had never brought up the concept of giving everyone a voice, because then we wouldn't have to hear Mordred's whiny one.

"He saved my life," I butt in from my position on the sidelines. Damn it, if everyone gets a voice, then that means I do, too. "I'm his sister. You think he should have stood around and let his own sister die?"

"If 'twere for the good of Camelot, aye." Mordred says, sitting back down on his throne. "What is one life when the kingdom is at stake?"

"Puh-leeze!" I roll my eyes. "The kingdom was *so* not at stake. You guys had, like, five hundred soldiers there."

Mordred frowns. He knows I've got him. He turns to Arthur on his left. "Who let this woman into court?" he demands. " 'Tis a forum for men only. Why is she not with the others, making preparations for winter? If she had kept to her place to begin with, we would not even be here, debating this."

"Yeah, well, if you're going to go there, how about the fact that if your *mama* hadn't been an evil, vindictive witch who liked to sacrifice innocent girls, I never would have needed rescuing in the first place," I say, stepping forward to stand beside my "brother," Lance.

Mordred's mouth drops open in shock. Oh, shit. I suddenly remember Lancelot hadn't exactly mentioned who my kidnapper was yet. My big mouth strikes again.

"His mother?" Arthur questions. "You mean to tell the court that the druid who deemed fit to sacrifice you to the goddess was Queen Morgause, my sister?"

"Yeah. Morgause, Morgan Le Fay, Evil Woman Who Tried to Kill Me, whatever name she's going by now," I say, trying to sound casual. I had kind of forgotten the witch was Arthur's half sister. "She's—"

"You killed her," Mordred interrupts, staring at Lancelot with icy dagger eyes. "You killed my mother."

"She was attempting to kill my sister at the time," Lancelot says, firmly meeting Mordred's eyes with his own. "By her actions, she chose her destiny. I did only what I had to do to save the life of my dearest kin."

I actually think I see steam coming out of Mordred's ears, making him look kind of like Wile E. Coyote. I feel a tiny bit bad for him. After all, losing one's mother has got to suck big-time. But what else was Lance going to do? Try to talk her out of it?

"I challenge you, Sir Lancelot," Mordred says suddenly, rising from his throne. "I demand blood justice for my mother's murder. Name your time and place and bring your favorite sword."

Lancelot groans, shaking his head in protest. "Do not do this, Mordred. I do not want to kill you."

"I should like to see you try."

"Mordred, you know I am the best knight in the land, and you are untrained with a sword," Lancelot tries to reason with him.

"You are so sure of yourself, du Lac?"

Arthur breaks in. "Silence!" he commands.

Everyone shuts up immediately.

"I have seen enough blood spilled already to last a lifetime," Arthur says in a hard but calm voice. "I have united Britain. I have ratified treaties with the Saxons. I will not let civil unrest between my knights and my kin tear apart all I have built up."

It's times like these that you know why Arthur's the king. Why, I bet if the guy had been king instead of King Solomon back in biblical times, he could have totally come up with that whole cut-the-baby-in-half thing on his own. I can see why Guen's so taken with him. He's strong, commanding, but fair and kind at the same time. A total winning combo.

"Mordred," Arthur continues. "My son. I am so sorry for your mother's loss. She was my kin as well. I promise she will be given a proper burial, and we will well honor her and the kingdom of Orkney. But please withdraw your challenge against Sir Lancelot. I cannot afford to lose either of you. There will be tough times ahead, and we need to be united, not divided."

Mordred frowns, but I think he knows he got off easy. He's proven his point and isn't stuck fighting the best knight in the land. "Very well, my king," he says, bowing stiffly. "For your sake, I withdraw the challenge."

"And Lancelot," Arthur says, "while you had noble intentions, leaving your post without reporting first to me is ill-advised at best. Did you think I would not have let you go if you had asked to take your leave? On the contrary, I would have offered you a small army to protect your sister. I only hope next time you will trust your king's judgment."

Lancelot hangs his head in shame. "Yes, my lord."

"Your actions cannot go unpunished. However, I think banishment too harsh a penance to pay for saving one's sister," Arthur continues. "Besides, as I said before, I need you in my service. Therefore, I command that you make monetary reparation to the kingdom of Orkney, which has now lost its queen. I also ask that you withdraw your application for this year's jousting tournament. Finally, I command you spend three nights fasting with Bishop Mallory on your knees by the altar of Christ, praying that he forgive you for your sins against God and king."

I see Lancelot sigh in visible relief. I'm sure he's not psyched to do the whole Christian-confession thing, him being a goddess worshiper and all, but it could have been a lot worse.

"Yes, my lord," he says to Arthur, bowing low. "I thank you for your fair discipline. And I vow to you 'twill never happen again while I am in your service."

Arthur smiles down at him. You can tell what good friends they are. Of course, so can Mordred, and he looks pissed at the very light sentence. As court breaks for dinner, I see the prince huddling around several of the other knights, including his Orkney half brothers Gawain and Agravaine. All three are whispering furiously.

"There is trouble ahead for Camelot," Lancelot says in my ear as he watches them alongside me. "Arthur should keep a close watch on his son."

I can't help but agree, and wish I had paid more attention in school, so I'd know just what this specific trouble entails.

Chapter Eighteen

Spring is beautiful in Camelot. The birds chirp. The flowers bloom. Everything is green and unspoiled and wonderful. And everyone's in a great mood, too, relieved to be out and about after being cooped up all winter.

On his days off from training, Lancelot and I spend long, lazy hours away from the castle, riding to a remote spot, picnicking by a lively babbling brook, making love on a large woven blanket. Heaven. I almost forget at times that I ever lived anywhere else.

On one especially warm day, I get the idea to lie outside and try to get a tan. I'm not normally a tanner—it's so unhealthy for your skin and all—but I figure in medieval times the ozone layer must still be pretty darn thick, since aerosol has yet to be invented, and so the skin-cancer risk should be way down. Also, this way, when I get back to NYC I won't need to stock up on any bronzing lotion, and everyone will be jealous, thinking I've been to Bermuda or somewhere else tropical.

Of course, tanning in a gown is pretty useless, so I grab a needle and thread and sew myself a two-piece, using material from an old dress. It's tough to design without a pattern or elastic, but I manage to come up with a cute little design. It's probably not seaworthy, but for tanning it'll do.

I find a vacant tower top, once used as a lookout when the country was at war, and spread out a wool blanket. I lie down, wishing I had sunglasses. But right as I close my eyes and prepare to bake, I hear a startled voice cry my name. I sit up. Guenevere is standing above me, hands on her hips and a horrified expression on her face.

"Kat? What on earth are you doing?"

"Tanning." I brush a hand over my arm. "I don't want to be this white."

She scrunches her face in confusion. "You mean to say you desire to become as brown as a peasant woman?"

"I don't know about the peasants." I shrug, sitting up. "But where I'm from, tanned is considered sexy, attractive, though somewhat deadly. But then, there's always a heavy price to pay for beauty."

Guenevere shudders. "Here, white skin is prized above all. In fact"—she lowers her voice—"there have been times when I have gone so far as to bleach my skin to ensure 'tis white as the winter snow. But please keep that knowledge to yourself. The queen should be naturally pale as the moonlight and need no enhancement."

"Yeah, you're probably better off with the whole white look," I agree. "Besides the whole cancer thing, the sun also causes wrinkles." Not that these people live long enough to get any. The average dying age in medieval times, I was horrified to hear, is, like, forty-something. I mean, people can still have babies when they're forty in my time. They don't even qualify for the senior discount at Denny's for at least fifteen more years. I, at the young age of twenty-nine, could almost be considered over-the-hill. (Yes, I'm still twenty-nine, even though my birthday has theoretically passed. I don't think I have to count it, since technically I haven't even been born yet.)

"However, I was not asking about your skin, but rather your gown. Or," she corrects, "your lack of it."

I laugh. "It's called a bathing suit."

"Bathing suit?" she questions. "Something to wear when you bathe?"

"Well, no. We still bathe naked, like you guys do. It's actually for when you swim, like in a river or the ocean. Or to lie out in, since you get more sun exposure without being all covered up."

"You would go in front of others in this bathe suit? It barely covers your . . ." Guenevere gestures to her private parts, her eyes wide.

"That's what makes it sexy."

Guenevere raises an eyebrow. "Do men like these bathe suits, then?" She's interested now. Probably thinking of Arthur—turning Arthur on with skimpy outfits, to be precise. I did mention that thanks to me they're majorly in love with each other, right? I'm talking Romeo-and-Juliet-level love, without the whole messy suicide part.

"Hell, yeah, men like bathing suits. In fact, in my time there's a whole TV show dedicated to them. They call it *Baywatch.*"

"TV? What is—"

Why do I bother? "Never mind. It's not important." Well, actually it is. In fact, I'd rank the television right up there with the most important inventions of all time. But it'd be way too hard to explain electronics to someone like Guen. I'll stick to bathing suits.

"So where did you get this suit to bathe?" Guenevere crouches down to her knees to examine the fabric.

"I made it."

She looks impressed. "I am sorry, Kat. If I had known

you were such a good seamstress, I would have not stuck you in the kitchen during the preparations for winter."

"No biggie. But yeah, I was a fashion major in college. We needed to make our own clothes. I'm quite handy with a needle and thread, actually."

"Will you make me a bathe suit?"

"I thought you didn't want to get your skin all brown?"

She blushes. "I mean, so I can wear it for Arthur," she says in a hushed voice.

"Ooh!" I throw her a knowing grin. "So we are no longer going shyly to the marriage bed, I take it?"

Her blush deepens at my implication. "I am learning to love like a woman," she admits. "And Kat, I must admit, I have never known such rapture could be attained by mere mortals."

"Glad to hear it," I say. "But I don't think you're looking for a bathing suit if your goal is to seduce Arthur."

"Am I not? Do you have another idea, then?"

"Do I?" I scramble to my feet. "You'd better believe it. I'm a fashion editor, remember? Okay, maybe you have no idea what that is, but I'll show you." I nod my head eagerly, thinking about what I can do. "It's makeover time, Guen. When I'm through with you, you'll be the very first fashionista in King Arthur's court."

Several hours of a nontelevised *Fashion Emergency* episode later, the queen emerges from her bedroom, looking rather sheepish and red-faced in her saucy new threads.

I whistle in appreciation. "You go, girl!"

"Go where?" she asks, all wide eyes and innocence. I laugh.

"Go directly to Milan. Paris. New York City. Do not pass Go, do not collect two hundred dollars. Wow, Guen. You could so be a model. Look at you!"

I size her up. She's successfully hidden a stunning pair of legs under her gowns this whole time. Her long torso compliments the ultra-low-rise skirt I've sewn. It hangs perfectly from her lean hips, showing off her flat stomach. (How'd she get that nice muscle tone without an Ab Roller?) And I'm a bit jealous of how her breasts fill out the corseted D & G top I let her borrow in a way mine never could. Back in good old Connecticut I thought I'd looked good wearing that top at the King Arthur's Faire, but Guen was stunning.

It's funny how much clothes define people and their time period. Looking at Guen now, you'd never know she's a medieval queen. She could be an NYU student in Central Park. A surfer babe at Malibu Beach. Actually, with her long, white-blond hair and tummy-baring outfit, she kind of looks like a petite Paris Hilton.

"What is a model?" the queen asks curiously as she skips over to me, playfully kicking out her feet. Evidently she's enjoying the freedom bare legs can give a girl. I only wish I had some panty hose for her.

"In my time we have women whose whole job is to wear clothes," I explain.

"But why?"

"To show them off so other people will buy them."

"Oh. I see. What a lovely job." She grins. "And where do they do this wearing of clothes? In the main hall of the castle?"

"No one lives in castles anymore, Guen. Well, the royal family of England does, I suppose, but I doubt they have models hanging around, strutting their stuff. Well, that is, unless Prince William's in town . . ." I'm getting off track. "In any case, usually they model clothing at special shows. And there's, like, a long stage—what they call a runway." I jump up to demonstrate. "And the women walk down the runway like this." I stick out my chin and sway my hips, doing my best catwalk impression. "And everyone sits on each side and claps."

"What fun!" Guenevere falls in behind me, trying to swing her hips like me. She's giggling so much she trips. "Sorry," she apologizes as she falls into me and nearly knocks me over. "I am not used to the shoes." She looks down at the two-sizes-too-big Manolos strapped on her dainty little feet. "Though they are quite lovely, I must say. I only wish I could own a pair. Perhaps several. Are they made in different colors? I should like one of each."

Ah. The first designer-shoe addict. Eat your heart out, Carrie Bradshaw.

"Stand up straight. Don't giggle," I order. "Models are serious. They don't smile; they pout. Like this." I stick out my lower lip, narrow my eyes, and glare. Guen attempts to mimic my serious face but can't stop laughing.

"Maybe you're not model material after all," I tease, shaking my head in mock dismay.

"No, no! I can do it. Wait." She dons a serious expression and starts walking again, sashaying her hips from side to side.

I clap my hands. "Now you've got it! Yeah, baby. 'You're too sexy for this crown, too sexy for this crown,'" I sing, paraphrasing the Right Said Fred song. "'Too sexy to, um, frown.'" Yeah. Not bad for a rhyme on the fly.

She turns back to me, her eyes wide. "What on earth do you sing about?"

"'I'm a model, you know what I mean, and I do my little turn on the catwalk,'" I croon, on a roll.

Guen puts her hands over her ears. "'Tis not music!"

"'I know,'" I sing, switching tunes, "'it's only rock and roll, but I like it.'"

"Stop, stop!" she begs, shoving a hand over my mouth to stop my murderous rendition of the Stones.

"'I wike it, wike it,'" I sing on, muffled by her hand. "'Es I dooo.'"

I stop. Guenevere lifts her hand away, shaking her head in amusement. "You are too funny, Kat. Thank you for the clothes. I love them. The things from your world are so wonderful. I only wish I could see the place for myself. It sounds heavenly."

Her words spark instant melancholy. *It sounds heavenly.* And it is, isn't it? All this time I've been getting used to the Middle Ages, I've forgotten all the stuff I'm missing out on. No matter how nice everyone is here, truth be told, I still prefer the rudeness of New Yorkers. No matter how good I get at horseback riding, I miss driving sixty-five miles an hour. (Okay, maybe eighty-five at times . . .) I can get used to roast pigeon, but I prefer filet mignon. Mmm. Filet mignon. Especially from Houston's. Mmm.

I miss my life. My home. My mother, my little sister, my brothers, my dog. I miss my magazine even—each shallow, fluff-filled page. I miss the bitchy models and my even bitchier editor. I miss telling the public that pink is the new brown, boots are the new flip-flops.

I want to go home.

Guenevere catches my frown and puts a comforting arm around my shoulder. "Soon," she says, all giggles gone. "You will be home soon. Summer solstice is but one moon away."

I look up in surprise. "One month? That's it?"

"Aye."

Suddenly my sadness magnifies as I realize what I'll be leaving behind. While I may be able to do without horse-back riding and roast pigeon, I am devastated to think of never seeing Lancelot again.

"You are thinking of Lancelot, are you not?" Guen asks gently.

"Yeah. I'm that obvious, huh?"

"'Tis a shame that you have found true love, only to have to abandon it so soon," she says, stating the obvious. "Maybe you should stay."

"Believe me, I've thought of that," I say. "Many, many times. I imagine Lancelot and me growing old together here at Camelot. At the same time, I can't pretend I don't miss my world. I miss my life. I don't belong here." I sigh. "The decision is totally giving me an ulcer."

"Maybe Lancelot will come back with you?"

I look over at her in surprise. "Do you think that's possible? I mean, if he wanted to, is it physically possible?"

"I do not know, Kat. But I would ask Merlin. Perhaps he could devise a way."

"Yes. That's it. It's perfect," I say, excited. "Then we'd never have to part." And Nimue and Merlin would never have to worry about Guenevere and Lancelot getting together. "He'll love the twenty-first century. I know he will."

A lingering doubt gnaws at my insides. Will Lancelot really love the future? What will the twenty-first century hold for a man whose talents consist of fighting with swords via horseback? He's a superhero here in Camelot. Will he be a laughingstock back in NYC? And if so, can I really justify asking him to come back with me? Will he be miserable? But we love each other. Isn't that enough? Can't we build a life together? A fulfilling twenty-first-century life?

"Kat, you look troubled."

"I just don't know." I shake my head. "I don't know what to do."

"You cannot make the decision for him," Guenevere reminds me. "Talk to him. Discuss your feelings. Open up and explore the possibilities." Now she's spouting the psychobabble back at me. I taught her too well.

"I will. Thanks, Guen."

"Now, please excuse me while I change clothes for court. Arthur has ridden to London for more peace talks. 'Tis up to me to rule over tonight's dinner."

"You're not going dressed like that?" I tease.

She shakes her head. "This outfit is for the king's eyes only."

"Oh, boy. He's in for a surprise when he gets back from peacekeeping. I'm sure he'll love it."

"I do hope so." She smiles. "Kat, you have done so much for me. How can I ever repay your kindness?"

"Don't worry about it," I assure her.

"No. I do worry. If not for you, I know not where I would be right now."

I do. She'd be fornicating with Lancelot. I must admit she does owe me one, and she doesn't even know the half of it. Because of me she's three for three: happy, in love, and won't get burned at the stake.

"Seriously, I'm glad to help."

"I want to give you a gift," she says earnestly. "To thank you." She rummages around her chambers until she finds a long purple gauzy sort of fabric. "'Tis my most special veil," she says in a reverent whisper, holding it out to me.

"Guen, I can't take your veil. You love this veil. You wear it all the time. It's your favorite," I protest, refusing to take it from her outstretched arms.

"Are your shoes not precious to you? And yet you gave them to me without a second thought," she insists. She's wrong about that. I had second, third, and fourth thoughts about giving up my Manolos. But I finally decided I'd just raid the freebie closet at *La Style* for another pair when I got back.

"But isn't there some rule that only queens can wear purple?"

"Ha!" Guenevere snorts. "You are the last person I would expect to care about rules." She stands on her toes to lay the veil over my head. It falls down over my face, gauzy and light. "It looks beautiful on you. You simply must keep it, or I shall be dreadfully offended."

"Fine. You win."

"Ooh," Guen says excitedly. "You have to wear it when you go visit Lancelot tonight! For they say the veil was spun using magic threads by the fey folk who made it. The woman who wears it will be irresistible to her true love."

"Guen, darling, when are you going to learn that I already *am* irresistible?" I joke, lifting the veil and folding it over my head so I can see better. "But thanks. I'm sure it'll knock his socks off."

"And his tunic as well?" Guenevere asks, her eyes sparkling.

I laugh appreciatively. "Yeah, baby. I'm sure he'll be completely unable to keep a stitch of clothing on when he sees me in this sexy veil."

But, I think as I thank Guenevere and walk down the hall to my room, it's not whether I can seduce him out of his clothes that I'm worried about now.

It's whether I can convince him to come back to the future with me.

Chapter Nineteen

I lie in my bed, pretending to sleep, waiting for my midnight rendezvous with Lance. I ponder over how I'm going to phrase the whole your-time-or-mine conversation. The more I think about it, the more I convince myself that he's *got* to come back with me.

I mean, look, I've finally met the guy of my dreams. Someone loyal, strong, sweet, giving, loving. I could go on and on. And call me shallow, but I dig a guy who, even after almost nine months, makes my heart go pitter-patter like a schoolgirl's. No guy I've dated has ever come close. He is the complete package. Michelangelo's David, sculpted in flesh. So what if he's from another millennium? Obviously destiny (i.e., Nimue and Merlin) brought us together. So why does that mean that once we're finished changing history we have to break up?

I slam my head into my pillow, trying to get comfortable. I don't want to break up. I know he doesn't either. So why let a little thing like a millennium keep us apart? And since I've already spent quality time in the Middle Ages, isn't it only natural that it's his turn to come visit my little world?

Besides, *he* has to admit that the twenty-first century is a tad bit cooler than medieval England. It's got stuff like Krispy Kreme doughnuts, IKEA, and IMAX movie theaters for a start. Sure, it may take some getting used to. He'll have to learn slang, figure out how to type, and come to terms with the fact that the world is round. But hey, I got used to roast pigeon. (It really does taste a lot like chicken, by the way.)

Yes, I determine, Lancelot will like modern-day America, if only he agrees to give it a chance. Now I've just got to convince him to do so. But he loves me. And if that's true, he'll do anything possible to make sure we don't spend even a minute apart, won't he?

I think it's about midnight—they have no clocks, of course, so I'm stuck estimating. I slip out from under the fur covers and pull back the curtains of my canopied bed. All is quiet. Nosy Elen is sound asleep and snoring in the next room. Good. I tiptoe across the floor, slipping into my shoes and grabbing Guen's veil. She says it makes the wearer irresistible, and I'm going to have to turn on the charm big-time to convince Lance to pack up and move.

I open the door, cursing the squeak and remembering another great, formerly unappreciated invention: WD-40. I peer out into the hallway. No one. I slip the veil over my head. At least this way if I run into anyone, they'll think I'm the queen and won't ask questions.

I've got a long walk. The knights live clear across the castle from the ladies and the queen. I guess it's supposed to make sure everyone behaves themselves, but it's a pain in the ass when you're trying not to.

I reach Lancelot's door and knock lightly. Footsteps approach and his also-WD-40-less door creaks open. I smile underneath the veil; he's shirtless, and I have to resist the urge to reach out right then and there and run my fingers down his perfect chest. I can tell he fell asleep; he has major bed head and his eyes have that half-sleepy look I love.

But instead of smiling at me, his eyes widen. "Oh, I am sorry. I am sorry. I . . . You woke . . . I mean . . ."

Huh? We were scheduled to meet up. Why the surprise?

"Are you hurt? In need? What brings you to my chambers at this hour? Is it the king? Is he unwell?" Clear and utter panic crosses his face.

I suddenly realize he thinks I'm Guenevere 'cause of the veil. Too funny. I'm half tempted to keep up the charade. At least his fluster assures me he certainly has no intimate relations with her majesty. Not that I doubted the guy. Well, at least, not anymore.

"It's me, silly!" I say, throwing back the veil.

His jaw drops. "I thought . . ." He shakes his head. "That veil . . ."

"Yeah. Guen let me borrow it. Sorry—didn't mean to scare you like that." I step inside, and he shuts the door behind me. "Still, you'd think you'd recognize that I wasn't her. I mean, I'm a good three or so inches taller, for one thing."

He draws me into his arms, silencing my rebuke with a hard, passionate kiss that takes my breath away. He's always doing things like this. And I, the sucker, usually give in immediately, succumbing to the pleasure and forgetting what I was about to say.

But today I have other things on the agenda. I pull away, walk over to the bed, and sit. I look down at my hands. They're shaking. Why am I so nervous all of a sudden?

He joins me at the bedside. "What is it?" he asks, perhaps sensing my unease. He strokes my knee with a warm hand, and I nearly give in to the seduction once again.

Focus, Kat. This is important.

"I need to ask you something, Lance," I say, placing my

hand over his to stop the stroking. This, of course, invites him to instead intertwine my fingers with his, his thumb lightly grazing my palm. The shivers start again.

"Anything, my love." He squeezes my hand. I stare at the floor, feeling his questioning eyes on me, but I can't look up. One look into his eyes and I'll lose it. Discussion first and, if all goes well, making love afterward. Man, I can't wait till the afterward part.

What if he says no? Then there can't be any afterward, can there?

I shove the negative thought from my head and clear my throat. He won't say no. He loves me. He's pledged his loyalty. He already nearly lost his job and got banished from Camelot for me.

"Summer solstice is only like a month—er . . . moon—away," I remark casually, still staring at the ground.

"Aye." Out of the corner of my eye I can see his nod. "Do not think I have not thought of it. Especially on nights when I have been away from you. Wasted nights that could have been spent in your arms."

Aw. He's so romantic. Maybe once we're back in the twenty-first century he could hold motivational seminars for guys who don't know how to talk to women. I can see the Learning Annex catalog advertisement now: *Chivalry 101. Taught by ex–knight in shining armor Lancelot du Lac.*

His hand lets go of mine, and his fingers trail up my forearm. I close my eyes, enjoying the sensation. I wonder if he'd be interested in taking a class on tantric sex when we get back. I always wanted to try it, and I bet he'd be amazing.

"I don't want to lose you," I say, opening my eyes and turning to look at him. Our gazes connect, and I once again marvel over the pure sapphire of his eyes. Forget motivational speeches; he could so be a male model. I could introduce him to some agents. Chas Lowery would love him. We could feature him in *La Style* or maybe our brother magazine, *MenX*. That is, if I want to share him. Maybe instead I'll lock him in a closet and keep him all to myself. I grin wickedly at the thought.

His hand has now reached my shoulder, and he plays with strands of my hair. "What?" he asks, of course not understanding my smile.

"I love you." Simple, open, honest. Yet I could never have said those words that way before I met him.

He smiles back at me. "No more than I love you; I am sure of it. You are sunshine and rainbows to me. How can I ever let you go?"

"Then do you think . . ." I draw in a breath, hope bubbling through my stomach like so many clichéd butterflies. "I mean, if it were possible . . ."

"Aye." He reaches out to catch a tear I didn't notice falling from my eye. My desire for this to work out consumes me, and his ready agreement to change his whole life for little old me makes me a little emotional. "I would like nothing more than to spend the rest of my life with you."

"Really?" I'm thrilled. This was so much easier than I thought. He doesn't even need a lick of convincing! He's practically packed for the trip. Oh, what was I so worried about? Of course he'd want to come with me. He loves me. I love him. We're destined to be together. He's not going to let a little thing like time travel stand in the way. "Oh, Lance," I bubble, "this is wonderful. I'm so glad you feel this way. I'll talk to Merlin in the morning and make sure it's all possible. Oh, I'm so happy. I was afraid—"

He silences me with another one of those breath-stealing kisses, and this time I don't resist. I throw my arms around his neck with wild abandon, pushing him back on the bed. After reaching down to hike up my gown, I straddle his thighs and continue to ravage him with kisses.

I'm so happy I could sing from the rafters. He's going to come back with me! I'm going to get to show him all the wonders of the twenty-first century. He'll love it.

I sit up, too excited to kiss and not talk. "I'll buy you all new clothes," I say. "I bet you'd look stunning in Armani. And you'll get to meet Gucci, my Lab. Of course, you'll want to get a job eventually. Maybe you could be, like, a bouncer at a nightclub or something. Use all that physical prowess of yours. Though I have no idea how I'm going to wrestle up a Social Security card for you. But if the illegal immigrants can get fake ones, I don't see why you can't. Or maybe they'll pay you under the table."

His eyes darken, and a shadow of confusion flickers over his face. "Slow down, Katherine," he says, sitting up. "I have no idea as to what you are going on about."

"Sorry." I grin, dotting his nose with a kiss. "I guess I'm getting carried away, blabbing on and on. It's just that I'm so psyched. I mean, it's not every day that a guy agrees to change millennia for you."

"Kat—"

"Guess that's how we know it's love, though, right? Love sweet love. You know, I always used to swear I'd never fall in love. Too much risk, I guess. Like, you give so much of yourself to one person and then if they let you down—which they so often do—you've left yourself vulnerable and hurt. But our relationship is different. I mean, you're willing to leave everything behind to be with me. I love that."

"Kat, I didn't—"

I put a finger to his mouth to silence him. "Wait. I'm not finished. I want to tell you everything that I feel before I lose my nerve. I'm in love with you, and for once I'm not scared to admit it. I know you won't hurt me. Sure, it'll be tough at first, living in a new time period, but we'll make it work. Because with you by my side I feel invincible. To paraphrase the great Sonny and Cher, 'they say our love won't pay the rent'—or mortgage actually. I've got a condo—but 'I've got you, babe.' " I lean over and plant a great big kiss on his lips. It's actually tough to purse my lips, as I'm grinning ear-to-ear.

"Kat! Listen to me!" he cries, pushing me away. I stare at him in surprise. He stares back, his eyes wild. What's wrong with him?

I bite my lower lip. "What?"

"I think you must be confused over my words. I cannot go back to the twenty-first century with you."

Bastard! Fucking bastard!

I grab Guen's veil and throw it over my head as I storm toward the door. Lancelot calls out to me, but I ignore him. There's absolutely nothing more to say to the loser. I slam the door behind me, no longer caring who hears.

I can't believe I ever let myself trust him. Allowed myself to fall in love. This is why—precisely why—I don't get into serious relationships. Guys suck. They're selfish. They think only of themselves. Bastard!

I can't believe he thought the entire time that *I* was saying that *I* would stay in Camelot. That I was asking if he wanted to get freaking married, not come back with me! Why the hell would I want to stay in Camelot? The place is a freaking shithole without flush toilets. Here I am offering him the travel opportunity of the millennium, and he wants to stay here out of some ridiculous displaced loyalty to the stupid king.

" 'The king needs me,' " I mimic under my breath. Utterly pathetic. Like the king doesn't have a billion other knights in shining armor knocking down the castle doors. Why, he'd be able to hire a replacement immediately. Wouldn't even need to send out for a temp. And besides, Lance would be giving way more than two weeks' notice.

"Oh!"

Lost in my anger and hurt, I'm not looking where I'm going, and I slam straight into a person walking in the other direction. I look up. Oh, great, it's flaming straight boy Mordred. Just what I need.

Maybe Mordred should come back to the future with me instead. He'd probably appreciate the opportunity to try something new and not be so pigheadedly stuck in his ways. Maybe it'd even help him come to terms with the closet he's in. I know plenty of guys who would love to help him find his way out of it.

"Your Majesty, I am sorry." I raise my eyebrows in surprise as he steps back and bows stiffly. "I was remiss in looking where I was going."

It suddenly dawns on me: the veil. He thinks I'm Guenevere. Thank goodness. Now I can duck out of here and escape hearing him bitch at me about my murderous brother or my failure to act like a proper lady in court.

I nod at him, not wanting to give myself away by speaking, and walk by. I know it's rude, but I'll have Guen apologize tomorrow or something. Right now I need to get out of here. Get back to my room before I burst into tears.

I feel his stare burning a hole in my back as I continue down the hall. Thank goodness for this veil. I seriously could not have dealt with him right now.

I turn my thoughts away from the prince and back to Lancelot's lame-ass excuses. I mean, I was so sure he'd say yes that I'd been mentally picking out china patterns for our wedding in the Hamptons. But I was wrong. This is what I get for trusting a guy.

I arrive at my room and swing open the door, throwing myself onto my bed. So unfair. Where does he get off expecting *me* to stay here? Tears run like rivers down my cheeks, and my nose gets all stuffed up and runny. I hate crying. It makes my eyes look puffy and gross, and I don't have any cucumbers to put over them to bring down the swelling. But I can't help it. It hurts so much to know that the guy I am so in love with doesn't want to spend his life with me. I knew it was too good to be true. I should have let him fall in love with Guenevere. Not that she deserves his shit either. She's got Arthur. I bet *he'd* give up his entire kingdom if she asked.

I ache. I literally ache inside. I feel like vomiting. I try to control myself, rein it all in, but I can't, knowing that soon I will never talk to him again, never make love to him or laugh with him. I must separate myself from him for the rest of my Camelot prison sentence. Keep a distance. There's no way I'm letting him have his cake and eat it too. If he's not willing to sacrifice for me, I'm not willing to share myself with him.

And soon I'll be gone for good. Then I'll never see him again. Ever. It's not like twenty-first-century breakups, where I might run into him at Starbucks. I can't spy on what he's up to by Googling his name.

Because when I get back to the twenty-first century, Lancelot will be dead. Long, long dead before I am ever born.

I wake up the next morning feeling like I've run a marathon. In a way I have—a sleep-deprivation one, anyway. All night I tossed and turned, thinking about Lancelot and his refusal to go back with me. And when I finally did get a minute or two of sleep, wouldn't you know I was completely haunted by bad dreams. In my dreams, unlike in reality, Lancelot had come to the future with me. Which would be a good thing if he didn't insist on wearing a pink tutu around Manhattan. The shrinks would have a field day with my brain.

I get dressed and walk down to Guenevere's room. I'm sure she'll be more than willing to let me bitch about my guy troubles. After all, I listened and gave her good advice when it came to her and Arthur. She's actually become quite the friend here in Camelot. I'll definitely miss her when I'm gone.

Ina escorts me inside and then disappears into the next room. I find the queen sitting alone at a large table, hands cupping her chin, looking glum. She misses Arthur; I can tell. I wonder when he's coming back from London.

I plop down beside her and toss the veil in her direction. "Here. You can have it back. The 'irresistible' thing didn't work for me. Maybe you have to be a queen or something."

She looks up. "Things did not go well with Lancelot, I take it?"

"They couldn't have gone worse." I give her the short version of his rejection.

"I am so sorry, Kat," Guenevere says with a long sigh. "That must have been terribly heartbreaking to endure. Perhaps he is scared and is retreating into his cave."

"Yeah, yeah." I love it when she spouts back my psychobabble. "What's wrong with you?" I ask, deciding to change the subject.

"I do not know," she says. "But something bad is brewing inside the castle walls this morn. Since I have awoken, I have been given the strangest stares. I walked in on Gawain and Agravaine whispering amongst themselves. They stopped talking the second they saw me. Their faces looked guilty. I wonder what game is afoot?"

"Who knows?" I say with a shrug. "They're probably plotting their jousting strategies. The tournament's in a couple weeks, right? I wouldn't worry too much about it."

"You are right, I am sure. It was just . . . odd." She sighs. "I will be happy when Arthur is back from London. Camelot is not the same without him."

I smile. "You really love him, don't you?"

"Aye." She glances over at me with shining eyes. "More than anything."

I shake my head. "You're so lucky. Your relationship is, like, way simple compared to Lance and me."

"You once said you had thought of staying here. What of that?" Guenevere asks.

I nod reluctantly. "Of course I've thought about it. But I don't know. I have a life there. A family. A dog. I can't abandon them all. And there is so much stuff I'd be missing out on, too. The twenty-first century has a lot of amazing stuff you guys can't even imagine."

"Perhaps Lancelot feels the same way."

"You'd think, but no, he's perfectly content to stay in the dark ages."

"No," Guenevere corrects me. "What I mean is that perhaps he feels attached to his own time, the same as you are to yours."

Her words hit me like a ton of bricks. She's totally right. Even though I, who have experienced both worlds, think going to the twenty-first century is a moving-on-up situation, Lancelot has no idea if it's better or worse than the world he lives in now—the world he loves. He has a job. Friends. A life. All the things I refuse to give up for him. Who am I to dictate that he lose everything simply because I miss shoe shopping and French manicures?

"Oh, Guen," I moan. "What am I going to do?"

* * *

I leave Guenevere and head down the hallway, thinking I'll take a walk or something, try to clear my head. I step out into the courtyard, squinting in the sunlight. Summer is definitely on its way, and so is my scheduled trip back to the twenty-first century. But now I'm more sad than excited.

What should I do? Should I consider staying? But then that means I'm surrendering who I am and where I belong. Either way, if we want to stay together, one of us will have to make the ultimate sacrifice.

I always swore I'd never again succumb to the long-distance-relationship trap after the time I hooked up with this guy from California. Now it's funny—plane tickets and massive phone bills seem inconsequential compared to my current dilemma. A geographical long-distance relationship would be a hell of a lot easier to put up with than a time-differential one.

As I walk toward the castle gates, I come upon two of the Orkney knights—the big, beefy Gawain and the sniveling Agravaine—whispering furiously. Hmm, Guen was right. Something *is* foul in Camelot.

Sensing the potential for good gossip, I sidle up to the knights and clear my throat to make my presence known. After all, while they may shy away from informing the queen of dirty doings in her kingdom, surely they won't mind enlightening Lance's very charming visiting sister.

"Good morn to you, Lady Kat," Gawain says, bowing respectfully. His brother Agravaine simply sneers. He doesn't like me much, namely because of the kick in the balls I gave him on my first day in Camelot. I've apologized for that, like, ten thousand times, but King Lot's son seems determined to hold a grudge. Plus, he's all friends with Mordred and stuff now, which doesn't help matters.

"Good morning, Gawain." I smile pleasantly. Gawain,

on the other hand, is like a big, gentle giant. A fierce teddy bear—all brawn, no brains, and loyal to Arthur to a fault. With Lot and Morgause dead, he could have left Camelot to become king of the Orkneys, but chose to stay here in service to Arthur. "How are you enjoying the Round Table?"

"It's a wonderful thing," Gawain gushes, nodding his head. "The idea that no knight can sit at the head. Bloody marvelous."

"Yes. It helps keep certain knights from putting on airs," Agravaine growls under his breath, while staring at the ground. Did I mention he doesn't like Lancelot either?

"Oh, really? Was someone doing that?" I ask, all wide-eyed and innocent, even though I know exactly whom he's referring to. Jerk.

"Oh, don't listen to my brother," Gawain says, slapping Agravaine on the back. The knight scowls and steps away. "He's jealous of your brother's prowess at arms."

Agravaine looks even more pissed at this. He narrows his eyes and glares at Gawain. " 'Tis his boasting that sours me, not his skill."

"Yeah, yeah," I say amicably. "Well, you know how Lancelot is." As a gossip queen, I've learned it pays not to get angry and instead make them think you're on their side. Then they open up to you more and you can get the whole story.

"I thought I did," Agravaine mutters.

"I'm sorry, what?" I'm getting close to the good stuff; I can feel it.

"We thought we knew your brother," Gawain butts in. "The only knight who would not take a lady to his bed. Pure as the driven snow."

The other knights, I had learned, were not so honorable as Lance when it came to damsel rescuing. He might have the whole celibacy thing going on before he met me, but from what I've heard, most knights would screw anything in a skirt, whether Arthur approved of it or not.

"Yeah, he's an honorable one, that's for sure." *Though not so virginal as you might imagine,* I think as I try to visualize their shock if they saw Lance and me together.

"Ah, then you do not know your brother as well as you think," Agravaine replies, a twisted smile distorting his hideous, battle-scarred face.

"I don't?" I put on an innocent expression. Here it is— the big gossip of the day. What the hell is it going to be? They obviously haven't figured out Lance and I are a couple, since they're not treating me oddly. So what then?

"Well, you see, it turns out the great Lancelot du Lac is not so honorable after all," Agravaine says, rubbing his palms together in glee. He's really enjoying this. "In fact, it turns out he is a traitor to Camelot."

I raise my eyebrows, beginning to get a little worried. Are they still talking about the whole abandoning-Arthur thing? He did his punishment. How about we move on? Unless there's something else?

"A traitor? How so?" I ask.

Gawain frowns. "Brother, maybe we shouldn't—"

But I can tell Agravaine's determined to finish telling whatever sordid tale he has up his sleeve. "Late last night the crown prince Mordred caught Queen Guenevere leaving Lancelot's bedroom. The two of them are lovers."

"What? But it was—"

I gasp as I remember the veil. Seeing Mordred. Pretending to be the queen so he wouldn't talk to me.

Oh, shit.

Chapter Twenty

I had to say something. Correct their mistaken identity. Oh, why hadn't I opened my mouth when I saw Mordred in the hall? Now I've screwed everything up, just because I didn't want him to yell at me. Stupid, Kat. Truly stupid.

I have to make things right. To come clean.

"That wasn't Guenevere," I say, trying to sound casual. They're never going to believe this. No way in hell. "That was me."

Both knights stare at me as if I've lost my mind.

" 'Tis noble of you to try to protect your brother and your friend," Gawain says gently. "But Mordred has made no mistake. He saw the queen with his own two eyes and has sworn to it on his mother's grave."

"Well, sure, I know he *thought* it was the queen," I argue. "Because I pretended to be her. And I was wearing her veil."

"The queen gave you her veil?" Agravine looks suspicious.

"Yes. It was a gift."

"Show us."

"Well . . ." Damn it. "I actually gave it back to her this morning."

They exchange bemused glances. "Do you expect us to believe Queen Guenevere gifted her royal veil to you? That you then walked around the castle late at night pretending to be her and paid a visit to your brother?" demands Agravaine. "Only to give her back the veil the next morn?"

"Well, um, yes!" Though I have to admit it sounds pretty far-fetched when he puts it that way.

Gawain raises an eyebrow. "But why?"

Should I tell them? What would they do to me if they knew I've been lying to them all along? That I'm not Lance's sister, but actually his lover? Could Lance get in trouble for lying to the king? Even so, isn't it better to get in a little trouble now than let fester a rumor that has the potential to lead to the downfall of Camelot?

I can't make the decision on my own. I don't have all the info. For all I know, lying about one's brother could get one burned at the stake. Especially if they think that I am a spy, and Lancelot has been aiding me the whole time. As much as I want to save Camelot, I'm so not dying for the place. Plus, I don't want to get Lance in trouble again. Mordred would probably take the opportunity to further his Lancelot-should-be-banished campaign.

"Well, fine. You don't have to believe me," I say, putting on a hurt expression. "Believe that sniveling inbred moron instead, for all I care."

"The problem, you see," says Agravaine with a sneer, "is that Mordred has no reason to lie. You, on the other hand, have a brother and friend to protect."

Touché. "I know how it must look," I protest. "But trust me, it isn't true. Guenevere is madly in love with Arthur and is dying for him to come back from London. She's got no interest in Lancelot whatsoever."

"If you say it, lady," Agravaine says with a patronizing smile, "it must be so."

Oh, forget it! There's no convincing these guys. I give Agravaine a dirty look and stomp back into the castle, trying to still the adrenaline pumping through my veins.

This is bad. Really bad. I mean, what good is it for Guen and Lance never to fall in love if everyone believes they have? Same result without the orgasms: end of Camelot.

Nimue's going to be so pissed when she hears of this. I can't say I blame her. What had I been thinking, pretending to be the queen? Of course, I hadn't known Mordred actually saw me leave Lancelot's room. . . . Still, all the rationalizing in the world doesn't make a difference now. The rumors have begun.

I wonder if this means I have to go back and do this all over again, like in *Star Trek, Buffy the Vampire Slayer, Stargate SG-1,* and every other TV series' requisite stuck-in-a-time-loop episode. Will I remember that I've done it before? Come to think of it, maybe I already have and just don't remember. Maybe this is my billionth time of looping, and I've still messed it up.

The thought makes me want to throw up. I don't want to do this over and over again. I want to go home and live a normal life. I want to drink mojitos on South Beach. Go on safari in Africa. Seek wisdom in Tibet. Hell, I even want to visit Stonehenge—but in a touristy drive-there-and-hit-the-pub-for-a-pint-of-Guinness-afterward kind of way. There's so much in the twenty-first century that I have never gotten to experience, and I'm dying to go back to do so.

There's only one thing I can do now: come clean to Lancelot. He'll know what to do. These are his people. Maybe he'll say, "Oh, sure, Kat, let's tell them about us. It's no big deal. We'll sort everything out."

Somehow I doubt it will be that easy.

If only I hadn't left things such a total mess between us. Why, oh, why did I storm out of his room last night? I could have stayed, talked it through. Listened to his side of the story. Then not only would I not be worried about telling him the rumor right now, but there would be no rumor to tell, since Mordred wouldn't have seen me and mistaken me for Guenevere.

After vowing never to let my explosive temper get the better of me again, I swallow my pride and head for Lancelot's chambers. My heart pounds as I knock on the door. Will he welcome me in? I wouldn't blame him if he didn't, after the temper tantrum I threw last night. In the light of day it all seems so petty and immature. Why couldn't I have had a normal conversation with him? A debate, if you will, on the pros and cons of each millennium? But no, I had to storm out the second he told me he couldn't abandon his life at Camelot, even though my doing so proved I felt the same way about my life.

Mature, Kat. Real mature.

The door creaks open. Lancelot's fully dressed, but his droopy, red eyes tell me he hasn't had much sleep.

"Kat." His voice is tired, drained, sad.

"Hi, Lance." I smile at him, my heart breaking. I love him so much, I can't bear to be angry at him. Oh, please let him forgive me for my stupid temper! "Can I come in and talk to you for a minute?"

He nods and ushers me in, closing the door behind me. He turns. "I—"

"I'm so—" I start at the same time. We both stop. Our eyes meet. A millisecond later I'm in his arms, letting his strength support me both physically and mentally. I nestle my face in his chest, enjoying the rigid contours of his muscles.

"I'm sorry," I murmur. "I'm so, so sorry." My tears soak his tunic, and he runs a hand through my hair.

"No more than I," he whispers.

"I was selfish to expect you to give up everything to come back with me."

"I have stayed up half the night thinking on your words," he says, leading me over to the bed. We sit on the edge, and I look into his sapphire eyes, only to realize he's fighting tears of his own. "I love you, Kat. I cannot bear to live without you. I have made my decision. I will leave Camelot. If 'tis possible, I will come back with you."

"No," I cry. "I'm the selfish one. You've got, like, this whole life here, and I just expected you to drop everything to come with me."

"What is my life without you? 'Tis better if I die than spend one moment out of your arms."

Does he mean that? Could there really be a person in the world who feels so strongly about me? It seems impossible, like what he's saying is some romantic bullshit. But somehow, as I study his earnest face and feel his hands squeezing mine a little too tightly, somehow I believe him.

"I've never met anyone like you," I whisper, trying not to choke on my sobs. Why couldn't he have been born in my world, or I in his? That way we'd have no regrets. Now, no matter what time we decide to stay in, the other person might start longing for their own world.

"I don't want you to have to give up everything for me," I insist.

"Do you still not understand?" he scolds. "You *are* my everything."

His words, his gaze, cause my heart to flip-flop like a fish out of water. I have to remember to breathe. With a desperate roughness he pulls me into his arms, claiming my lips with his own. It's not his typical soft, slow kiss—this time his mouth is hungry, demanding, wild. Parting my lips, I allow his tongue full penetration, matching its thrusts with my own.

His hands fumble with my dress, yanking down the front to expose a bare breast. I gasp as he cups it in his hand, running his calloused fingers over the tip, his touch sparking a tremendous ache between my legs.

He lowers me down onto the bed, his mouth no longer content to let his fingers have all the fun. I moan and dig my fingers into his tousled black hair, dragging my nails along his scalp. Dying to end the ache, I try to wrap my legs around his waist, but he pushes me away, unwilling to satisfy me so soon. His hand reaches under my dress and finds my inner thigh, caressing it, higher and higher until he's stroking the aching part. I squirm against him. He knows exactly how to touch me to make me want to scream. Not too rough, not too gentle. If he could market his skill, he'd make a fortune. Not that I'd want him to. I'd rather keep it all for myself, thank you very much.

"Oh, Lance," I moan as his tongue glides over my nipple. "I want you inside me."

He lifts his head, his eyes dark with lust. He unties the sash around my waist and lifts the dress over my head. Then he quickly loses his own clothes and climbs on top of me.

There's something nice about flesh against flesh. Especially rock-hard, muscled flesh like Lancelot's. My body melts into his, and I stifle a cry as he enters me, as we become one. I want to scream from the rooftops as he rocks against me, thrusting deeper and deeper. But I must stay quiet. Someone could overhear.

I want to prolong the ecstasy, but my body has other plans, exploding almost immediately and rocking my world. I still can't believe how effortlessly he makes me come. Other guys have tried everything, to no avail. I usually end up faking it to make them feel better. But no more. Now, having experienced the Ritz of orgasms, I'm never going to settle for Motel 6 again.

He comes with me, another thing I've rarely seen guys be able to do. I can see him biting down on his lower lip as he stifles a groan of pleasure. Then he collapses on top of me, his breath labored and erratic in my ear. I reach around and hold him, squeezing my arms, never wanting to let him go.

"I love you," I whisper.

He lifts his head to look into my eyes. His gaze is full of wonder, awe. Do I really have that effect on him? He reaches to brush a wayward strand of hair from my face.

"As I you," he says with a small smile. "Though the word *love* seems a feeble understatement. If I knew a stronger one to describe my feelings for you, I would surely use it."

I giggle. Man, I love chivalrous speeches like that. "We could invent one," I suggest coyly. "A brand-new word that's stronger than *love.*"

He nods solemnly. "How about"—he squints his eyes and scratches his chin—"abba? As in, I abba you."

I shake my head, laughing. "No, no! ABBA's, like, this terrible seventies disco band. I am *so* not going to be your dancing queen."

He smiles uncertainly, by now used to me babbling about things he doesn't have a clue about. "Well, then how about . . . bubba?"

I shake my head. "Former intern-screwing-president or a big ol' Southern man. Try again."

"Rubba?"

I groan. "New England–accented word for *condom.*"

He groans in mock exasperation. "You pick then." He grins. "For your world seems more cluttered with words than mine."

I laugh appreciatively, putting a finger to my temple, trying to think. "How about . . . lubba? Yeah. That's it. From now on *lubba* means the feeling that's greater than mere love."

He smiles, kissing me softly on the forehead. "Well, then, I lubba you. More than anything on this earth."

I laugh. He laughs. I feel warm and safe. I never want to leave his arms. Screw the twenty-first century. Screw lattes and fashion week and 7-Eleven. Screw TV and elevators and DVDs. None of the material things I remember are worth leaving what I have here.

"I'll stay." I can't believe I'm saying this, but I mean it. "I'll stay in Camelot. I can't leave you."

"No."

I furrow my brows. "No?"

"No. I have given this a lot of thought. I will come back with you."

"But—"

"No buts." He rolls off me and onto his back, staring at the ceiling. "You have already lived in my world. It is my turn now to see yours."

I scarcely dare to breathe. Is he serious? Or is this one of those reverse-psychology things where I'm supposed to argue that I really think we should stay here? Then again, reverse psychology has yet to be invented, so he must be for real. He wants to come back with me. Oh, happy day!

"Are you sure?" I ask, praying that he is. "I don't want you doing something you'll regret, just for me. I mean, once we get there there's most likely no going back."

"I'm sure. Very sure." He props himself on his side, hand cradling his head. "I want to live out my days with you by my side. Besides, you have said in your world that people can live a hundred summers. That will give me many more days to spend making you happy."

Very true. Though I'm not quite sure the damage to his

body hasn't already been done—lack of nutrition and inoculations and all. But I don't think I'd better spoil this by mentioning the pesky details.

"What about the king?"

"He has other knights. And I fear that soon his son, Mordred, will be the one leading the Knights of the Round Table. Do you think the prince would allow me to remain in his service once he becomes king?"

Mordred. Oh, shit, I almost forgot. I rise from the bed, grabbing my dress. "Listen, Lance, we've got other problems." I relate what I heard from Gawain and Agravaine.

He shakes his head. "Silly gossip. Nothing to concern ourselves with."

"I think it is." I frown and pull the dress over my head. "What if it got back to Arthur? They could try you for treason. You know Mordred's completely out to get you after the Morgause incident."

"Arthur would not believe idle tales over the word of his first knight and lady queen."

"Maybe we should come clean," I suggest. "We could tell everyone that we aren't really brother and sister, but boyfriend and girlfriend. Or we could say we're married."

Lancelot looks aghast. At first I think it's 'cause I mentioned the dreaded M-word, feared by men everywhere, but then I realize he's more worried about the idea of letting his boss in on our relationship.

"To admit we have been lying to the king for months? You cannot be serious." He shakes his head. "What you heard is merely careless talk that will evaporate in a day. 'Tis not worth the trouble admitting our lie would cause. The truth would only give Mordred a chance to declare you a spy and me a traitor. And for that we could be not only banished, but executed."

"I'm not sure what's worse, Lance," I say, not ready to

give in. This is too important. "After all, remember what I've told you: in my future, everyone thinks you and Guen were lovers. Maybe this is how it all starts. Maybe the legends are due to a case of mistaken identity. If this turns out how I think it might, it could lead to the destruction of Camelot. And that," I conclude, "is bigger than just admitting a lie that didn't hurt anyone to begin with."

Lancelot stares at the wall, evidently lost in thought. "I do not know," he says as last. "Perhaps we should wait and see if the rumor spreads. A few loose tongues do not the end of a kingdom make. I will stay clear of the queen for the next moon, and there will be no new stories to feed the fire. Thus, 'twill die out."

"I know, but . . ." I pace the floor, trying to quell the nervous ache in my stomach. What he's saying makes sense, but at the same time, knowing how the legends are supposed to play out, it still makes me nervous.

"Besides," Lancelot adds, "they have no proof to their claim. For a case of treason to be substantiated, they must catch us in the act. Which," he says with a grin, "certainly will never happen."

He's got a point there. According to the legends, the knights catch him and Guen in bed together. They don't burn Guen on account of a rumor. Maybe I'm overreacting.

Then again, maybe I'm not.

The next month goes by quickly. Lancelot and I spend many hours discussing our future together. I inform him of everything a man needs to know about twenty-first-century life: what he'll wear, how he'll talk, what he'll eat. I teach him about never wearing navy blue with black, the importance of shaving regularly, and how to make a perfect dirty martini. When I get through with him he'll be a regular metrosexual. *Queer Eye* Fab Five, eat your hearts out.

I also talk to Merlin and ask him if it's possible for Lance to come back with me. He says yes—once the portal has been opened, anyone can step through. In fact, the old magician is more than thrilled at the idea of Lancelot taking off with me. This way, he says, there'll be absolutely no chance the queen and her knight could ever get together once I'm gone. I think about mentioning the rumor I heard, but since it seems to have died down, I figure it's not worth it.

I tell Guenevere that Lance is coming back with me, and she's totally psyched, though a little sad for herself, being left behind and all. She will miss me, she says. I have become her best friend. I ditto that. If she wasn't all in love with Arthur, I'd suggest she come back too. She'd adore the twenty-first century; I know she would. But she'd never leave her true love; that's for sure.

Not that Arthur's been spending much time at the castle lately. His dealings with the lords and other kings over how to keep the precarious Saxon peace are taking up a lot of his time. He's hardly ever home, and I know Guen misses him dreadfully.

Of course, there's now a proxy king in place at Camelot. Whether officially sanctioned or not, Mordred has stepped up to the plate and embraced his role as heir to Arthur's often-vacated throne. He talks a good game—of action, battles, and blood. In reality, the dude's probably never picked up a sword in his life, but his ideas ignite a fire under the knights' feet, and they become restless. Fighting breaks out frequently between those still loyal to Arthur and Mordred's growing regiment.

Guenevere is especially worried at Mordred's popularity. She obviously has no interest in seeing her husband's throne usurped, and has sent messages to London on several occasions to try to convince Arthur to return and reclaim his kingdom. But when Arthur does return for short periods of time, he laughs at Guenevere's worries and insists his son is simply exerting the power of his birthright and has every right to do so. In fact, I think he's kind of proud of the prince. I guess it's a dad thing. Or maybe one where love is blind. Oh, well, what do I care? I'm leaving soon anyway. I'm simply looking out for Guen.

Three nights before summer solstice, I find myself in Lancelot's chambers. Our last night in the castle. Lance, Guen, and I have decided to leave for Stonehenge a couple of days early so she can practice her spell casting. She's extremely nervous about messing it up, which, of course, puts me on edge, too. I don't want to have it fizzle, and end up stuck in Camelot for another year.

"Are you excited, my darling?" Lancelot asks, pulling me into his arms. We've just made love, and I'm feeling warm and fuzzy all over.

"You don't know the half of it," I purr. "Just think, the next time we go at it, we'll be in the twenty-first century."

"Aye," he whispers, dragging a finger down my bare shoulder. "And I am sure you will feel as delicious."

I roll over to face him. "Do you have any regrets?"

He shakes his head, and I see his eyes are clear, with no worry or doubt clouding their brilliant blue. "Nay," he says, leaning over to give me a soft kiss on the lips. "In fact, I'm greatly looking forward to it—to spending the rest of my life with you."

"Ditto." I sigh contently. "This has worked out perfectly. I only wish I had a chance to thank Nimue personally."

"Nimue?" Lancelot's eyebrows shoot up in surprise. I gulp. Oops. I forgot for a moment he doesn't know Nimue and Merlin's plot. Major duh. "Why would you thank her?"

"Er, um . . ." *Shit, Kat, think!* "I would thank her for, um, saving my life when I was ill."

Lancelot frowns, sitting up in bed, and taking my hand.

"You are a terrible liar, Kat. What is it you are not telling me?"

"Nothing. Really." I pull my hand away and stare at the ground. What am I supposed to say? That I was brought back in time to make sure he stays away from Guenevere? I can't tell him that now! He'll totally freak.

"Kat . . ." His voice sounds a stern warning. "What are you keeping from me?"

"Keeping from you?" I ask, laughing nervously. "I would never keep anything from you."

"Woman, I am leaving my whole world for you. It is not fair for you to keep a secret from me."

"I know." I sigh, resolving to tell him the truth. He deserves to know. Besides, he's usually very understanding. In fact, I don't know why I'm even nervous about it. "Um, well, it turns out I didn't travel back in time randomly. Evidently I was sent for by Nimue and Merlin."

Lancelot's eyes widen. "What? What ever for?"

Okay, here goes. "For you. They say I'm the only one you would fall in love with."

"And they would care about my love life why?" he asks in a tight voice. Uh-oh. The hands-balling-into-fists thing he's got going on is not looking good in terms of his easy acceptance. But it's too late to turn back now.

"So you wouldn't fall in love with Guenevere and thus start the roller-coaster downfall of Camelot and the rise of Christianity." I try to make it all sound very casual.

"You knew of this?" Lancelot says in a loud and very angry voice. "So that means you seduced me on purpose in order to help them in their political gain?" Lancelot rises from the bed and grabs his tunic, throwing it over his head. This is not going well—at all.

"No!" I cry. "That's not how it was!" I get up from the bed and try to pull him back. "Sit. Let's talk about this," I beg.

He shrugs my hand away. "When did they tell you this?" he demands, grabbing me by both shoulders. "How long have you known of their plan?"

I know I should be lying through my teeth at this point—like, say I found out yesterday. But stupidly, the truth spills from my lips. Blame it on love, I guess, but something inside me insists he deserves to know everything. "When I was sick. At Avalon. Nimue told me."

"So all these moons you have been deceiving me?" Lancelot says in a furious tone, dropping his hands. "By the goddess, this all makes perfect sense. Your jealousy and suspicion of the queen and me. Your following us to Camelot Cottage and accusing me of lying with her. Your insistent attempts to save the marriage of Guenevere and Arthur. Your begging me to come back to the twenty-first century." He slams his fist against the wall, actually cracking the stone with the force of the gesture. "What did Nimue promise you in exchange?"

I bow my head. I'm a loser. A total loser. "She said she would send me back to the twenty-first century." My heart aches as I see his face turn white with rage. The man I love more than anything now thinks I hooked up with him only to secure my one-way ticket back to Connecticut.

"Of course. You would sacrifice anything to get back to your precious twenty-first century." He paces the room, his steps eating up the distance between walls. "What would you have done when I got to your world, Kat? Deserted me? Left me to fend for myself in a foreign land?"

"Lance, it wasn't like that!" I cry, desperate to explain. I grab his hand, try to still his pacing, but he shrugs away. "I fell in love with you. It was never a lie. It was a total coincidence that Nimue asked me to seduce the one man I already wanted. And besides, it's for the best. If you and Guen got together, history says you'd be caught by the other knights.

And Guen would be tried for treason and burned at the stake. You would be cast out of Camelot forever. This is a much better scenario."

"Rather you should have murdered me in my sleep," he growls. "Then I would not have gotten together with the queen as well, and 'twould have spared me this agony."

"Please try to understand. I didn't manipulate you. I realize I should have told you, but I didn't know how. I was worried that you'd act like you are acting now. And I thought that, since I really do love you, it didn't make any difference in the end."

"It makes a great difference. How can I ever trust you now?" He turns and stares at me, and I ache to see the hurt and confusion in his eyes. "I would have gladly given you my life, Katherine. Instead you have torn out my heart while I still live."

Tears blur my vision as my mind races for a way to explain, to make him see that he's taking it all wrong. How can I convince him that I love him so much? That the times we have spent together have been the best of my life?

"Lance . . ." I try, not knowing what I'm going to say. "Please try to—"

Suddenly there's a knock on the door. We both stare at it.

"That will be the queen," Lance says in a low voice. "Dress yourself. And if you have any love for her in your heart, do not tell her what you have told me. I would spare her that pain."

"But—"

"If you keep silent I will continue to offer you my protection by accompanying you to Stonehenge. If you speak out I will leave you to fend for yourself."

Well, that's something, I guess. That'll give me a couple more days to convince him I'm telling the truth about my feelings for him.

And besides, he's right. I can't let Guen in on the whole thing so she starts hating me, too. I throw the dress over my head and allow him to open the door to let the queen in.

"Greetings! I have came down to see if you are ready to leave for Stonehenge," Guenevere says, stepping into the room, completely oblivious to what has transpired. "Ina arranged for the horses. Everything is in order."

"Actually we're not quite ready," I say, hoping to stall her. I have to talk to Lancelot—to make him see that I really do love him, that I need him and can't live without him. "Can you come back in, like, an hour?"

"What, so you can crawl back into bed?" Guenevere scolds, hands on her narrow hips. "You will have plenty of time for that when you reach your new life."

Oh, if only she were right. But the look on Lancelot's face tells me that as far as he's concerned, he'd rather share his bed with a cockroach.

"Go now, and get your things," Guenevere commands. "We will wait here. But hurry. I have slipped the outer guards a sleeping draft, and I do not know for how long 'twill work."

I look at her and then at Lance. He turns his head, refusing to meet my eyes. What am I supposed to do? I swallow hard. It'll have to wait until we get to Stonehenge. I still have three days, I remind myself. Plenty of time.

"Okay. I'll be back in, like, five minutes."

I rush back to my chambers and grab my purse. Then, remembering my cell phone, I run to the other end of the castle to Merlin's tower to retrieve it from the old magician. After all, I'll need it if I have to call for a cab when we get back. Who knows how much time will have passed? The fair may be gone, my car towed. Luckily the old magician willingly gives it up this time and wishes me good luck.

"You have done well, Kat," Merlin says, actually smiling. "Nimue was right to have chosen you to save Camelot."

If only you knew, I think as I smile back and thank him before heading back down to Lancelot's room. I've now screwed up everything. In fact, if I don't make things right, for all I know once I'm gone Lance and Guen will turn to each other for comfort. And then this whole year will have all been wasted.

No. I can't think like that. I have to have confidence that I can convince Lancelot that the whole Nimue thing doesn't matter a hill of beans. That I would have fallen in love with him anyway. That he is my soul mate, my true love. That no one else fills the void in my life like him. I feel a tear slip down my cheek. It really hurts to know that right now he thinks I've completely betrayed him.

What's that up ahead? Flickering lights? Is someone shouting? I squint, trying to make it out. I definitely need to visit the eye doctor when I get back to the twenty-first century. Is someone up and about? I don't want to run into anyone, like last time. Especially not creepy-king-in-training Mordred. At least I'm not wearing that stupid veil. I tiptoe down the hall to keep my presence unknown as I scope out the situation.

I turn the corner, and my eyes widen as I realize the hallway is alive with torchlight, flames casting dancing shadows on the otherwise darkened walls.

Guards. Shouting. Screams. Swords drawn. Chaos everywhere.

I see a porter rushing by. "What's going on?" I demand, grabbing his sleeve.

"Treason," he answers, his eyes wide. "The queen has been caught with her favorite knight. With Lancelot."

"What?" I cry. "But you've totally got it wrong. They were just waiting for me to come back."

"No mistake, lady." The porter shakes free of my grasp and runs down the hall.

I run to Lance's room at the far end of the hall. Gawain stands at the door, sword drawn, his eyes red and wild. He stares into space as if he's lost his mind and is waiting for the men in white coats to show up and take him away.

"Gawain!" I cry. "You guys are making a huge mistake."

He doesn't answer. Doesn't acknowledge me at all. It's as if he can't even hear me.

"No mistake," a cold voice corrects, stepping out from the chambers. Gawain flinches as Mordred, dressed entirely in black, puts a white hand on his broad shoulder. The prince's piercing blue eyes stare right through me, and I stifle a shiver. He looks evil. Powerful. Ruthless. He may never be a warrior, but he has learned the look of a king.

An evil king, that is.

"Lancelot and Guenevere were caught together in his chambers," Mordred says in an icy tone. "They have betrayed their king. The whore has shared her bed with a man other than my father. Now she must pay for her sins with her life."

"But—"

"That is not all," the boy king interrupts. "In his haste to escape, Lancelot attacked my half brother. By his very hand, Agravaine is dead."

Gawain lets out a tortured moan at the sound of his brother's name. No wonder he looks so crazy. I feel kind of bad for him. I mean, Agravaine was a total jerk, true, but he was still Gawain's brother—and a Knight of the Round Table. What was Lancelot thinking? Did he try to talk his way out first? Explain that things weren't as they seemed?

"Where's Lance now?" I demand.

Mordred frowns. "He has fled Camelot like the coward that he is, leaving his whore to stand alone for their sins."

This is not good. This is really, really, really not good! I taste blood in my mouth and realize I've been biting down too hard on my lower lip, piercing the skin the same way I want to pierce Mordred's black heart. I squeeze my hands into fists and wonder what I should say, what I should do. I take a deep breath, forcing myself to stay calm. Flying off the handle and sputtering the truth is not going to help anyone's case.

I look past Mordred into Lancelot's chambers. The bed is just as we left it—unmade, rumpled, probably reeking of the musky smell of sex. I can see why they assumed something went on here, and, of course, they're right. It just wasn't with who they think it was. And there can be no DNA testing in this time to prove it.

I pull my eyes away from the bed and scan the room. I see Agravaine's limp body on the floor, practically floating in a large pool of crimson. My stomach heaves at the sight of it, and I swallow back the bile that rises in my throat.

I raise my eyes and see, at the far end of the room, Queen Guenevere standing with her head bowed, her golden hair covering her face. I look down at her hands; they've been tied in front of her. Two guards flank her on each side, swords drawn.

"Guen!" I cry. She looks up, tears staining her white cheeks, a defeated look on her face. I attempt to go to her, but Mordred raises his sword, quite effectively stopping me in my tracks.

"Stand back!" he commands.

"But she didn't do it!" I sob, losing my self-control, my resolve to stay calm. Seeing the queen there, in shackles, has completely freaked me out—mostly because I know the part of the story that comes next. I dreamed it a thousand times.

Guenevere to be burned at the stake. For treason. For sleeping with Lancelot.

But she didn't sleep with Lancelot! I did! How can I convince them of that? And what will they do to me if they believe me? Will I end up serving as their human marshmallow instead?

It doesn't matter. I have to take the risk. I can't let Guenevere take the fall for something I did. She'll lose her true love, Arthur, over this. She may even lose her life. And all the people will lose their kingdom of Camelot.

I take in a deep breath and look Mordred straight in the eyes.

"It wasn't her. It was I!" I proclaim, forcing my voice to stay calm. "*I* slept with Lancelot. He's not really my brother at all. It was a lie to throw you off track. I'm his lover, not the queen. If anyone should be burned, it should be me."

Chapter Twenty-one

Mordred laughs, a venomous, cold sound that gives me the chills down to my toes. He addresses the guards waiting with Guenevere. "Take her away. To the dungeons."

He turns to Gawain. "My dear half brother, I beg you go to Bishop Mallory and see that he comes to perform last rites on our poor, dearly departed brother."

Gawain nods, agreeing like a mindless puppy dog and scampering off to do his fool's errand.

Now, alone with me, Mordred turns and smiles. "What was it you were saying, my dear?"

I let out a breath. "I am the one you should be arresting. I slept with Lancelot. Not Guenevere."

He laughs again. "It makes no difference to me who did the actual rutting, my sweet. It is enough that the people believe 'twas the queen."

Huh? "What are you talking about?" I demand.

"Well, you see, now my dear father is put in a rather bad position," Mordred explains. "If he pardons his true love, he will turn his people against him. After all, how can an old cuckold who cannot bring order to his own household control a kingdom? Arthur stands for the law, and even the king is not above the law. Therefore she must be held accountable for her sins. And once she's out of the way," he sneers, baring his crooked teeth, "he will be too distraught to rule." He cackles, evidently pretty proud of his plan. "Cast your lot with me, Lady Kat," he says with a wink. "For I am the future of Camelot."

"Never!" I cry, hoping I sound braver than I feel. This is bad. Really, really bad. The dream is over. Camelot is done for. I have no idea whether or not I'll ever see Lance again. Without Guenevere's spell casting, there's no way I'm going back to the twenty-first century. Could things get any worse? And here is this little twerp who thinks he's so cool, actually trying to get me to join his team. Yeah, right. He's got a better chance of raising the *Titanic*. (Which, considering it hasn't even sunk yet, would be extremely challenging.)

"You do not have to decide now," Mordred informs me oh-so-graciously. "But when I take the throne, I shall need a queen by my side. I see no reason it could not be you."

What? And here I thought he hated me. "How romantic," I spit out sarcastically. "But don't you think you're counting your chickens before they hatch? And forgetting one very big contingency to your taking-over-Camelot plan? Namely Lancelot."

Mordred's eyes darken. Evidently I've struck a nerve. But he quickly regains his composure. "That coward?" he sneers. "He took off faster than a hart being chased by the hounds."

"Ah, good comparison. You being a dirty dog and all." I'm sorry, but he walked right into that one.

He frowns. "Watch yourself, lady," he suggests with a gleam in his eye. "I can easily have you join your little friend down in the dungeon."

Okay, he's got a point there. Guess I should behave. There will be time for heroics later. Like when he's not wielding a big sword, for example. "Sorry, Your Highness," I apologize, backtracking like crazy. "I meant no offense."

"Very well. But remember what I said." He sheaths his sword into a jeweled scabbard slung low on his waist. "We could rule Camelot, you and I. Together."

"Okay. Definitely a tempting offer. I'll think long and hard about it. Um, catch ya later." I back away, and then turn and try to casually walk down the hall without breaking into a run. As I round the bend, I drop all decorum and sprint to my chambers, my heart beating wildly.

What now? What now? *Think, Kat!* I've got to make this right. Make sure Guenevere doesn't get burned at the stake. This is all my fault. Stupid, stupid, stupid!

I reach my chamber door and throw it open. Elen takes one look at my crazed face and backs away, her own face draining of its color in reaction to my fright.

"What is wrong, lady?" she asks.

"Guenevere. She's been caught with Lancelot. They are going to burn her at the stake for treason."

"That is insane," Elen scoffs.

I stare at her, uncomprehending. "What?"

"Well, 'tis very apparent that Lancelot has eyes for you alone."

My mouth drops open. "You know?"

Elen sniffs. "I may be a servant, but I am not blind, milady. I should think anyone could see how he looks at you. Kin or nae, the two of you are in love. He has no business with the queen."

I sigh and flop down on a chair, scrubbing my face with my hands. "He's not really my brother."

"I did have a feeling 'twas the case." Elen walks over

and squeezes my shoulder affectionately. I regret all the mean things I've said about her. "Where is Sir Lancelot now, milady?"

I look up at her, my vision blurred by fresh tears. "I don't know. He evidently killed Agravaine and took off. I'm sure it was self-defense. But now he's like an outcast. And I have no way to reach him."

I take back all the times I've complained about people using cell phones everywhere. I'd give every shoe in my closet to equip Lancelot with one so I could get hold of him, work out a plan. But now I'm completely on my own.

Fear claws at my heart as reality sinks in. Everything's completely messed up. I'm going to miss the portal to go back to the twenty-first century. Guenevere, even if Lancelot does rescue her from burning, is never going to be able to return to Camelot. Neither is he, for that matter. Even if I can convince him I love him, what will we do?

Maybe we can all be banished roommates together. But where will we live? Will we be poor? Will Lancelot have to become a mercenary just so we'll survive? The careers for women in this day and age are few and far between, and certainly not high paying. How long will we have to wait till the next portal? Is there one every year, or is this a once-in-a-blue-moon type of thing?

The thoughts are too much. Nausea consumes me, and my stomach heaves. Elen grabs a chamber pot and thrusts it under me just in time. "I'm sorry," I moan after emptying my stomach's contents into the vessel.

" 'Tis perfectly normal, given the circumstances." Elen shrugs.

"If only I could find Lancelot," I moan. "Elen, if you were a knight in shining armor on the run, where would you hide?"

"Well, if I were Sir Lancelot, I guess I would go to my

castle," she says matter-of-factly, answering my rhetorical question.

I look up. "Castle?"

"Joyous Garde."

"The guy has a freaking castle?" I cry. "He never told me that."

"Having been in the service of King Arthur, he has likely not been there in many a summer. However, he was bequeathed a castle long ago. A place to retire to when his servitude to the king is completed."

"How do you know all this?"

"Again, you underestimate me because I am a servant," Elen rebukes me with a frown. "Before you I served a lady named Elaine. She was much in love with Sir Lancelot." The maid looks somber. "She died by her own hand when he would not return her devotion."

Ah, I remember Nimue talking about her. The first attempted hookup to keep him away from Guen. Poor girl. "And she told you about the castle?"

"Aye. And," Elen adds with a gleam in her eye, "sent me to deliver messages to him. So I well know the path to get there."

"That's great!" I say, scrambling to my feet. "What are we waiting for? Let's go!"

Suddenly a loud rapping sounds on the door. Elen and I exchange worried glances. I point at my inner chamber and to myself. She nods. I rush into the other room and shut the door. *Please don't let it be Mordred.*

I press my ear to the door to listen to the conversation. "The lady is not in," I hear Elen say. "Nae, you cannot enter. Sir, I am sure . . ." Uh-oh. Sounds like the unwelcome guest is giving her a hard time. Who could it be?

I hear a shuffling and then a knock on my door. "Milady, there is a cloaked gentleman here to see you," Elen whispers. "He will not give his name; nor will he go away. Should I call for the guard?"

Could it be Lancelot? My heart pounds in my chest. I take a deep breath and decide to face the unknown visitor. I open the chamber door.

"See him in."

Elen nods and opens the door. A tall man dressed in a long black cloak enters the room. Not Lancelot. I'd know my knight's walk and build anywhere. Not Mordred either. That twerp's much smaller than the guy standing before me. So who . . . ?

After Elen closes the door behind him, the visitor pulls back his cloak. I gasp in surprise.

King Arthur.

"Your Majesty," I say, dropping to my knees. He reaches down and takes my hands, pulling me up again.

"I do apologize for the intrusion, Lady Kat," he says in a hoarse voice. "But I simply must speak with you."

"Of course." I motion for him to sit on one of the chairs while Elen discreetly exits the room.

Once seated, he clears his throat before speaking. "You may well have heard the rumors by now. My wife and your brother, Lancelot, were discovered together in his chambers." He sighs deeply. "The knights believe they are lovers."

"They also believe the world is flat!" I burst out, wringing my hands together in anger. "Listen, Your Majesty, I hope you don't believe any of this bull. Lance and Guen are so not lovers. She loves *you*. Like, with all her heart. In fact, it's almost nauseating to hear her go on and on about how much she adores you."

"It is lovely for you to say so, my dear," Arthur says in a tired voice. "After all, I have never wanted anything but for my beautiful wife to feel the same way about me as I do her." He smiles a half smile. "But the bedding does not lie. 'Tis clear a relationship has been consummated in Lancelot's bed."

"Well, yeah, sure. That's true," I say, shifting to the edge of my seat. "But not Lance and Guen. Lance and *me*. We're lovers, he and I. And have been for months."

"But you are . . ." Arthur begins, evidently trying to put it delicately, even though he's no stranger to the kissing-cousins thing. "He is your . . ."

"Actually he's not my brother. No relation whatsoever. First time I saw the guy was the day on the jousting field. Listen, Arthur, I'm sorry we lied to you. It started out as a small thing. To protect me, Lancelot said I was his sister, 'cause I have no family around, and everyone thought I was some spy. Then we started getting hot and heavy, and it was too late to go back and tell you we made it up. Though we should have, I guess. Then we wouldn't be in such a mess."

Arthur ponders my words for a moment. "It does make sense," he admits. "And it explains well why Lancelot was so quick to abandon his post when he believed you to be in danger."

"Exactly." I nod. "He loves me. I love him. There's nothing going on with him and your wife. The whole Lance-and-Guen thing is a total setup by Mordred. He even admitted it to me. He wants to make you look bad in front of your people so he can take over as king."

"I fear you may be right," Arthur says, rubbing his beard with his thumb and forefinger. "Guenevere and Merlin have been trying to convince me of Mordred's ill will for some time now. But I refused to see it. It is difficult for me to accept the fact that my own flesh and blood, my only

311

son, would seek to destroy everything I have worked my entire life to create."

"No offense," I say carefully. "He may be your kid and all, but he's got a heart as black as his mother's."

"Aye," Arthur agrees. He stares down at the floor, kicking the stone with his boot. "Mordred was conceived through deception. Now in life he has deceived me as well. He is not interested in a father. He wants a kingdom—my kingdom. And while I would happily give it to him in time, he is not content to sit idle, waiting for his turn." He curls his hand into a fist. "And now it is my love, my Guenevere, who pays the price for my stubborn blindness."

"But Arthur, you're forgetting one major thing here. You're king!" I remind him. "You can free her. Just say the word. Unlock her cell. Let her go."

He shakes his head. "It may seem that simple to you, Kat," Arthur says sorrowfully. "And how I wish you were correct in that assumption."

"What do you mean?"

"Mordred has hardened the hearts of my knights against me. He has told them that because I seek peace instead of war, I am weak. He promises them battles that will conquer nations and create a British empire as vast as the one Rome once held. They are bored, thirsty for blood, and he excites them with his boastful predictions."

"Guess the soccer matches aren't cutting it then, huh?" Obviously David Beckham isn't a descendent of the Round Table. "I was so hoping some team sports would give them a healthier outlet for their violent tendencies."

Arthur stares off into space as he continues: "Now Mordred has framed Guenevere and my last loyal knight. If I set her free, he will say I hold my own household to a different set of standards than my kingdom. He will use that to turn the people against me, as he has already turned my knights. He will demand I abdicate the throne, and I will have no army to defend my right to be king." Arthur sighs. "He knows well that I must choose: my Guenevere or my kingdom."

"Yeah, but that seems like a pretty easy choice. I mean, no offense, but material things aside—"

"You see this from your heart, not your head," Arthur interrupts, rising from his seat. He walks over to the window and stares outside. "Yes, if I give up the throne and live out my days with Guenevere, I will die a happy man. But there are thousands of serfs living on the land under my protection. Who knows the brutality they will suffer under Mordred's rule? He wants war, which costs money. He will tax them to death. Beat them and throw them in the prison. Force them to become soldiers, destined to die on the battlefield." Arthur clears his throat. "So I am left with the decision: do I save one or thousands? My people, whom I have vowed on my life to protect? Or my wife, whom I love above all?"

Okay, I can see where he's stuck between a rock and a hard place. Geez. No matter what the Mel Brooks movies tell you, it's not always good to be the king.

"If it makes you feel any better, Lancelot got away," I remind him. "I'm sure he's concocting a rescue plan at this very moment." Either that or he's off sticking pins in a voodoo doll that looks remarkably like me.

Arthur turns from the window, a dash of hope clear in his eyes. "That is why I have come to see you, Kat. To ask your and Lancelot's assistance in rescuing Guenevere. I can officially sentence her to death to save the kingdom, but I refuse to let her die. I will do everything in my power to aid you. You and Lancelot must see that she is safe." He swallows hard. "Even if I am never to see her again, it will be enough to know that she lives."

My heart aches in my chest as I see the love practically radiating from his bearish frame. He really, really cares about her, as much as Lancelot cares about me. Or did, before I opened my big mouth and let him think I was in it only for the time travel.

"Guen is my friend," I tell Arthur. "I will do everything in my power to save her."

Arthur rubs his chin, thinking. "Here is what we will do. I will schedule a public execution at high noon. I will leave the castle gates wide-open and schedule the weakest guards to stand watch—ones who can be easily manipulated or overpowered to gain entrance. In the stables I will have the fastest horses saddled and ready to go. The other knights will be invited to stand at a place of honor on a high dais with me, so they will be nowhere near the pyre. This way Lancelot will be able to swoop in without battle, rescue Guenevere, grab a horse, and go."

I have to admit it's not a bad plan. "But you can't let on that you're doing this," I remind him. "You've got to pretend you want her to die. Like you're a totally jilted husband pissed off at her infidelity." It'd better be an Academy Award–winning performance, too, if he wants to convince Mordred.

Arthur nods. "Aye. 'Twill be a hard act, to be sure. For the truth is, I want nothing more than to hold her in my arms once again. To love her as she deserves to be loved."

My heart aches for him. For all of us. Why has fate been so cruel? "You will," I assure him, lying through my teeth. The last thing he needs to hear is that, according to history, Guen's going to be spending the rest of her days in a convent. "Someday."

"Perhaps you are right," Arthur says with a fond smile. "While Christians believe in heaven, Guenevere is still fond of the old ways, where a circle of love may be reborn anew every generation. If matched with true love in one lifetime, so shall one be reunited in the next," he explains, eyes shining. "Perhaps in my next lifetime I will find her again. Love her again."

"Yeah, exactly," I say, not wanting to hurt his feelings, but not believing any of this druidic nonsense about reincarnation either. "Still, maybe we should concentrate on saving Guen's butt this time around and not think too much about the future."

I know—that's rich coming from me, since I come from the future and all I ever think about is returning. But now it seems I've got to straighten out this mess before I can go back. Besides, to tell the truth, even if there *were* a way to return to the twenty-first century without Guen's help, I can't imagine leaving here without making sure she's okay. And, of course, I've got to straighten things out with Lance.

Arthur walks over to me and takes my hand. "You are right, Lady Kat," he agrees, pulling my hand to his lips and kissing it fervently. "And I am trusting you with her precious life."

Arthur nods a good-bye and walks out the door. Poor man. Such an awful position to be put in. This kind of thing used to always happen to Captain Kirk on *Star Trek* too. I'm glad I'm not the one stuck making the decision.

The annoying thing is, it could have all worked out so perfectly too, if not for a stupid case of mistaken identity. Lance and I could have gone back to the future. Guen could have lived happily ever after with Arthur. The people of Camelot could have been happy-go-lucky for the rest of their days.

Yup, it has to be said: sometimes destiny sucks.

* * *

Dior is exhausted by the time we've galloped all the way to Joyous Garde to find Lancelot. At least Elen's directions are better than MapQuest's, and we don't get lost once.

It's a beautiful castle, on the small side, and nearly hidden by a maze of climbing vines. But I'm not here to enjoy the architecture. I leap off my horse and run to the front door. Locked. I bang my fists against it, yelling. *Please let him be here!*

"Lance!" I cry. "Lance, are you there?"

The door creaks open. Lancelot stands on the other side. Unshaven. Dirty. I've never seen him look so tired. Old. Defeated. Not at all like a guy concocting a brave rescue plan.

"Kat," he notes, without a hint of enthusiasm in his voice.

I frown. "Lance, what are you doing here? They're going to burn Guen at the stake. We have to rescue her!"

He turns and walks back into the castle. I run after him. "Where are you going? Didn't you hear me?"

He slumps down into a chair and puts his face in his hands. "I should have listened to you when you told me about the rumors to begin with. Then none of this would have occurred."

I shake my head. "Doesn't matter now. Point is, unless we get back to Camelot, the queen's going to be executed."

"What can I do? I cannot fight a whole army." He sighs deeply, picking at a fingernail. "I cannot fight my fellow knights and my king."

"Lancelot du Lac, this isn't like you," I protest, hands on my hips. "You're the bravest, noblest, most chivalrous knight in all the land. You don't just sit around and let your friend die because of a stupid misunderstanding. What would Arthur—"

"Arthur," Lancelot interrupts, "thinks I betrayed him."

"No, he doesn't. I had a long talk with him. He totally

knows you and Guen would never hook up. In fact, he's counting on you to go rescue her. He can't, 'cause it will destroy the kingdom and stuff, and so that leaves you. If you don't save her, no one will, and she'll die. You don't want her to die, do you?"

"No. Of course not." Lancelot stands up and walks over to the far wall. Pressing his hand against it, he bows his head. "But there will be an army guarding her. The knights will be out for my blood. They think I killed Agravaine."

"Well, yeah, but they have to understand it was total self-defense," I argue.

"No. It was not."

I scrunch my eyebrows. "It wasn't? Then—"

Lancelot turns around, meeting my eyes with his bloodshot ones. "Mordred killed him—stabbed him in the back to make it look like 'twas me." He clears his throat. "He wants to ensure I am not pardoned for my supposed rutting with the queen. Sex is one thing. Many a man can forgive a night of passion. A violent murder of one of my sworn brothers, however, is a sin worthy of death. An eye for an eye, as the Christians say."

I pace the floor, trying to think of a plan. "Still, there's got to be a way to help Guen. Arthur's setting it up so it's like a big public execution—gates thrown open, knights out of the way, stuff like that. He's going to make it as easy as possible for you to rescue her. And, of course, I could help, too."

"Why? What's in it for you?" Lancelot asks angrily. "Ah, I know. You need Guenevere alive so she can send you back to your future."

I stare at him, horrified. Is that what he really thinks? Does the man I love more than anything really believe me to be such a monster?

317

"I need Guenevere alive because she's one of my best friends!" I say furiously. "I need Guenevere alive because she's innocent and doesn't deserve to die for something she didn't do. How can you stand here and say I'm only interested in what she can do for me? How"—I choke back a sob—"dare you? Is that what you really think of me?"

Lancelot sighs deeply. "I do not know what to think anymore. However, it does not matter, I suppose. Whatever your motivation, you are right. The queen must not die for something she did not do. And as a knight loyal to Arthur, it is my duty to protect her at any cost." He walks back to the table and sits. "Thank you for bringing this to my attention. You may depart now and inform the king he need not lose sleep over that matter."

Oh, he thinks he can get rid of me that easy, does he? Boy, he's got another thing coming! "No way," I protest, plopping down on a seat next to him. "You may not believe me, but I care about Guenevere, too. And, like it or not, I care about you. I'm sure as hell not going to sit back and watch you fumble this rescue because of your stubborn refusal to believe I'm telling the truth. As you said yourself, you can't fight an army alone. So, like it or not, I'm helping."

Lancelot snorts. "I hardly think a woman—"

I shoot him a glare. It's so obvious he's being all chauvinistic in hopes I'll get mad—maybe even take off. After all, me being a kick-ass twenty-first-century chick is what drew him to me in the first place.

"Puh-leeze. I've said it before and I'll say it again," I proclaim. "Girls can do anything boys can do . . . usually better."

He raises an eyebrow. "Can you fight with a sword?"

Oh, he's going to pull the whole men-are-stronger-than-women argument. Figures. "No. I can't," I say honestly. "Though I'm pretty handy with a stick sword." I grin, trying to lighten the mood. No luck. Why are men so pigheaded? "Okay, fine. You got me there. I'm not an accomplished swordswoman. However, I can do other things."

"Like?"

"Like . . ." *Come on, Kat. You can think of something.* "Like create a diversion."

"Diversion?"

"You know, to distract everyone. Then you can swoop in and rescue her."

"And what do you plan to do?"

I tap a finger to my temple, trying to think. "I could whip off my dress and dance naked on the Round Table."

Lancelot laughs bitterly. "While I imagine that would certainly distract some, I am not sure 'tis enough—no offense—to detract from a burning."

I sigh. "You're probably right." What would be big enough to get everyone's attention? Ooh, ooh, I know! "What about a bomb?"

"A what?" At least he's listening to me.

"Well, it's this thing that explodes. Like, um, a burst of fire. Everything blows up," I explain. "When I was in first-year home ec at Brooklyn Community College I accidentally blew up the kitchen when mixing cleaning chemicals to clean milk mold out of an old bottle. Believe me, it got everyone's attention, including the school's chancellor. In fact, I almost got expelled."

"Where would you get one of these 'bombs'?"

"I'll make one. Somehow." I frown, realizing I have no idea how I'd do that. I mean, I know mixing bleach and ammonia makes an explosion, but I don't have access to Clorox here. There's got to be another way, though. Where's *The Anarchist Cookbook* when you need it?

I brush a strand of hair from my face as I try to think. My hair's grown so unruly lately. Guess it's lack of regular conditioning. Of course, it's probably a lot healthier since I no longer blow it dry and use my limited supply of hair spray only on special occasions—

"That's it!" I cry, grabbing my purse and rummaging through it. I pull out my travel-size can of hair spray and check the label. *Flammable. Avoid heat, fire, and smoking during use until sprayed hair is fully dry.* Thank goodness I refused to listen to all the environmentalists at work who ragged on me for not switching to the pump kind.

"What is that?" Lancelot asks, walking over to check out the can.

I smile broadly. "Lancelot, my dear, meet Aqua Net. Savior of Camelot."

Chapter Twenty-two

You'd think there's a carnival in town, the World Series taking place, or Elvis performing live from beyond the grave, the way people have turned out for the burning. I mean, this has got to be bigger than Lady Diana marrying Prince Charles. Everyone who's anyone—and some who aren't—have all dressed in their queen-burning best and have made the trip to Camelot. It's sick—really sick, if you ask me, which of course no one has.

The courtyard is filled, the pyre piled high; they could probably burn a dinosaur with the amount of wood they've stacked. Talk about overkill. And Mordred's front and center, looking as eager as a little kid ready to toast marshmallows when the coals get hot. Everyone else is milling about, talking excitedly. If they lived in the twenty-first century they'd be total rubbernecking ambulance chasers.

Arthur sits on a makeshift throne, high on a platform above the courtyard, flanked by his knights and Merlin. Even from down below I can see he's trying to compose himself, to keep the illusion of being in power. But there's no doubt in anyone's mind who's running the show: the little bastard Mordred, giving orders down on the ground. He's acting like a celebrity, basking in all the attention from the ignorant peasants.

Trumpets sound. It's starting. My quickening pulse throbs under my wrists. Will this work? It has to. There's no plan B.

Cheers and jeers erupt as Guenevere is led into the courtyard, dressed in a simple shift dress. Her golden hair hangs tangled over her pale face. Her hands are bound in front of her, and I can tell she's finding it difficult to keep her balance as the guards escort her to the stack of wood—her intended grave.

She stops in front of me, shooting me a desperate look with her heartbreaking eyes. "Kat," she whispers. "I am sorry I could not help you. Maybe Nimue . . ."

I'm awestruck. Here she is, moments away from what she believes will be her last breath, and she's still concerned about me. My heart lurches, and I want to reach out to hug her, whisper the plan in her ear, tell her not to worry, that I would never let her die. But the guard shoves her forward, causing her to fall onto her knees. Then he roughly grabs her by the arm and yanks her to her feet.

"Get up, ye filthy whore!"

His brutality toward the sweet, innocent girl pisses me off, and as the man pushes by me I can't help but stick out my foot to trip him. He falls flat on his face, causing several bystanders to snicker. Scrambling to his feet and whirling around, red-faced, he tries to figure out who's to blame, but I'm already making my way through the crowd. He's lucky I have to keep a low profile, or I would have so kicked his ass.

I head to the outer gates to deal with the guards, balancing a pewter cup of mead in my hand. I can't believe they even had the nerve to open up a medieval-style concession stand. If they had the technology, they'd probably be selling souvenir cups and "My Grandma went to Guenevere's execution and all I got was this lousy T-shirt" paraphernalia.

Standing at attention by the outer gate are Andre the giant and his smaller, grouchier friend. I remember my first day at Camelot, when I talked them into letting me leave what I thought at the time was just a theme party. So much has happened since then; so much has changed.

The guards have been stationed like bouncers at a nightclub or airplane security people. They've been searching everyone who enters to make sure no one sneaks in with a weapon. From the large pile of confiscated swords resting at their feet, I take it this is not merely a formality at Camelot.

"Hey, guys," I say amicably. Andre glares at me. He's not as nice as he was that first day. Funny how a little thing like Mace in the eyes can ruin a developing friendship. Well, it couldn't be helped then, and I can't be held responsible for what I have to do now. "How's it hanging?"

"I do not know about any hanging," the grouchy guard says. "But it seems the burning is right on schedule."

Ooh, good one. "Wow, you definitely ate your clever vitamins this morning," I say with a snort.

"What brings you to the outer gates?" asks the big guy. "Are you not staying to watch the queen burn?"

"Nah. I've never really been into the whole *Faces of Death* thing." I shrug. "Figure it'd be more fun to come hang out here with you guys."

They scowl at me simultaneously.

"Hey," I protest in a wounded voice. "Why the mean faces? And here I am trying to do something nice."

"Nice?" the giant one asks, his curiosity overcoming his unfriendliness.

323

"Well, I figured you might be thirsty, being stuck at the gate and all. So I sneaked you out some mead from the concession stand." I produce the cup from behind my back. "I know it's probably not PC to drink on the job, but I won't tell anyone if you won't. The way I figure it, what happens at the outer gate, stays at the outer gate."

They exchange glances. "Are you trying to trick us?" demands the grouchy one. "What is in the cup?"

I put on a hurt face. "Dude, I told you—it's beer. Mead." I place the cup to my lips and fake taking a big gulp, keeping my lips pursed. "Mmmm. Beer," I say in my best Homer Simpson voice after lowering the cup.

That's all it takes to convince them—typical men. They'll believe anything for free alcohol. The bigger guard takes the cup from me and slurps greedily. The other guard scowls at him for taking more than his share and yanks the cup from his grasp, also sucking it down.

"Thank you, milady," Andre says, moments before his eyes roll back in his head and he slumps to the ground. The grouchy guard joins him moments later.

"No, thank *you!*" I say, kicking them to make sure they're truly unconscious. "And thank Ambien." I didn't think the I'm-afraid-of-flying-so-I-keep-it-in-my-purse sleeping pill would work so fast. But then again, I did crush up about twenty pills into their drink to be on the safe side.

With the guards indisposed, all we need now are some fireworks. I go back into the crowded courtyard, weaving in and out of the throngs of people. Their eagerness for death makes me almost reconsider finding a nice quiet place to set the bomb.

But out of respect for Arthur, who seems dearly to love these moron subjects of his, I head to the back of the courtyard where no one stands. Against the stone wall I find a little crumbling niche just big enough to wedge a can of hair spray into. I tie a length of cotton that I've dipped in candle wax around the can and stick it in the slot. I pad the slot with a bit of extra cotton to make sure it burns long enough to ignite the can. Then I roll the length of cotton away from the wall, giving myself a good long wick. I'm so not interested in getting blown up.

I reach into my purse and pull out the lighter I have stashed there. I don't smoke, but have found it's always good to have one on hand for when a cute guy at a bar asks if you've got a light. Thank goodness, too, because Guen would be dead by the time I managed to rub two sticks together, me being a Girl Scout dropout and all.

I look over at the main stage. I've got to get the timing right—not too soon and definitely not too late. Looks like Bishop Mallory has taken center stage.

"Guenevere of Cameliard, the court has found you guilty of the sin of adultery and therefore treason against the king, your people, and God himself," says the priest, reading the verdict from a long scroll. "The sentence dictated by the court is death by burning. Do you have any last words? Remember, God is listening."

Guenevere draws her petite frame to its full height, her mouth set in determination. "Arthur, I love you," she says loudly, raising her eyes to the king above. I can see Arthur's face crumple. I'm half convinced he's going to call the whole thing off. *Stick to the plan, Arthur. We don't need any spontaneous heroics.*

"Executioner, please begin," the king says finally, his voice cracking with grief. Poor guy. I watch as he turns and walks back to his throne, slumping down on the seat, his face in his hands. The joy of seeing Guenevere rescued will be bittersweet to him. She will live, but he will never see her again. It's all so tragic, I can hardly stand it.

The executioner lowers his torch until it touches the kindling at the base of the pile. Flames lick at the lower timbers, and I realize the time has come. I flick the lighter and set fire to the end of the cotton wick.

Then I run.

Fast as my twenty-first-century legs can carry me I dive into the crowd and push my way through the masses until I reach the other end of the courtyard.

Until I hear . . .

Kaboom!

Chaos everywhere as the explosion rocks the ground. I picked just the right unstable spot. The wall crumbles, large boulders crashing down, creating a graveyard of stones and dusty rubble. Everyone's screaming, running.

"We're under attack!"

"An army has penetrated Camelot's gates!"

"Grab your children! Run!"

I duck into the stables and free Dior and another horse that Arthur had arranged to have saddled. I peek out the door. Is Lancelot here yet? He'd better hurry. This plan is completely dependent on timing.

I watch as a brown-cloaked monk approaches the pyre with defiant strides. I draw in a breath. What is he doing?

Lancelot, hurry!

The monk leaps onto the pyre—pretty agile for a scholar of God—clearing the flames and approaching Guenevere. His hood falls from his head, and I gasp as I realize who it really is.

Lancelot.

Pride and love swell in my heart. He hadn't told me about the disguise. Damn, he's good!

Once freed, the queen collapses in a dead faint into his arms. Is she okay? Lancelot cradles her like a groom carrying a bride over the threshold and runs toward the gates. In all the confusion and dust, no one seems to have comprehended what is happening.

I leap onto one of the horses, keeping hold of the bridle on the other. Then, digging my heels into the mare's flanks, I urge them out into the courtyard and play dodge-the-frightened-medieval-peasant until I make my way out the gate and to the meeting spot. Already I can hear Mordred's voice above the din.

"A trick!" he cries. "Lancelot has used the devil's magic to save his harlot from hell. We must go after them! We must stop the sinners and persecute the injustice."

I reach Lancelot and Guen, exchanging a glance with the knight. His eyes reflect my worry, and I know exactly what he's thinking.

Not much time.

He hoists the unconscious queen onto the horse and slides on in back of her. Then he urges his mare onward, and I follow as best I can. The skies open up and rain pours down in buckets as we gallop fast as our horses can go to Stonehenge.

As we fly down the hill toward the village, I look over at Lancelot's horse and notice that Guenevere seems to have gained consciousness. That's one relief.

Okay, Kat. Time to cross my fingers, cross my toes, cross myself, and invoke getting-to-Stonehenge-on-time karma.

We need all the luck we can get if we're going to pull this off.

About an hour later Lancelot slows his horse and turns to me. We're deep in the woods now, having taken countless twisting turns. Luckily he knows where we're going. He comes to a stop by a small stream. The rain has tapered off, at least momentarily.

"I think we have lost them," he says. "We must rest the horses for a moment, or they will surely drop dead."

As his horse greedily slurps water, Lance slips to the ground and helps Guenevere off. She looks shaken and weak, sinking to her knees. I dismount and approach her.

"Are you okay?" I ask, kneeling down in the mud and pulling her into a warm hug. I can feel her body tremble against mine as she wraps her arms around me and holds on tight.

"Thank you for rescuing me," she murmurs. "I truly thought I would die at that stake."

"Nah! We wouldn't let that happen to you!" I say with a grin that I hope looks more happy-go-lucky than I feel. Inside, I'm still extremely worried. I'm sure a search party of knights wielding swords is out in full force. If they find us, we're doomed. If they don't, then what? Guen certainly can't go back to Camelot. She could head for her dad's place at Cameliard, but who knows if she'd even be safe there? Mordred and his army could easily take the small kingdom.

"Guen," I say carefully, not wanting to upset her, "I know a lot has happened. Do you have any idea what you want to do now?"

"I do not know," she wails, tears slipping down her pale cheeks. "Perhaps 'twould be better if I had died at the stake. I have nowhere to go. When you are gone I will have no one." She wipes her tears away with a dirty hand, the grime streaking across her face. She looks more like a homeless waif than a queen. But still beautiful. Innocent.

Anger stirs inside me as I think about all that's happened. About how everyone got it all wrong. Throughout history this sweet, vulnerable girl will be known as a slut who fucked over her husband for a dashing knight. I wonder, when and if I get back to the twenty-first century, whether I should write a tell-all book. Disguise it as fiction if I have to—to let people know the true story behind the infamous love triangle that, if you count me, is actually more of a square.

"What about Avalon?" I suggest. "Won't they take you back? You love it there."

Guen shakes her head. "My going there would endanger them all. I do not want to introduce violence into their peaceful world." She sighs deeply. "A convent may take me in, but I do not desire to live out my days with those who deny themselves all the pleasures of being a woman. 'Twould be a living death."

I try to think, then mentally smack myself upside the head when the most obvious idea in the world comes to me. "Duh!" I say. "I can't believe I didn't think of this. Why don't you come back to the twenty-first century with me?"

Guen looks at me, her eyes wide. "D'you think . . . ?"

"Yeah, that'd be great!" I exclaim, scrambling to my feet. "I've been wishing you could come back with me anyway, but of course I knew you had a total life here and stuff. But now that you don't, there's nothing stopping you."

Her face falls. "If I come back with you, I will never see Arthur again."

"That's true, but Guen, chances are you won't anyway." I hate to break it to her, but I'm going the tough-love route here. "And anyway, don't you believe in reincarnation?" I add, remembering Arthur's speech. "That if lovers are joined in one life they will find each other in the next?"

"Yes, but—"

"So I bet you have a good chance of running into the twenty-first-century version of your husband. How cool would that be?"

Her eyes light up, and I know I've sold her on the idea.

Lancelot finishes tending to the horses and approaches. He motions for us to mount. "We must ride on, or we risk getting caught."

"Aye," agrees Guenevere, a smile shining through her tears. "Let us be off to Stonehenge."

Lancelot looks at her, then me. "So Your Majesty still plans to perform the spell to send Kat home?" he asks in a deliberately emotionless voice. It almost sounds as if he's hoping I'll miss the portal.

"Aye, and myself with her," Guenevere tells him. "I have nothing left to keep me in Camelot. Better I start a new life than have mine end here."

"I see," Lancelot says quietly.

The queen scrunches her eyebrows in confusion. "But do you not travel with us, Sir Lancelot? I thought Kat said—"

"Things have changed," Lancelot interrupts. "I will accompany you to the portal, but that is as far as I go."

Guenevere glances over at me, confused. I shrug. What can I say? The last thing I want is for her to hear about Nimue's plan and freak out, as Lance did.

Lance. I look over at the knight as he boosts Guenevere up on his horse and then mounts himself. My heart feels like it's being torn in two, and I literally ache from my head to my toes. I wipe away the tears that are determined to fall. I can't leave like this. Even if we can never be together, I can't let him go through life thinking I used him for personal gain. And now it looks like there's not going to be much of a chance to talk things through.

Suddenly an idea comes to me—hits me like a ton of bricks, actually.

I will stay.

Sure, I'll still go to Stonehenge and let Guen open the portal. But at the last moment I won't jump. I'll let it close forever. And then, maybe then, Lancelot will see that I mean it when I say I love him. That he means more to me than some stupid millennium. And once he forgives me, then he, Guen and I can gallop off into the sunset. Go back to Lancelot's home county of Little Britain or something and live happily ever after. Maybe even get Arthur to come join us so Guen can have her true love back. After all, the chances of him keeping his kingdom at this point are slim to none.

It's the perfect plan. I only hope it works.

The rain picks up. Lightning streaks across the sky, followed by earth-shaking thunder—the kind Gucci likes to hide under my bed from, whimpering. I feel like doing a little whimpering myself, but there's no time. On and on the horses press into the rain-soaked night. The drops bang against my face with such intensity I'm afraid I'll end up bruised. The wind whips my hair into a Medusa-like tangle.

Summer solstice indeed. More like monsoon solstice, if you ask me.

"This is it!" Lancelot cries. I can barely hear him over the storm. But I can see his hand, pointing to the top of a hill before us. And I can see the familiar stone structure standing tall and true.

Stonehenge. The gateway. Home.

I hear noises behind us and whirl around. In the distance I can see flickering torches. The knights. They've found us!

"Hurry!" I cry, urging on my horse. "They're almost here." My heart pounds in my chest and blood roars in my ears as we gallop to the top of the hill.

I slide off my horse and look back. The torches are closer. We've got only a few minutes and they'll be here.

"Guen, we've got to hurry!"

The queen dismounts, her eyes wild and wide. "I am not sure if I can—"

"There is no time for talk," Lancelot interrupts, his eyes not wavering from the approaching army.

"I understand," Guenevere says. She turns to the Stonehenge and begins her incantation. "*Solstice en hirum au callibar . . .*"

The torches are closer now—so close I can see the men who hold them in their grimy fists. It's an angry mob, determined to kill Lancelot. To kill the queen. Me, too, probably, if I stand in their way. I turn to Guenevere. Her eyes are closed in concentration. Her voice quavers as she speaks the words.

"*. . . arruliam de tona los garillium . . .*"

Lancelot places a hand on my shoulder. "They are here," he says, softly stating the obvious. "She will not have time to finish."

I turn to him, panicked. This was not at all how I wanted my big sacrifice drama to play out. "But she has to!" I cry.

Lancelot nods, distracted. Then he squares his shoulders and draws his sword. He looks powerful, breathtaking, wielding the mighty blade. A true hero. "Make sure she keeps her concentration. I will hold them off."

Wait! I don't mind him looking like a hero, but this is not the time for him to act like one! I grab his arm, a futile attempt to hold him back, as panic engulfs me. "No!" I cry. "There's too many of them. You'll die!"

He turns back to me, his troubled, fierce gaze grabbing my eyes and not letting go. I feel my body tremble into a near faint, my heart banging against my rib cage.

"There is no other way. Better they kill me, and you two escape."

"No!" I shake my head, my lips tasting the tears that

spill down my cheeks. "You don't understand! I'm not going to leave you. I refuse." I take a deep breath, swallow down my sobs, and continue: "You told me once that no matter what, you would always choose me. Well, I choose you. The time period doesn't matter. Wherever, whenever I am doesn't make any difference. I choose you." I break down, sobbing. "I choose you."

Lancelot suddenly grabs the back of my neck, fiercely pulling me toward him and planting a hot, rough kiss on my mouth. His lips are demanding, fierce, but I can feel his tears splashing onto my cheeks. For a moment there is nothing else. No past, no future, no time, no place. Just him and me. Together. One. Nothing matters except his touch.

"Kat," he murmurs. "I am so sorry I doubted you."

"I'm sorry I didn't tell you the truth," I sob. "I ruined everything."

"No. 'Tis my stubbornness that caused you this grief," he insists. "I want to be with you above anything."

"Then I'll stay."

"No." He shakes his head. "The current situation here is perilous at best. At this point, 'twould be far better to journey to your world."

I nod slowly. He's right, of course. But before I can answer, an angry voice cuts through the moment.

"There they are! After them, men!"

We break apart; looking down the hill I see the mob has found us. They raise their weapons: swords, arrows, clubs. It's like that big battle in *Lord of the Rings*. We're totally outnumbered. And unfortunately we have no Gandalf the Great or fighting trees to save us.

"Shit!" I cry. "What are we going to do?"

"When the portal opens, jump through," Lancelot instructs. "I will join you when I can."

"No! I can't go without you. What if you don't make it?"

He kisses me on the forehead. "Trust me, Kat. After all, our destiny is written in the stars. How can a little thing like time keep us apart?"

He kisses me again, a hard, desperate kiss against my lips, and then pulls away, running down the hill to meet the mob. I watch him with a dead, sick feeling inside.

"Please stay safe," I murmur, tears and rain streaming down my cheeks.

I turn back to Guen. She's still incanting, her face white and tense, almost old-looking. Her voice has taken on a new quality, no longer musical, no longer girlish. The voice of the priestess she never got to be.

Lightning strikes the center of Stonehenge, illuminating each stone pillar. But instead of sparking a fire, it creates a strange circular doorway in the center of the circle, seemingly made of light itself. I release the breath I didn't know I was holding.

The portal. Will this really lead me back home?

Guenevere opens her eyes and looks at the circle, then at me. "This is it," she says in a reverent whisper. "The doorway to your world."

I step into the circle, my pulse pounding, my hands shaking. I take one last look behind me. I can see the fight has commenced between Lancelot and the gang of men. Can I leave him? Maybe I should—

"Kat!" Guenevere grabs me by the hand. "We must go. Now!"

I feel like my insides are being ripped out. "But Lance—"

"He would want you to. You know that."

"Yeah, well, he can be a chauvinistic idiot sometimes!" I cry, breaking free of her hold. I dash out of the circle and scream down the hill, "Lancelot! Come now!"

I watch as he slashes at Mordred, cutting him down

where he stands. As the prince distracts the mob by screaming bloody murder, Lancelot takes the opportunity to dash up the hill. I look back at the portal; its brilliance is already fading. How long will it hold?

"Guenevere, go now!" I cry. She opens her mouth to protest, but I put out my hands and shove her through. She stumbles, disappearing into the swirling blue mist.

I turn back to Lancelot. "Hurry!" I cry.

He almost reaches me. But suddenly he falls, screaming in pain. The dying Mordred's well-aimed arrow has pierced him in the back. I run over and grab him, dragging him with all my might toward the portal. I feel the way that woman who lifted up the truck to save her son must have felt, my adrenaline giving me superhuman strength. I'm sure that any minute I'm going to get one of those arrows right in the heart, and it will all be over.

But call it destiny, fate, or just damn good luck—I make it to the portal. Pulling Lancelot into my arms, I stumble through, our bodies disappearing in the swirling sea of light.

We made it. But will Lancelot be all right?

Epilogue

The low-battery beep of my cell phone startles me into consciousness. I slowly open one eye, then another. Are we home?

I sit up. The landscape is dark. I fumble around in my purse until I find my lighter and flick it on. The quick glow reveals Guenevere and Lancelot lying beside me on the grass, both still unconscious. Nothing else is in sight except a vacant, grassy field.

We made it. But where are we? Are we on the fairgrounds I left from? Perhaps some time has passed, the fair moved on? Will my car still be there? I pick up my cell phone, but the battery completely gives out before I can place a call. Damn.

Then I remember: Lancelot is hurt. I flick the lighter once again and examine the spot on his back where the arrow pierced his flesh. It's still there. Evidently time does not heal *all* wounds. It looks bad, too. Is he going to be okay? I swallow back my sobs. It would be just my luck to get him back to the future, only to have him die. I've got to find him a hospital.

"Mmmm." I hear Guenevere moan as she regains consciousness. "Are we here?" she asks sleepily.

"I guess so," I say. "Though I'm not exactly sure where." It feels so weird to be back. Surreal, I guess. Like I'm a visitor to my own world.

"Is Lancelot here?" Guen asks. "Did he make it?"

"Yeah, but he's unconscious. And badly hurt. We've got to get him to a hospital," I tell her. At least he can get some good old-fashioned twenty-first-century healing. If we were still in medieval times, we'd be doomed. "Damn Mordred and his arrow."

"It's strange." Guenevere sniffs. "I can't believe that my Arthur is dead. That he died a thousand years ago. I wonder if he triumphed over Mordred's mutiny or died the day we left. I guess it makes no difference now." She sighs deeply. "I miss him already."

"Oh, Guen, I'm sorry," I say, feeling out her hand and giving it a squeeze. Poor thing.

After consoling her, I turn back to Lancelot. What are we going to do? We can't move him. And we can't leave him here and head out into the pitch-darkness. We might never find him again. Damn the cell phone battery! Maybe there are some houses around. If I yell real loud . . .

"Help!" I cry at the top of my lungs. "Someone please help us!"

Guenevere touches me on the arm. "What if someone evil hears you? A marauding bandit or such?"

"Nah, we're in twenty-first-century upstate New York. There are no marauding bandits here," I assure her before starting my loud plea again.

About five minutes later I'm totally hoarse from yelling. No one's come. Lancelot's still bleeding. Worried, I rip off a section of my gown and press it against his wound, trying to stop the blood flow.

"Stay with me, Lance," I murmur in his ear. "I need you. Please."

"Look!" Guenevere cries. "A light approaches."

I look up. Sure enough, a bright halogen flashlight flashes toward us. Rescued! I stand up and wave my arms in the air. "Over here!" I cry.

The light brightens as it approaches, and I'm blinded, so I can't see the person behind it. But who cares who it is? We're saved!

"What in bleeding hell are you doing out here?" asks an English-accented male voice. I shield my eyes as his light shines in my face.

"Thank God you're here," I say, pointing to Lancelot. "He's hurt. Do you have a car? Can you get us to a hospital? Or call an ambulance maybe?"

"Don't be daft; he doesn't need a hospital," says the voice, after the man flashes the light onto Lancelot's back. "I can fix him myself."

"You can?" I ask, rubbing my eyes. "Are you a doctor or something?"

"Nah. But it's only a flesh wound," the man says. "A kid could heal him."

With the light focused on Lancelot, my vision somewhat returns, and I can see our rescuer. He's a tall, good-looking blond man, probably in his mid-thirties, wearing a very oddly cut silver suit—something you'd see in a couture show, but never on a real-life person. Is he for real?

"Are they having a medieval fair around here somewhere?" the man asks after looking at our clothing. Ha! And here I am thinking his outfit is weird. We must look like total freaks.

"Yeah," I say, not knowing how else to explain. "Um, battle re-creation. Lance here got hurt. Where are we anyway? We're kind of lost."

"On my land. About five miles outside Poughkeepsie."

Ah, so we did come back to the same area I'd left from. Phew. I was a little worried when I heard the English accent. But we're not too far from home at all. If I can't find my car, I'll call a cab. Sure, it'll be expensive, but totally worth it. I'm exhausted and just want to collapse onto my own bed and sleep for about a year.

But my relief is short-lived as the man pulls a strange object from his pocket. It looks kind of like one of those *Star Trek* communicators. He presses it against Lance's wound and pushes down on a button. A red laser light shoots out.

"What the hell are you doing?" I demand. Great, the first person we meet back in the twenty-first century is a total nutball. Guen's going to get the totally wrong impression.

He looks up at me. "Surely you've seen a gamma reconstruction wand before. I can't imagine you got insurance to play your medieval re-creation without one on hand."

Uh-oh! I'm getting a bad feeling here. Especially as I watch Lancelot's wound shrink and disappear under the red laser. Could Guen's spell have worked too well? Could we have . . .

The man turns off the gamma recon-whatever and touches Lancelot on the shoulder. "Hey, mate, wake up."

Lancelot stirs and sits up. My heart swells with love, as I forget our situation for a moment. He's going to be all right—that's all that really matters. I reach over and hug him.

"I thought I'd lost you," I cry, overjoyed. He hugs me back and kisses me on the forehead.

"Did we make it?" he asks in a weak voice. "Are we in the twenty-first century?"

"Twenty-first century?" the man exclaims. "Oy, mate, were you hit on the head as well?"

"What?" I cry, suddenly shivering with fear. What the hell is going on here? "Please tell us, sir. Who are you? And, um, when are we?"

"Oh, I get ya. Still role-playing," the man concludes with a chuckle. "Well, luv, I don't want to burst your medieval bubble, but since you asked, I'll tell you. It's the year 2110." He holds out his hand. "And I'm Arthur, CEO of Camelot-dot-com."

Oh, man. Beam me up, Scotty; here we go again.

SANDRA HILL
WET & WILD

What do you get when you cross a Viking with a Navy SEAL?

A warrior with the fierce instincts of the past and the rigorous training of America's most elite fighting corps?

A totally buff hero-in-the-making who hasn't had a woman in roughly a thousand years?

A wise guy with a time-warped sense of humor chanting grody jody calls?

A dyed-in-the-wool romantic with a hopeless crush on his hands-off superior officer?

Hoo-yah! Whatever you get, women everywhere can't wait to meet him, and his story is guaranteed to be…

WET & WILD